the
other
passenger

ALSO BY LOUISE CANDLISH

the *other* passenger

— a novel —

LOUISE CANDLISH

ATRIA PAPERBACK

New York London Toronto Sydney New Delhi

ATRIA
PAPERBACK

An Imprint of Simon & Schuster, Inc.
1230 Avenue of the Americas
New York, NY 10020

First Atria Paperback edition July 2021

ATRIA PAPERBACK and colophon are trademarks of Simon & Schuster, Inc.

For information about special discounts for bulk purchases, please contact Simon & Schuster Special Sales at 1-866-506-1949 or business@simonandschuster.com.

The Simon & Schuster Speakers Bureau can bring authors to your live event. For more information or to book an event, contact the Simon & Schuster Speakers Bureau at 1-866-248-3049 or visit our website at www.simonspeakers.com.

Interior design by Jill Putorti

Manufactured in the United States of America

1 3 5 7 9 10 8 6 4 2

Library of Congress Cataloging-in-Publication Data has been applied for.

ISBN 978-1-9821-7410-1
ISBN 978-1-9821-7411-8 (ebook)

For everyone who has ever been tempted to compare up . . .

1

December 27, 2019

Like all commuter horror stories, mine begins in the mean light of early morning—or, at least, *officially* it does.

Kit isn't there when I get to St Mary's Pier for the 7:20 river bus to Waterloo, but that's not unusual; he's had his fair share of self-inflicted sick days this festive season. An early morning sailing calls for a strong stomach at the best of times, but for the mortally hungover it's literally water torture (trust me, I know). In any case, he always arrives after me. Though we live just five minutes apart and he passes right by Prospect Square to get to the pier, we gave up walking down together after the first week, when his spectacularly poor timekeeping—and my neurotic punctuality—became apparent.

No, Kit prefers to stroll on just before they close the gangway, raising his hand in greeting, confident I've secured our preferred seats, the portside set of four by the bar. At St Mary's, boarding is at the front of the boat and so I'll watch him as he moves down the aisle, hands glancing off the metal poles—as much for style as balance—before sliding in next to me with an easy grin. Even if he's been up late partying, he always smells great, like an artisan loaf baked with walnuts and figs ("Kit smells so *millennial*," Clare said once, which was almost certainly a criticism of me and my Gen X smell of, I don't know, stale dog biscuits).

Get us, he'll say, idly scanning the other passengers, snug in their cream leather seats. It's one of his catchphrases: *Get us*. Pity the poor saps crushed on the overland train or suffocating on the Tube—*we're* commuting by *catamaran*. Out there, there are *seagulls*.

Also, sewage, I'll reply, because we've got a nice sardonic banter going, Kit and me.

Well, we used to.

I clear the lump in my throat just as the boat gives a sudden diesel rumble, as if the two acts are connected. On departure, information streams briskly across the overhead screens—*Calling at Woolwich, North Greenwich, Greenwich, Surrey Quays*—though by now the route is so imprinted I pay little attention. Through the silver sails of the Thames Barrier and past the old aggregate works and industrial depots of the early stretch; then you're at the yacht club and into the dinghy-strewn first loop, the residential towers of the peninsula on your left as you head towards the immense whitehead of the O2 Arena. Strung high above the river is the cable car that links the peninsula to the Royal Docks, but I won't allow myself to think about my only trip to date on *that*. What was done that night. What was said.

Well, maybe just briefly.

I turn my face from the empty seat beside me, as if Kit is there after all, reading my mind with its secret, unclean thoughts.

"Back again on Friday," he grumbled on the boat on Monday night, bemoaning his firm's insistence on normal working hours for this orphan weekday between Boxing Day and the weekend. "Fucking cheapskates." Normally, if he misses the boat, I'll text him a word or two of solidarity: *Heavy night?* Maybe some beer emojis or, if I was involved in the session, a nauseated face. But I don't do that today. I've hardly used my phone since before Christmas and I admit I've enjoyed the break. That old-school nineties feeling of being incommunicado.

We're motoring now past the glass steeples of Canary Wharf towards Greenwich, the only approach that still has the power to rouse my London pride: those twin domes of the Old Royal Naval College, the emerald park beyond. I watch the bar staff serve iced snowflake cookies with the teas and coffees—it's surprising how many people want to eat this stuff first thing in the morning, especially my age group, neither young enough to care about their silhouette (such a Melia kind of word) nor close enough to the end to give a damn about health warnings. Caffeine and sugar, caffeine and sugar: on it goes until the sun is over the yardarm and then, well, we're all sailors in this country, aren't we? We're all boozers.

Only when we dock in front of the *Cutty Sark* do I finally reach for my phone, reacquaint myself with my communications of Monday night and the aftermath of the water rats' Christmas drinks. I scan my inbox for Kit's name. My last text to him was spur-of-the-moment and tellingly free of emojis:

Just YOU wait.

Sent at 11:38 p.m. on Monday, it's double-ticked as read, but there has been no reply. There *have* been, however, five missed calls from Melia, as well as three voicemails. I really should listen to them. But, instead, I hear Clare's voice from yesterday morning, the "proper" talk we had under a gunmetal northern sky four hundred miles from here:

You need to cut ties.

Not just him, Jamie. Her, as well.

There's something not right about those two.

Now she tells me. And I slip the phone back in my pocket, buying myself a few extra minutes of innocence.

———

At Surrey Quays, Gretchen gets on. The only female water rat, she's prim in her narrow, petrol-blue wool coat, carrying one of those squat bamboo cups for her flat white. Though I'm in our usual spot, she settles in the central section several rows ahead. Weird. I move up the aisle and drop into the seat next to her. You can't usually take your pick so easily on the 7:20, but the boat is half empty—even excusing the lucky bastards who don't have to return to work till the New Year, I have to admit the river's no place to be in these temperatures. It's one of the coldest days of the year, breath visible from people's mouths on the quayside and from the heating systems of the buildings.

"Jamie, hi," she says, not quite turning, not quite smiling. Her lashes are navy spider's legs and there's a feathering of pink in the whites of her eyes.

"Thought you were blanking me there," I say, cheerfully.

"Good Christmas with your family?" She's been somewhere like Norwich, if I remember. There are healthy, uncomplicated parents, a brother and a sister, a brace of nieces and nephews.

She shrugs, sips her coffee. "It's all about the kids, isn't it? And I haven't got any."

There's really no need for her to spell this out: we're connected, our little group, by our childlessness, our freedom to put ourselves before everyone else. To self-indulge, take risks. No parent would do what I've done this last year, or at least not so readily, so heedlessly.

"What about yesterday? Do any sales shopping?"

Gretchen blinks, surprised, like I've suggested she rode a unicorn naked down the middle of Regent Street. She's clear-skinned, delicately feminine, though in temperament a woman who likes to be one of the boys, who laments the complexities of her own gender and thinks men simpler allies (a dangerous generalization, in my opinion).

"You all right, Gretch?"

"Yeah, just a bit tired."

"I don't know where Kit is this morning. I'm sure he said he was working today. Did he say anything to you?"

"Nope." There's an edge to her tone I'm familiar with, a peculiarly female strain of pique. I've wondered now and then if there might be something between Kit and her. Maybe there was some indiscretion on Monday night, maybe she worries what I saw. Did I say something I shouldn't have? God, the "shouldn't haves" are really building: shouldn't have got so drunk, shouldn't have let him goad me.

Shouldn't have sent him that last text.

"What happened there?" she asks, noticing my bandaged right hand.

"Oh, nothing major. I burned my thumb at work. Didn't I show you on Monday?"

"I don't think so." Noticing the music piping through the PA—the same loop of festive tunes we've been subjected to since early December—Gretchen groans. "I can't take any more of this 'happy holidays' crap, it's so *fake*. You know what? I think I might just book a trip somewhere sunny. Call in sick for a few days and get out of here."

"Could be expensive over New Year."

"Not if I go somewhere the Foreign Office says is a terrorist risk."

I raise an eyebrow.

"Anyway," she adds, "what's another grand or two when you're already in the red?"

"True." But I don't want to talk about money. Lately, it's the only thing I hear about. We pass the police HQ in Wapping, close to the zone change at which the westbound boats are required to reduce speed precisely as passenger impatience starts to build. We're entering the London the world recognizes—Tower Bridge, the Tower of London, the Shard—and as the landmarks rise, Gretchen and Kit and their troubles sink queasily from my mind.

"Enjoy Afghanistan, if you go," I say, when she prepares to disembark at Blackfriars for her office near St Paul's.

She smiles. "I was thinking more like Morocco."

"Much better. Let us know." My joker's grin shrinks the moment the doors close behind her and I rest my cheek on the headrest, stare out of the window. Seven fifty in the morning and I'm already done in. The water is high as we sail towards Waterloo, sucking at the walls with its grimy brown gums, and the waterside wonderland of lights that glows so magically after dark is exposed for the fraudulent web of cables that it is. It's as quick to get off at Westminster Pier and walk across the bridge as it is to wait for the boat to make a U-turn and dock at the Eye, but I choose to sit it out. I hardly register the pitch and roll that once threw me into alarm or, for that matter, the great wheel itself, its once miraculous-seeming physics. Disembarking, I ignore the waiting ticket holders and stroll up the causeway with sudden sadness for how quickly the brain turns the wondrous into the routine: work, love, friendship, traveling to work by catamaran. Or is it just me?

It's at precisely that moment, that thought—right on the beat of *me*—that a man steps towards me and flashes some sort of ID.

"James Buckby?"

"Yes." I stop and look at him. Tall, late twenties, mixed race. Business-casual dress, sensitive complexion, truthful eyes.

"Detective Constable Ian Parry, Metropolitan Police." He presses the ID closer to my face so I can see the distinctive blue banner, the white lettering, and straightaway my heart pulses with a horrible suction, as if it's constructed of tentacles, not chambers.

"Is something wrong?"

"We think there might be, yes. Christopher Roper has been reported missing. He's a good friend of yours, I gather?"

"Christopher?" It takes a moment to connect the name to Kit. "What d'you mean, missing?" I'm starting to tremble now. "I mean, I noticed he wasn't on the boat, but I just thought . . ." I falter. In my mind I see my phone screen, alerts for those missed calls from Melia. Her heart-shaped face, her murmured voice humid in my ear.

We're different, Jamie. We're special.

The guy gestures to the river wall to my left, where a male colleague stands apart from the tourists, watching us. Plainclothes, which means CID, a criminal investigation. I read somewhere that police only go in twos if they think there's a risk to their safety; is that what they judge me to be?

"Melia gave you my name, I suppose?"

Not commenting, my ambusher concentrates on separating me from the groups gathering and dispersing at the pier's entrance, owners of a hundred purposes preferable to my own. "So, if we can trouble you for a minute, Mr. Buckby?"

"Of course." As I allow myself to be led towards his colleague, it's the coy, old-style phrasing I get stuck on. *Trouble you for a minute*, like trouble is a passing trifle of an idea, a little Monday-morning fun.

Well, as it transpires, it's fucking neither.

2

Still, at least they're not escorting me back to their base in Woolwich.

DC Parry suggests we go to my place of work instead—"if that's more convenient?" They'd aimed to catch me at home before I left, he adds, only to get stuck in traffic and turn the car around—in effect, chasing the boat along the Thames. I suppose I should be grateful they didn't board the thing and arrest me in front of my fellow commuters.

Calm down, Jamie. No one said anything about an arrest.

"So I don't need a lawyer for this?"

"No, it's just an informal chat for now," the second detective says (*for now?*). He is light-skinned, shorter and slighter than his colleague, a little less polished. A few years older, too—midthirties, I would judge. Whereas Parry gives every impression of having been born to apprehend suspects, this one is closer to my model of a man. A little less goal-orientated.

9

Don't be a fuckwit. What are detectives if not goal-orientated? This "informal" business will be an illusion designed to catch the kind of blurted secrets that are not so easy to come by in the interview room, some killjoy solicitor at hand to crush any mode of questioning too maverick.

"To be honest, I'd prefer not to go to my work. It's a small café and there's nowhere private to talk." The idea of squeezing into the staff room, little more than a walk-in locker, with two detectives from the Met, while Regan, my manager and a keen follower of local crime news, hovers outside vibrating with curiosity, is excruciating. "Could we just find somewhere quiet near here instead? I'd be really grateful." The implication is I'll be more cooperative and, to my relief, the ploy works.

"Fair enough, I don't see why we need disturb your customers," the second guy says.

I can't keep calling him that so I ask him to repeat his name.

"Andy Merchison." He speaks brightly, as if we're meeting at a party or a sales conference. Though the name sounds Scottish, his accent is one of those smooth, neutral ones that's impossible to place. "How about up there?" He's spotted a corner of the upper terrace of the Royal Festival Hall, both secluded and deserted, since the place hasn't opened yet.

Jesus, they've come for you so ridiculously early public places are still shut!

Calm down. It's just routine.

"Yes, fine," I say.

A friendly nod to a passing security guard and we're alone, seated at a table and sheltered from the December wind that, fifty feet away, whistles off the water like a warning. No one can hear us here.

"I need to text my manager and tell her I'll be late." I produce my phone, tilt the screen away from the light. My eye catches the most recent message: an alert for those voicemails from Melia. Melia Roper now, but still listed by her maiden name, still Melia Quinn to me.

I remember Clare telling me last night that she'd had missed calls from her too, though no voicemail had been left. Should she call her back, Clare had asked, her reluctance clear.

Leave it, I told her.

I blink, aware of the detectives' scrutiny as I dither; they're surely noticing my bandage, changed this morning but already grubby. I select the contact for Regan, who will by now have dealt with the deliveries of milk, sourdough, and pastries and be grinding her first coffee orders. It's her habit to get in half an hour early, make herself a premium-grade matcha, and open up solo. Her flat share sounds like hostel conditions and those thirty minutes before I arrive are the only ones she'll get all day to spend in a room alone.

Going to be late, sorry. I stare at the screen as if an answer will come at once, something to rescue me, but of course she won't have time to look at her phone. By eight thirty, the queue is out the door.

"All done?" DC Parry asks with an edge, like I'm taking the piss. Clearly he's less accommodating than his partner and the moment I put the phone down, he gets down to business: "So, according to Mrs. Roper, her husband failed to arrive home on Monday night and you were the last person to see him . . ."

There's a significant pause where the word *alive* should fall.

I answer politely. "You mean on the boat home? To be fair, Melia wasn't with us to know who that was."

But this pedantry is water off a duck's back. "Members of the crew witnessed you both disembarking and we've also spoken to another passenger who saw you alone together. Mrs. Roper has spent the last few days contacting family and friends and is certain no one else has seen him since then."

"I've had missed calls from her myself," I concede. "I haven't had a chance to get back to her." I wonder about this other passenger. Obviously not Gretchen, since I've just seen her and she made no mention of having been contacted by the police. Steve, perhaps? The last person besides Kit that I remember noticing, he got off at North Greenwich fifteen minutes before us. He's off work now till next week, but I'm fairly sure he would have phoned or texted me if the police had been in touch.

I remain composed. "I suppose you've already checked the security video on the boat?"

"We have indeed. So, your recollection of Monday night . . .?" Parry prompts.

"We got the last boat home together, that's right. A few of us got on at Blackfriars after Christmas drinks at Henry's on Carter Lane."

"The others being?"

"Gretchen Miles and Steve Callister. We've got to know each other on the commute, had drinks a few times. We always sit together."

The names don't appear to be new to them, though Merchison jots an extra note I can't decipher. Both detectives have big A4 pads in front of them, but only he has produced a pen.

"But it wasn't that late when we got to St Mary's—the last boat gets in at eleven thirty. Someone else must have seen Kit after that, surely?"

"That's what we're trying to discover," Parry says, frowning. I can tell he's finding me unusually sanguine about a friend having been reported missing. "Did you and Mr. Roper pass anyone in the street on your way up from the pier?"

"Not anyone I particularly remember. We didn't walk together, actually, so *he* may have."

His gaze sharpens. "You didn't walk together, even though you live a few streets away from each other?"

"No. Normally we do, but . . . Come on, you obviously saw from the video that we got into a bit of a row on the boat? I marched off ahead. I didn't want to spend another minute with him." The statement hangs between us, I can almost hear it spinning around a wood-paneled courtroom—*I didn't want to spend another minute with him*—and I'm not surprised by the doubtful look they exchange.

"What was this row about?" Merchison asks.

I sigh. My throat feels painful and gritty. "Nothing much. We were both the worse for wear. But I didn't want to hang around arguing. I had a very early start in the morning, a train to catch from King's Cross, and, like I say, I assumed he followed."

"Are you and Mr. Roper in the habit of arguing?" Parry says. Unlike his colleague, who shifts constantly in his seat, he has the sharp-eyed stillness of an owl.

"No, not at all. We're mates. We were drunk, that's all." Without thinking, I bring my bandaged hand to my face and of course he makes the association I'd prefer he didn't.

"Injure yourself in this fight with your mate, did you?"

"No. This is a burn from the coffee machine at work. Speaking of which, is there any chance we can get some coffee?" My first, a double espresso at home, has worn off. Usually by this time I'd be at work and firing up my second or, if I'm lucky, being handed one on arrival by Regan. "Look, there must be security cameras between the pier and the high street, so why don't you check them and you'll see it was exactly as I'm telling you?"

I happen to know that the route back to Prospect Square took me past at least one other CCTV camera. "Maybe ask at the bar on Royal Way? Mariners, it's called, on the corner of Artillery Passage, less than two minutes from where the boat docks. We often go there after getting off the late boat, so maybe he went on his own this time." I pause, convincing myself. "Yeah, I bet he stopped for a drink there, met someone and, you know, continued his evening."

Merchison's pen scratches the paper throughout this speech and when he raises his gaze I see a flare of interest in his eyes. "Are you saying you think he spent the night with someone other than his wife?"

"Maybe. If he didn't go home, then I'd say it's a possibility."

"Is several nights a possibility? The whole Christmas break?"

Both detectives' skepticism is plain to see. I shrug. "Look, I'm not saying he's eloped bigamously, just that he might have

14

carried on partying and got caught up in something and now he's sleeping it off. I mean, he must have been *somewhere* these last few days, mustn't he? He's not some loner, he's a very social animal."

Once, in the summer a few weeks before the wedding, Kit and I stayed out all night. It was a Friday and we'd got off the boat at North Greenwich, found a club near the O2 that stayed open till dawn. I remember there was a charity walk starting at midnight and it was surreal to watch thousands of women in leggings swarm by all bright-eyed, before limping back six hours later in a miasma of exhaustion. Melia, staying with a girlfriend across town, was not around to disapprove, but Clare was spitting blood when I finally skulked home at 8 a.m. "He's young, Jamie, he can take it physically, but you might have a stroke!" And for the rest of the day my inbox pinged with links to articles about middle-aged men falling down dead after binge-drinking.

I don't say any of this to the police. Instead, I look from one detective to the other, spreading my integrity evenly between them. "Seriously, any minute now, he's going to come strolling back in, probably not even sorry he wasted your time. So I should probably go to work now—my colleague will be struggling on her own. Plus it's not the kind of job where you get paid if you're not there, you know?"

There's a short, sweet moment when I think I've swayed it and they're going to say, Fine, off you go, our apologies for the overreaction. But they don't. Maybe they're remembering Melia's face, distraught at the thought of her new husband injured or abducted or worse. She's so appealing, even in red-eyed, nose-running distress; so persuasive.

She's obviously persuaded you, Jamie, Clare said, not long ago.

"If you don't mind filling in a few more gaps for us," Merchison says. "Would it help if we had a word on the phone with your manager?"

"Or perhaps it's best we head to the station, after all," Parry says. He flicks Merchison a dismayed look and I know I'm right about them bending the rules talking to me unofficially like this. It's probably not even legal. But the last thing I want is for my words to be recorded and run through some lie-detection system (is that even a thing?). Or for a medical examination to expose the ugly bruises on my collarbone, safely hidden by the high neck of my sweatshirt, evidence of the true viciousness of that grapple with Kit. "No, please." I huddle inside my jacket, fold my fingers inside the cuffs for warmth. "Whatever you need. I just need to keep work informed."

"Thank you, James," Merchison says, "we appreciate your co-operation."

"Jamie. No one calls me James."

And no one calls Kit Christopher. The police's use of our full names only emphasizes the fact that they don't know anything about us, about this.

"Jamie. So how about we make this easy and start at the beginning. You tell us everything there is to know about Mr. Roper."

Sweet Jesus. They of all people must know that "everything there is to know" is *never* as simple as it sounds. As a seagull squawks overhead, I nod my consent.

"How long have you known each other?"

"Almost a year," I say. "We met at the end of January."

"January this year?" They both look up, surprised. "Not that long, then."

"No." And it's true, it's no time at all.

On the other hand, it feels like the longest year of my life.

3

Before I start, I should like to point out that it wasn't me who got us tangled up with the Ropers, but Clare. The woman who is now their fiercest critic was also their discoverer and erstwhile champion. For a while there, she thought they were the bee's knees—both of them.

Melia came first. Whatever complications arose later, there is one thing I have no doubt about: the collision of our two worlds was pure chance. Of all the estate agents in all the towns in all the world, she walks into Clare's.

Clare mentioned her on one of her first days back at work in January. "I had lunch with that new girl who started last month. Melia, she's called. It turns out she lives near here."

"Girl?"

"Well, she's in her late twenties. Possibly thirty. I honestly don't know."

Hurtling towards fifty as we were, we found it hard to judge younger adults' ages. They all looked like sixth formers to us.

"Anyway, she's the new junior Richard hired. To work with the re-lo consultants? She's fitting in really well, he's getting fantastic feedback about her."

The relocation from overseas of corporate highfliers and their families was a healthy slice of the lettings business and I knew from Clare's stories that some clients could be hard to please. "So she's gorgeous, I take it?"

"That sort of remark gets reported to HR, these days." Clare's mouth curled. One of our shared convictions was a loathing of extreme political correctness. "If you ever hear me use the word 'woke,' shoot me," she liked to say, and I'd reply, "What, even in the context of, 'My devoted partner woke me up with a cup of tea and a bacon sandwich'?" (Oh, the banter.)

"Very gorgeous, yes," she added. "Dark hair in a bob, lovely eyes, a kind of tawny color. Her skin is off-the-scale elastic."

I chuckled. "How can you possibly know that? What scale measures skin elasticity, anyway?"

"The human eye, Jamie, the human eye." Clare plucked the back of her hand with an expression of fascinated disgust. "All I know is it doesn't pleat like *this*, so it must have plenty of natural elastin. Or is it collagen?" She was, lately, a proud discusser of menopausal symptoms, referring openly to decreasing estrogen levels and the shutting down of wombs. I'd learned not to show how revolted I was by such talk. In any case, Clare still looked all right to me. She was tall and slim (-ish, but I was hardly rocking a six-pack myself) with blonde hair swept from her face for work but worn fringed and punky off-duty, kind of Debbie Harry circa "Heart of Glass." A well-raised girl from Edinburgh, she'd been the beneficiary of an excellent state education, followed by university in London, where she'd stayed on account of a boyfriend, who exited the scene soon after. By the time, in her late thirties, she'd met yours truly at a Christmas party, her career in property sales had led naturally and lucratively to the establishment of her business with Richard. (It had helped to be free of any derailment wrought by motherhood, which by the way was a question of personal choice, not any biological malfunction or enforced preference by her current mate.)

"So what did you and Melia the Millennial talk about, besides work?"

"Loads of stuff. Life, family, our relationships. Oh, I told her about the career coaching and she thinks it's an inspired gift."

Because she has no idea what it signals, I thought. The clearly very costly Christmas present to me of a course of sessions with some guru or other marked the end of Clare's tolerance of my noncareer. While she didn't deny that my prospects were threatened by ageism—how many of her own hires were over thirty, let alone late forties?—the gift had come just weeks after a renewed campaign for me to set myself up as a freelancer. "I *am* a freelancer," I'd told her. "A freelance café assistant."

"Eight one-on-one consultations, wow," I said, on receipt of the gift voucher. I would strongly have preferred a new shirt. "'Dream job. Real results.' That's my New Year's resolution taken care of, then. In 2019, I will finally find a way to work with white tigers."

Clare smiled. "You joke, but maybe you'll surprise yourself with what you decide to do next."

Maybe I would. "What about you? Any resolutions?"

"Actually, I do have one," she said. "I've decided I'm going to embrace the new. I read that's the key to aging successfully."

"I think all aging is unsuccessful, ultimately," I said, grinning. "New what, exactly?"

"New everything. New hobbies, new ideas, new friends." She grew emphatic as she searched for the right phrase and I saw she was very determined about this: "I'm open to submissions."

Enter Melia, and, a step or two behind her, Kit, with their winning submission of youth, fun, freedom. Everything Clare feared she was losing.

I suppose what I'm trying to say is this whole thing began with exactly the midlife crisis you might imagine—just not mine.

————

They came to dinner on the third Saturday of January. I was in the kitchen when they arrived and Clare ushered them straight off for a house tour, so my first impression was of two heads of glossy dark hair yet to lose its pigmentation in a single strand, of alien and seductive fragrances that lingered in their wake. As I opened the wine, I could hear their voices in the stairwell saying the things people always say when exploring our four-story Georgian town house:

"Oh my God, this is, like, my dream house." (Her.)

"Seriously, isn't it completely beautiful?" (Her.)

"It's fucking amazing." (Him.)

"Look at this stone staircase. I feel almost *depressed*, it's so grown-up." (Her.)

And Clare's delighted laughter, at odds with her murmured modesty.

As I say, we were accustomed to the house being an object of envy, even among our peers. Prospect Square, a five-minute walk from the Thames, is an intact Georgian conservation area sometimes used in the filming of period dramas and number 15 still has many of its original glories: hand-cast ceiling roses, internal shutters, that kind of thing. From the rear window of our bedroom, which occupied the entire top floor, we had a view of the river; out front there was a private garden square. We were fortunate by anyone's standards and every so often the realization would take possession of me: *I've got it made here. I'm #Blessed.*

Maybe this gushing Melia girl was taking pictures right now for her Instagram feed, so busy cropping, filtering, hashtagging, she didn't notice she was leaning a little too far over the curved banisters. A gruesome image sprang to mind of a young woman hurtling through the tubular void and landing splat on the flagstones of the hallway, hair fanned around her head, absorbing the blood and turning sticky.

What the . . . ? I shook my head clear.

When the party came back down and settled in the sitting room, I distributed large glasses of Burgundy. Helpfully, the other couple had chosen to sit opposite us on the smaller of the two sofas, a pale high-backed piece that showcased their strikingly twinlike good looks. Both were slightly built, she a beautiful tomboy dressed in an odd but winning combination of velvet shorts, glossy tights, and a glittery top the color of blue hydrangeas, he girlishly handsome in black jeans and a shirt in a paler blue. On closer inspection, of course, they weren't so similar. She was finer-boned, a proper beauty with large eyes the amber of Pears soap, whereas he had flaws: unusually wide-set eyes, asymmetrical eyebrows, a slightly beaky nose.

"This is a relief," Melia said, gripping the wineglass in two hands as if it might at any moment be confiscated. Her nails were yolk-yellow. "Everyone else seems to be doing Dry January."

"We do it every other year," Clare said, which made us sound not only dull but dull on an advance-notice basis.

"Wait, so you already know next January is going to be completely miserable?" said Kit. He was lithe with animation, clenching and twitching in his seat. "Why not leave it to the last minute to decide? Give yourselves the gift of hope?"

"And what if something awful happens just before, like you're splitting up and you really need a drink?" Melia spoke with a blurting charm, immediately apologizing: "I can't believe I said that! Of course you're not going to split up."

"If we do, then plans for sobriety will need to be reviewed on an individual basis," Clare reassured her, with mock formality.

"You've never been tempted to go dry, then?" I asked Kit and he gave a loose, roguish smile.

"Mate, I'll quit when I'm dead."

Cliché though it was, we were all excitable enough to splutter at this and at the playful smack Melia landed on the back of his head. They touched and gasped and gestured frequently, I noticed, reinforcing each other's presence.

"That's a refreshing attitude for your gen," Clare said to Kit. She was already very taken with him, I could tell. "We've been led to believe you prefer soya oat flat whites to the strong stuff."

"Soya *or* oat," I corrected her. "It's one or the other."

"Jamie works in a café," she explained.

"Really?" Kit said. "Where? Here in St Mary's?"

"No, Waterloo. It's called the Comfort Zone, which is appropriate since it challenges about as much as it pays."

"It's only temporary," Clare said, loyally, "and it actually sounds exhausting."

"Well, physically, I suppose," I said, and as Melia's gaze rested on me I wondered what she saw. In the flatteringly soft lamplight of our living room, a still-attractive man, I hoped. Tall, well-built, hair enduringly thick, jawline reasonably sharp. At forty-eight, I wasn't so far off my prime, was I?

"I know what those jobs are like," Kit said. "We've both done our share of bar work, haven't we, Me? That's what you do when you're an actor." His tone became droll. "You never actually act."

"I thought Clare said you worked in insurance?" It had struck me as a staid career choice for a millennial when she'd briefed me; even more so now I'd met him.

"I do. De Warr Insurance. I've got debts to pay off before I can do anything interesting. But for a while there, I was, you know, deluding myself I might be the next big thing." He shrugged the easy shrug of someone to whom such acceptance had not come easy at all.

"That's where we met," Melia explained. "Drama school."

So they were both failed actors: Clare hadn't told me that.

Though I hardly knew them, the detail made sense of them, of their physicality, their confidence, their need to be noticed, if not admired.

"How much professional acting work did you do?" Clare asked.

"Melia was in a rep for a season," Kit said. "I did a whole load of unpaid stuff, but I gave up after a few years."

Melia sighed. "I stuck it out for a bit longer, but it was the same story every time. You'd be down to the last two and it would go to the girl with the father in the business."

"Showbiz does seem like it runs purely on nepotism," Clare said.

"It's becoming one of those professions where only the rich can do it," Kit said. "They're living rent-free in their parents' house in Hampstead, while you're running up massive debts just to share a stinking mattress in Catford. You can't compete."

There was more than a trace of resentment in this remark. Though they'd brought beautiful flowers and an expensive bottle of wine, a theme of financial hardship was already established and, by the time we'd finished the main course—I cooked beef on the teppanyaki grill—and Clare was serving her cherry and pistachio trifle, had found full voice.

"I would literally give *blood* to live on this square," Melia said.

"People 'literally' give blood all the time," I told her, grinning. "It's called paid donation. But I think you only get a hundred quid, not a house."

"Okay, but you know what I mean. I would give an organ or something." She'd closed her eyes as she said this, as if she were making a wish before blowing out her birthday candles. Her eyelids were glittery bronze, the lashes extended in some mysterious way. Under the table, restless legs crossed and uncrossed constantly. She was, I acknowledged, insanely cute.

"Well, you're in the right job if you do choose to buy around here," I said.

Eyes open once more, she licked the trifle spoon in front of her face as she studied me. "It's not a question of *choice*. We've got no chance. Even one-bedders are pushing half a million, at least they are in the buildings *we* would want to live in."

She and Kit glanced about them once again, not asking what they wanted to know: how much we'd paid for our place. How much it was worth was public knowledge since a similar house on the square was currently on the market for £2.3 million. In Greenwich or Camberwell, it would be a million more; in Kensington, five million more. It was all relative, but I'd lived long enough to know that people compared up, not down—and not only in terms of property.

"Luckily, we're ancient enough to have bought when St Mary's was a no-go area without a direct train into town," Clare said, her standard line, though neither of us had in fact been involved in the transaction. The property had been acquired by her parents when they'd lived in London briefly in the eighties and theirs remained the names on the deeds. Clare, an only child, would be the sole beneficiary of their estate when the time came. My decade of contributing to the bills was easily offset by the absence of rent; even if I wanted them to—and I didn't—no lawyer was going to argue that the house was anything but an Armstrong treasure.

"Believe it or not, you used to be able to get a mortgage for a place like this on just one person's salary," Clare added, as if imparting word of a juicy scandal. "The average price of a house in London in 1986 was fifty-five thousand."

"Stop!" Kit groaned, alcohol lending a camp extravagance to his manner. "To be told that if we'd just been born a few years earlier, we could have had what we wanted without lifting a finger."

"Well, not quite," Clare said, with a note of correction.

"You'd still have to have had a nose for up-and-coming areas," Melia agreed, her professional instincts allowing a more nuanced envy than Kit's. "*And* work incredibly hard to save for the deposit."

He scoffed at this. There was an ingredient to his manner I couldn't quite identify. Something childish, a propensity to sulk, perhaps. "Yeah, but compare that with now. We could work 24/7 and still never come close. We couldn't even buy our rental on Tiding Street."

Tiding Street was a road of narrow terraces on the other side of the high street from us, not long transformed from near slums to desirable starter flats unaffordable to starter people.

"Nice street. How long have you lived there?" I asked.

"Six months. We were over in Blackheath before, so we're still getting to know St Mary's."

"What do you think of us so far?"

He smirked. "I think you're great—except for all the mums and babies."

"Kit!" Melia protested. "You can't say that!"

"What? It's true. They charge down the high street with their buggies, expecting you to jump out of the way. I mean, for fuck's sake, they'd rather you got hit by a bus than they should have to slow down for two seconds."

"I think new parents don't always notice. They're in a different mental zone from us," Clare said, amused.

"They're mental all right."

There was that moment of collective elation when a group understands it agrees on something fundamental. As child-free fortysomethings, Clare and I were getting rarer by the year, marooned in a neighborhood that had grown ever more family-friendly now the inner zones were unaffordable for most. Though Kit and Melia were still young and, presumably, fertile and might very well change their minds, they were for now at least in our camp.

"The only real downside is the commute," Kit said. "The overland is a nightmare, isn't it? I'm always late for work and that's if I can squeeze on in the first place."

Clare and I exchanged a look.

"Those rush-hour trains are more than twice over capacity," I said. "Well over legal limits. I've complained repeatedly."

They listened nonplussed as I detailed the complaints process. They hadn't taken me for a consumer rights activist.

"I'm quite claustrophobic," I explained, "so public transport is the bane of my life."

"He had to cut out the Tube completely," Clare said in a confirming tone. "He doesn't like tunnels."

"I don't like being *stuck* in them." I didn't say that I found the overland passenger experience only minimally less panic-inducing. The trains had sealed windows and were supposedly climate-controlled, but in reality were overheated, commuters crushed against one another like lovers. London would soon need those Tokyo-style paddles to wedge people in.

"He had to have CBT. Cognitive behavioral therapy," she spelled out, but she needn't have: this age group knew its therapies better than ours.

"What gets me," Kit said, "is there's always some twat who's jumped on the tracks or whatever. There was one the other day hanging off the bridge. Couldn't make his mind up. I mean, if I wanted to end it all, I'd fuck off and do it privately, I wouldn't hold up an entire rail network. That smacks of egomania if you ask me, not lack of self-esteem. This person shouldn't be topping himself, he should be auditioning for *Britain's Got Talent!*"

So much for being more mental health literate! "Your compassion for society's most vulnerable is a beautiful thing," Clare joked over Kit's shouts of laughter at his own comments. So he was a controversialist, I thought. A provocateur—in short, a man after my own heart.

"I've been thinking about switching to the river bus when my season ticket runs out," I told him. "They've just extended the route to St Mary's and it doesn't take much longer to get into town."

"I heard it's pretty expensive," he said.

Melia took out her phone to google. "There's an introductory discount for annual tickets from St Mary's bought before the end of January. What d'you say, boys?"

"A year's quite a commitment," Clare said.

Kit took the phone from Melia and peered at the timetable. "What time do you start work?" he asked me.

"Quarter past eight. Monday to Friday. Not so different from you corporate drones, eh."

"The seven twenty looks like the one then. Gets into Waterloo at eight-oh-five. You're on my way, I could swing by here at ten past."

I played along. "Five past, to be on the safe side."

"The safe side! You're showing your age there, Jamie."

Clare shrieked with delight. "You tell him, Kit—he's turning into such an old codger!"

Not the most flattering remark—the sweet little protest Melia made didn't pass me by—but I couldn't begrudge Clare her high spirits. She was really sparking off this pair. Normally by now she'd be winding down, cooperating fully with guests' murmurings about calling an Uber, but tonight she begged them to stay, insisting on sharing her love of 1980s power ballads, vintage videos of which were ceremoniously aired.

"You've never heard 'Alone' by Heart?" She pressed her burning cheek to mine as the lyrics began and I felt the muscles in her face working as she sang. I mouthed along gamely, while our guests mocked the band's haircuts, speaking of the era as if it were Elizabethan. They were both pie-eyed now and elegantly swaying. Costumed differently, they could have been in Warhol's Factory, adult children wafting into shot behind a dancing Edie Sedgwick.

"Play us something *you* like!" Clare urged them, when her own favorites had run out.

Melia overruled Kit to choose a lullaby by some R&B star, which finally defeated our second wind and at last, just after two, they stood to leave.

"So great to finally meet you," she told me, at the door, as if she'd known of me for years, not weeks.

"Likewise. Delighted to have had the opportunity to see your famously elastic skin close-up."

"Oh!" She giggled. "Clare *said* you were funny." Amid farewell hugs and kisses on hot cheeks, her mouth caught the corner of mine.

"They're great, aren't they?" Clare said, upstairs. "I didn't mean it about the old codger."

"Oh, I don't care," I said, thinking that I would only care if I *was* one. Even so, she was kissing me in apology, and I wasn't going to argue with that. These days, sex was neither frequent nor frantic and to be taken in whatever spirit it was offered.

But midway, a terrible, unforgivable thought ignited before I could stop it and I confess I almost burned my eyeballs on the flame before blowing it out:

Shame it's you and not her . . .

4

The next morning, Clare received a thank-you text from Melia, who requested my number on Kit's behalf. A few minutes later, a text arrived from him, complete with a screenshot of his river bus season ticket confirmation:

See you on the 7:20 tomorrow?

My first thought was shamefully childish, *That was my idea, not yours*, though it was by definition impossible to claim ownership of a form of public transport. I was uncommonly fired up, though, and while Clare was in the shower I bought my own annual ticket for £1,500.

"I've done it," I told her, when she reappeared.

"Done what?"

"Booked the river bus season ticket. So you won't need to hear my moans about the train anymore."

"Oh, really?" She looked disconcerted, began toweling her wet hair with excessive vigor.

"What? Is it the money?" I'd used the joint account, set up a decade ago for household expenses. Separate finances had served us well until my removal from white-collar security the previous summer, and what savings I'd had had rapidly dwindled. Now we'd entered a gray area, discussed only in vague terms: I could use "whatever" joint funds I needed till I was earning "properly" again.

Clare draped the damp towel around her neck and smoothed her hair from her forehead. At the roots, there were little worms of silver. "Those one-time offers are nonrefundable, aren't they?"

"Is that a problem? I'll get a refund on the rest of my train ticket," I added, an unexpectedly personal note in my voice.

"No, it's just I didn't realize the idea was to stay in that job for another year." She stood in front of me, her face bathed in natural light from the huge skylight; without makeup, her skin was heavily patterned with lines, a diagram of life lived, and I thought, with a jolt, *How weird that we're getting older*. I understood exactly why she'd declared herself open to newness: time was running out!

"I'll still need to travel in, whatever I do next," I pointed out. "There aren't any decent jobs around here, as we know." When I'd searched locally for a stop-gap position like the one I held now in Central London, it had been a dismal experience; on the two occasions I'd been invited for an interview, I'd been rejected as overqualified, beaten out by candidates half my age.

I could see Clare appreciated my effort to meet her halfway. She nodded, smiling. "Well, I think it's great you've made the change. No more train dramas. Kit as well?"

I know it sounds crazy: I'd known him only for a few hours, but just like that he'd proved himself an agent of change in my life. Just like that we'd committed ourselves to seeing each other once, perhaps twice, a day, Monday to Friday, for the rest of the year.

"Yes, Kit, as well."

The conditions that first morning did not make for the sparkling debut commute we might have imagined. For starters, it was midwinter and still dark when Kit called at Prospect Square at 7:05; sunrise, when it came, had no more effect than a frosted glass lamp with a failing bulb. And the brackish smell of the river was just a little repellent.

The boat was more familiar to me from the website than real life. Amazing how you can live by a world-famous river for years and not notice a thing about the craft that go up and down it. It was a 150-seater high-speed catamaran called *Boleyn* (the others in the fleet were also named after abused Tudor queens) and, compared to the train, was palatial. Plenty of space, big leather seats. A bar. TV screens showing the news.

"First day of the rest of our lives, eh?" Kit said, in general mockery, but I could tell he was as exhilarated as I was to have changed something fundamental so suddenly. He was immaculate in a costly looking wool coat with an equally high-end leather messenger bag slung over his shoulder. Next to him, in my jeans and North Face jacket, I felt shabby, a slacker relic from the nineties.

"Hope it sticks to the schedule," he added, as the engines fired and we set sail so smoothly as to be anticlimactic. Lit by the boat's powerful lights, the river was the exact color of black Americano. "I've got a new boss who likes to start the week with an eight-fifteen 'motivator.' Marks you on some register if you're late; you'd think we were still at school." As I would learn, work was a necessary evil for Kit. He expressed none of the vaunted "passion" his generation had been taught they were entitled to—and that was required of mine if we were even to begin to compete.

"It's an insurance firm, right? You must get great benefits? Car insurance, that kind of thing?"

"Haven't got a car, mate," Kit said.

"All right, life insurance, then?"

"Well, yeah, Melia would get a fortune, but that's no use to either of us since I plan to stay alive."

"Don't we all. Pension? Let me guess, you don't plan to get old? Fine, we won't speak of your package ever again."

He laughed at that. His laughter was an automatic weapon, firing and firing after you expected it to stop, and as heads turned to look at us I experienced a schoolboy's satisfaction that I was sitting with the cool kid.

Already, we'd reached Woolwich, where more commuters took their seats. Boarding was fast, the crew slick. It was a well-heeled crowd: I could see I was the only minimum-wage worker on the boat—other than the guy serving coffee—and I said as much to Kit.

"How long have you worked in . . ."

"Catering? It's a recent thing, only four or five months. Before that I was in marketing, internal comms, but the company I worked for was in North London and the commute was a bit of a saga. The Northern Line, you know."

"Oh yeah, the claustrophobia. How do you even catch that?" He made it sound like syphilis or something, the result of promiscuity.

"Could be a posttraumatic thing, could be inherited. The therapist I saw told me it's people with a keen need to defend their personal space who are more likely to develop it."

He rolled his shoulders, gestured to the generous seating and wide aisles. "Not sure there's gonna be any problem with that here."

We were tourists that first day, Kit and I. Naming the neighborhoods and buildings we'd only ever seen before from land, willingly disorientated by the curves in the river you forget exist when you're traveling by road or underground; ticking off the bridges, one by one.

"Did you ever go on the Millennium Bridge when it was still the Wobbly Bridge?" I asked him, before remembering he would have been a kid back then. The raw, unsophisticated London I remembered from my twenties meant nothing to a man who'd spent his with onboard Wi-Fi. I'd met them by the truckload in my old line of work, grown-up kids who had no experience of self-sacrifice, of paying your dues, and who, understandably, viewed me as an old fart. "God, I sound like I'm your father, droning on about the old days."

"You sound nothing like him," Kit said, darkly. "He's a dead-beat loser."

"Really? In what way?"

"Oh, loads of ways. Like, when my mum died, he sold the house and spent the whole lot at the bookies. We had to move in with my gran."

"Wow. I'm sorry."

"Don't be. I have nothing to do with him now. Melia hardly sees her parents either, we always joke we're orphans."

Rather a bleak joke, I thought.

"Yours still alive?" he asked.

"My dad is. We get on pretty well. He's closer with my sister, Debs, they live in the same town and she's supplied the grand-kids, which suits me fine. And Clare's folks are great. We just saw them over Christmas—we always spend it at their place in Edinburgh."

"Lucky for some. Just move back a bit, old man, will you?" He used his arm to ease me back a fraction. "You're messing with my view of St Paul's."

"You got it, son."

Was there something paternal there? Even a trace of the vicarious? Or was it straightforward rivalry, right from the get-go?

God knows. Back then, I was just elated to not be battling compressive asphyxia on the commuter train.

At my place of work, Kit would have been the old-timer. Though the staff used Waterloo Station daily, not one of them knew what I was talking about when I quoted "Waterloo Sunset." "Terry and Julie, Friday night? You don't know the Kinks? Tell me you've heard of the Beatles, at least?"

(They'd heard of the Beatles.)

My manager, Regan, was twenty-four and from the Midlands. She was an exponent of that weird contouring young women do to their faces, like stage makeup, so I can't say in all honesty what she looked like, other than she was chestnut-haired, brown-eyed, and stocky of build. A resident of the Smoke for not quite eighteen months, she had an obsession—in the mornings, at least, fresh from a browse of the news—with "lawless" London's murder count: the recent stabbing of a teenage pizza delivery driver had occupied her for days. Thankfully, she considered our stretch of Belvedere Road, SE1, civilized, even cool, what with the proliferation of hipsters among the tourists and commuters, the local students, and residents of the sleek new apartment blocks. The café occupied the ground floor of a neglected building of the same vintage as Prospect Square, with a large window at the front made of nine panes (once, overnight, someone sprayed a game of noughts and crosses on the glass. The noughts won). The decorating budget must have been about a fiver, bits of old mirror and objects made of shell that you'd find in dumpsters, and cushions everywhere—that was the comfort element of the zone (in all my months of service, I'd never known them to have been cleaned). People came for our artisanal coffee, but we also served pastries and "hand cut" a limited menu of sandwiches. Regan Instagrammed latte art in her downtime.

I don't mean to sneer. My point is just that we weren't surgeons. Indeed, our utensils had IKEA stamped on them and I'd brought our only decent knife from home, the ones provided being too blunt for slicing the prosciutto we layered in our best-selling prosciutto and fig on sourdough. We handled hiccups like the contactless handset playing up or the Wi-Fi going down with aplomb, safe in the knowledge that none of it mattered and that at the end of our shift we would stroll away, free of all responsibility. Our only frictions involved battles over music and I seem to remember that Regan had prevailed with Billie Eilish when, midmorning, Clare called.

"How was the river commute?"

"Amazing. A business-class experience. I feel like a new man."

"Oh, good. Just so long as you don't feel like a new woman."

"Ha." Though my gaze was on Regan, consolidating two half-empty baskets of pastries into one full one, I thought unexpectedly of Melia on Saturday night, the way her legs emerged from her shorts on the sofa opposite, pale under sheer tights.

"While I'm on the phone . . . I just had an email from Vicky Jenkinson."

"Vicky who?"

"Your career coach." An edge of exasperation entered Clare's voice. "She says you haven't scheduled the sessions and she wanted to warn you that she books up over a month in advance."

"Okay, I'll get on to it."

"Actually, I don't mean to be controlling, but . . ."

In my experience, when people said they didn't mean to be something, it was usually in the spirit of apology, not denial. "But?"

"I've already put some dates in her diary for you, just provisionally. I hope that's all right."

"Fine." It hardly mattered, since I already had my suspicions that the only career guaranteed to benefit from this transaction was Ms. Jenkinson's own.

As I hung up, I reached out a hand to stop a leaning tower of takeout cups from toppling to the floor.

———

On the trip home, everything slid by in reverse, as commutes have a habit of doing. I'd never seen my city before from the water at night and was charmed by the thousands of acid-blue bulbs along the South Bank and, inside the office buildings, the ceiling lights of open-plan floors, stark and beautiful as art installations.

Kit got on at Blackfriars, picking up a pair of Peronis from the bar before joining me with the air of someone whose day had only now properly begun. Having not done so in the morning, I was reading the emergency instructions and slid the laminated card back into the pocket in front as he thrust the beer at me.

"You're not reading the safety card," he mocked, taking his own from its pocket and reading aloud in a scoffing tone: "'Your crew are trained in emergency procedures . . .' I should bloody well hope so!"

"It's not funny," I said. "You obviously haven't heard of the *Marchioness* disaster."

He slurped his beer. "No. What was that?"

"A collision. Back in eighty-nine. Happened the first year I lived here." And just like that, we resumed the morning's dynamic. (Perhaps I could propose to my career coach that I become a tour guide? It would not, I suspected, fulfill Clare's brief.) Having taken the edge off his postwork euphoria with my account of the worst loss of life on the Thames in living memory, I cast about for other historical pearls to impart. "Did you know the Thames Tunnel is somewhere below us now? It was the world's first underwater tunnel. London's the most tunneled city in the world. Built on clay."

"I've been in the foot tunnel," Kit said, as we approached Greenwich, where the dome of the tunnel entrance glowed in welcome. Used by thousands of pedestrians daily on this bridge-less stretch, it linked Greenwich on the south with Millwall on the north. "What about you, Jay, would you be able to go in that?" He must have been thinking about our morning conversation about claustrophobia. I'll say that for Kit: unlike many of his generation, he asked questions, he was interested in other people.

"I'd be able to go in anything, I just might not like it." I *had* been in the Greenwich Foot Tunnel once, in fact, back in the day. As twentysomethings, a pack of us had raced through the long, narrow pipe, too competitive to be unnerved by the discovery of its being twice the distance it looked from the riverbank. "If it wasn't too crowded, I'd know I'd be okay. I could run."

"What would you be running from?" Kit asked.

"Nothing. I'd just want to get back outside, above ground."

He considered this. "The way I see it, it's safer down there than up here."

I glanced at him. "Why would you not be safe up here?"

He smirked. "Visibility, mate, know what I mean?"

I didn't, and as he turned to his phone and began chuckling at something on Twitter, I found my thoughts trapped in the tubular worlds far below us. Running near the foot tunnel, much deeper, was the DLR between Cutty Sark and Island Gardens stations. It was all too easy for me to imagine the crush of people below us right now, held in a black tunnel at a red light, some rush-hour incident ahead having caused all moving stock to halt. Was sweat beading under layers of winter clothing as commuters grew uncomfortably conscious of being sealed in, the engines eerily still? Were they starting to ask themselves—or one another—*What's going on? Why aren't we moving?* Was there someone down there whose mind, like mine, spun faster, towards terror, someone thinking, *When will the oxygen run out?*

"You all right?" Kit peered at me, more curious than concerned. He lowered his phone. "You look like you're having an allergic reaction to that beer."

"I'm fine. Fancy another one?"

"Does the sun set in the west?" But noticing how speedily we'd progressed—there were no signal failures on the water—he proposed we drop in at the Hope & Anchor instead, the nearest pub to St Mary's Pier, situated on the river path leading east.

What with my nervous system having previously mistaken the Northern Line for the trenches of the Western Front, I had never before strolled into a pub at rush hour for anything other than a solo pulse-lowering double vodka and it was a thrill to submit to this commuter's rite—or right, as Kit would have seen it. In spite of having lived in the area only half a year and been to the pub a fraction as frequently as I had, he was on first-name terms with the bar staff.

"Nice spot in the summer," I told him as we took seats in the deep bay overhanging the water. "Did you know this is an old smugglers' haunt?"

He lowered his pint. "What did they smuggle? Drugs?"

"More likely wool. Because of high taxes. If you look in daylight, there're gallows hanging over the water."

"Harsh." As the alcohol deepened his complexion, Kit turned mischievous. "So, Jamie, *you* ever done anything illegal?"

"Like what?"

"Y'know, the usual."

"I don't know what *your* usual is, but I imagine the answer is yes. Hang on, you're not recruiting me into some bomb-making cell, are you?"

"Absolutely not." And he smashed our glasses together so hard I thought they might crack, letting out that machine-gun laughter that caused faces to turn towards us and soften at the sight of such bonhomie. "Clare seems up for a laugh, as well."

"Well, that was her New Year's resolution. Trying new things. New people."

"Trying new people? I see." His eyebrows waggled. "Why aren't you two married? I thought it was better for rich people to get married for inheritance tax reasons?"

"We're not the marrying kind." I didn't point out that Clare was the rich one, not me, and it was obvious enough why: I wanted him to admire me. Envy me. To believe I had something he didn't besides an archive of historical facts.

"You don't know how lucky you are, mate, being able to do whatever you like without worrying about bills. If that was me working in a café, I wouldn't be able to pay my rent. I'd just be some loser."

It was the same word he'd used to describe his father that morning. His face took on an expression I would come to know as peculiar to him: part coconspirator, part tormentor. An oddly destabilizing kind of look. As he got to his feet to get another round in, I made a mental note never to make an enemy of Kit Roper.

5

Under a luminous white sky, the river flickers silver, as if re-branded for the holiday. A riverboat appears from the east, sleek and low: *Seymour.* Henry's third wife, queen for just a year. I can make out figures already queuing in the aisle to disembark at Westminster, eager to start a new shift making money for other people—or perhaps spending it on behalf of some government department. Stretching my throat, I raise my eyes and stare directly at the sun, dangerously pale behind dense cloud. I'm having one of those acute out-of-body rushes: *This is really happening. This is really me with two detectives from the Met!* I feel a sudden knifing of fear. Am I handling this okay? If I don't act the right way, will I be arrested and put in a cell with a gangster or a pedophile?

"All right, Jamie?"

I blink away the glare and pass a hand over my eyes. "I'm fine."

Worrying perhaps that I'm losing concentration when we've scarcely begun, Merchison tasks Parry with fetching coffee, and as soon as we're alone the atmosphere alters perceptibly. He's like the teacher dismissing the bully to release me from my own face-saving survival instincts.

Now you can feel safe enough to tell the truth.

"What rank are you?" I ask him. "An inspector or something?"

But he's a constable, like Parry, it turns out. This can't be that important an investigation then, I think, heartened. "Look, whatever you seem to have decided about Kit and me, we're not joined at the hip. Most weeks, I only see him on the boat."

He rotates his pen, a miniature baton between his fingers. "So you're *not* close friends, as Mrs. Roper thinks?"

"It depends how you define close." I wish I had a transcript of Melia's interview. Knew what she's revealed, what she's chosen to draw a veil over. "We've socialized a bit at weekends as couples. Drinks, dinner, you know. And we sometimes have a drink on the boat after work."

"You carried on drinking on the boat on Monday, did you? Before this bust-up between you?"

"We had one or two more for the road, yes."

He taps the pen nib on his open pad, leaving little marks on the page. "Mr. Callister and Ms. Miles were with you, you said?"

"Yes, though they both get off before us. Gretchen lives in Surrey Quays, and then Steve is on the Greenwich peninsula."

Don't think about the peninsula.

The apartments, the bedrooms, the secrets.

I feel myself flush. "After that there's only one more stop before St Mary's. We were the last on board."

"Among the last," Merchison corrects me, mildly. "As we said, there's another witness we've spoken to already. I wouldn't mind seeing if your account matches theirs."

I don't like his assumption that this unnamed stranger's story is the benchmark against which others must be judged. Nor do I like my own incomplete recollection: I don't remember noticing a single other person, other than the crew, after Steve got off the boat. I do know it was only then that the scene turned ugly; before that I had been high-spirited, even raucous. A memory breaks from earlier in the evening, when we were still at the bar: *Christmas*, I declaimed with drunken exaggeration, *season of goodwill to all men—or so all men hope . . .*

Oh, God. These days, you have to judge your audience before you make those sorts of jokes. You have to be careful no one's filming you on their phone. Is that what's happened here? Did this other passenger find something we said so offensive they *filmed* us?

No, that's crazy. Come on.

"This passenger you've been talking to, is it a man or a woman?"

There's an involuntary flicker in Merchison's gaze when I say *woman* and I pounce. "Who is she? What's her name?"

The pen is motionless in his grip. "You know I can't tell you that."

I don't know that at all. On TV, detectives constantly taunt interviewees with testimony from witnesses freely named and I argue as much now.

"That's telly, Jamie," he says, with a little show of kindness. "This is real."

"At least tell me what she's said about Kit and me. Why did you speak to her before anyone else?" Before *me*, apparently established as the last person to see him alive. It makes no sense—unless . . .

Unless *she* went to *them*. The next day, she contacted the police to report our altercation as suspicious. That has to be it. *I saw these two guys fighting and I just wanted to check nothing bad has happened . . .*

"We'll come back to that," Merchison says. "Let's talk about these other two mates of yours first. Steve and Gretchen. Where do they fit in?"

There's a nasty twisting sensation in my gut as the drumroll in my chest accelerates, steals my breath.

I think, *I don't like this.*

6

February 2019

One of the joys of commuting without the risk of losing my mind was being able to indulge my curiosity in the people around me, to enjoy the incongruities in the way they presented themselves to the world. There was the man in polished handmade brogues and silk socks of cornflower blue, but with the neglected hair of a vagrant; the younger guy in a cheap suit, with a vinyl backpack from which he unpacked a bento box of perfectly sliced tropical fruit; and the woman who wore tan leather gloves with green piping and whose poker-straight black hair had turned-up ends tinted pink. You grew to match morning faces with evening ones, like a game of pairs: in the morning, animated with purpose or at least nervous tension, by the evening collapsed with exhaustion or relief.

Kit—surprise, surprise—was no mute observer. He would throw out comments, seizing on the slightest reciprocation to get a bit of banter going. I soon learned that he was drawn to a mood of hard living: with Steve, who boarded at North

Greenwich one morning, there was something about the way he pitched himself into his seat across the aisle from us that appealed, as if he'd been on his feet all night and only now been offered rest.

"The peninsula's a decent place to live, is it?" Kit asked. "Are you in one of those new towers?"

Needing no second invitation, the newcomer launched into a long complaint about having worked from home the previous week and been bedeviled by noisy construction work. "Apparently the whole complex'll be finished in twenty years, so that's all right then."

"So you'll cash up and retire rich. You're getting no sympathy from me," Kit said.

"Yeah, maybe, but will I still have my hearing? Will I still have my *soul*?"

Smirking at each other, they exchanged names and slipped their phones into their pockets to signal their intention to engage for the duration. Sitting in the window seat and obscured by Kit's turned shoulder, I peeked sideways at Steve. He was in his late thirties, broad-shouldered, fleshy, and very shortsighted—when he removed his glasses to wipe the lenses, it was a surprise to see how large his eyes were and how rich a graygreen color. His voice was nasal. Unlike Kit, whose diction was well-projected, he spoke as if through a grate.

"What d'you do?" Kit asked him, after ten minutes of ambitious—some might say fabulous—talk about a friend of a friend's electric scooter start-up he hoped to get in on once his debts were cleared.

"I work at Finer Consulting. Internal comms."

"Isn't that your game, Jamie?"

"Was." Leaning forward, I began to explain that I'd left my job following a health scare, but it was obvious Steve thought that whatever story I was peddling I'd have been sidelined soon enough anyway because of my age. (He was almost certainly right: in media, fifty is the new seventy.)

"Jamie lives in one of those massive houses on Prospect Square in St Mary's," Kit told him, "so he must have done *something* right."

I couldn't tell if this was meant in defense of me or accusation, but Steve said he didn't know St Mary's at all and the subject was dropped in favor of hangover war stories.

The next morning, when Steve took the same neighboring seat, Kit gave him a heads-up on the evening service we caught, which prompted a move to the two pairs of seats facing each other next to the bar and a round of Peronis for three. Discovering they both smoked, they slipped out onto the deck for a cigarette. When they came back, buoyant, like they'd discovered fresh air, I had a ridiculous feeling of being put out, as if my friend had been stolen from under my nose in the schoolyard.

"Get us," Kit said.

"This is the fucking life," Steve agreed.

He'd come up with a name for us, Kit reported: the water rats.

"Isn't there a pub called that?" I said.

"There is? Even better."

They stopped just short of high-fiving each other, before screwing up their faces and making nibbling noises like rodents.

I supposed that at least, what with his getting off two stops before us, Steve wouldn't join us at the Hope & Anchor, which had by now, inevitably, become a daily staging post in the Jamie-and-Kit river commute.

In those early weeks, Kit rarely mentioned Melia. Every evening, while I texted Clare my ETA and negotiated the shopping and cooking chores ahead, he made no contact with his girlfriend; I'd even seen him decline her calls, flashing Steve or me the sitcom grimace of the long-suffering male evading his shrew. Meanwhile, Clare would pass on complaints from the other direction, though in such a way that it was impossible to tell if the criticism was Melia's or her own. "You saw how stunning she is, but he pays her no attention. What an idiot."

"He's one of those men who prioritizes the charming of new people," I said. "Maybe it's the drama training. Every situation is an audition, a bid for approval. I'm amazed she even *wants* his attention. They've been together almost as long as we have."

If this implied that I had no desire for *her* attention, Clare took it in good part, cheerfully arranging a date for the four of us to get together again. Kit and I got off the boat at Woolwich to meet Melia and her in a new food hall that had sprung up in a disused factory to dispatch pho, roti, ramen, fennel blanched in ostrich urine (not really, just testing) and cocktails with sprigs of Thai basil served in enamel camping mugs with striped paper straws. In spite of—or because of—high prices and taxing acoustics, the place was heaving, the simple accomplishment of securing a table enough to bring about a release of endorphins.

We sat, as we had on first meeting, in facing couples, Clare opposite Kit and me Melia. "I'll tell my clients about this place," Melia said, sucking her drink. "If they take a flat on the peninsula, they can hop on the boat and come here for dinner. Make a little trip of it."

Clare nodded approvingly. "Maybe we'll be like Brixton Village soon."

"Hope so, it'll be a lot easier to get coke," Kit said and Melia gave him one of her playful slaps.

"Look how she abuses me," he appealed to me with a twisting smile.

"There are men who would pay good money for a slap from your missus," I said, which was no more than the truth, for Melia was looking good enough to draw the gaze of most, if not all, passing males. The legs were not on display this time, but other assets were: her inky hair was pinned up to reveal a pale nape; she removed her work blazer to reveal a top with a neckline wide enough to slip off one shoulder, exposing a lacy black bra strap.

I'd dressed a little more smartly myself for the occasion, had even had a haircut in my lunch break and spritzed myself with some of the posh French cologne Clare had given me on my last birthday.

I realized Kit was responding to my last remark, repeating a question: "How much, d'you reckon? Enough to sort out the student loan?"

"Oh, definitely." I wasn't sure how much the average student loan was, to be honest. Already, I'd learned not to refer to the financial injustices of our age gap: to say, for instance, that I'd been to university when it was still free—I'd even received a grant—would be to provoke a bitter rant.

Less familiar with the danger, Clare began talking to him of her undergraduate budgeting, leaving me to devote myself to Melia and her lovely golden gaze.

"So how are you, Jamie?" An emphasis on *you*. She leaned a fraction closer. "I was thinking on my way here that I hardly know anything about you. I feel like Kit hogs you. I can just imagine him snuggled up to you on that boat."

I grinned. "I can assure you there's no snuggling."

"He says you know things. About the river, the buildings. All the old pubs."

I smiled. "Well, I've made a life's study of *those*." I watched as the end of the paper straw began disintegrating on her lower lip, causing her to pick off soggy fragments with matte-black fingernails. "How are you getting on at Hayter Armstrong?"

"Oh, great. I love seeing all the amazing flats, especially the riverside ones. Those terraces where you can just stand and look out at the water."

"You're lucky to be working at the higher end of the rental market."

"Not as lucky as if I got to live in one of them," she said, with a girlish flounce of self-pity.

I raised an eyebrow. "Some of them are unoccupied, right? You could always go back after hours and hang out. Pick your favorite and meet Kit there. Lie on someone else's sofa and enjoy their view free of charge. Stay the night."

I remembered making a similar comment when I first met Clare and she'd insisted that the scurrilous practices for which estate agents had once been known were long since outlawed.

"What a brilliant idea!" A smile broke over Melia's face, light cracking the cloud. "When I'm caught in the act, I'll tell Clare it was all your fault."

"I'll deny it," I said and we grinned at each other over our sprigs of basil. "What's your family background, Melia? You have such an unusual eye color."

"Half jaguar, half lion," she said, deadpan, and our laughter interrupted our partners' conversation. There was faint relief in Clare's expression, I saw, and I knew to expect the complaint that arrived later over a glass of wine in the kitchen before bed.

"Kit's easily whipped up about money, have you noticed?"

"I certainly have," I said. "He's very aspirational."

Clare sighed. "All the youngsters at work are. They want more, more, more and then feel persecuted if they don't get it. Richard says that generation were raised to expect it all to be handed to them on a plate and take it personally when it isn't." She paused to glance around her elegant elder-and-limestone kitchen, relocated from basement to ground floor before my time to capitalize on the high windows and gracious proportions. The dining chairs were wittily mismatched, including the Shaker antique draped with sheepskin that she always chose.

I thought, a little disloyally, *Wasn't all this handed to* you *on a plate?*

"Kit's the worst I've met, though," she went on. "You should've heard him tonight, talking like he thinks there's some Anti-Roper League meeting every week to dream up new ways to thwart his ambitions."

"You have to admit life *is* tougher for them than it was for us," I said, with as much—or little—delicacy as my four cocktails and large glass of red would allow. "Because of people like you driving up property prices."

She smirked. "That's right, blame estate agents for all the world's ills. We only propose what the punters are prepared to pay."

"Is that Hayter Armstrong's new slogan?"

"Ha! But seriously, how do they afford their lifestyle, Kit and Melia? They plead poverty and obviously have these debts and yet they dress so well and they go out constantly. Kit hinted at a coke habit, didn't he? That can't be cheap."

"I think the way it works is they spend their salaries the moment they're paid and then put the rest of the month on credit cards," I said. "They live the way they think they have a right to live, not the way they can afford to."

Clare's eyes flared. "That's not the way I would want to run *my* finances."

There was a hint of superiority in her dismissal that riled me. "To be fair, they haven't been supplied with a home by their parents."

She said nothing, though she'd be forgiven for objecting to my sudden piety, given the unquestioning ease with which I'd benefited from her parents' generosity all these years. All of a sudden it seemed impossible that we'd rubbed along for so long with this fundamental imbalance. If I didn't reinvent myself adequately in the time frame she deemed appropriate, would I be out on my ear?

"Would you swap? Would you go back to being young, even with all the hardships?" All at once, she was very earnest. She was a magical realist, Clare; she took hypotheticals as seriously as true dilemmas.

"God, no," I said. "Would you?"

"Maybe. I don't know."

Which meant yes. "Really?"

"Maybe if I were a man I'd feel like you do."

"What's the difference?" I asked.

"Duh. People still find you attractive—I've seen them looking at you. But women our age are invisible."

It was natural that I should think of Melia earlier that evening, the pleasurable glow of her gaze. I wondered if she'd have paid me so much attention if she knew of my lack of assets. "Men our age without money can be just as invisible, believe me," I told Clare.

———

Well, perhaps the feted Vicky Jenkinson would be in a position to offer a solution to aging in an unfriendly marketplace.

It wasn't until I sat face-to-face with my career coach in a pair of midcentury chairs upholstered in Delft blue that I understood why I had needed Clare to step in and schedule my consultations for me: I didn't want to look for a new job. I was quite content with the one I had.

That wasn't to say I didn't like Vicky or her very cool live-work unit in a former spice warehouse in Shad Thames that I passed twice a day on the boat.

She invited me to choose from a collection of herbal teas, individually packaged and with names like Rejuvenate and Reinvent. I scanned for one without a "re," but there was none and so I chose Reawaken.

She spoke in brisk certainties. "You're demoralized from applying for jobs and not being invited for an interview. We hear a lot about unemployment figures, but not very much about the million-plus people who want to work but don't get fairly considered for the roles they apply for."

"Try not even having the application acknowledged," I said, though the truth was that since starting at the Comfort Zone I had not applied for a single job in my old sector.

"The thing to bear in mind is that hiring someone is a risk-weighted investment decision. You need to lean on your gifts."

I felt myself wince, and, noticing, she dialed down the jargon. "Jamie, I can help you return to marketing by expanding your network and refining the way you sell yourself, or, alternatively, identify a new career, one that has a healthy supply of roles. Do you have a sense of which it will be?"

"Neither," I said, slurping the hot green Reawaken potion. "The thing is, I kind of like the job I've got. I'm happy there for now."

She was not discouraged. "Is your current salary acceptable?"

"It matches the unskilled work, I suppose. Clare says it's pin money, but it's not pin money to the millions of people who earn it. It's how they put a roof over their heads and feed their kids."

"While studying for qualifications in some cases, I imagine," Vicky said. "Qualifications that you already have, Jamie." She talked about earning power, self-esteem, and peer status, which made me remember Steve's casual disregard and, to an extent, Kit's.

"The issue is, Vicky, I have a public-transport phobia, so how I get to work is more important to me than the kind of work I do when I get there or what my friends might think of it. So any new job will have to be within walking distance of London Bridge—or commutable by river bus."

"River bus?" This sparked a connection and she opened a nearby storage box. "I have an exercise I do to discover how someone feels about their current position when they can't identify it easily in words. Let's try it."

I thought I'd identified my position perfectly well in words, but I looked anyway at the picture cards she laid on the low table between us. They all involved a man and a boat of some sort, including one of an athletic type in a canoe heading towards a tsunami, another of a drudge on a ferry looking blankly out of a rain-spattered window, and a third of a rakish sort steering a yacht, with friends in the background drinking champagne. I had to say which one was me.

"One client said she was none of these," Vicky commented. "She said she was in the water, drowning. Now she's a vice pres-ident at a nonprofit organization. Her dream job."

"This is easy for me," I said, pointing. "I'm the one on the ferry."

"Are you heading to work or back home?"

"I'm heading home." I paused, starting to enjoy this. "But my season ticket's run out. I'm a fare dodger."

"Interesting," Vicky said.

"Were the teas a test too?" I asked, sipping.

"The teas? No." There was a pause. "Let's take a look at your A to Z of skills, shall we?"

———

One evening on the boat, we got talking to a red-haired woman who boarded at Blackfriars with Kit and Steve and beat them to the bar for her G&T before removing all outer garments and settling into a seat near ours as if in her own home. When she called out hello in a celebratory tone, I realized she'd already had a few.

"What we need on this thing is a bit of decent music, don't we? Not this soporific crap."

Weary after a shift at the café so manic I hadn't been able to take my breaks, I smiled only thinly at the prospect of a floating dance floor.

"There's always the option of a silent disco," Kit said, laughing. "Plenty of space to dance."

Our new friend was called Gretchen, a digital project manager whose ambition was to be an artisan gin distiller. I put her at thirty-five but knew better than to do so publicly in case she was in fact twenty-three (later, I found out she was thirty-six). We offered our elevator pitches: Kit the insurance drone, Steve the marketing maverick, I the dropout who frothed milk and mashed avocados for a living.

"Good on you, Jamie," she said, as if I'd said I volunteered in a hospital for terminally ill babies. "I would *never* have put you in insurance," she told Kit. "How do you even stay awake in that world?"

"I have my ways." Kit winked at her.

When he and Steve disappeared for a cigarette, it was no surprise that she should interrogate me about him. "Is he married?"

"No, but he lives with his girlfriend."

"What's she like?"

"Really nice."

"Really nice as in not at all pretty and you're being kind to her or really nice as in unbelievably pretty but you're being kind to me?"

I gave her a look of exaggerated horror. "Is this *really* how women think?"

"Just put me out of my misery, Jamie."

"I'm afraid she's gorgeous." I smiled, ruefully. "He's a lucky man."

"Damn. You got some sort of love-triangle thing going on?"

"Not at all. Kit's very happy with Melia. I'm very happy with Clare."

As I made these statements, my voice smooth and convincing, I was aware of a twitch of uncertainty inside my chest.

Anyway, Gretchen joined the gang with or without any prospect of bagging Kit. Now, the fourth seat was saved for her. Now, on the evening boat, a round was four beers, which at £4.50 a go was almost twenty quid, over two hours' worth of my working day (what with the drinks at the Hope & Anchor on top, I'd soon be working at a loss).

I realize I'm making it sound like we were Ocean's Eleven, assembling our crew, one by one, for the heist of the century, but we stopped at four.

And the idea of crime of any description never entered my head. Though I suppose I can only speak for myself.

7

December 27, 2019

Two young female tourists swish by in biker boots and bobble hats, glancing appreciatively at DC Merchison, and I'm thinking he's actually a bit of a dude. He's got a certain poise, an unshockable way about him that reminds me just a little of Kit. If I wasn't already confident of my own innocence on Monday night, I could easily be lulled into a false sense of security by someone like this—or, rather, a false confession.

Because this isn't one of those stories of murder dispensed in drunken blackouts or PTSD fugues. I am one hundred percent confident I did nothing wrong at Monday night's drinks, other than knock back a bit more than planned, and if we're going to call *that* a crime then this city's going to need a couple of million more police cells.

"Did Mr. Roper confide in you about any worries he might have at the moment?" Merchison asks.

This is easy. Everyone knows what Kit worries about most. "Yes, he's got money troubles."

The detective gestures for me to elaborate.

"Debts. Student loans, and more recent loans as well. Even though he's on a good salary, he spends every penny he earns and complains he'll never be able to get on the property ladder."

"He's shared details of his salary?"

"Well, no, but it's sure to be decent. He works for a big insurance firm and the benefits package alone is supposed to be fantastic. You've spoken to them, presumably? He's meant to be in work today, I think."

"We will be in touch with his employer shortly," Merchison says, as if to dispel my fears, but in fact merely confirming that I am not only a priority over Kit's other commuter mates, but also ahead of his colleagues. I make a painful attempt to gulp, but my saliva glands seem to have failed. God knows where Parry's gone to get the coffee. Has he left town? I should have sent him to the Comfort Zone for the Indonesian guest bean that's been so popular this month. I imagine Regan serving him, ignorant of the connection.

Then it strikes me that he might be taking his time because he's making a phone call about me—or receiving one. Maybe he's sent someone to hammer on the door of Mariners and take a look at the late-night footage from Monday. Good. But, wait, what if there's a problem viewing the material? What if the camera wasn't working that night for some reason and there's literally no evidence that I walked home alone?

Aware of the expanding silence, I refocus. "Anyway, recently, he's become fixated on me. He can't bear that I get to live in a great house and he doesn't, even though mine is actually my partner Clare's and in reality I've got as little as he has. But he doesn't see it that way, he thinks I've got it made. He resents Clare, as well. He was very rude to her the last time we all went out." I give a hollow chuckle. "I mean, if you can't handle the idea of inherited wealth, then London's really not the place for you, is it?"

DC Merchison observes me with increased attention. "You're sure the resentment towards you is in relation to your perceived differences in financial assets?"

"What do you mean?"

He pauses, gives the impression that he's choosing his words with special care. Then he moves fractionally closer, a little gesture of discretion, though there is clearly no one to overhear us. "You should know that Mrs. Roper has been very honest with us. She understands we need the full picture if we're going to find her husband. Holding back important information only wastes time and you're probably aware that in a missing-persons investigation you *really* don't want to waste time."

"Oh. Right. Okay." My tone is as wary as my gaze.

"You mentioned Mr. Roper might have continued drinking at this bar, Mariners, and possibly gone home with a woman other than his wife. Assuming this was the case, is it possible he might have done it as some sort of tit for tat?"

Inside my cuffs, my fingers clench. "Tit for tat? You mean towards Melia?" Unexpectedly flooded with shame, I meet his eye. "Yes. Yes, I suppose it might be that."

"So you and Mrs. Roper . . ."

"Please, can we just call her Melia."

"You and Melia," he says, agreeably. And he angles his head as if to appraise me afresh, to assess whether I'm plausibly appealing enough for a woman of her caliber. There's a flicker in his gaze and I imagine him thinking, *Yes, I can just about see it.*

"When exactly did you start sleeping together?" he asks.

8

March 2019

I'm really attracted to you, Jamie . . .

It was so simple a seduction, so direct. My response? So *predict-able*. Frankly, I never expected to hear words like these from my long-term mate, much less from a wildly attractive younger woman.

We'd known each other six weeks or so by then and were to-gether once more as a foursome, this time at Kit and Melia's place on Tiding Street. Just before it could start to be conspicuous by its absence, a dinner invitation had come for a Saturday night in March.

They'd spoken of their flat as a hovel, but it was no different from the first flats of my own youth, albeit at a vastly inflated rent (Clare knew the going rate off the top of her head: eighteen hundred a month). The difference was that I'd been quite con-tent with such accommodation at their age; I'd scarcely given it a thought from one month to the next.

The sitting room was dominated by an acid-yellow velvet sofa, a raft of vivid color in the ocean of rental neutrals. Whatever had been at the window had been torn down, an exhibitionist move on their part in a street this narrow or perhaps simply an act of negligence by their landlord. Other than the flowers we'd brought—purple tulips, with some sort of foliage that smelled of the woods—a framed Spanish poster for the movie *Niagara* was the only decoration, its star pictured lips parted, mid-protest.

"Who's the Marilyn fan?" I asked.

"Who *isn't* the Marilyn fan?" Melia said. She wore a zipped floral jumpsuit of mauve and buttercup-yellow and high cork-soled platforms that would have looked ludicrous on anyone else but on her looked, well, ravishing. "Kit bought me that for Christmas," she added.

Vintage posters were not cheap, I thought.

There were few personal items in evidence. Clare and I had dozens of photographs and spent a fortune on frames, but our hosts had only one (I supposed their memories were mostly digital). It was of a group of actors in front of a plantation house set, a baby-faced Melia, dressed in a slip dress, identifiable in the center.

"Was this your fifteen minutes of fame?" I asked her.

"Sure was. Guess the play."

"It's got to be *Cat on a Hot Tin Roof*?"

"Very good! I played Maggie. Rich but unfulfilled." Adopting a sultry Southern accent, she added, "*I* should be so lucky."

"You pull off the Liz Taylor styling pretty well."

"Thank you. Sadly, we didn't get to keep the costumes." Her gaze lingered, and I suppose mine must have too for me to know hers had.

I scanned the other faces in the photo. "Have any of these guys made it big?"

She moved to my side so we were shoulder to shoulder and I felt electrified by the touch of her arm against mine. "Freya's understudying at the Gielgud at the moment. Oh, this guy, Rollo, he's touring in the Far East with a great company. The problem is, you get a gig like that and then it ends and you're back to square one. Back to bar work to pay the rent."

"I've done it the wrong way round," I quipped. "Maybe now I've got the café job, I need to become an actor?"

Melia cocked her head. "I actually think you'd be good, Jamie."

"Based on what?" Clare asked her, laughing. I hadn't realized she'd been listening. "I can always tell when he's lying."

"There must be a slight difference between acting and lying," I pointed out. "Otherwise half the population would be auditioning for the RSC."

Melia repeated the remark as if committing it to memory. In her own home, there was a subtle difference to her manner. She was more adult, challenging, even a little intimidating, as if she were in the one place where life worked on her terms instead of other people's.

We chatted about my career counseling—"I'm going to be master of my own narrative"—and when I next looked I saw that Kit had Melia's cast photo on his knee and was dividing a small pile of powder into lines, vertical arrows through the bodies of each of the figures. I glanced at Clare, knowing I would need to take her lead, which was almost certainly to abstain since we hadn't done drugs in years. But when Kit passed it to her, she peered at faces in the photograph and laughed.

"I need to know who I'm abusing here."

"Go for Si, on the right," Kit said. "He works in Harrods in small electricals now. He was the one we all thought would make it, as well."

"You get Melia," Kit told me, indicating the line running up the center of her skimpily costumed figure.

I could tell the coke was finer quality than in the old days. I felt instantly, shockingly pleased with myself, a sentiment reflected in the dilated gazes of the others in the room. God knows how much time was spent finding one another fascinating before Clare said, "Are we actually eating this evening?"

"Oh, yeah, there's stuff in the oven," Melia said, as if she'd forgotten quite what.

"I can check for you," I said. "I need to get some water."

I congratulated myself on the water, which I felt showed a level of self-preservation.

"Grab another bottle of red from the rack, will you?" Kit said.

The layout of the flat was from the original conversion, the galley kitchen at the back, next to the bathroom. Its sash window was half open, and in a neighboring garden a dog barked and was loudly shushed by its owner.

Having filled the water jug and picked up the wine, I turned to find that Melia had arrived in the narrow space and was standing with her back to the door, blocking my exit. I smiled, wine bottle in one hand and jug in the other. "Any particular reason you're barring my way?"

"I just wanted you to myself for a minute."

"That's nice," I said, uncertainly.

"It *is* nice." She took a step towards me, her platforms soft on the tile, and added, in case I'd misunderstood, "I'm really attracted to you, Jamie."

Well. Without the chemical boost, I'd have assumed I was being pranked; even *with* it, I thought this was not a declaration to be taken at face value, though she'd inched so close I could feel her breath. Was this some prearranged wife-swapping proposal? But hearing Kit and Clare in the living room arguing about Brexit, I thought not.

"You don't believe me, do you? Why would I lie?" She gave a smoky sigh. "I'm going to have to show you."

With both hands full, I was completely exposed to her wraithlike embrace, arms snaking around my chest, her fingers moving over the back of my neck, small high breasts compressed between our rib cages. Her confidence was audacious, even insulting, and in my mind I pictured myself shaking her from me, asking her what the hell she thought she was doing. In reality, however, I was kissing her, responding to the pressure of her instinctually, mindlessly. Occasionally the silky fabric of her jumpsuit would touch my bare skin, its frictionless contact wildly erotic.

I have no idea how long this went on for—thirty seconds, perhaps even a minute—but we came to only when we heard Kit's voice from the other side of the door. "Me? Can you bring another bottle of white, as well?"

Melia detached from me as efficiently as she'd attached herself. "No problem, babe," she called.

There was the roar of the extractor fan as the bathroom light was turned on and then the sound of the door closing. In a few deft moves, she swiped a bottle from the fridge, eased the red from my hand, and swiveled, hooking the door open with her foot. Left alone with the water jug, my sleeve drenched from the motions of our clinch, I could only wonder if what I'd just experienced had been a quantum leap with consequences for all four of us or the opposite: ephemeral, weightless, a sweet suburban lapse never to be mentioned again and remembered in old age with fond nostalgia.

Back with the others, gender lines prevailed, Melia plunging instantly into some deep heart-to-heart with Clare while Kit and I co-DJed. The food, unchecked, had to be abandoned and a takeaway ordered.

———

"I think we overdid it last night," Clare groaned, delivering tea and Advil to the bedside the next morning. No longer morning, in fact, I saw, nudging my phone from under the pillow and seeing the time. Sitting back on her pillows beside me, she looked like I felt: destroyed. "Good to remind ourselves why we don't do drugs. *They're* too old for it, let alone us! Never again."

Struggling upright, I ignored the white streaks in my vision and downed the tea while she googled a story about a middle-aged couple going to bed after a cocaine binge and not waking up again. In the cold light of day it struck me as extraordinary that in these straitlaced times Melia should have done drugs in front of a work superior. But, then, that wasn't the only line she had crossed so incautiously last night—my memory functioned well enough for me to be clear that it had been she who initiated our kiss. What had I been thinking, kissing her back like that?

I hadn't been thinking, that was the problem.

"Who's this Steve bloke Melia told me about?" Clare asked, cradling her mug. With her head lowered, the shadows under her eyes were dark, ghoulish.

"He's a friend from the boat. I don't think she's met him, has she?"

"No. What's he like?"

"He's okay. A bit full of himself."

"Everyone's full of themselves these days. Where did all the shrinking violets and wallflowers go?" Clare groaned. "Anyway, Melia's very suspicious of him. I wondered if you two had words about him in the kitchen."

I made a sound in my throat like a blocked pipe. "No, not at all. Why?"

"Just that when you came back, she went on and on about him, how he's a bad influence on Kit, that kind of thing."

"Maybe he is," I said.

"Yeah, or maybe *Kit* is." Draining the last of her tea, she set the mug on the bedside cabinet and sank lower into the bed. "I imagine she'll be fine once she meets the guy and his tongue is hanging out like every other man she's ever encountered."

"I'm sure you're right." Though confident there was no insinuation in her comment, I turned onto my front and buried my face in the pillow. There was nothing for it but to sleep off my shame.

9

It was a relief on Monday morning when Kit made no move to lure me onto the deck and bundle me overboard. Evidently, he knew nothing about what had taken place in his kitchen. In any case, rain was lashing down and the deck was closed. The buildings at ground level were slick from the downpour, their tops obscured by low cloud. Umbrellas, mostly black, formed jagged walkways of shelter.

"Saturday night, mate," he said by way of a greeting. As tradition dictated, Clare had sent the thank-you text, not me, and would slip a card through their letterbox later, even though either of us could have handed it over directly. Those Edinburgh manners prevailed.

I pulled a classic lads' expression: sheepish, but unrepentant. "Can I give you some cash for, you know?"

"No, you're all right. Just being good hosts."

Free drugs and a grope of his girlfriend—or, more precisely, a groping from her. Remembering my hands-free help-

74

lessness, I felt a surge of desire, turned my head from Kit and pulled myself up from the seat. "Let me at least get the coffees."

"Great. Oh, get me a pastry as well, will you? Didn't have time for breakfast."

There was a queue at the bar and by the time I returned, we'd reached the peninsula and Steve had joined us. As they discussed the weekend's football scores, Kit tore at his pastry as if he hadn't eaten for days. Everything he consumed, he consumed so vigorously.

"You're quiet today, Jamie," Steve remarked. "Having a bit of a Zen moment, are you, before you clock in at the Cabinet Office?"

"Yeah, yeah." It hadn't taken me long to recognize him as one of those people skilled at making a sneer sound like a bit of harmless fun. I turned from their cackling to look at the river.

By the time I got to work, I'd dismissed Saturday's canoodle as an isolated incident (how could a woman as beautiful as Melia possibly fancy a man who used words like "canoodle" unironically?). Even so, the subconscious is a powerful thing and I found myself humming that old Special AKA song, "What I Like Most About You Is Your Girlfriend." I played it to Regan—she'd never heard of the Specials—and started thinking it might be one of my Desert Island Discs (I didn't dare ask her if she'd heard of Desert Island Discs. Or just *discs*).

Then, midmorning, a text came:

Enjoyed Sat. Want to meet just U & me?

I stared at it for some time before replying, *Is this you, Melia?* and breathing in painful snatched gulps until the next text appeared:

How many of us R there? Yes, M. Thurs 7:30?

I began typing, *I'm flattered, but,* and found myself pausing. I can't claim that events ran away with me, that I was swept along like some hapless antihero, because I actively stopped mid-composition and considered my answer from a bigger-picture perspective. Even a long-lived life is tragically short—would I ever get an offer like this again?

I hit the delete key, tapping away at that little cross, and then typed:

Yes. Where?

Simple as that. As treacherous and opportunistic and—I would like to think—uncharacteristic as that. Never mind that I'd be sitting side by side with her boyfriend every morning between now and then in a seat paid for by my partner, never mind that Melia worked with that partner and was several ranks her junior. I was a cad, a heel, and other terms Kit and Melia would never have heard of. She was whatever passed in millennial vernacular for the female equivalent.

Her message came back with an emoji I'd never used before but that I guessed meant "my lips are sealed":

Goody. I'll send address deets.

It was easy enough on the evening in question to tell Kit I was getting the usual boat and then deliberately miss it to get the one after. Even in minimum-wage work—especially in minimum-wage work—you got held up, and so he took the 5:55 and I the 6:25.

I was meeting Melia after her final appointment of the day. The flat was on the twelfth floor of a new development on the east side of the peninsula, with a view downriver towards City Airport. It was dusk, the lights of the planes piercing the smog.

She was already there, waiting for me as the lift doors parted and kissing me boldly on the mouth before singing hello. Her hair was loose, little flicks of auburn at the ends that I hadn't noticed before. She wore close-fitting black trousers and a rose-pink silk blouse.

I followed her high-heeled steps down a narrow, carpeted corridor and through the door of a low-lit corner apartment. Unlike in the movies, we didn't fall wordlessly on each other the moment the door closed behind us, but instead acted as if we were the first to arrive at a gathering of many. I unscrewed the bottle of wine I'd picked up, filled the takeout coffee cups brought from work, and made a little circuit of the open-plan living space. The windows had those gauzy white drapes you find in beach hotels in Bali, the furniture black and sleek. On every sofa and chair there was a complex scheme of throws and cushions, unlit candles in porcelain pots on the low central table, even a photography book open on a spread of a rooftop pool. It had obviously been professionally staged, a notion I'd always found ridiculous when Clare mentioned it, but entirely appropriate for this, a drama with adult scenes, a running time of, what, an hour? Ninety minutes? "Who owns this place?" Had Melia misused work properties before or had I sown the seed in that jesting exchange at the food hall?

"A buy-to-let investor," she said. "She's never lived here herself. I'm not sure she's ever set foot in the place."

"And I assume she has no idea you're using it for your extramarital assignations?"

Her lips pressed together in amusement. "I'm not married, Jamie."

And nor was I. "Extracurricular then."

"And only one assignation. We won't come here next time." She watched for my reaction to this casual assumption that we would continue in subsequent locations, and nerves flurried in my stomach.

Nothing has happened yet. You could still walk away.

"Come and see the bedroom."

I tailed her to a lamplit box of fashionable charcoal hues, as pristinely arranged as the rest of the place. Whereas the living room had a deep balcony beyond its walls, the bedroom window was a single-pane cliff face of glass.

"You don't have a fear of heights as well, do you?" she said.

"As well?" I laughed. "You see me as completely maladjusted, don't you?"

"Maladjusted, that's a great word. But no, of course I don't. We're all maladjusted in some way. We all have The Fear." She held out her hand to me, palm down and fingers outstretched, almost as if she expected me to kiss her hand. Wild impulses sparked.

"What's yours?"

"I think I have, maybe, a fear of boredom."

That was when we moved towards each other, the combined velocity giving the impact an unexpected violence. Then we were kissing hard, tumbling sideways onto the bed, fingers reaching for zips and buttons. Naked, she was smooth and milk-pale, hot to the touch and in constant motion; spine arching, legs hooking, mouth searching. She was so unlike Clare it helped me keep Clare from my thoughts, which was convenient.

"I can't believe we're doing this," she giggled afterwards, with lighthearted relish, as if we were skipping school or stealing apples. Not that she'd have known the concept of the last: she ordered everything on her phone, even another woman's man, and everything came to her in the delivery slot she'd selected.

"Don't you worry someone will walk in?" I said.

"No. We're the sole agent."

"But yours can't be the only set of keys. What if Richard or someone came for some impromptu viewing? You'd lose your job."

"Then I'd get another."

"Good luck with references. 'I cannot in all conscience recommend Melia I-Don't-Know-Her-Surname as a property negotiator because she was found in a high-end apartment abusing the client–agent trust by sleeping with the partner of a company director . . . '"

Melia's lips curled. "Sounds bad when you put it like that."

I was beginning to understand that she was a person with a strong sense of having nothing to lose—and she assumed no one else did either. It was easy to see why she and Kit were together.

"It's Quinn," she added.

"What?"

"My surname."

"So we can't come here again, Ms. Quinn?"

"Probably not, it'll be let soon, maybe by the morning. I showed a couple just now and they're keen. But there are other places. I just need to pick ones without doormen and schedule a viewing for the end of the day. Then I take the clients down afterwards, wave goodbye, and come back up."

"What about security cameras?"

Her eyes widened, roguish, conspiratorial. "Who's watching? And if they were, you're just another client looking at a flat."

To demonstrate our anonymity, or perhaps her own recklessness, she slipped from the bed and stood at the window, completely nude. When I protested, she wrapped herself in the gauzy drape, winding twice, three times, until she became an opaque Melia-shaped dummy at the edge of the window. I tried not to imagine the feeling of confinement wrapped like that.

"Come back, Melia, come back! You're like Cleopatra," I said, as she unfurled. "That was how she was presented to Caesar. Not in a curtain, though, in a carpet."

Melia returned to the bed. "Was he pleased?"

I gripped her against me, ran my hands over her back and bottom. "Very, I would have thought."

After we'd dressed and smoothed the bedding, I went to the window myself, nose almost to the glass. It was impossible not to feel a kind of holiday high. Sex with a woman twenty years younger than me in a bedroom in the sky. Lights from the planes climbing from the City as if staged for our adventurous urges and not those of the passengers within; the illuminated riverboat mapping its course silently below. It must have been the service that arrived at St Mary's just before nine thirty.

As Melia consulted a photo on her phone to reorder the throws and cushions precisely as we'd found them, I took one last look out and knew, with total certainty, that whatever it was we'd started this evening, and no matter how strenuous the deception or debilitating the guilt (and I *did* feel guilt, whatever anyone might think of me), I would not be able to stop.

"What?" Melia said, beside me again, ready to depart.

"I can't believe you like me," I said, truthfully.

She smiled. "I told you. You know things. You're funny."

I was moderately knowledgeable and amusing, I conceded, not to mention euphoric enough to push from my mind the more obvious explanation of this miraculous pairing: she also thought I was rich.

10

December 27, 2019

"Well, you're certainly not the first man to find himself in this position," Merchison says, and I assume he means tempted into infidelity generally as opposed to by Melia Roper specifically. I wonder if in his dealings with her he'll infer that it was *I* who tempted *her*, she who was "not the first" to be tricked and misled. A little police mind game to divide us, loosen our memories.

I'm saved from answering by the sight of DC Parry marching into view, a cardboard tray of Costa takeout coffees in hand. Though I'm not a Costa fan, at this stage in the game I'll take the psychoactive boost in whatever form it comes. But at the corner of the building he pulls up to speak to someone out of sight and, to my horror, that figure reveals herself to be a uniformed officer. Is she there in support of the two detectives, poised to step forward the moment she gets the nod? On TV, they just hit a button on their phone and bark, "Request backup NOW!" and two minutes later it's there, officers fanned out, all escape routes covered.

She glances in our direction before dipping out of sight and I breathe a little easier.

Parry rejoins us. "I guessed black, no sugar," he tells me, delivering the tall cup with a thump. His ungloved hands have the grayness of cold.

"That's fine. Thank you." Coffee is expensive, should I offer to pay for mine? Then again, they're preventing me from earning money here. Unlike Kit, I don't get paid if I fail to turn up.

He remains standing. "Shall we move inside, warm up a bit? They've opened up."

I appeal to Merchison, who is already on his feet and sipping at an espresso-sized cup: "How much longer do you think we'll be? I really need to get to work." In actual fact, I can see Regan's response to my text on the phone screen: *WTF? Take as long as you need*!

"Just a little longer," Merchison says, "if that's okay with you?"

Again, I read between the lines: *It's either here or we take you in. Charge you.* Charge me with what? They clearly already knew about the affair, so that can't be what he was hoping to extract from me in Parry's absence, and whatever briefing Parry might have received while gone, he's not announcing it any time soon.

"Of course." I follow them into the vast public hall and across the acres of marble to a table far from the central bar and obscured by a broad supporting pillar. My cheeks are stiff with cold, aching as they thaw in the heated interior.

"So we've just been getting up to speed on the current status between Jamie here and Mrs. Roper." Merchison updates Parry, who grimaces as he listens. I sense he doesn't care for the sex subplot, at least not the details of it.

I'm thinking, meantime, of Clare. The deceived partner. *This is not just about you, Jamie.* "Can I just ask, have you spoken to my partner, Clare Armstrong?" It strikes me that Melia must surely have let her colleagues know her situation; she can't possibly have gone into work this morning. I picture her sitting in pajamas on her yellow sofa, pale and tearful, with one of those family liaison people who nod gently and know the right lines to say—"It's important to stay positive. We mustn't catastrophize."

"Not yet." DC Merchison is scribbling her name, asking for the correct spelling. "Do we need to?"

"No, I just wondered." *Idiot.* I wish I could take the pen and score a line through his note. If they do decide to phone her, or pay a visit, they will surely tell her about Melia and me; they're not in the business of diplomacy. I can only pray that her shock will be obscured by the greater horror of a friend having vanished.

"Maybe you should call her," Merchison urges me, with a glance towards Parry. "Tell her where you are."

This is obviously a test. They want to hear what I say about Kit.

Fine. I fish my phone from my pocket and select Clare's name, trying not to show my relief when I connect straight to voicemail. I'm starting to feel that time has lost its reliability, a minute expanded, a half hour compressed.

I speak in a low, cautious tone: "Clare, it's me. Something's going on with Kit. Apparently he's gone missing. I'm with the police at the moment and wanted to let you know they might phone you."

To confirm my alibi.

"Maybe you already know this from Richard," I add, "or Melia herself. If you've seen her, I hope she's holding up okay."

As I end the call, Merchison observes, "I take it she doesn't know what you've been up to then?"

Rattled both by the sound of Clare's recorded voice and the implication in his that he's identified a new form of leverage, I let my politeness slip. "No. And I'd prefer to keep it that way."

"I'm sure you would." He jots a line or two on his pad before sitting back and smirking at me, giving off a one-lad-to-another vibe that feels pretty authentic, and I can only guess at his own success with women. His innate understanding that in our new culture of scrupulous equality most men and women still want to enjoy the original game of opposite sexes. It doesn't just recede because we say it should. "No guarantees, I'm afraid," he says, with faux regret, and flattens his hair with both hands.

My gaze dips to his notepad, momentarily unprotected, and I attempt some upside-down reading. *Probs with CA*, I decipher. *CA doesn't know about MR*?

Why the question mark? He hasn't taken my word for it? I speak more firmly: "Look, Clare's not relevant to whatever's happened to Kit."

Parry, who's been listening to this exchange, must have an asbestos throat because he's already tipping back his coffee to drain the last drops. "Until we know exactly what happened to him on Monday night, we have to assume *everything's* relevant," he says, close enough for me to catch the scent of americano on his breath.

The table is smaller than the one outside, more of a bistro table for two, and I have a sudden image of Kit at our Christmas drinks (*inaugural* Christmas drinks, he kept saying in that significant way of his, like he'd just invented the word, like it was some kind of legacy, a gift from him to us); appearing at our tiny table in the bar with a round of drinks, empties swept to the edge. His voice was thick with mockery as he raised a glass in my direction: "To Jamie, who thinks his generation's the only one that knows how to drink . . ."

Was there . . . was there some sense of farewell in that thespian flourish? What was it he said to us that time about suicide? *If I wanted to end it all, I'd fuck off and do it privately . . .*

Even as I resolve not to repeat his words to these detectives, I'm visited by a sense of loss so profound I find it hard to breathe.

11

March 2019

Fortunately for me, Clare was out at a client dinner the night of that first liaison, giving me time to scrub the smells of adultery from my skin and feign sleep by the time she returned. In the kitchen the next morning, I took my customary position at the coffee machine, blue-lit buttons aglow as the beans ground, while she sat at the table eating mango chunks with a cake fork and checking her email. She seemed exactly as she always was until she suddenly exclaimed, "Oh!"

I handed her a cappuccino and stood slightly out of her eyeline with my own coffee. "Bad news?"

"It's from Vicky."

"Vicky?"

"Your career coach." She regarded me with dismay. "She says you missed your consultation last night."

Feeling my face redden, I eased into the seat next to her. "God, I completely forgot about that."

"*Jamie.* You need to put this stuff in your phone calendar so you get reminders. You can't just keep it in your head."

"I thought it was tonight," I said, proving her point.

"It's only the second one, isn't it? What must she think? If you can't even make the sessions, how can you expect to carve out a new career?"

The language was grating—*Maybe "carving out" and being on time are different skill sets*, I thought—but I was not about to start an argument with the pressure of another woman's fingers still burning on my skin.

"I'll apologize and reschedule," I assured her. "Why is she emailing you, anyway?"

"I guess because I set it all up." She returns to the message. "She says she won't charge for the no-show. That's very decent of her."

"Great. I'll thank her. And, Clare? I'd prefer to communicate with her directly from now on. What with my being forty-eight years old and all, I think I can handle it without an intermediary."

"Of course." And she looked across the table at me meaningfully, like a pet that expects its owner to understand its needs without having to ask.

Or maybe *I* was the pet.

Later that day, I waited for Melia's confirmation of our next meeting—*7:30 Weds*—before composing an email to Ms. Jenkinson suspending our course indefinitely owing to work pressures. *I will be in touch as soon as my diary clears again* . . . Her response was prompt and professional: an agreement to await my preferred dates as and when I became available (*I must point out that the fees have been paid in full and are nonrefundable*). I followed up with my thanks and then told Clare I'd rescheduled for the following Wednesday at seven thirty.

Potentially, I had six further iterations of the same cover story.

Of course, the downside was that Clare was now alert to the need for closer supervision, on my case the moment I returned from my second meeting with Melia, a glass of wine ready for our self-consciously informal debrief.

"How did it go with Vicky?"

"Great. She's very inspiring. We did exercises to identify desires."

Don't think about sex with Melia. The animal pleasure. The commitment, as if it's our last act on earth.

"Has she given you homework?"

"I have this whole thing to download with possible new career directions."

"What are you thinking at the moment?"

"Maybe a comms job in education. Or even teacher training."

"I suggested that ages ago!"

"I know you did, and now I'm thinking about it properly."

"Retraining is definitely the key," Clare enthused. "Unlike the baby boomers, we'll be working till we're at least seventy."

I dismissed the flare of objection I felt that she should include herself in this cohort; with her private wealth, she'd have no need to work a day longer than she chose.

"When's your next session?" she asked.

"I'm not sure yet—Vicky'll confirm in the next few days. Look, I'm knackered. I'm just going to have a quick shower and then you can tell me about your day. How did the viewing go at the Woolwich riverside complex?"

Clare nodded. "Really good, it's just a question of deciding on the unit. Nice couple, early thirties. They've been scrimping for years, doing all these side-hustle jobs. Unlike our young friends, who want what they want when they want it."

She began crooning the song in breathy Marilyn-style vocals, but, Melia still on my mind, I didn't stick around to hear the next line.

———

Of course, Clare was not the only chess piece on the board I needed to consider if our liaisons were to continue undetected: there was also Kit. Easy enough to tell him the same story of career coaching sessions; more difficult was the fact that the flats Melia and I used were in the Greenwich area, mostly on the peninsula, and therefore on our route home. Though the water rats had a WhatsApp group to let one another know which boat we'd be getting, I was still caught out twice over the course of the affair. The first time, Kit joined me on the later boat without warning and I claimed to be meeting Vicky in North Greenwich instead of Shad Thames, an unlikelihood not challenged.

The second time, Steve was on the same boat and there was no way I could hope to say I was getting off at his stop and not be accompanied at least part of the way. ("I'll just leave you here, Steve. This is the building where I meet Kit's girlfriend for a spot of fornication.") I had no choice but to text Melia a cancellation, turning my head from him to hide my frustration. I remember the boat's windows were veined with dried rain from heavy showers earlier in the day and in a better mood, I'd have thought their tracks beautiful. Instead, I wanted to smash the glass with the heel of my hand. Turning up at home with some tale of Vicky having been double-booked with a VIP client, I then had the collateral unpleasantness of Clare holding my hand while I tackled a teacher training application I'd never wished to make and had no intention of submitting. Some extremists punish faithlessness with death, but, believe me, this ran it a close second.

———

"Do you feel guilty?" I asked Melia, as we lay entwined after sex. It was the fourth meeting, if I remember. A town house on the peninsula, an ultramodern version of my own home, though a meaner slice, a cheaper construction (the rental rate? £4,000 a month). The bedroom we commandeered was at the rear of the property, where the light wouldn't be noticed by neighbors, the bed a preposterous cushioned velvet thing, its inelegant proportions reflected to infinity in two facing walls of mirrors.

"About Kit? No way." In the low light, her irises were burnt umber, her black mascara smudged.

"Have you ever thought about ending it? I mean, if he makes you so unhappy you're doing this. If you think he's not good to you."

Was there a splash of hope in the glance she gave me before lifting a slender arm and flicking her fingers as if to bat off a wasp? "I don't think he's good *for* me, is that the same thing? And where would I even live if we did break up? My credit rating is a disaster, I wouldn't be able to raise a deposit."

"You could get something through work?"

"Nothing comes up even close to what I'm paying now—and I can't afford *that*. And I've got no intention of living in one of those awful flat shares with no heating and mold on the walls, so don't try hooking me up with your friend at work. She obviously has no pride."

"She obviously has no money," I corrected, gently. "Regan would kill for your flat. How much do you and Kit owe, anyway? What kind of figures are we talking about?"

Her answer was mind-boggling: well over a hundred thousand pounds between the two of them. The debt earned almost as much in interest as she did from her job. Was this normal for her age group? It was like a high-interest mortgage on your life.

"Can your family not help?"

"My parents haven't got a bean—we don't speak, anyway. And my sister would rather finance, I don't know, a Free All Pedophiles campaign, than help me."

I'd heard a little from Clare about the enmity between Melia and her sister and it sounded to me like straightforward sibling rivalry, albeit one that had extended to a falling-out on Melia's part with her parents. The gist seemed to be that Melia had had the looks and talent growing up, the promise of stardom as an actor, but now the sister had eclipsed her by acquiring a wealthy husband, producing twin sons, and launching a business designing school satchels that had already won an entrepreneur award.

"I wish I could help you, but I haven't got a whole lot myself." I took a long breath. "You know the house is Clare's, don't you?"

There was a silence and then Melia raised herself onto a bent elbow. Her face blazed. "Seriously? I didn't know, no. I thought you owned it fifty-fifty."

"Nope, it's a hundred percent hers—held in trust by her parents, in fact, to protect her from thieves like me. I'm as poor as a church mouse." Though I sounded blithe enough, I could feel, once more, that new burn of umbrage at the inequality of my position.

"I had no idea," Melia said. There was a darkening in her eyes and I thought, *This is it.* She thought she'd line me up, she thought we'd set ourselves up with half the proceeds. It made sense that she'd be the sort of woman who didn't bother with gaps between relationships (in my experience, the better looking someone is, the more likely they are to be an overlapper). And in intuiting this, I understood that I'd exploited her. Let her seduce me when I knew all along I had nothing to offer her, not even an expensive trinket on her birthday.

But she surprised me with her sudden squeezing against me. "Well, that makes sense because I'm only ever attracted to men who have nothing. Nothing in monetary terms, I mean." Her tone was tender, consoling. "You still get to live in an amazing home, have this amazing lifestyle."

"You want to make soya lattes for tourists, be my guest. I'll see if we've got an opening." Seeing her unable to muster a chuckle, I said, "You could have anyone, Melia. Ditch Kit, ditch *me*, and find someone who can give you what you want. There's no shame in wanting a great lifestyle. There must be thousands of bankers or tech rich kids who'd be happy to go out with you."

"I just told you, I'm not attracted to those guys," she said.

It struck me that I would have expected someone Melia's age to protest that she preferred to be totally self-sufficient, the good feminist, and I said as much now.

"How am I supposed to be self-sufficient?" she demanded. "I'm paid peanuts at Hayter Armstrong."

"You're a junior in a structured training program," I reminded her. "Everyone loves you, you'll get promoted soon."

"It takes too long!" she cried, frustrated. "I don't want to be rich when I'm old, I want to be rich while I'm young! It would be different if I was starting from scratch, but debt is the worst. It's like knots tying you to the starting blocks. Every time you move, they just tighten."

"Well, don't marry Kit, whatever you do," I said. "You'll only be liable for his debts, as well as your own. Do you not have anything you can sell?"

"No. Nothing. If the bailiffs came, they'd take the clothes from our backs."

"If that happens, come round to Prospect Square and we'll give you a room for the night. Meanwhile, I think we both need to buy a lottery ticket." I cuffed one of her wrists, felt the pulse quicken, and soon I was inside her again and doing my best to take her mind off her misfortunes, if only for the short term.

Later, in a smaller voice, more maudlin now than angry, she said, "I can't have anyone I want. There's something about me, something that puts people off."

Her mind had looped back to what I'd said about bankers. "What do you mean? What thing?"

"I don't know what it is. If I knew, I'd eliminate it and bag a billionaire. Fuck feminism."

Superficial though her desires were, I was nonetheless impressed with her self-awareness. Because she was right, there *was* something, something that might have brought pause to a man less devil-may-care than Kit: a sense that she would not be satisfied by convention. These men had had an instinct, perhaps, that there could be trouble long term.

We lay in silence for a while, staring at the ceiling. For all the house's technological bells and whistles, the ceilings were featureless. No cornicing and ceiling roses, just the smooth blank lid of a box.

No, in this room, the only beauty, the only poetry was in Melia's face. The line of her nose and jaw, the rich blaze of her eye. I thought, *Doesn't she realize being young is priceless?* Clare had as good as admitted she would trade her fortune for a second stab at youth; unlike love, unlike happiness, you couldn't buy it.

Only as we dressed and tidied up after ourselves did she abandon the subject of money—not that I was any keener on the next one.

"She's worried about you, you know. Clare."

"Is she? How do you know that?"

"We had lunch yesterday and she confided in me."

I frowned. "You had lunch, just the two of you? Now that we're, you know, wouldn't it be more politic not to do that?"

"More 'politic'?" Her smile was mischievous. "Why? You think we'll compare notes and plot against you?"

I couldn't believe how cavalier she was. "But aren't you worried you'll slip up?"

"I'm a good actor, remember? Seriously, don't worry, she doesn't suspect. She's fixated on Kit, thinks he's leading you astray with all the drinking."

"Really? Well, she told me you said Steve was leading *him* astray."

"I did say that, yes." Melia kissed me, long eyelashes skimming my skin. "Misdirection, darling. This Steve guy's the big bad wolf. Doesn't matter who it is, really, just so long as no one's looking our way."

Evidently, she'd come into this affair with skills honed. On the wall beyond, I caught her narrow smile in one of the mirrors. They were like cameras in the room, catching hidden angles, exposing guarded emotions. Making strangers of us.

12

April 2019

We had our first sun in April and there were colors in the river besides the familiar brown: metallics of silver, pewter, and gold. The city's magnolias were flowering and, when the boat's doors opened, there was even the odd snatch of birdsong. As we sailed under Tower Bridge towards ultramarine skies, it was impossible not to feel the rejuvenating spirit of a new dawn. Not to mention the resurgent arrogance of a new adulterer.

Melia's assessment was accurate: Clare had no idea. To her, Melia and Kit continued to be the younger couple we socialized with, the couple who were hedonistic, provocative, occasionally explosive.

I remember one scene at Prospect Square—it must have been several weeks into the affair—when we found ourselves refereeing a row between them.

Kit, obviously knowing which buttons to press the deepest, had made some admiring remark about Melia's sister. There'd been a photo of one of her product lines in the previous week-end's *Sunday Times* Style section. "Looks like I picked the wrong sister," he said, and even a casual bystander would have picked up on the goading.

"Should've thrown your hat in the ring, see how you got on," Melia said, coldly.

"Yeah, I should."

"You'd have soon found out she's only interested in money."

"Well, that doesn't sound at all familiar, does it?" Kit taunted her.

It was childish stuff, but soon Melia was weeping in the kitchen and being comforted by Clare, and he, claiming he wasn't going to pander to her oversensitivity, went out to the front doorstep to smoke.

Instinct told me to even up the numbers. Outside, the wind was high and the tops of the lime trees shivered and swayed like cheerleaders' pompoms, fanning the scent of a thousand spring evenings before this one: the stone underfoot, balsam from the trees in the square, the faint briny scent of the river.

"Sorry about Me," Kit said, his mouth obscured by smoke. "She's always been weird about her sister."

"Clare said something about that," I said, vaguely.

"Actually, she's weird about everything at the moment," he added.

I didn't like to think when it was that the two of them had begun bickering, that it might have been about the same time that she began a relationship with me. Was she angry with him because he'd failed to notice he was now sharing her? The thought made me dizzy with unease. Why on earth hadn't I made adjustments by now, maneuvered Clare and myself into distancing ourselves from them as a couple? I suppose I feared it might have the opposite effect and stir her suspicions. It's the classic giveaway, after all: avoid someone you've always got on with or act less relaxed when you've previously been perfectly at ease.

The problem was that all four of us were boozers and drinking together made it dangerously easy for either Melia or me to make some insider allusion we shouldn't, or give an absentminded physical touch that just-good-friends never would.

I was saved from commenting on Melia's "weirdness" by racing clouds uncovering the moon, its soft light falling on the square in front of us and stealing Kit's attention.

"Do you need a key to get in there?" he asked.

"Yes. All the residents have one. It only opens to the public once a year on an open garden scheme." I had no idea if Melia had yet passed on the information that the house was owned by Clare's family, but standing there on the old, broad steps, I felt as deep a sense of surrender as I ever had to the intimate power of my home square.

"What are those trees, even?" Kit said.

"They're 'even' planes and limes. There're loads of shrubs in there, as well. Some flowerbeds. We all contribute to a fund that pays a gardener."

He sighed, exhaling a mix of awe and resentment. "How the hell do you get to live in a place like this? I bet there's not a single resident here under forty." Sod's law, a taxi pulled up at that very moment on the west side of the square, releasing a chorus of upmarket middle-aged voices.

"Actually, there are quite a few families with grown-up kids still living at home," I said.

"Poor little posh kids," he sneered, and the look he cast me was unnervingly knowing. Knowing of something specific, like my intimacy with his girlfriend? Or generalized, the hardwired superiority of youth? He knew better, he just hadn't yet had the chance to prove it to the world.

"You're not the only one, Kit, you know," I said, in a low voice.

"The only one what?"

"Suffering from the housing crisis. Some would say you're doing pretty well. You've got a place to yourselves, you don't have to share a kitchen and bathroom with strangers. There's not *that* much to complain about."

He blew smoke in my direction. "Okay, boomer."

He had a way of defusing conflict, of making me laugh. "Gen X, thank you very much, snowflake."

We stood for a minute listening to the music coming through the living-room window, the sixties hits playing on in spite of the breakdown of the group.

"Great playlist," he said. "Who's this again?"

"The Zombies."

"Yeah, I'm liking all your sixties stuff. Music was definitely better in your day."

"You know I was born in 1971, right? And I wasn't actually alive when these songs were out?"

"I do have some basic numeracy," he scoffed. He lit a second cigarette, lifting his chin as he did. The song played on—*It's too late to say you're sorry*—and I ignored the quiver the words sent across my skin. "Want one?" he offered.

"Go on then." When you haven't smoked for years—Clare and I had given up together on her fortieth birthday—the first hit is painful, like self-harm. Then again, inhaling fumes from the London roads is said to be equivalent to smoking ten a day. "I remember when ciggies were two quid," I said.

"I fucking don't want to know," Kit said. "Crap music, over-priced fags, extortionate rent. What other reasons do I have to slit my wrists?"

"Climate change?" I said, not without sympathy. Life was exciting for me—perilously so—but I didn't envy the world Kit and Melia had inherited. Thank God Clare and I had no kids, no stake in the future.

As if to mark the sentiment, there was the distant blare of a vessel on the river, a reminder that the water was right there and would flow long after we'd left this city. In response—or so it seemed—a fox cried out from some hidden corner of the square, sharp as a tile-cutter.

"Jamie," Kit said.

"Yeah?"

"Don't do it, will you?"

My breath caught in my throat. "Do what?"

"Take her side. Melia's, I mean. I know Clare will, women always stick together, but *you* don't need to fall for her drama."

"There are no sides to take," I said firmly, though raised

voices behind the door announced Melia's continued distress and plans for an immediate departure.

As she burst onto the doorstep, Kit and I moved to one side, making no eye contact.

"Kit, you'd better walk her home," Clare said, a concession not to the three or four mean streets of St Mary's that separated our houses so much as a criticism of Kit's neglect of his girlfriend's emotional needs.

"Sure," he said, and we watched them leave, Melia stalking away in heeled boots, Kit keeping pace, the end of his cigarette burning orange by his side.

He made some attempt to touch her—put an arm around her perhaps—and her screech split the night: *Do NOT touch me!* And then they were gone from the square and our surveillance.

"That went well," Clare said, as we set about wedging wineglasses into the dishwasher and scraping leftover food into the bin.

"Didn't it?"

"Why's she so sensitive? And why does he have to be so *in*-sensitive? You know she thinks he's screwing that woman on the boat."

I was taken aback. "What woman? You mean Gretchen? I very much doubt it."

Clare raised an eyebrow. "And yet you knew who I meant straightaway."

"Only because we don't know any other women on the boat." Though suspecting another sleight of misdirection on Melia's part, I was nervous of talk of infidelity, regardless of the participants, especially so soon after that exchange with Kit. What would Clare do if she found out about Melia and me? Grab a knife and slice my throat, or turn away, rocking with laughter? "I honestly think this is how they like to conduct their relationship. They enjoy tormenting each other," I said.

"I agree. Probably this is how their parents behaved," Clare said. "They think it's normal."

Even with the advantage of sleeping with one of the subjects, I couldn't match her psychological insight.

"Don't get me wrong, I like Kit, but I wonder if she might be better off with a different kind of guy. Someone who gives her what she craves."

I gulped. "What does she crave?"

"To live her dreams." Catching herself in a rare moment of sentimentality, Clare gave a self-deprecating chortle. "What she *thinks* are her dreams, I should say. Anyway, if they go on like this, something bad could happen."

"I was just thinking that," I agreed.

13

It's approaching 9:30 and our coffees are finished. Though I could get up and leave any time I choose, I have to admit there's a rogue part of me that's appreciating this opportunity to order my thoughts, to take my disjointed history with Melia and turn it into something more cohesive. I've warmed up, I suppose.

Still busy, I text Regan.

Parry collects the cups and flattens them in one fist, placing them on the rough cardboard tray. It seems to me his fingers have the potential for precision, even cruelty—I imagine him plucking the legs from an insect. I look beyond him, scanning the banners in the space below us, marketing for a series of festive concerts by the London Philharmonic in the New Year, until he says, almost kindly, "What you have to remember, Jamie, is one person's version of events is never the only one."

Does he mean that Melia's said something different about our affair? That's hard to believe. Or is he referring then to this other witness they've got up their sleeve? Either way, I'm not delivering the easy solution to the mystery of Kit's disappearance that they'd hoped for. I'm guilty of sleeping with his wife, I've admitted that, but they want more. They're stuck.

"In my experience, no two people ever remember things exactly the same way," I say, equably. "Sometimes you wouldn't know it was the same event."

"Yes, of course," he agrees. "You must know that from previous incidents."

"What d'you mean?" My brows rise so high I can feel my forehead corrugating. My injured thumb is starting to itch inside its dressing.

"I mean, maybe now might be a good time to talk about what happened in July of last year."

It's a swerve of direction so violent, I feel whiplashed. What could possibly link my helping them with their inquiries involving my missing friend with a mental health episode suffered a year and a half ago among total strangers? Is *this* what he discovered in his prolonged coffee run? Did it come up on the police database or was it the result of a quick google? Certainly, there is no reason for Melia to have mentioned it. I hold his gaze, defensive, almost proud; let him know I'm unimpressed with these tactics. They obviously don't realize yet that they can trip me up a hundred times and it won't change the fact that I have not harmed Kit.

Or maybe they don't care about facts. Maybe they only care about statements. *Versions.*

"July of last year?" I repeat, playing for time.

"Yes. 2018. The last time you were involved with the police."

He makes it sound as if I'm some serial offender, in and out of Wormwood Scrubs. "If you mean the business on the Tube, I don't see what that's got to do with this."

"I would say it suggests a certain impulsive streak in you that very well may have reared up again on Monday night," Parry says.

I flush, angry now. "'Impulsive streak'? You've got to be joking? What is it you want to know about it that you can't read in the statement I made to the police at the time?"

He isn't backing off. "Just give us the highlights, Jamie. Or do I mean lowlights?"

I glower at him. I don't like the edge of disrespect to his tone, which echoes, if anyone, Kit. Not a generational fault, however, since his partner is casting him a glance that suggests a level of disapproval of his own.

"Mental illness isn't like that," I say in a flat tone. "It's complex, personal. Different for every sufferer. Weren't you taught that in training? Half the people you deal with must have mental health issues."

Parry bows his head in apology. No doubt he's remembering warnings of the myriad new ways members of the public might complain about how they've been misspoken to or wrongly defined by police officers. The organizations that will rally to support them, the activists and the trolls. He tries again: "Let me rephrase. Please would you tell us how any mental health issue *you* suffer from specifically affected your actions last July."

"Do I have a choice?" I direct the question at Merchison, but it's Parry who has the baton and he's keeping a tight grip on it.

"You always have a choice, Jamie," he says. "A man like you."

14

It had been building, I knew that. But the problem with phobias involving commuter transport is you either face them or lose your job. You have to get to places at a time that suits other people's preferences, not your own.

I didn't work at the Comfort Zone then, I was still in my "real" job, an erroneous distinction if ever there was one, since standing for nine hours serving coffee feels a lot more real than nine hours sitting in a meeting talking shit, drinking coffee served by someone else. Anyway, the office was in North London and to get there for 9:00 I'd catch the 7:35 overland train into London Bridge and then take the Northern Line to Chalk Farm.

The train was without exception overfull, but at least you could position yourself at the window facing out, deceive the brain into thinking you could touch the world beyond. The Tube offered no such trickery: look out of the window and you'd see only how terrifyingly close you were to the black walls of the tunnel, tunnels built for compact trains intended for a working population a fraction of today's size. No walkways, no escape routes; only the popping veins of the cables and the blackened, peeling panels.

As for overcrowding, the Tube made the overland train look like the Orient Express: bodies were crammed into every last column of vertical space, the necks of those who'd pressed on last bent painfully forward in line with the curve of the doors—doors that locked like a crocodile's jaws.

But I had no alternative. The roads were clogged, making driving as slow-moving as walking. The bike I'd bought was stolen from outside the Hope & Anchor even before I'd had a chance to test my fitness for it, and still so new it hadn't yet been insured. And now, in July, there was a heat wave. The papers were full of the soaring temperatures, the inhumane conditions. *Tube Hotter Than Legal Limit for Cattle!* The older, deeper lines took a hammering: close to forty degrees, with explanations of how the extra heat was caused by a combination of friction from braking and inadequate ventilation.

The Northern Line is the oldest and deepest of all. It is also the longest continuous tunnel on the network at over seventeen miles.

The day it happened, I had a gut instinct there was something different about the journey. I was like the birds that bolt when the earth quakes ten thousand miles away—except I didn't bolt. I couldn't. I was trapped.

As the train swung between Euston and Camden Town, the mass was swaying towards me, forcing me painfully against the protruding flap of the emergency lever. I'd read so much about crush dynamics, I was practically an expert. A crush is seven passengers per square meter, when bodies are so jammed together they start to move as one, like fluid. A typical Northern Line train of six carriages had a capacity of eight hundred, but there were thousands on this one, and now it was happening—it was really happening: I couldn't inflate my lungs.

Cheek flat against the partition, I gasped a plea to anyone who would listen: "Please can you move a bit, give me some space."

"No chance, mate. It's sardines in here. Same for everyone."

I thought, *I need a doctor, I'm going to die.*

A press of hot faces, hot chests, hot breath. My vision red and black, crinkling at the edges. Scrabbling waist height with my right hand, without even being able to see what I was doing, I lifted the flap and pulled the emergency lever.

At once, an alarm rang out, though the train continued to move. Dozens of low voices asked the same few questions:

"Has something happened?"

"Did someone just pull the alarm?"

I know now that when the alarm sounds while the train is in a tunnel, the driver will override the automatic brake and continue towards the next station; he'll call ahead for help but must get his train to the next platform before that help can be administered. Obvious, when you think about it.

But what happened that July morning was that the train *did* start to brake, about five seconds after I pulled the lever, before coming to a halt in the tunnel. Instantly, I understood that I had made the situation much, much worse, and now I was assaulted by hate-filled voices:

"Was it *you*?"

"For fuck's sake, why did you do that?"

The cause of our captivity passed through the carriage and into those beyond, provoking a thousand muttered curses, the collected humidity of that human breath raising the temperature. My ears were primed to pick out the most frightening comments, the ones that served my own catastrophic thinking:

"There's *literally* no air in this thing."

"It's like an oven, isn't it?"

"When are we going to get out of here?"

The shock of what I'd done receded and in its place roared a need to escape that was so extreme, so fanatical, I lost my mind and began scratching at the partition with my nails. My hearing was briefly fuzzy—I must have been on the verge of passing out—before returning with hideous clarity at the sound of my own roar, a wild, animal response to captivity. A babel of voices and accents:

"He's a maniac, what's the matter with him?"

"Fucking idiot."

"Don't be so horrible. He's having a panic attack, he needs help. We need to give him some space."

"There *is* no space."

I thought how unexpected it was that the angriest voices were female and the only helpful one male. It was he who appealed to seated passengers, calling out, "Will someone give this guy a seat. He needs to calm down."

"Don't look at me, I'm pregnant!"

"Someone else, then!"

No one would do it. Even in my hysteria I knew not to succumb to the instinct to drop to the floor, which would create a hole in the crush into which others would fall on top of me. I managed to keep standing, legs juddering, eyes screwed shut—if I couldn't see, the brain might forget the confinement! But the image of the carriage and its hellish press of bodies remained on my retinas.

Above the arguing, the driver's voice droned through the PA system: "We're being held behind another train. Can the person who pulled the passenger alarm please hang on, we'll be on the move again soon and we'll get assistance to you as soon as we reach the next station."

The commentary altered:

"He didn't make the train stop, it was stopping anyway!"

"They'll be queueing for the platform. I was once trapped for twenty minutes."

"*Twenty minutes?*"

That was when the lights went out, a marginal relief for me, but a development received with universal angst by the others.

"Oh my God, is this some terrorist thing?"

"Is this guy in on it?"

"Don't be stupid, you heard what the driver said."

But the "T" word had been released and all down the carriage people were losing their minds. Someone began sobbing and the voice I recognized as the pregnant woman's grew wild and raging:

"This is unbearable! I feel faint! It's so hot!"

"Should we force the doors and let some air in?"

"There is no air, we're a million feet underground!"

"Here, I've got some water."

I opened my eyes, childlike in my gratitude, but the water was being offered to the pregnant passenger.

"D'you think there's been a power cut above ground, as well?"

One of the hundreds of things I knew about the Tube was that forty-seven million liters of water are pumped from the system every day and if there *had* been a mass power cut above ground, or an earthquake that caused the power to shut down indefinitely, then the pumps would have been down too. Would putrid water arrive at our feet and slowly rise?

I won't relive it minute by minute, but we were in that tunnel for half an hour with no power, no messages from the driver. My skin burned as if I'd been shoveled into a furnace and yet somehow I stopped myself from passing out. Light radiated from torch apps, but all I could think of was the heat of a thousand devices turned on at once.

At some point, news arrived, passed from carriage to carriage: we were to be detrained. The train in front had broken down and was now being evacuated. We would have to walk through the tunnel and through this other train to reach the platform at Camden Town.

There was a gradual easing of the crush as the doors between carriages were opened and those further up began shuffling towards the front of the train. Then came the first sight of London Transport staff in hi-vis vests and directing powerful torchlight. "Is this gentleman all right?"

Gentleman. I remember that. A low calm voice, fractionally consoling. My throat was dry as tinder. Water was passed to me and my hands shook as I tried to drink, so I spilled it onto my shirtfront.

"We need to start moving to the front of the train, sir."

I was escorted, hands gentle on my arm, through the evacuated carriages, past the faded seats littered with newspapers and discarded garments. Being on the tracks was even worse. It was just as airless but with the smell of scorching. We were rats in a clay oven. As I began to groan, my escort reassured me. "It's just a bottleneck at the back of the train in front. Stay calm. We've put down boards to make it safe for you to climb up onto it."

Breathe, breathe. But the air was so thin. My head throbbed, out of time with the thudding of my heart.

At last, we shuffled through the train in front. It had broken down just outside the station and light was visible from the platform, onto which we were assisted via a ramp. I was deemed capable of taking the escalator on foot and not stretchered to the area above ground, where those needing medical assistance were being assessed in the ticket hall. The northbound service had been temporarily suspended and at the barriers a crowd waited. Among the general rubbernecking, there were a fair few unkind looks and comments.

"People get very agitated in this weather," a uniformed officer said to me.

The pregnant woman, coming up the escalator behind me, was mouthing off: "It's *got* to be a criminal offense to use the emergency lever without a proper reason? He could be a terrorist for all we know!"

"We will need a statement from you," I was told, just loudly enough for the nearer reaches of the waiting crowd to hear.

There was a fresh outbreak of jeers.

I wasn't charged with anything, of course, but who needs police prosecution when we have our fellow citizens?

Someone had videoed the "action" in the carriage, others the aftermath at Camden Town, and it was all over social media the rest of that day.

In the press coverage, my name was given, along with an erroneous attribution of guilt:

Mass Panic in Crush Hour
as Train Evacuated in Tunnel

Overheated commuter James Buckby, 47, brought the Northern Line to a standstill today when he pulled the emergency lever and set in motion a complex sequence of delays. Three trains were evacuated and passengers led through darkened tunnels to safety. Emergency services treated Buckby and several others on site in temperatures of almost forty-degree heat and a woman thought to be eight months pregnant was taken to University College Hospital with suspected dehydration.

"It was hell. Mass panic, started by this one bloke. If he'd just hung on, he would have been out of there in a couple of minutes. Instead we all had to suffer," said Abbie McClusky, a 26-year-old software consultant.

"We were trapped in the tunnel for almost an hour," said Charlotte Silva, a working mother of three. "I thought we were going to die. We had to walk single file because of the live lines. I didn't see the man who started it, but if I was him I'd go into hiding."

A spokesman for TfL explained that Mr. Buckby's call for help was incidental to the factors that led to the emergency evacuation. "Extreme heat conditions caused the train in front to break down less than twenty meters from the station platform. Trains were backed up at stations and in tunnels all down the line. It was a perfect storm, I'm afraid." He added that rumors that Buckby's act was in any way related to a foiled terrorism attack were entirely false.

Even so, commuters have continued to round on Mr. Buckby for the inconvenience he has caused, many using #Commuter Hell to share their anger. Were YOU trapped on the train? Contact us with your eyewitness account!

Twitter went into overdrive, if overdrives can be distinguished from the general tone of emergency, and one *#Com muterHell* tweet went viral: a picture of me balled up in a seat, hands crossed over the top of my head, the carriage having half-emptied around me, with the single-word caption: *This.*

An email came to my personal account that gave me palpitations: *I went into labor after what happened. The baby almost died!* No name was given, only the email address sbm1989 @gmail.com.

"There must have been some preexisting medical condition," Clare said, when I showed her.

"It was very hot." Even talking about it made my lungs burn.

"But that wasn't your fault, Jamie. You didn't control the temperature down there. It's basically a clay furnace, you said it yourself."

"Should I reply? You know, ask about the baby?"

"I wouldn't. It might be interpreted as an admission of guilt and she'll come after you with some civil lawsuit. It might be some sort of scam."

On medical advice, I took a week off, and my GP helped me book a course of CBT sessions. Returning to work, I took a cab, but the traffic was so bad my commute took almost two hours. Next, I tried a complicated route involving only surface trains, but panicked after a stretch through a tunnel and had to leap off at the next station, making my way on a succession of crammed and crawling buses.

I resigned. While procrastinating about setting up as a freelancer and working from home, I looked for a job, any job within range, and, failing that, widened my net to within walking distance of London Bridge. The Comfort Zone was hiring.

I'd already begun there when another mail came from my antagonist: *Too much of a fucking coward to get back to me? Should of known.*

"Not a grammarian, then," Clare said.

You shouldn't be allowed to get away with this, said the next.

And then: *What goes around comes around. Remember that.*

"You need to close that email account," Clare advised.

I did. "Weird that it's a woman who's got so angry. It was the same at the time, as well. The men were fine."

"The tide is turning," she said, and perhaps because I was still mid-breakdown she didn't add what I was fairly sure she was thinking: *Get used to it.*

15

May 2019

It was hardly a surprise to learn that Melia had googled me and read about my disgrace. What was surprising was how long it took her, given that I'd searched *her* name as soon as our affair began. This was what lovers did in 2019, they coolly investigated each other. No more subtle gleaning, no more telling your backstory in your own time. Privacy was a setting now, not a human right. And so I'd scanned various three-line reviews of her acting performances from years ago, as well as out-of-date employment listings. Instagram was her favored form of social media, her activity veering from wild enthusiasm one week—#LoveLondon Life—to total abstinence the next (#HateLondonLife, I guess).

"We read about that Tube thing," she told me. It was about two months into the affair by then, late May. Another workday evening, another one of her apartments, sleek and impersonal crucibles of intense human passion. I lived for our assignations now; I was a trained animal. "We didn't realize you'd made the news."

We. Kit and her. I imagined the two of them propped on their pillows, sharing the iPad, dark heads side by side. Did he cradle her head the way I did, the way I was right now, my thumb stroking the soft down of her hairline?

"Sounds like a real drama," she added.

"Yes, it was. And a lot more of a drama because people tweeted about it. The *Standard* totally stoked it."

"Kit loves that Hashtag Commuter Hell thing on Twitter."

"That's still going strong, is it?"

"Yes, he says people are really witty."

"Believe me, it's not so witty when you're the one they're trolling. Did the article you read mention that it was the train in front that broke down? Nothing to do with me. And did it mention that we're unbelievably lucky not to have had a mass crush in one of our stations? The platforms are as overcrowded as the trains. There's literally no margin for error, one person could trip and fall and that would be it. Hundreds could die."

She shuddered and took my hand. The backs of our hands were a portrait of age: mine crinkled, discolored skin and raised blue veins, hers pale and smooth. Was her blood brighter too? Were her bones glossier? "Maybe you should have cycled?"

I explained about my bike having been stolen. "It was out of range of any CCTV, but even if cameras *had* picked up the thief, I'd never have got it back."

"Have you thought about moving somewhere else? Where you could drive to work."

"Maybe. But Clare would never leave London. Her business is here. That trumps any of *my* concerns," I added, displaying more pique than I'd intended.

There was a silence. Sometimes with Melia it felt as if her silences were messages in invisible ink; you applied the magic fluid and revealed the words at your own risk. This time, I read: *What's Clare got to do with anything?* Though I'd asked her if she'd considered leaving Kit, she'd never asked me if I'd leave Clare.

Dropping my hand, she ran her fingers over my chest, fluttery as moth wings. "I quite like crushing up against men on the Tube. Sometimes, you can feel, you know."

"What?"

"That he's getting excited."

I had to laugh. "You're admitting you're a sex pest? Careful I don't report you."

She shrugged. "It's not a crime if the victim doesn't object."

"You're on shaky ground there, darling, legally *and* morally." I wondered if she'd given any thought to the short-term nature of her sexual power. In a decade or two, she might press herself against some guy and be called out for it, humiliated. A new generation of Melias would be quick to deride her.

"I had a panic attack once," she said.

"Oh yeah? When it occurred to you that you were cheating on your boyfriend and he might find out . . ." That reminded me of something else. "Clare said you think something's going on between him and Gretchen?"

"I wouldn't be surprised," she said, displeased.

"Was that why you got so upset at our place?"

No reply.

"Come on, Melia, even if he is, you're not really in a position to object, are you?"

She turned, eyes furious. "He hasn't got a clue about us. What I *object* to is he thinks he can do whatever he likes. Say whatever he likes."

It was hard to reconcile her assessment with my own: to me, Kit was a man perpetually frustrated by what he couldn't do. I said no more and she returned to the story of her panic attack.

"It was on a flight. There was really bad turbulence and I freaked out. I only stopped when they threatened to restrain me. I was still whimpering and I could hear people saying, 'Can't she shut the fuck up.' People are so mean; that was almost more upsetting than the turbulence."

As she began to detail individual examples of hatefulness, as if it were hers that had been the career-ending, life-altering trauma, it was hard to tell whether her original aim had been to empathize or simply to talk about herself.

"There's a reason 'Melia' gets shortened to 'Me,' " Clare said, later, on a cold morning in Edinburgh. "It's because she's a complete narcissist."

But I'm getting ahead of myself.

———

The Tube drama wasn't the only thing about me that Kit and Melia had been discussing. *Or* the water rats.

I remember Kit and Steve were bonding over terrible bosses one morning, a well-worn topic—Kit disliked his line manager, called her the Cold Fish, and over time this was abbreviated to the Fish; Gretchen, out on the deck, worked for the Psycho; and now they'd settled on a name for Steve's, a fitness freak: Iron Snake.

"What about you, Jamie?" Kit asked.

"Oh, my line manager's a great girl. I really like her." There was an echo of our conversation about fathers: his a waste of space, mine decent.

"It's probably you that's the one with the nickname," Steve said. "Come on, spill. What do they call you over at Starbucks?"

"It's *not* a Starbucks," I muttered.

"Maybe they call you the Escort?" Kit said. "They do know you're a kept man?"

I felt myself flush. So Melia *had* told him. What had I expected? Presumably, she'd given him the impression the information had come via Clare.

The two of them guffawed. As they riffed on other words absurdly unsuitable for a middle-aged bloke—gigolo, playboy, cocksman—I gave up and went to join Gretchen outside. Under a fresh spring sky, the river shimmered with light, almost as if it were heat, almost as if the temperature, which was low enough to cause cold water shock all year round (yes, I'd read up on it), wouldn't cripple the strongest limbs and cause a gasp reflex that drew filthy water into the healthiest lungs.

She was sitting with her eyes closed and head back, hair lifting onto her face in the breeze.

"Gretchen? Are you asleep?"

"No." She acknowledged me through a squint. "If you close your eyes, you can pretend you're on holiday, not on your way to spend the day with a nest of vipers."

Jesus, the trip was a real pity party this morning. "Is work really that bad? Why don't you move somewhere else?"

Gretchen opened her eyes and I expected her to take the opportunity to talk once more of the gin distillery of her dreams, but to my astonishment, tears brimmed. "Oh, I'm looking, don't worry. I wish I could take time out in between, but I can't afford to. There's no one to bail *me* out."

So she knew too. They'd discussed my unusual situation, and far from considering me an asset-free vulnerable as they might if I were the woman in the relationship, they'd decided it was unfair that I should be subsidized when they were not.

"It's not a bailout when you're a long-term couple who care about each other," I said, and it was surely the hypocrisy of my own words that took my breath away and not the bracing river air. Clare still believed I was attending sessions with Vicky, a ruse I'd extended by claiming to be interspersing them with networking events, but their usefulness as an alibi was due to expire. I'd need a new hobby of some sort, something Clare wouldn't be tempted to join me in (taxidermy, perhaps).

Gretchen was not to be roused from her gloom and so I went back inside, slipping into a seat at the back rather than rejoining the men. Melia's disgruntlement with work was one thing—I shared her pain because I was besotted with her—but to hear constantly how these young adults thought themselves entitled to jobs more prestigious and better paid than those they'd actually earned was tedious. Grow up! It was a reminder, I supposed, that friendships born of convenience were as flimsy as the pages of our *Metros*.

As we approached Tate Modern, a series of reflections in the glass made the city tip to the side, the Millennium Footbridge like a ladder to the sky, the people climbing, heads down, unable to escape the slanting water.

I could see it would start to scare me, the river, if I let it.

―――――

If I was a little glum at work after this commute, Regan trumped me—*and* Gretchen. She trumped all of us. "I'm being thrown out of my room next week. The original friend is coming back from traveling."

"Well, a curse on Original Friends," I said. "I didn't know it was a sublet."

"They've said I can sleep in the utility room but there's no window and the boiler's dodgy." Regan pushed up her sleeves. She had a tattoo of a spider on her left forearm, its legs encircling her arm like binds.

"No, you don't want to die of carbon monoxide poisoning."

"I know someone with a spare room, but it's right near where that kid was just shot. Did you read about it? In a car park in Plumstead? That's why it's cheap, I suppose. You might get gunned down." She earned, I knew, precisely 40p an hour more than I did, but that did not raise her rate to the living wage, which in London was currently £10.55 an hour. "My mum wants me to leave London and come home. She thinks there are gangs going around stabbing people every second of the day."

"It does feel like that at the moment," I agreed. "But you probably need to have provoked them in some way and I don't think you're in any danger of doing that, are you?"

There were a succession of coffee orders and we lost ourselves for a while to the grinding and hissing and thumping of the machine—it got noisy in that café, sometimes you'd think we were bricklayers or electricians. When we were clear again, I said, "Let's put a notice up here. Room Wanted."

As Regan hooted at the notion of a physical, handwritten notice stuck with a pin to a board, and asked if maybe *I* had a spare room, ideally one with an *actual window*, I wondered what she would say if I showed her a picture of 15 Prospect Square, with no fewer than nine windows visible from the street. No, if the water rats' reaction was anything to go by, I was better off keeping the grandeur of my accommodation to myself.

"People still read things on paper," I told her. "Otherwise we wouldn't have a shop full of flyers and leaflets, would we?" As if to disprove this, I took a card payment from a customer who apologized for not having cash for a tip. People used contactless for purchases in the pennies. We'd turned money invisible, rid ourselves of the vulgarity of its metallic chink, and yet I'd never heard people talk about it more. I'd never known it so hungered for, so fetishized.

On the way home, alone for once, I noted Clare's text about ordering a takeaway while remembering with a stab of guilt the leftover bread and pastries Regan took home most days. As we passed One Blackfriars, its silver-blue skin bruised with evening shadow, I studied the commuters around me. Who of them had just been paid a bonus and who was spiraling into debt? Could the woman in the floral silk wrap dress reading the Booker Prize winner pay her rent? Was the balding guy covertly watching porn on his phone set up for a comfortable retirement? What did *they* make of *me*? It was impossible to tell a pauper from a prince in this city.

———

"Should we take a lodger?" I asked Clare, as we unpacked a dozen tacos delivered from the food market by a boy who didn't speak English. I'd tipped him a fiver.

"Why would we do that?" she said.

"Just, you know, there's a housing crisis. We've got spare rooms."

She grimaced. "Yeah, but we help in other ways. We pay forty percent tax."

"*You* do."

She took a bite of taco, expertly keeping the contents from dripping down her top. "Do you seriously want a total stranger wandering around the place?"

"They wouldn't be a stranger for very long. Or we could have a friend."

"That's worse. Everyone always falls out and then you can't get rid of them."

I swallowed half a taco without chewing the contents, felt it slithering in my gut like something still alive. Scooping guacamole with a fat bubbly chip, I made a point of chewing the next mouthful properly. I tried a different angle. "Does it make you feel bad, knowing there are all those apartments along the river sitting empty while sellers and landlords hold out for crazy prices and yet we both work with people who are living in horrible conditions?"

"They're not empty for long, not if I do my job properly." She twitched her eyebrows, but I no longer felt willing to share her hubris, however droll its expression. "Speaking of people we work with, I had an interesting chat with Richard today."

"Oh yeah." My heart drummed. He couldn't have discovered Melia's abuse of her duties, could he? We were always meticulous about leaving our meeting places precisely as we found them.

"Given that you've decided against teacher training, and the coaching sessions and networking events haven't led to anything concrete—"

"Yet," I interrupted. "They've been really useful, though. I'm miles ahead of where I was psychologically. Confidence-wise." I didn't need Clare spreading the word that poor Vicky Jenkinson was a charlatan or, worse, demanding a refund from her.

"What I was going to say is there might be an opportunity in lettings soon and I suggested Richard has a chat with you. I know you haven't got any experience, but nor did Melia when she started and she's doing fine."

I spent a moment ordering my objections to this latest proposal. First of all, of course I couldn't work for my partner alongside my lover. Second, it was one thing to be a ladder's worth of rungs below one's partner when in separate professions, but another in the same *company*. Third, I wasn't keen on the salesman's confidence with which Clare had raised the suggestion, as if there could only be one reaction to it and it was the same as her own.

"No," I said.

She selected her next taco. "No what?"

"No, don't put Richard in that position. It's not fair. You wouldn't like it if he asked you to employ his wife." Sour cream slopped onto my T-shirt and I smeared it with my fingers.

"Actually, I'd snap her up, but since she's an independently wealthy interior designer with clients all over Europe, he'd be unlikely to do that." She passed me a square of kitchen roll. "The thing is, I already said you'll call him. I thought we could do a practice interview this weekend."

It was the face that did it, the casual assumption that I would fall in line: I was suddenly enraged. "Clare, I said no. The coaching sessions were a very generous gift, but will you please leave it to me now to sort out my employment and stop acting on my behalf all the time. Have some sensitivity to my feelings!"

As her gaze grew opaque, I tried to examine my own fury, which I could see as well as she did was a wholly ungracious response to an offer of help. Perhaps it was referred pain, a manifestation of my guilt in the wrong location (it should have been in the balls), or perhaps fear—God, had she emailed Vicky with this job idea of hers? Would she soon receive some baffled reply?—but whatever the case I could express only so much moral indignation before my nose grew. Before the gods sided with the innocent and left clues for her to find.

I muttered an apology.

"No, it's fine," she said. Her cheeks were stained pink under her makeup. "I should have consulted you. I'll tell Richard you've got other plans."

"Thank you."

"Maybe you'll share those plans with me sometime," she added, because she *had* to have the last word and who the hell was I to deny her that?

I pushed my food from me, no longer hungry.

16

July 2019

Melia and I developed a rhythm to our liaisons, an agenda for our meetings no doubt familiar to anyone conducting an affair: drink and small talk, sex, proper conversation—"big talk," we called it because we were saying all the cute stuff I'd completely forgotten got said in the early days and that Melia loved.

Sometimes the most important things were said as we were dressing, as we were one July evening when something happened outside of the normal routine. The meeting place was a penthouse apartment with smart technology, wide-angle views of the Dome and Canary Wharf erased and magicked at the press of a button, and I would have enjoyed lingering, but Melia had other ideas.

"You know we were talking about our panic attacks that time? I had such a good idea and I think we should do it right now! It will be good for both of us—like, I don't know, therapy."

"What therapy?"

"You'll have to pay, though," she continued, merrily. "I'm completely broke. My bank card keeps getting rejected, I must have gone over my overdraft limit."

"How much will it cost?" I asked, mindful of my own minimum-wage limitations.

"We'll find out. Come on, have you got another half an hour?"

We left the building and walked towards the O2. There was some cool Euro DJ playing and everyone we saw seemed high, naturally or chemically, maybe both. Though we didn't pass Steve's building, and in any case I knew from the morning commute that he had a work event this evening, being outside together felt like a much more daring game—and I knew that daring gathered momentum and turned into recklessness.

"Here we are," Melia said. "Your claustrophobia, my fear of flying. Two birds with one stone."

It was the station for the cable car that linked the peninsula with the north side of the river. Nearly a hundred meters above the water, the gondolas were alight against feathered gray cloud. I'd never taken it before, had had no need; I considered those glowing square bulbs to be purely decorative.

"I thought your great fear was boredom?" But I could see the fever in her excitement: there was no getting out of this. "Do you even know what's on the other side?"

"It doesn't matter because we won't get off. We'll come straight back over. They call it the Three-sixty."

We'd had a bottle of wine together in the apartment and I was just about relaxed enough to pay for the tickets and follow her through the turnstile without protest. Long after the rush hour, it was easy to claim a gondola to ourselves.

"How long does it take?"

"Ten minutes there, ten minutes back. So, the point of the therapy is to take our minds off our irrational fears." She pressed herself against me, her breath hot as she dropped the words in my ear. "What can we do in twenty minutes?"

As the terminal building shrank below us, to my appalled amusement she sank to her knees. "Melia."

Her voice rose from between my legs. "What, not your thing?"

"Cameras," I said. "Right at this moment, some guy is sitting in front of a bank of monitors watching us."

She was unzipping me. "So what's he going to do? Stop the thing and zipwire along to arrest us?"

There ended my pathetic words of caution—I was powerless to her by then, if that's not already self-evident. It was the weirdest feeling, a stomach-dropping arousal, the city diminished and out of reach, until the towers and the Dome and the docks, the airport runway and the ribbon of river all lost their meaning entirely and I closed my eyes and succumbed.

Then, a sudden, aching removal, Melia's voice in interruption: "Don't freak, but I think we've stopped."

She struggled up to sit next to me and brushed the dust from her knees. I zipped myself up. The gondola was still. In the next car along, a man stood and looked back at us. I had no idea if he'd been able to see what we were doing. None of us made any sign.

"I'm sure it's okay," Melia said. Her arms encircled me. "Is it because of us?" she whispered, as if there were microphones in the car.

"I don't know." Oh, the solipsism of us, as if a couple enjoying each other could cause an entire transport link to grind to a halt. It took a moment to realize I was holding my breath, as if to hold the silence, hold us safe. I thought, *If the winds were stronger, would we sway and creak?* What would it feel like to know you were about to plunge three hundred feet to the river? Would the doors spring open on impact or would we be sealed, figures in a snow globe?

"We're moving again," Melia breathed.

And we sat side by side, backs straight, fingers entwined, for the rest of the ride, neither speaking; it seemed to me our breathing was synchronized. When we disembarked, I avoided the eyes of staff, but Melia thanked them, gleefully innocent. "See? No arrest. No one's interested in us, Jamie." She led me back through the station and out onto the concourse. "The point is, did you feel claustrophobic?"

"Not claustrophobia, exactly, no. It was more a fear of falling." I steered her into the shadows. "How about you?"

"The same. Like it was going to come loose and we'd just drop like a stone. I'm calling that progress: we replaced our phobias with a new one!" She punched the air, her exhilaration contagious. "I feel something else new," she whispered, and her face was close to mine, her eyes wide and confessional. "I won't say it, though. It's too soon. Too crazy."

"Say what?"

"You know." Kissing my cheek, exactly as if we were friends saying goodbye after a chance meeting, she turned and walked away from me, past the ticket office, in the direction of the Tube.

I remained where I was. What was going on here? Living a lie was one thing, forging a secret subplot, but this was becoming the main plot, the truth. For the first time, we'd taken our affair outside. Our aborted sex act might have been high above the city but it was still public transport, with cameras, possibly even with another passenger watching. It had been an appalling risk, an act of lunacy, unless . . .

Unless we were edging now towards wanting to be caught. Wanting to be asked to choose.

And, if we were, would we make the same choice?

I walked the short distance to the ferry pier in a fugue, glad that there was no one on the boat to St Mary's for me to have to talk to, to ask me what I was doing getting on here, or even just if I'd had a good day because theirs had been *terrible*. I could taste the gin in the warm cabin air, hear the chimes of bottles as the assistant restocked the fridge with beers.

As we docked at St Mary's, I looked back to the peninsula and Canary Wharf beyond, the towers silhouetted against the late dusk sky; in the foreground, the red-eyed sentinels of the Thames Barrier. I realized I felt as happy as I'd ever felt. I felt *elated*.

Then, moments later, I got a shock. Not far from the pier, a few steps down Artillery Passage past Mariners, I saw Kit. He was with a tall, bony guy in jeans and trainers, a pair of over-sized headphones around his long neck like a scarf. I assumed he was a mate, though by the time I'd reached Prospect Square, I'd convinced myself he was Kit's dealer.

Head down, I hurried past before he could see me, before he could summon me close enough to smell his wife's saliva dry on my skin.

———

The next morning, Kit arrived on the boat eating a doughnut oozing peanut butter and jam, scoffing it in that way people did when their body has been starved of nutrients the night before.

"I thought I saw you outside Mariners last night," I said. "About ten o'clock?"

As I kicked myself—what if we'd in fact been on the same boat and he'd half-noticed me get on at the peninsula and only now had his memory jogged?—he merely shrugged.

"You were with some guy," I added.

"Give me a break, Jay, it's not like we're exclusive." This he said in a theatrically camp tone, his breath smelling of peanut butter. His eyes were rimmed red, pink lines patterned the white.

"I just thought he looked a bit dodgy, that's all."

"Maybe dodgy by *your* standards." But he didn't say who the guy was and, next thing, Steve had boarded and was drawing our attention to a black figure crawling like a monster insect on the slanted roof of one of the waterside towers.

"Suicide?" Kit said, without concern.

Steve chuckled at his heartlessness. "No, you Good Samaritan, you. He's a cleaner."

"Or a technician of some sort," I said, "fixing something on the exterior."

"How the hell is he attached?" asked Kit.

"Ropes," Steve said. "I read about it the other day. They work on skyscrapers and bridges, crazy places. I bet they get danger money."

"I bet they don't," Kit said glumly. "I bet they get paid a fucking pittance."

"Don't get him started on money," I told Steve.

"Don't get *him* started on being a twat," Kit said, his expression clouding.

Admittedly, I'd been a little thoughtless, but I didn't think I deserved that. What was his problem? When Gretchen arrived, he moved away from us, throwing me an unfriendly look.

"What's eating Gilbert Grape?" I said to the others. "Hangover?"

"It must be because he didn't get that promotion," Gretchen said.

"What promotion?"

"Oh, *Jamie*, he told us all about it yesterday."

"I got a different boat home," I reminded her.

"I'll see if he wants to come out for a smoke," Steve said and Gretchen said she'd come too.

"Make sure you stand one on either side, you don't want him jumping in," I joked, but neither of them cracked a smile. I sighed. I knew Kit better than they did and even though he'd made that reference just now to suicide, he would *never* attempt it himself, especially not over some work setback. Some other commuter might, though. Any one of them could board alone one night after a work disaster, wait for the boat to reach a stretch of particularly evil-looking currents, then stroll out onto the deck and find a spot to do it. Just drop overboard without a word, never to be heard of again.

But, no, the crew kept count. I'd been aware of them using those handheld clicker devices every time I crossed the gangway: it was maritime law probably. If the numbers didn't tally, they'd know soon enough.

17

December 27, 2019

My phone buzzes and, ignoring the detectives' scrutiny, I read Clare's reply to my earlier voicemail:

Yes, Melia told Richard about K. So strange! I hope he's OK.

I judge from her use of "strange," as opposed to tragic or horrific, that she is skeptical about Kit's being in any real danger.

"Not him, is it?" Merchison says.

"No." It strikes me that I haven't tried Kit's phone myself since that text on Monday. "His phone is off, is it? You haven't found it abandoned somewhere? Come on, you can tell me *that*, surely?"

"No. It may be on his person, but it's out of service," Parry says.

"That's definitely unusual."

They don't dignify this with the response it warrants—*Gee, thank you for confirming we've done the right thing to launch an investigation!*—and I feel foolish.

"Were you aware of anyone in his life who might have a grievance against him?" Merchison asks. "What about his colleagues?"

I think. When you and your fellow commuters all work in different industries, you discuss your work very little. Gripes about bad bosses notwithstanding, who wants to start the day sharing their dread of the meetings and deadlines ahead? "No," I say. "Sorry. He's pretty popular. I imagine his colleagues like him a lot."

"What about family?"

"Hasn't Melia filled you in on that? She's fallen out with hers. His are mostly dead."

"'Mostly' dead?"

"His mum died young, when he was ten or eleven. Not suicide, if that's what you're thinking."

There's a short, frozen moment when I realize that in trying to deny a theory I've only gone and proposed it. I strongly doubt Melia has introduced the notion. "His mum died of cancer and his dad sold their house and spent the proceeds on the horses. Kit hasn't had much to do with him since, from what I can gather. He was pretty much raised by his grandmother." It occurs to me that this summarizes quite neatly Kit and his bitter aspirations. "But I'm sure Melia's told you all about it," I add.

"So there's no one he argued with recently, even over something small?"

"No, I met some of his friends at the wedding and they all seemed nice enough. Some were from his drama school days, a couple from work."

My answers are intentionally bland: my aim is to neutralize my interrogators, regain some of the power I lost with that blurted error about suicide.

"You and your partner were witnesses at the wedding, I gather," Merchison says. "That must have been a bit awkward."

"Melia told you that?"

"Must have made you feel a bit, what's the word they use?" He pauses. "*Conflicted.*"

"I was happy for them." I have a sudden unprompted image of Melia spinning herself in that length of diaphanous fabric in the first of our borrowed bedrooms. *Come back, Melia,* I say in a sing-song voice, the yearning only half-mocking. *You're like Cleopatra.*

God, have we been too caught up in self-mythology? Have we cared too much about what our feelings *mean*?

Merchison is watching me, reading me. "Come on, Jamie, you're only human. You must have felt a bit envious seeing him marry the woman you were . . ." He pauses for the right word, but this time it feels as if he's withholding it as a taunt. "In love with," he supplies, at last, and I'm unsettled to see that he's grinning at me. For the first time I see his teeth, perfectly straightened, as they always are in the mouths of men younger than me (if you want to see the famed British dental neglect you have to go to the forty-plus age group).

I sigh. "Look, I'm not in therapy here. What's your point in relation to the investigation?"

"Our point is it all seems to lead back to you," Parry says. "You're the one who was there on Monday night. You're the one with the history of emotional outbursts. You're the one Kit trusted to be a witness at his wedding, even though you were in fact betraying him in the worst possible way."

It sounds bad when he lists it all like that. You could say indefensible.

"He's right, you know," Merchison says. And he looks almost saddened, as if he's tried to defend me, he really has, but he simply cannot find a way through to a truth that might serve me better.

"You're his only known enemy, Jamie."

18

August 2019

The wedding, on a Saturday in late summer, struck me as an act of insanity the moment I heard about it, still buried by pillows in our bedroom, black-out blinds drawn.

"Jamie! You need to get up!" Clare was in the doorway, waiting for me to raise my head before crossing to the windows to snap open the blinds and flood the room with daylight.

I shielded my eyes with my arm. Kids shrieked in the square out front and dogs barked in reply. "Why?"

"Seriously, get up now." Her voice was alive with emergency. "You're not going to believe this: Kit and Melia are getting married!"

She was right, I didn't believe it. I sat up, seized by a forceful jabbing in my chest, my heart protesting the news before my brain could formulate a spoken response. "That *is* news. I doubt it will actually happen, though." I gave a grudging little laugh before sinking against the headboard. "You know what they're like."

Clare was at the wardrobe, moving the hangers along the rail with a horrible metallic scraping that shredded my nerves. "No, you don't get it, it's happening *now*. Today at twelve o'clock! They want us to be their witnesses. We need to get ready, it's already past ten."

Immobilized and gaping, I found it all too easy to put myself at the center of this development: Kit must have found out about Melia and me and proposed in order to reclaim her, lock her in. But no, who invites their new wife's lover to be a witness? That was perverse, even for Kit. More to the point, how the hell were they going to pay for a wedding? It could only create deeper debt, tighter knots. I remembered my advice to her, much too recent for her to have forgotten: *Don't marry Kit . . . You'll only be liable for his debts, as well as your own.*

Clare tossed me her phone. "Look at Melia's text. Can we meet them at the register office at eleven thirty. I said yes."

It was unnerving seeing my lover's name on my partner's phone screen, the long string of messages between them, evidence of firm ongoing friendship. My relations with Kit had conveniently been camouflaged by the group, our last night out alone an all-nighter in June at a club on the peninsula that had taken me a week to recover from and seen me dispatched to the spare room for days afterwards for "breathing alcohol through your pores." *Please say you can do it?* Melia had pleaded. *Exciting!* She'd added an emoji of a veiled, blushing bride.

I swung my legs to the floor. "Kit didn't breathe a word on the boat last night." There'd been the usual onboard beers and he'd asked what everyone was up to the next day, but there'd been no secret smile that I remembered, no conspiratorial wink. "Don't you have to give notice when you get married?"

Clare, who'd selected a dress, was now assembling underwear and accessories. "Yes, twenty-eight days, isn't it? But I suppose you can spring it on your guests as last-minute as you like!"

My heart renewed its ghastly thumping. So Melia had known about this morning for four weeks. Four assignations with me—including the cable-car excursion—and not a word breathed. What was she playing at, expecting me to be a witness at her wedding when she'd told me she loved me?

Not told. Implied. I felt myself deflate: what kind of a middle-aged sap was I to be thinking in terms of love? In the shower, I turned the water to the most savage cold in an attempt to extinguish my smoldering thoughts. Melia and I were over. It had only been five months and yet there'd been times, when I woke in the morning and the fragments hadn't yet pieced together, that I couldn't begin to fathom the double life I'd been leading. How had we survived as long as we had without detection? Kit, I'd understood to lack sensitivity to altered cues, but Clare was something else. If this marked the end of Melia and me, which surely it did, then I had to consider my exit as having been made by the skin of my teeth.

Easier said than done.

Scrubbed, shaved, and dressed halfway smartly, I dashed down to join Clare, who looked delightful in a poppy red dress, her hair in a big blow-dry, a chunky chain-link necklace sitting on her collarbone. Next thing we were in the taxi and pulling up at Woolwich Town Hall, a grand edifice with domed roof and a clock tower.

"I forget what a nice building this is," I said.

"Edwardian Baroque. Wait till you see inside. There's got to be a waiting list as long as your arm for this venue. Melia must have got a cancellation."

She automatically assumed Melia had driven this and I didn't challenge her.

She was right about the interior, a surreal sight for eyes accustomed to gazing into a coffee cup at this hour on a weekend: a vast domed ceiling with checkered flooring, stained glass, a staircase worthy of a sultan, all presided over by a marble Queen Victoria.

We found the happy couple in a waiting area on the upper level. Perhaps because of the opulence of the venue, they both looked slight and innocent, particularly Melia, who was in a simple dove-gray sundress and sandals that were little more than flip-flops. Long earrings made of dangling silver strands threatened to get tangled in her hair, which she wore loose and natural on uncovered shoulders. Other than lipstick and mascara, she presented herself to her husband-to-be barefaced. Kit was in tailored dogtooth check trousers and black shirt—a young mod—but the sharpness of his dress seemed only to accentuate his lack of life experience. He'd never looked so out of his depth as he did now.

"Is this Mum and Dad?" the official said to Melia and I pretended not to hear. I had a very strong feeling that no good was going to come of this for any of those present and accepted Kit's handshake with such reluctance he began laughing.

"I know you don't believe in marriage, Jamie, but you can do better than that."

Embarrassed, I pulled him into a hug. "Sorry, mate, I'm just a bit thrown. Had no idea this was on the cards."

Clare kissed them both. For a self-proclaimed wedding cynic, she was exuberant, even joyful. "Hang on, do you not have flowers, Melia? You have to have flowers. I'll nip out and get some for you."

No sooner had she departed than Kit was asking for directions to the loo and Melia and I were left alone. Her cheeks were the exact soft pink you'd apply with a brush to a bride's skin, only natural. Her eyes, when turned towards me, were ardent, radiating devotion—a highly disconcerting sight, given the circumstances.

"Jamie," she murmured, "thank you for this."

This? I hardly knew where to start. "Why didn't you tell me?"

Her smile was hard to read, combining excitement and apology and another emotion oddly like guile. "I was going to when we met on Wednesday, but . . ."

"But it didn't make the news headlines?" It had all happened so quickly I wasn't certain if my agony was caused by her decision to marry Kit, an unsuitable husband by anyone's standards, or her decision to marry at all. I was sick both with envy of him and self-loathing for the way I'd betrayed him—and Clare.

She stepped closer, cupped my elbow. Her touch was tender, full of commiseration. "Look, there's not time now, but I'll explain everything next time we meet."

"You don't need to explain, darling." I pulled myself together, tried to look pleased for her.

"Don't I?" She was suddenly full of sorrow. "Are you saying you don't *want* me to?"

"I'm saying I don't expect you to. If this is what you want, then—"

"Next week," she interrupted, taking the risk of placing a finger on my lips.

Next week? She couldn't mean . . . I knew her well enough to know she was unusually willing—some might say entitled—to have her cake and eat it, but surely that didn't include wedding cake? Gently, I brushed her finger away. "I'm going on holiday next week, Melia. I told you. We leave on Wednesday. I'll be away for two weeks."

"Oh yes. As soon as you get back then. I haven't got my schedule yet for that week, so I don't know which day is good. Wednesday or Thursday, though, same as usual."

"Same as usual?"

"Yes." Her eyes gripped mine with an almost fanatical desire to persuade. "Trust me, Jamie. I need you. I really—Oh, Clare, they're so pretty!"

Clare had returned with a sweet bunch of wildflowers, which Melia clutched demurely over her abdomen while Clare took photos on her phone. She had taken on a semi-officiating role, it seemed. "Are you planning a honeymoon, Me? I hate to be the bad guy, but you haven't booked any leave, have you? The holiday roster was worked out ages ago. Should I talk to Richard for you?"

Melia smiled as if sharing a joke. "Oh, we're not having a honeymoon. We can't afford *that*."

Kit, who'd spent so long in the loo I could only guess what he'd been doing there, reappeared by her side. "We can't afford anything," he agreed, cheerfully. "We begin our married life as beggars."

And then the beggars' names were called and it was happening. The official was full of genuine good cheer, even if it was a comically short service in an empty room, there being no readings or additional vows and no other guests besides Clare and me.

Afterwards, like a star and his hippie child bride, the newlyweds fled the opulent interior for the stone steps outside, feet kicking confetti from the unions that preceded their own. They were holding hands, giggling together. You'd never guess one of them had promised to continue her adultery with a third party just moments before taking her vows and the other had inhaled illegal drugs he couldn't afford. Then they got on their phones and invited people, seemingly at random, to join them for drinks at the Stag, a big pub on the river at Greenwich.

We shared a taxi there, Melia sandwiched between Kit and Clare in the back. I could smell the jasmine of her scent and wondered, with sudden fright, if Clare had ever smelled it on me. No, she couldn't have or we wouldn't all be here together today.

God forbid it rain on their special day: a thin sun was rising, warming our skin and shooting light at us from the water as we walked in a line like some dysfunctional Fab Four (or perhaps *The Usual Suspects*). As we approached the doors of the pub,

Clare said to Melia, "Will you let us buy the champagne as a wedding present?"

I couldn't bear to look at Melia's traitorous face as she accepted, so kept my eyes on Clare's. She was beaming, wholehearted in her goodwill, and I saw that it was not so much the act of marriage itself that had stirred her as the rock 'n' roll spontaneity of the occasion. I also saw the emotion that would succeed it, if not later today then soon: disappointment in herself for having eschewed tradition when she could simply have subverted it like Melia had.

"Nice of you to pick up the bill for the champagne," I said, when we were on our own.

"I just thought, you know, we need to remember how lucky we are," she said, which I knew from previous declarations was code for, *We need to remember how talented and hardworking we are*—because people who've been helped never accept that their success is a simple consequence of that. They think they'd have been just as successful without it.

Also, since I was being pedantic, she meant *I*, not *we*. She hadn't consulted me about the champagne because she had no need to. Conversely, I couldn't have made the gesture *without* consulting her. The truth was that by leaving my white-collar career I'd rendered myself as economically helpless as the Ropers themselves, and in the year since, I'd failed to take advantage of career counseling and turned down a direct leg up from Richard. Instead, I'd focused my energies on a secret extracurricular opportunity that was about to be withdrawn, regardless of what Melia had appeared to claim at the register office.

Same as usual . . .

Not possible, my love, not possible.

I tipped my glass to my lips and swallowed Clare's champagne in one.

———————

Over the course of the next couple of hours, as the temperature rose and the rain held off, the Ropers' friends arrived at the river. Clare met Steve and Gretchen and I met various colleagues from Melia's division at Hayter Armstrong. Her director and Clare's business partner, Richard, was away on holiday in his cottage in Brittany, the very one Clare and I would be occupying the following week. How did he feel about Melia, I wondered? Was he as charmed as everyone else, as compelled to possess that slippery beauty as I was? Had she considered *him* for her affair? (*I need a man without all this debt!*) Or did his three kids present an obstruction that was helpfully missing in my case?

But this was bitterness talking. Anguish. Melia had not cynically chosen me any more than I had her. We liked each other—loved, if only briefly. And Richard, had he been here, would probably simply have offered the cash-strapped couple his holiday home for a few days' honeymoon, thrown in flights as a wedding present.

"Well, this is completely nuts," Gretchen said to me, not exactly through gritted teeth, but with an edge to her enthusiasm. In this realm of actors and deceivers, she was real. It was clear she'd mobilized quickly for the event, her hair flat and in need of a wash, lacy dress a little crumpled, toenail polish chipped. I remembered Melia's accusations that she and Kit were involved and I had the sudden thought that this was both humanity's curse and saving grace: our biological need to know who liked who. To keep the whole thing going, generation after generation. The same negotiations, the same vows, the same ratio of winners to losers. A zero-sum game.

"What's nuts?" I said. I was grateful for the brightening sky; with sunglasses on, I was less fearful of exposing emotions inappropriate for the occasion. "You mean Kit getting married so suddenly?"

"I mean at all. I would have thought he was the last person to spend money on something like this and, to be honest, the only time I ever hear him talk about her he's complaining."

"And vice versa," I admitted.

"Well, you would know, Jamie."

"How do you mean?"

There was a long moment. Did Gretchen know? If she did, how? The only possible means was Kit himself. I remembered my first thought when I'd heard the news of the wedding was he wanted to formalize his claim to Melia, to warn me off. But instinct told me that Clare was right: Melia had driven this. Had *she* found out about *his* infidelity and this was the result?

Trust me, Jamie. I need you.

The thought made me shiver.

Finally, Gretchen answered. "I just meant you're the only one of us who knows them both. Steve and I have never met her before. Or Clare."

"Right." I felt a sudden lurch of disorientation. A year ago, I didn't know a single one of these people. Even the Hayter Armstrong employees present were from the lettings arm and therefore under my radar. The only constant was Clare and I was aware that I was avoiding her as discreetly as I could, terrified my mood would give me away.

I excused myself to use the loo. Returning, I could hear Kit and Steve talking at the bar, indiscreet enough to be discussing the very question on their guests' lips.

Steve's normally indistinct voice was helpfully amplified by drink. "So whose idea was this, mate?"

"Melia's, of course."

My scalp prickled.

"It was either this or split up," Kit added.

"Seriously. Wow." Steve whistled. "Classic ultimatum. You'd think after Me Too and all that, women wouldn't want to get married, but they do, don't they? There's hope for me yet. Speaking of which, I like the look of—" He broke off, his tone altering to one of amusement: "What're you doing loitering there, Jamie? Earwigging on us, were you?"

"I was." I stepped forward to join them. "If you want my two cents, fear of turning thirty can be a powerful motivator. My colleague Regan thinks she's ancient at twenty-four."

"Yeah? Or maybe Me wants kids?" Steve suggested, with the disgusted resignation of someone discovering he'd got a parking ticket.

Kit, however, looked genuinely shocked. Shocked at the thought of having a child or shocked that Steve had guessed the truth, I wondered? I had an image then, of Melia being pregnant, of the baby possibly being mine but the paternity never challenged. My mind burned through the catastrophized consequences: an email from a teenager who'd been alerted to a DNA match; Clare urging me to investigate, to welcome the youngster into our lives.

A few minutes later, back outdoors, when Melia and I were next alone and out of earshot of the others, I asked her. "You're not pregnant, are you? Is that why you've done this?"

"Uh, this is 2019, Jamie, not 1950." She laughed, raising her glass to my face. "And I'd hardly be drinking like this, would I?"

On cue, Kit came tripping over with a champagne bottle to top us up. Over his shoulder, I saw Clare and Steve standing together, her head tipped to listen, smile broad. The weather had turned quite beautiful by then; just two or three careless blotches of cloud remained, as if sponged onto the blue by infants. Our group had colonized a stretch of river path and someone played music on their phone, tinny as a music box. Melia began dancing with a friend, a girl with a solemn, angular face and tanned lean legs. The song was Lana Del Rey's version of "Doin' Time" and the women moved as if unaware of anyone but each other. Tourists, identifying the center of the afternoon's energy, formed a loose ring around the party, taking pictures, watching the girls dance. *I'd like to hold her . . .* I mouthed, trying to remember the lyrics from listening to the original track years ago, when I'd been young myself.

I became aware of Kit looking at me and let the song drift from my attention. "Congratulations, mate," I said, with a decent impression of cheer. "You're a lucky man."

"Yeah, thanks, Jamie." He turned his face to the water as if overcome by the force of my goodwill; as if I had made all of this happen. The river, for once, looked almost wholesome, a body of fresh water, its temperature agreeable and currents benign.

But, you only had to take a few steps forward and the way the sun flashed off the vertical silver surfaces of Canary Wharf could blind a man. Knock him right off his feet.

19

September 2019

The routine of our annual late-summer holiday with my father was well-worn. We always collected him from his place near Winchester and took the express ferry from Portsmouth to Cherbourg, then on to somewhere in Normandy or Brittany. We always agreed how fantastic it was to be childfree and able to travel in term time to beautiful places rendered insufferable in August in the presence of screaming kids (we always agreed this *before* we picked up Dad, who we knew privately regarded our not having children as a tragedy).

"Imagine the traffic in school holidays!" Clare said, word perfect, as the A3 slid by without a single snarl-up.

"I know. Horrific."

"I much prefer September weather, anyway."

"Best of both worlds," I agreed.

So far, so familiar, but she surprised me then by straying from the next part of the script—the financial savings to be made by avoiding August—and plunging into heavy silence. My eyes were on the road, on the incessant lane-changing of a van just ahead, but after a while I glanced across and saw she was glaring at the dashboard. "What's up? You look annoyed."

"I was just thinking about Melia and Kit. The wedding."

Ah. As I mentioned, following occasions of high excitement, Clare was more prone than most to the forces of anticlimax and so I'd been expecting this downturn in mood. For my own part, in order to conduct myself on the holiday with appropriate cheer—in order to save my sanity, frankly—I'd chosen to regard the Ropers' nuptials as a hallucination.

"I mean, *they're* the ones always arguing," Clare said. "We thought they were close to splitting up, didn't we?"

They're the ones: she meant in comparison with us.

"Maybe all that volatility is just passion," she added, glumly. "I thought millennials didn't have sex. That's what I read in the *Telegraph*."

I laughed.

"Why are you laughing?"

"Because what you just said was funny! Why should you care about it, anyway? It was *their* decision to get married."

She turned defensive. "It's tradition after a wedding, isn't it, to question your situation? Your choices."

I indicated to exit the A3, inhaling for exactly the length of time my foot eased the brake. I knew I had no chance of closing the lid on this, the criticism of me about to spill out. I couldn't regard my relationship with Clare as a hallucination too.

"It's been rough for me, you know, Jamie," she said, all fired up.

"What has?"

155

"Supporting you."

"Supporting me? I don't see why it should be rough on you." On the roundabout, some twat tried to undertake and my mood turned incautious. "You don't need my salary, you could live exactly as you are without any contribution from me. It's me who's taken the risk and downgraded myself."

I shut up, at risk of protesting too much. She was quite right to doubt us, she just didn't yet know why. I saw suddenly that the number plate on the car in front had the same first three letters as ours. What were the odds?

"I wasn't talking about financial support," Clare said, coolly. "The wedding made me take stock, that's all."

I experienced a rush of fear. "You don't mean *you* want to get married?" My confidence wavered. "You want to split up?" For a moment, I wondered if we'd reach France. I had a sudden urge to follow our matching number plate wherever it took us.

"Neither of those," Clare said. "I just think something needs to change."

Well, it was too late for children, our biological own at least. I prayed she wasn't going to suggest adoption or surrogacy or something that involved official examination of my habits.

"I'd like a bit more honesty," she said. "I can't plan otherwise."

I noted the singular. Was she subconsciously framing her future in terms of independence or was guilt making me oversensitive? She'd literally just denied wanting to separate. I glanced at the satnav's predicted time of arrival. We were six minutes from my father's house.

"Honesty is good," I said, with as much commitment as I

could bring to such humbug. "But maybe we need to park this for now and concentrate on the trip."

She nodded. "You're right. Let's get the holiday out of the way and then see where we are."

As she reset her mood, I felt the imminent clutch of a gloom of my own. I hadn't liked that exchange one bit. What was she withholding? A secret affair of her own? (No partner could have been less mistrustful than me.) It struck me that I was totally at her mercy—hers and Melia's—robbed of my autonomy by these two women.

Wouldn't that be the definition of irony? To be ditched by *both* of them.

Irony or just deserts, one of the two.

————

The Channel crossing was smooth, the onward journey by car soothingly familiar. The blue autoroute signs, the scalding coffee from petrol station vending machines, the big-sky promise of breathing space, of emptiness.

I was pleased we were basing ourselves in Brittany this time and not Normandy. The Normandy beaches are vast and beautiful, but to step onto them is to pass through the ghosts of war. I didn't want to think of stolen lives that holiday; I didn't want to reflect on my own rank ignobility.

We'd stayed a few times in Richard's "cottage," a blue-shuttered farmhouse surrounded by wildflower meadows and pine woods, meticulously renovated and decorated by his wife, Agnès. We were instantly at home there, our groove easily got back. One thing I would say about Clare and me: we wanted the same thing out of our holidays, the same thing every day: sleep, walk, swim, cook, eat, drink. My father was no trouble; he partook of all of the above with the exception of the walk, and he'd always loved Clare. All things considered, we were happy holiday makers—at least, at first.

"This is *so* inspiring. I think gardening will be my new thing," Clare said, over lunch on the fourth or fifth day. All meals were taken on the canopied stone terrace, surrounded by a botanical garden's worth of hydrangeas, whose blues perfectly complemented the hue of the local rosé and made me remember the colors Kit and Melia had worn the first time I met them.

"Who's looking after that big house of yours?" Dad asked.

"A lovely local girl called Delilah," Clare said. "She's just left university and she's working on a screenplay, so it will be somewhere quiet for her to write for a couple of weeks. It was Jamie's idea."

Delilah, I thought, rolling my eyes. Writing a *screenplay*. Though I'd suggested a house sitter, it had certainly not been my idea to offer the house to the daughter of a wealthy friend of Clare's. My first choice would have been Regan, who was now sharing a single room in South Croydon with a friend of a friend who worked night shifts at the hospital, hot-bedding, basically. But I still hadn't revealed that I lived in a house designed to accommodate a large family and their staff, and so had dithered over the proposal and, instead, a local rich kid moved from her parents' luxury crib in Greenwich to ours, a few miles downstream. In any case, it was becoming clearer by the day that Clare made the decisions about "our" house, not me.

"Not quite the starving writer in the freezing garret," I said. "What hardships is she going to draw on in her writing? Dickens worked in a shoe-blacking factory, didn't he?"

Clare ignored this. "I'm happy to support creative endeavor in this small way," she said, directing her words at Dad. "It's so hard to keep afloat unless you're really successful. We have friends who used to be actors, but they couldn't afford to keep going after a couple of years. They were just racking up debts and never actually earning anything."

At the mention of Kit and Melia, nerves flared across the surface of me.

"I get the feeling they're both really talented, as well," Clare added. "It's a real shame."

"Would I have seen them in anything?" Dad asked.

I found my voice. "No, they weren't on TV. She was in a couple of plays. One even had a short run in the West End, I think."

"She works with me," Clare told him. "She's excellent, when she turns up."

I picked up the carafe of rosé by its neck and began refilling our glasses. "She doesn't turn up?"

"Well." Clare pulled a face. "She's not the *worst* I've come across, but she has more than the average number of sick days. We used to troop in with a broken leg, didn't we? But that gen is just a lot more precious. Anyway, Tony, they've just got married and because of all these debts they can't even afford to go on a honeymoon."

This led, as I'd expected, to a comparison between the Maldives getaways of today's romantics and the out-of-season B&Bs in Margate of Dad's prime. Clare and I had a great photograph of him and Mum in the sixties at the haunted snail ride in the Dreamland amusement park. If we split up, I would need to make sure I took that picture.

If we split up. I reached for my water glass and felt the icy liquid wash through my gullet.

"You should have lent these actors your house for their honeymoon," Dad suggested.

"They'd be far too proud to accept," Clare said. "Anyway, I'm not sure I trust them. We'd get back and find they'd sold the contents. Or the house itself! Property fraud is a massive problem, you know."

"Oh, come on, they're not thieves." I thought of the picture Kit had sent me that morning of a river police launch sitting alongside the river bus like an escort:

Water rats had a brush with the fuzz this morning. Just a drill, but almost gave me a heart attack!

Time for a bit of clean living? You'd save money.

Drop in the ocean, mate.

This last came with a water wave emoji, followed by a money bags emoji. Finally, before he signed off, he sent a crying face. It was impressive, when you thought about it, that he hadn't borrowed to fund a honeymoon. For the first time, he and Melia had deprived themselves of something they actually had a right to expect. (I was lucky Clare hadn't extended her champagne largesse to the offer of a holiday share.)

"You sure you want someone like that working for you?" Dad was saying to Clare, laughing.

"She just said she's excellent," I snapped, to his surprise.

"She is," Clare agreed. "She's one of the most persuasive people I've ever met. She's obviously persuaded you, Jamie—look how you're defending her."

"Because she's our *friend*," I said. "We just took part in her *wedding*."

As Clare stared at me, a memory surfaced from that dinner at the Ropers' flat, back when it all started, when Melia said I'd be a good actor: *I can always tell when he's lying*, Clare said.

There was a sudden itch on my neck and, scratching, I felt the hard lump of an insect bite. I excused myself to go inside and fetch something for it.

————

A day or two later, about half an hour into our daily walk through the pine woods, Clare startled me by announcing, abruptly, "I know, Jamie."

Under my sweat, I froze.

"I thought I could wait till after the holiday to deal with it, but I can't. That's what I was thinking about when we argued on the drive down to Winchester."

"Deal with what?" My words were lost in a cowardly gulp.

Her face had flushed deeply and I felt mine do the same. "I know you asked me to butt out, but I just wanted to touch base to make sure the advice I was giving you was along the same lines as hers."

It took me a few seconds to realize she was talking about the career coach. I could have hooted with relief. "Oh, you mean Vicky."

"Yes, of course Vicky." Her voice rose in accusation. "I know you haven't been back since the first session."

"Not yet." Though clearly in a hole, I at least had a foothold in it and was not about to be cracked on the head with a spade and buried alive.

"When were you going to? I booked those sessions months ago. It's September now!" With a sharp crackling underfoot, she drew to a halt. "And why pretend you were doing them, when you weren't? I don't understand. What were you doing instead?"

Hoping she might make a better suggestion than I could, I played for time.

"Let me guess: drinking with Kit? You were, weren't you? Trust him to cover for you. For fuck's sake, Jamie, you're going to be fifty in less than two years and every month you let it slide, it's going to be harder getting back into the workplace."

"I'm already *in* the workplace," I said, stonily. "I'm on my feet nine hours a day. And the reason I pretended is because I'm well aware that you care way more about it than I do. Why *do* you care so much? If it's not about finances, then what? You're ashamed to have a partner doing a menial job, is that it?"

Clare's brow knitted, her gaze as aggrieved as I'd ever seen it. "I think that's a bit reductive."

"Reductive? Expand it then? Tell me how I can be more than I am. Please, I'd love to know!"

There was a tremor in her hands as she gripped them together, presumably to stop herself from slapping me. "After everything I've done to try and help you, you have no right to make out that *I'm* the one at fault." She strode off ahead, sick of the sight of me, and I didn't blame her.

Trudging on alone, I disgraced myself further by brooding not on her, but on Melia. I was missing her with a ferocity I hadn't anticipated. The wedding had been no delusion and the thought of her in renewed intimacy with Kit made my chest ache. I was, I supposed, grieving: whatever she'd said at the register office, I didn't believe for a moment that we would resume our affair. No, I had to make a virtue of our parting and concentrate on shaping up in Clare's estimation.

I got back to the house first and told Dad Clare had decided to drop in to the neighboring village, where the boulangerie sold stacks of the fresh galettes we all loved. She arrived an hour later bearing exactly this treat and I wondered if she'd read my mind.

(If so, what else had she seen while she was at it?)

"Sorry about earlier," I said, helping with preparations in the cool stone-flagged kitchen. "I was out of order."

She busied herself making tea. "You should have at least told me you didn't want to do the course. I could have transferred it to one of the team at work. Melia, maybe." As the tea brewed, she gave me a long, impaling look. "What's going on with you, Jamie?"

"What do you mean?"

"*I'm* asking *you*. Ever since you've been friends with Kit and that group on the boat, something's been off."

I tore off an edge of galette and chewed. "There's nothing

off. You met them at the wedding, you saw they're just regular people. Steve's a bit of an arsehole, sure."

"I liked him," she said, more in the spirit of contradiction than truth, it seemed to me, but at least she removed her gaze. "He seems like a straightforward guy. Maybe the dynamic will change, now Kit's married," she added, lifting the teapot and gesturing that I should bring the plates.

She said nothing more on the subject. But several times over the course of the rest of the trip, I imagined her thinking, *You lied to me, Jamie.*

Why should I believe another word you say?

———

On the ferry home, there was an odd moment. A crowd had gathered on the narrow rear deck, their chorus of urgent cries audible through the open doors. Dad was in the loo, Clare plugged into an audiobook, so I joined the gathering alone, fearing there must be a man overboard. And I admit to a certain excitement, in spite of the risk to this poor person's life. I imagined myself at the heart of the fray, making the crucial suggestion that saved a soul, or at least succeeding in calming a hysterical spouse—something to make me the hero of the hour. But when I eased through the throng to the front, it turned out someone had spotted a dolphin, evidently now vanished. As far as the eye could see, the sea was gentle, silver-skinned, scarred only by our own wake.

No word of a lie, it was at exactly this moment, as I stood regarding the water, that a text arrived from Melia:

Are you back yet? Fuck, I've missed you.

The speed of my reply surprised me, though possibly not her:

Same.

I know you must be confused. I'll explain when we're together.

I could see the dots moving.

I love you.

Quite some PS. Perhaps I gave it too little thought before responding:

Same.

Tomorrow?

Yes, tomorrow.

"That's how boats capsize," Dad said, when I rejoined Clare and him and recounted my misapprehension about a man having gone overboard. "People attracted by the rumor that someone else is in danger, they end up creating it for themselves."

He had no idea.

20

September 2019

This sounds crass, but when I think about that reunion with Melia, I prefer to think about the sex, not the words. I think of her skin glued to mine, the warm, wet squeeze inside her, the scrape of toenail on shinbone. Hair with a complicated new fragrance—dark and earthy, like the forest—covering my face, fingers gripping my neck, baby-pink nails as hard as almonds.

There are some words I *will* replay:

"I've married one man and fallen in love with another."

I wish I could think of a brilliant metaphor to express the irony, the theater, of our situation, but I can't. I do remember telling her I loved her too and repeating it like a prayer. (There's a simile for you, anyway.)

The encounter took place in a converted factory unit, with soaring ceilings, exposed brickwork, and polished concrete floor. Though it was a mild evening, we'd huddled in bed as if freezing, our brains deceived by all those cold materials.

There was a break in my voice as I asked her about the text: "So you love me, do you?"

And smooth honey in her reply: "I thought you already knew that."

"Getting married to another man might be considered a bit of a red herring." I twisted the cheap wedding band on her finger; though it was a little loose, she claimed to have no intention of getting it adjusted.

"You should see my sister's," she said, wistfully. "It's a massive diamond. Must have cost, I don't know, twenty grand."

"She'll probably be mugged and have her finger broken for it," I said, eager to amuse her. "So you have no qualms about breaking your vows, do you?"

Now I'd amused her. Her laughter was soft, a puppy bark of approval. "You obviously weren't listening at the register office, were you? We said nothing in our vows about being faithful."

"Didn't you?"

"No. Let's hope Clare didn't notice, either."

I told her about the arguments in France, the exposure of my dishonesty, and we agreed to take greater pains than ever to keep our secrets.

"It would definitely have come out, if she knew," Melia said. "She sent me some photos from the wedding, actually. Sweet of her."

"She took quite a few, I remember." I reached for my phone. "Did you know *I* took one?"

"One? Wow. I hope it was worth the effort." She examined the image, a smile on her lips. "That's from when we were dancing, Elodie and me. I'd forgotten about that."

"It was kind of magical, actually. You were like, I don't know, pixies or something."

"Pixies?" She giggled. "Don't they have weird pointy ears?"

"Fairies, then. Sprites."

Holding on to the phone, she said, "Tell me your iTunes password."

"Why?"

"I want to download a song for you."

I watched her, her delicate profile, the gleam in her eye. Minutes passed, during which I understood that I was not only in love, but also addicted, a different kind of brain disorder altogether. "How many songs are you downloading there?"

"I got you a whole album. Well, you got it yourself, technically."

I closed my eyes, drunk with contentment as, at last, she played the track they'd danced to by the water and began kissing me with fresh urgency. "Did you ever feel for Clare . . . you know, *this*? At the beginning. What *we* feel."

"No," I said, as much because she demanded to hear it as because it was true. Though it was true, it really was.

When the song played a second time, I made out the line I'd only half-heard that Saturday in August by the river:

I'd like to hold her head underwater.

21

December 27, 2019

At the next table, a man settles with a lurid green smoothie, speaking very loudly to the empty seat opposite: "Tell them that's fine, but I would need to know by four at the latest, yeah?"

I spy the AirPods and realize he's not deranged. Meanwhile, DC Merchison's fingers play with his notepad, thumbing its edges like a pack of cards he's about to shuffle. I will the pages to fall open on something that might help me—reassure me. This is the problem with the police: they defend information as fiercely as they seek it.

I need to get real here. If this goes on much longer, I'll admit defeat and phone a lawyer, but for now I take comfort in the fact that the note-taking is hardly extensive, judging by what I can see; they obviously think most of what I've said is irrelevant.

"So you continued the relationship with Mrs. Roper after your holiday?" Merchison says.

"Yes." *She was the one who got married*, I consider saying, but there is no point, because Clare was—is—no less a victim than

169

Kit. We are equals, Melia and I. This is something I've come to trust in. We're not identically unscrupulous, but we align. Our respective moral gaps fit together like a smooth-running zip.

The guy at the next table suddenly adjusts his seat and the scraping of chair legs on marble seems to travel through my legs and into my pelvis. Perhaps experiencing the same discomfort, Merchison straightens and places his palms on his thighs. Freed of his fiddling, the pages of his book drop apart and I see, under the heading "C. ROPER" and a reference number of some sort, another name in capitals. "SARAH MILLER," it looks like.

"Who's Sarah Miller?" I blurt, before I can stop myself.

Looking down, he sees his mistake and angles the pad so the notes are no longer visible to me. By his side, Parry frowns, but says nothing.

"She's a witness in a different investigation. Not relevant here."

He brings just the right edge of dismissal to convince most people, but I feel I understand him well enough by now to sense danger.

If Sarah Miller is part of *this* investigation, then it's not hard to guess who she might be. She's the loose cannon whose projectile is coming my way. The other passenger.

And I've seen her name before, I'm certain of it.

"Can I suggest a theory?" I say. Because suddenly, chillingly, I know it is not enough that every word I've uttered is the truth. These days, the truth comes in inverted commas, as owned and defined by the listener as by the speaker. Unless these two detectives believe my story, it might just as well be fiction.

Merchison rotates a shoulder, grimaces at the evident discomfort of it, and urges me on: "Sure, let's hear it."

"I think Kit's disappearance might be to do with drugs."

They go rigid, soldiers on parade, and I know my timing is perfect. After all my objections and denials, my self-indulgent account of infidelity, I'm suddenly the one offering something, something I hope they'll think about when they're driving back to the station. Something they'll tell their supervisor when they're reporting on their progress and awaiting a steer.

"I've maybe played it down, but he's got a serious cocaine habit, probably other drugs as well, and it must be costing him. I've been with him a few times when he's left to meet his dealer."

"Where?" Parry says. Merchison starts to take notes.

"They have a regular spot on the river path, a black spot where there aren't any cameras."

"Where is this black spot?"

"Near the Hope and Anchor. You sometimes see homeless people there, or dodgy types, it's not the nicest stretch. Anyway, my point is he might have owed money, got into some sort of dispute. For all I know, he could have been dealing himself."

I stop speaking and assess their reactions. They're not smacking their heads and exclaiming, "Of course!", but they're not scorning me either. They're mulling the basics, checking the logic.

"This has just occurred to you, has it?" Parry says, his tone dubious.

"Not 'just,' but . . ." I hang my head a little. "I thought it might be relevant."

"You've taken drugs together, have you?"

I'd forgotten he wasn't here when I described the dinner party at the Ropers' flat. "Well, once or twice, but I'm too old for that game."

Both sets of eyes flare, but no comment is made. Merchison's pen is already dismayingly still.

"Anything else you'd like to share now your memory's cranking to life?" Parry asks.

"There is something, actually. He asked me if I could lend him some money. Back in October, I think it was."

"How much?" He looks as if he could thump me for waiting this long to share the most incendiary details.

"Five thousand pounds. He said it was for rent arrears, but now I feel certain it was a drug debt."

"Did you lend it to him?"

"No, I don't have that kind of money to spare. Look, I know it probably isn't that much in terms of his overall debts, but . . ." I falter.

"But even if you *had* had it, you still wouldn't have given it to him?" Merchison guesses.

I meet his eye. "You guys are in a better position to know this than I am, but what I was actually going to say was that people have been killed for less, haven't they?"

In the first instance of harmony among the three of us, there is a collective intake of breath.

22

October 2019

Admittedly, it was a bit late in the day that I began worrying about Kit's lifestyle choices, when the drug use I'd assumed to be recreational and self-contained started to feel as if it were defining him. As if it might bring everything crashing down. After the excitement of the wedding had faded, the backslapping and good wishes, he was visibly untethered, the very opposite of the new dynamic Clare had predicted. At least once a week, he failed to turn up for the river bus, which meant he must have been getting into work late, if at all.

I wasn't the only one to miss him. I'd clock Steve's disappointment when he approached our seats on *Boleyn* and saw it was just me—followed by Gretchen's, when she saw it was just Steve and me. It occurred to me that the low-level flirtation she and Kit had engaged in might have become less tenable now he was married and that he might in fact be avoiding her. The notion that he might be avoiding *me* only struck later, when we connected one morning on the later boat—I'd missed the 7:20 by seconds—and I caught the reflex of irritation in his eyes when he saw me sitting there.

"You all right?" I asked. His complexion was terrible, graying and blemished, his eyes glassy.

"Yeah, fine."

"How's work?" It had been a while since he'd talked of leaving his firm of dinosaurs (and, of course, the Cold Fish) to jump on some tech start-up or other cliché.

He didn't bother answering, but turned to look out of the window. The river was pale under a flagstone-gray sky; any minute now, the rain would come down. As we sat in strange, tense silence, I imagined myself saying, "Have I done something to offend you?" and the justifiably violent twist of his response: "You fucking know you have!"

But I wasn't a lunatic. My job was to thwart any airing of my own injurious part in his affairs and carry on acting as if his off-color mood was nothing to do with me at all. Instead, I tried a different angle. "Is there anything I can do to help?"

He jerked to attention. "You know what? There is, actually."

My pulse quickened as I caught the torment in his eyes. "Tell me."

"I need a loan, mate. Quick."

"How much?"

"Three or four grand. Five would be great." His voice wavered with a desperate hope that I knew it cost him to show. "I could get it back to you when I get my end-of-year bonus."

"Five grand?" I was stunned. (And if I knew anything about

his performance at work, he wasn't getting any bonus.) "I haven't got that sort of money, Kit. You know I work in a café."

He dismissed this, of course. "Yeah, but you could get it from Clare."

"It's not as easy as that. What's it for, anyway?"

"Just cash-flow problems. We owe a couple of months' rent." Rain began to slide down the window in diagonal lines.

"I don't know," I said, carefully. "I think you'd have to ask her yourself—or get Melia to. Could you ask work for an advance? You can't be the first employee they've had who needs a bit of help."

He lost his patience. "You're the one who just offered to help! Look, forget it." And he didn't look at me again, fingers rapping on his thigh in a ceaseless rhythm, as if counting down to the moment this torture would end. At last, well before his stop, he leapt up and made for the door, the first to disembark. Below, the river was liquid mud, stippled with rain, its lethal eddies and currents visible on the surface like feeding mouths, and I saw Kit glance down at it with trepidation. Hard to believe anything could survive in it for more than a few seconds, I thought, and I willed him to cross the gangway with greater care than usual.

I thought hard about whether to report his request to Clare, but after that row in France I ruled against drawing further attention to her financial might and my utter powerlessness. I could no longer deny my resentment, but I owed her a period of cooperation and would not involve her in this.

Instead, I raised it with Melia.

"I'm worried about him. He feels out of control. And he must be skating on thin ice at work—the last thing he needs is to lose his job."

She exhaled heavily, her nostrils flaring. "I'll talk to him."

———

The season was turning, daylight hours shrunken and precious, and the spokes of the Eye glowed neon against the darkening sky, delicate as harp strings. In the café, the young people in their pricey trainers and their zero-gravity activewear added jackets befitting a jaunt to the Lake District, not Waterloo. But, of course, we were close to one of the busiest railway stations in Europe. These people, they weren't all wage slaves, eschewing annual leave, denying themselves vitamin D; many, perhaps fifty percent, simply secured their coffees with our special biodegradable lids and escaped to wherever they chose. I envied them.

According to Regan, there had now been more than a hundred violent killings in London so far this year. "The bloodlust in the capital shows no sign of relenting," she read aloud from her *Metro*, in earshot of bemused customers.

It was an uneasy time, for sure, but at least Melia seemed to have cajoled Kit into getting his work attendance back on track, even if he did continue with his nervous roving on the boat—he couldn't stay in his seat for longer than five minutes.

One morning, when he disappeared to the deck for a second cigarette in half an hour, I broached my concerns with Steve. "Do you think Kit might have an addiction issue?"

Frowning, Steve peered at me through the powerful lenses of his glasses. "Leave it out, Jamie."

"I'm serious. As someone who's, you know, struggled in the past, I know how it feels when people don't step up to help. Everyone assumes someone else is doing it."

"You had a phobia, mate. Kit's just letting off steam now and then."

As he returned to his phone, I took the easy option. "Maybe you're right."

"I am. Live and let live, yeah?"

Another time, on the evening boat, I observed an interaction that should have worried me but in fact had the opposite effect. Kit was at the bar getting in the beers, and Gretchen had gone to the loo. On her return, she approached Kit at the bar and murmured something in his ear. A change of order, I supposed, but then she touched his hand. It wasn't erotic, like the way Melia touched me, but sisterly, as if reassuring him there was closeness in his life, kinship. I watched as he acknowledged it, a look on his face I found impossible to read, just a scrawl of general human despair. Though Gretchen waited, and the lump of his Adam's apple moved as he cleared his throat, no words were spoken.

I pretended not to notice, of course.

23

I didn't know it at the time, but the double date Clare and I had with the Ropers soon after would be our last. It was early November, several days into a run of dreary and oppressive weather, and we hadn't been in Mariners half an hour before I realized Kit's mood was going to make the evening untenable. Whatever phase of drug abuse it represented—I suspected involuntary withdrawal—he was irritable, unrestrained, lucid to the point of withering.

And predictable by then, so very predictable. Melia had joined us directly from showing a rental on Prospect Square to a re-lo consultant who represented a family from Switzerland and she was expressing amazement at the annual running costs, when Kit spoke rudely over her: "Oh, the kind of people who live there wouldn't even notice."

"Why wouldn't they?" Clare asked, accepting a challenge that by now provoked little more than an eye roll from me. "Isn't it possible 'the kind of people' living there are actually working their arses off to pay those bills? Fretting about keeping their heads above water like the rest of the world?"

"Of course," Melia said, placatingly, but Kit was not about to concede so easily.

"So it was all hard work, was it, Clare? You paid for that massive house by working your arse off?"

She glared at him. "Yes." It was unfortunate that she glanced at me then and caught the doubtful look on my face. I sucked in my breath. This was just the sort of territory I had always dreaded us entering, confidences that could only have come from me being recirculated between the two couples as common knowledge, and it seemed incredible it had taken this long to happen.

"Give us a break," Kit said, sneering. "You make out you're this self-made businesswoman, but we all know your house was bought for you by your parents."

"It's none of your business," Clare snapped, casting me an outraged look. I could only hope she presumed I'd told Kit directly, not Melia.

"Kit," Melia warned, and I could read the message she hoped to transmit to him: *Stop. Remember the wedding champagne. Remember I work for her company.*

Remember your fucking manners, was what *I* thought. Clare had always been generous to him, she didn't deserve this takedown. "Don't speak to her like that," I said, but I could tell it was a beat too late for Clare's liking.

"Of course *you're* happy about it, Jamie," Kit scoffed. "You're like those grown-up kids on your square, living for free, someone else paying the bills. We'd all like to be a glorified lodger like you."

"I am *not* living for free," I protested, feeling true dislike for him, but Clare lifted a hand.

"For goodness' sake, why does everything have to be about money with you lot?"

You lot. She meant me, too, all three of us, and I registered in myself a complicated blend of insult, fear, and release at the change of status.

"Only someone *with* money would say that," Kit pointed out, correctly, and when Clare spoke again her tone was less hectoring.

"Okay, so it's not fair, but we all know life *isn't* fair."

"No, it's a precious gift," Kit sneered. "We should just be grateful to be alive, right? To be allowed to buy the chosen ones a drink?"

"*Kit,*" Melia said again. "Clare's the one who's always buying *us* drinks. You're being really rude."

Clare laid a reassuring hand on her arm. "It's fine, Melia. If he's offering, this chosen one will have another glass of pinot grigio."

While I admired her for the way she'd recovered herself, I suddenly felt a far simpler emotion than any other so far that evening: sadness. Sadness for the circularity of our association with the Ropers. As a foursome, we seemed to have returned to where we'd started, at the subject of Clare's house, but what had begun with a joyous dinner hosted in its rooms seemed to be ending with so much bitterness she'd be forgiven for fearing a brick through her window or a lit match through the letterbox.

Unsurprisingly, she left after that next glass, insisting I stay, but two tetchy rounds later, Melia and I followed. Normally, we avoided leaving on our own together, but Kit was determined to stay out, his eyes already scanning the bar for likely playmates as we said our farewells.

So long as we didn't touch, it was no risk for me to walk her home to Tiding Street. Instead, we drew as close as was decent and spoke in low voices about Kit, what was wrong with him, how his urges might be reined in before he said something that *really* got him into trouble. Though it wasn't late, their neighbors' windows were mostly dark and I wondered what they made of the Ropers, with their partying and histrionics.

I waited, shuffling my feet, as Melia found her keys.

"Come up," she murmured into my neck.

"I can't, darling."

"I like you calling me that. *Please* come up. Just for a few minutes."

"No. Kit could come back any time."

"Killjoy."

"I know, but it's for selfish reasons, believe me. I don't want it to end tonight."

"I don't want it to end *ever*," Melia said, and even in the face of her inebriation—and my own—I allowed my vanity to accept her tribute as nothing more than I deserved.

———

As I let myself back into Prospect Square, Clare watched me with a thunderous expression from the sitting-room window. I strode towards her, tripping on the curled edge of a rug, which worsened my own mood, and the row erupted the moment she turned to face me.

"What the hell's going on?"

I didn't quite meet her eye. "What do you mean?"

"Something's going on. For you to tell Kit you're a—what was it?—a 'glorified lodger'? You know that's nonsense."

"I didn't use that term, *he* did. Just forget it, you know what he's like." Through the old glass behind her, the square was a still life in a hundred shades of black, the streetlamps casting a thin amber light onto the tips of the railings.

"Look at me, Jamie. This is the second time I've asked you what's wrong and I'm not sure I can keep on asking. If you can't tell *me*, who can you tell?"

It was an excellent question—Clare's were, as a rule—but I had no intention of giving an honest answer. I did look at her, though. Her eyes were glistening with hurt, lids drooping with fatigue.

"I'm just worried about him," I said, feebly.

"Who? Are we still talking about Kit? I've heard enough about him to last me a lifetime."

I knew the feeling.

"Well, if that's *really* it, you're on your own. Far be it from me to interfere in your friendships."

She'd withdrawn into pomposity, but that didn't mean she wasn't upset and confused. "You don't consider him a friend of yours anymore?"

She gestured, hands upturned. "I consider him Melia's problem—and I don't know why you persist in making him yours."

The clarity of her assessment took my breath away. All those evenings with our younger, wilder counterparts that had ended with our good-natured discussion of them: they were over now. What had been implied in the bar was categorical: Clare considered herself the only responsible adult left standing. And maybe I did too.

―――――――

Towards the end of November, Melia paid her only visit to the Comfort Zone. It was three o'clock and Regan was on her break when a tour party descended in search of a midafternoon lunch. Melia, off work that afternoon, playfully offered to help me out. "Go on, I've done loads of café work. I bet I can work that monster on my own." And before I knew it, she was behind the counter and standing in front of the shiny chrome coffee machine.

I knew it would be a health and safety breach if she so much as touched it. "Don't, you need training for that. But you can do these sandwich orders, if you like? The fillings are in Tupperware in the fridge."

For forty-five minutes we worked in harmony and then, with a glance at her phone, she prepared to leave as suddenly as she'd arrived. "We should think about running a place together. It'd be fun."

I felt the surge of pleasure I always did when we spoke of our having a future together. After Kit, after Clare. After *this*. She flashed me a wicked smile and patted the tote bag at her hip. "Aren't you going to check I haven't stolen from the till? I *am* a known debtor."

"I trust you." I smirked. "Tell you what, when we divvy up the tips, I'll save my share for you."

She kissed me goodbye on the lips and a departing customer sent a curious backwards look. *How did* he *get her? He must have some hidden talent . . .*

After she'd gone and Regan had returned, I felt a strange, elevated mood, almost fanciful, as if I'd imagined the whole thing.

24

You can lead a detective to water, but you can't make him drink.

Having recorded my drugs intelligence in his notebook in frustratingly scant detail, Parry insists on leading *me* to water, back to the river and the water rats' Christmas drinks.

"If you'd stopped getting on so well, why go for drinks?" he demands and I feel a painful pressure building in my chest. We are reaching our conclusion. This is the part of the story that matters.

"We hadn't stopped getting on, not really, it just wasn't the same."

"Whose idea were the drinks?"

"I don't remember. Kit's, I think."

"You're sure it wasn't yours?"

I shrug.

"How long in advance was the date planned?"

"I remember it as being pretty spontaneous. Look, if organizing Christmas drinks is your idea of foul play, you're going to be working a lot of overtime this month."

But I know exactly what he's getting at: premeditated behavior. Malice aforethought. For the first time in this encounter, I challenge them to spell this shit out: "So you think I had something to do with his disappearance, do you?"

"You tell us," Parry answers, inevitably.

"That would be a good slogan for the Met: *You tell us.*" I decide it's time to take this interview by the scruff of the neck and show my winning card, if you'll excuse the run of clichés. After all, it's not as if they won't see it soon enough when they requisition my—and Kit's—phone records. "I know you'll be checking the cameras on the route, but I want to show you something that proves I couldn't have seen him after we got off the boat." I pick up my phone and display my last text to Kit.

Parry reads the words aloud—"'Just YOU wait'"—before turning a baleful eye my way. "What does that mean, exactly?"

"It was a response to what *he'd* said to me. He threatened me, said he knew people I had no idea existed. 'Just you wait, Jamie': that was the last thing he said to me, I swear to God. I sent that text because I had to show him I wasn't intimidated. I had to get the last word."

There's an unwelcome sinister edge to this last phrase, given the context, but I can't take it back.

"What did he mean by people you had no idea existed?"

"I assumed he meant criminals. His drug buddies, men he could ask to hurt me. He said they were animals."

While Parry scans the previous messages between Kit and me, Merchison watches me with a certain skepticism. "Maybe 'threaten' is too strong a word," I correct myself. "I'm not scared of Kit, it was more low-level harassment. But the reason I'm showing you is the timeline." I take the phone from Parry to remind myself. "I sent this when I got home. See the time? Eleven thirty-eight. The boat docks at eleven thirty. I was texting as I walked through the door, Clare can confirm I was home at that time."

"I'm not sure I understand your point," Parry says.

"My point is, he's opened it, see? It's marked as read. Since he couldn't have opened it before it was sent, he was obviously still alive and kicking after I got home."

I wish I didn't keep saying "obviously"; if I were a police officer, it would make me think a lie was being fed to me. "Then, at seven a.m., Clare and I got a taxi to Kings Cross for our train to Edinburgh. She'll tell you we were on the eight-fifteen train together or, if you don't believe her, check the station's CCTV—and the train's."

Parry raps the nails of his right hand against the knuckles of his left. "You seem very confident of the cameras. Almost as if you've gone out of your way to be seen."

I hold my nerve. "There've got to be some advantages to living in a surveillance state."

"So that was your last communication with Mr. Roper. What about Mrs. Roper? You said you hadn't had a chance to return her calls: it's quite a coincidence you were so distracted during the same period your friend went missing."

I've been expecting this to come up. "I was at my partner's parents' house, so I was hardly likely to phone my secret girlfriend, was I? I mean, I saw she'd left voicemails, but I just assumed that she was, you know, on my case."

"About not being in contact over Christmas, you mean? The ignored mistress?"

"Yes, if you want to put it like that. And since I didn't know Kit was missing, it wasn't much of a coincidence to *me*." If my gaze is firm, his is granite-hard. "Why don't you get hold of his phone activity from Monday night and find out when he opened this text? Find out if he made any calls after that, talk to the people he phoned. It will help your timeline more than talking to me."

Really, I'm the one who should be a detective here.

"Thanks for the tips," Parry says. As the din of voices in the hall suddenly rises, his, almost capriciously, grows very quiet, causing me to lean in to hear. "Here's a timeline for you, Jamie: you stalk off after this row on the boat and wait somewhere out of sight for when Kit walks by. You lure him to this black spot you told us about, where you continue your argument. Things get out of hand and you kill him, maybe using something you took from your place of work, which I assume contains catering equipment. Sharp knives." There's a significant pause. "Maybe you cut yourself while you're at it."

All three of us lower our eyes to my bandaged hand and I know what they're thinking. If I really *had* just burned it, wouldn't I unwrap the dressing and prove it? As if from the scrutiny, the wound begins to throb.

"You take his phone, so you can open the text you're going to send to him afterwards, to make it look like it's been read by him, then you dispose of his body over the river wall," Parry finishes.

The pull of my breath is audible. "Over the river wall? You're kidding, aren't you? It's pretty high—what am I, the world's strongest man?"

"He doesn't weigh that much. Not even eleven stone. Any fitness expert would agree it could be done."

Merchison watches his colleague with undisguised admiration. Whatever theory they came here with, Parry has developed it. A horrible notion occurs: what if I haven't cleared myself with this eleventh-hour seizing of momentum, but helped him fill in the details that might incriminate me? What the hell have I done?

"Prove it," I say, my voice returning to the growl of early morning, the animal protest at being singled out. "Prove that someone could do all that between when the boat docked at eleven thirty and when I was witnessed arriving home at eleven thirty-eight. Eight minutes! There's no way, no way on earth. Check the cameras, how many more times do I have to say it?" I stand, agitated. "I think it's time I got a solicitor involved here. You can't accuse me like this, it can't possibly be legal. I'm not answering any more questions until I've taken advice."

Merchison stands too, hands raised in appeal, gaze warm with fellow feeling. "No need for that, Jamie, we're only thinking aloud. This is all completely informal, none of it is on record.

And no one's accusing you of anything. We're grateful for your help, aren't we, Ian?"

"Absolutely." Nodding, even managing a smile, DC Parry taps his pen on the open page. "All we need now is for you to talk us through Monday evening and then we're finished."

I stare at him. Petty to glory in that rare smile, but I do. "Five more minutes," I say. And I sit back down.

25

Now I think about it, maybe it was Gretchen who suggested our little festive celebration. "Do you realize we've never had a drink together when we haven't had life jackets under our seats?"

"Don't forget Kit's wedding," I said. "We were on terra firma then. How about the last day we're all in work? When is that?"

All of us but Gretchen had booked Christmas Eve off work, which made Monday the 23rd the natural date and everyone plugged it into their calendars.

"Are you bringing partners?" Steve asked Kit and me, hopefully, and I hid a smirk. He must fancy Melia, just like Clare said he would.

"No, don't," Gretchen said, firmly.

In a strange—or perhaps inevitable—parallel to the breakdown in friendship between the Ropers and Clare and me, there was a strong sense that our days as a commuter quartet were numbered. Every morning now I looked forward to the short stretch of solitude after the others had left the boat. Through

191

the red-and-gold arches of Blackfriars Bridge I'd go in glorious silence, past the north bank barges with their cranes and groaning construction machinery and, on the south, the tiny sandy beach and wooden piers so picturesquely exposed by the low tide; then on past the magnificent Brutalist National Theatre, without risk of reopening Kit's thespian wounds about not being a contender. No, it seemed to me there was more to avoid now in my fellow commuters than there was to seek out, but I didn't feel sad about it, not like I did about the loss of friendship between the Ropers and Clare and me. A time to weep and a time to laugh—we all know the line.

The bar was insanely busy and horrifically loud, thanks to a polished wood interior and little in the way of soft furnishings to absorb the clamor of three hundred-plus binge-drinkers (this close to Christmas, every night in Central London was a Friday). Owing to that early morning train to Edinburgh, I'd promised Clare I'd go easy on the booze, but somewhere around the fifth drink I lost sight of that.

Gretchen, having banned partners, brought along a colleague killing time before a date, a girl in her midtwenties whose degree of attractiveness was wildly out of step with her self-importance; she presented herself as a celebrity graciously taking questions from a roomful of eager press. Within an hour, Gretchen had sloped off, followed by Kit, and Steve had been waylaid by a colleague he hadn't expected to run into, so I was saddled with the girl—what was her name? Maybe Yaya or Yoyo, some nickname she thought cute enough to foist on strangers. She made no effort to hide her lack of interest in a senior citizen like me and the dynamic of interviewer/interviewee continued. ("When did we lose the art of conversation?" I asked Clare once. "When Instagram told ordinary people their lives were extraordinary," she said, and I wasn't unkind enough to cite Hayter Armstrong's social media, which dangled the prize of star-worthy homes several times a day, like we all had an equal chance of winning.)

"Sending Yoyo to sleep, are you?" Kit said, when he and Gretchen finally reappeared. His expression was full of arrogance and I snapped.

"Fuck you, Kit."

"Nice," Yoyo said, and at last she peeled away to share details of living her best life with her unfortunate date.

To celebrate our liberation, I bought tequila shots, spending a good twenty minutes waiting to be served before rejoining the others and crashing the tray down with a drunken flourish. "Christmas! Season of goodwill to all men—or so all men hope!"

"You won't find *that* on any Christmas card," Steve said.

———

We left it late to catch the last boat eastbound, the four of us racing through the streets to Blackfriars Pier, cheering as the lit boat emerged under the railway bridge and skimmed towards us. In the sleek glass swathe of train station above, there was the fleeting, hideous illusion of impending collision as two trains crossed, before dark figures began mobbing the open doors. As we reached the onboard bar for more drinks we were still panting and wheezing, joking about heart attacks. There was another group, tourists or students, I judged, fanned across a couple of rows at the front of the cabin.

"Who the hell was Little Miss Self-absorbed, Gretch?"

"She's the insufferable assistant who just joined the team," Steve said. "Don't you listen to anything, Jamie?"

We were still competing to make the most lacerating denunciation of our gate-crasher, when Gretchen began shrieking that she'd almost forgotten, she had presents for us, and she was fishing from her shoulder bag three flat items wrapped in gold paper. They were Mr. Men books: *Mr. Grumble* for Steve, *Mr. Fussy* for me, *Mr. Wrong* for Kit.

Hardly the most flattering trio, but Steve and I took ours in good spirit, unlike Kit, who reacted sulkily, barely saying goodbye to Gretchen when she left at Surrey Quays. Even in my own state of intoxication, I could tell he was the most wasted of the lot of us. I don't actually remember seeing Steve leave the boat a few minutes later, but he must have, along with the other party, because the next time I noticed Kit and I were alone on an empty boat, torn gift wrap on the seats beside us. He flicked *Mr. Wrong* to the floor, muttering into the neck of his beer.

"Why did you do that? What's going on with you and Gretchen?"

"Wouldn't you like to know." His tone was antagonistic, making me prickle with annoyance. He was so fucking *childish*.

"Nothing Melia needs to know about, I hope?"

"Piss off." For a few seconds there was just the thrum of the engines, the strains of the Christmas soundtrack over the PA, and then he said, "I read something interesting the other day: people who accuse others of playing away are almost always the ones doing it. And here you are, accusing me." Thanks to the alcohol, his glare was more glazed than provocative, but there was no mistaking the tightness in his upper body, the tensing of his fists. "You can stop faking, all right, Jamie. I've seen the way you look at her."

"What are you talking about, look at who?" Our raised voices filled the cabin and I was sentient enough to wonder what the crew thought. I had a sharp picture of how we must appear: the feral two, the last to leave.

Kit tipped the beer to his mouth and, on discovering it empty, picked up Gretchen's half-finished bottle and drank that instead. "You must know by now she's a total slut, yeah? You said it yourself tonight: goodwill to all men—that's Melia."

I hit him then, causing him to drop the bottle, which rolled away, pumping foam onto the floor. Even mid-grapple, I registered the dynamic as warped, the lover defending the wife's honor to the husband. As the boat lurched in a sudden swell, we continued to trade slurs.

"You think you're so clever, but you haven't got a clue in your posh bubble on Prospect Square," he sneered. "I know the kind of people you wouldn't even know existed. They're animals. You'd be shitting yourself if they so much as *looked* at you."

Though I was taller and broader than him, he was becoming hard to contain, headbutting me freely, bruising me with the sharp pinch of his fingers. Seeing a crew member approach, I called out, "Excuse me? This man is bothering me!"

"'Bothering' you? Why d'you always have to sound like such a twat?" Kit said through clenched teeth.

"Let's break this up, please," we were told by the crew, and a second member of staff—the barman—helped prise us apart and keep us on opposite sides of the cabin. "Gentlemen!" he cried, and the word caused a disorientating flashback to the horror of the Tube tunnel incident, a slicing sense of self-loathing I had not felt since.

"Of course, sorry," I said, and when we docked at St Mary's, it was clear that I was to be allowed to disembark ahead of Kit. It pleased me that though I'd struck him first, he was the one being restrained, singled out as the agitator.

I could still hear him on the jetty behind me: "You'll wish you never met me, mate!"

"Took the words out of my mouth," I growled. "*Mate*."

"Just you wait, Jamie! I fucking mean it!"

I staggered onto the street. Cold and rage blocked my ears so my footsteps vibrated through my body, a monster's stomping. I didn't look to see if he was following. Mariners was still open, music and overloud voices pouring through the doors into the night. Smokers stood in a cluster in the alley, kicking their heels, restless in the cold, and I wished I could join them to scrounge a fag and draw the delicious toxins into my lungs. I longed to phone Melia, to see her, to take all the reassurance and calm I needed from her voice, her touch. Instead, as I reached the house, I texted *him*:

Just YOU wait.

Not waiting for a reply, already regretting my own message, I left my phone on the hall table to run out of charge. Upstairs, Clare had had an early night and was not overjoyed to be roused by the clatter I made hunting for Advil in the cabinet in the en suite. She reminded me of our horrifically early start, but I was in no mood for a teacher's telling off.

"That's why I'm back so early—it's not even quarter to twelve!"

"The cab's coming at seven and you haven't even packed."

"I'll do it in the morning."

"There's no way we're missing that train, Jamie. I'm not having you let Mum and Dad down."

"For Christ's sake, we won't miss the train and I won't let anyone down. Go to sleep." I didn't want to get into a second row, my nerves were roasted. All I could think was how sick I was of Kit. Sick of being with him, sick of thinking about him.

Navigating my way to the bed in near darkness, I swallowed a couple of Advil, drank a pint of water, and tried to steal a few hours' respite from my churning imagination.

26

December 24–26, 2019

If I'd been anywhere else but the Armstrong household over Christmas I might not have been able to compose myself, but Clare's parents, Rod and Audrey, were a balm for my inflamed pride, my animal wounds. Like their Georgian apartment in Edinburgh's New Town, they were elegant and patrician: there was little chance of a raised voice here, much less a raised fist.

The four hours' kip I got on the train helped. Clare had booked first class and it was comfortable enough for me to rest properly, even if she did toe me a couple of times from the seat opposite to try to jolt me from snoring.

"Three whole days without clients," she told her parents, luxuriating in the first fireside drink of Christmas Eve. The tree was hung with dozens of wooden figures from *The Nutcracker*, all with movable joints and golden chains. "I turned my out-of-office on last night."

"Well, I hope you don't die of heartbreak," Audrey said. She couldn't have known, of course, that her de facto son-in-law did have reason to pine—for his young, married lover, with whom he was unlikely to be able to connect over the Christmas break. As Clare talked about the freefalling London property market and an asking-price offer on a house in Blackheath she was hoping to receive on Friday, I realized how out of touch I'd become with her work news. I knew more about the lettings arm.

"What happened to your hand?" Audrey asked me.

"He burned it on the coffee machine at work yesterday," Clare said. "He didn't even notice it till this morning."

"I did," I corrected her, "I just hadn't bothered bandaging it. I had to run out to meet people for drinks."

"Enough drinks to kill the pain, presumably," Rod said. "Does it hurt?"

"It did when I woke up, but I'm maxed out on paracetamol now, so I can't feel a thing." The same went for the bruising to my collarbone caused by a savage headbutt from Kit. I wondered if I'd marked *him* in our squalid little tussle.

"Careful about mixing the painkillers with the booze," Rod warned, but he needn't have worried: I intended Christmas to be an exercise in moderation, right down to the pleasing economy of the single call I would make to my family on Christmas morning (never more than a few feet from an Armstrong, I would not be making one to Melia). On Monday night, I'd resented the lack of interest shown in me by Gretchen's young colleague, but now I relished sharing as little of myself as I could get away with, concentrating gratefully on my hosts. I could tell Clare was pleased with me. In the weeks since our argument after that unpleasant last drink with Kit and Melia, she'd not sulked—that was not her style—but I'd been aware of a with-drawal on various counts: physical affection, humor, the benefit of the doubt. In no position to object, I'd lain low and we'd coex-isted peacefully enough.

One useful side effect had been her not deigning to ask the reasons for my weekly—sometime twice-weekly—late arrivals home following liaisons with Melia, but, doubtless, blaming Kit on principle.

Not until we went for a walk on our own on Boxing Day morning to Calton Hill did either of us mention the Ropers.

"I had a bit of a row with Kit on Monday," I said, at the sum-mit, as if the subject could only be broached here, with the wind gusting in her ears and her eyes misled by the panorama. It was all there, solid and unchanging: the castle and Princes Street; Holyroodhouse Palace and Arthur's Seat; the Leith docks and the distant haze of the Forth Estuary.

Her head turned only fractionally. "What about?"

"Nothing in particular. I just think we rub each other up the wrong way these days. Like I said, I'm worried about him."

"Right." *Melia's problem*, that's what she'd said.

"To be honest, I'm not sure he's that stable," I added. "He's more of a cokehead than I thought."

We looked across to Arthur's Seat. Right in front of us a young couple preened with a selfie stick, adjusting their poses repeatedly.

"You haven't got involved on any deeper level, have you?" Clare said.

"What do you mean?"

"You know, sharing his habit. You don't owe any money or anything?"

"God, no." I paused. "*He* does, that's for sure."

"We all know *he* does. If this was the nineteenth century, he'd be in the Marshalsea. Melia as well, probably."

"He did ask me for a loan a while ago," I confessed. "He made me feel really guilty when I said no."

"Be careful. That kind of thing is only ever the start. He could end up blackmailing you or something."

I stole a wary glance her way: what did she mean by that? The conversation was burrowing closer to the bone than I cared to allow and I let a minute pass, willing the city—at once familiar and remote—to work its magic on me, on *her*. I had the sense that if we'd settled here and not London I'd never have accepted that I owned precisely nought percent of the home I lived in; I'd never have had to leave my job because the commute felt life-threatening; perhaps never have begun an affair with a woman like Melia—or any woman. In the end, was Kit right? Was it all down to property? Not just the financial security of it, but the pride of ownership. The power of possession.

My gaze settled on the National Monument, Edinburgh's unfinished Parthenon—unfinished because the money ran out.

"You want to know what I think?" Clare said.

"What?"

"I think you need to cut ties."

"With Kit? I was thinking the same myself. Thought

maybe I'll ask to change my hours at the café so I can get a different boat from him. It would mean working some weekends, but I—"

She interrupted: "Not just him, Jamie. Her, as well."

I swallowed. It was out of the question not to meet her eye, avoidance would only have broadcast my guilt, but when I did I found her gaze to be more cooperative than accusing.

"Both of us, I mean," she said. "There's something not right about those two."

"I thought you liked Melia."

"I do, but maybe not as much as I did. There's a reason 'Melia' gets shortened to 'Me.' It's because she's a complete narcissist."

Wow. I breathed cold clear air into my lungs, expelled it in a mist. "Okay. Well, that's fine in theory, but how can you do it when you work with her?"

"Not directly," Clare pointed out. "Sales and lettings are separate teams and we're all out of the office a lot on appointments. Anyway, I don't mean I want us to ghost them or anything, just stop hanging out. It all got too intense too quickly, didn't it? And I know that was my fault. It didn't develop the way a friendship should."

I fell silent, more than content for her to do the talking. The thinking.

"I don't want to hurt anyone's feelings," she added, with typical Clare decency. "Life's hard enough, isn't it?"

My heart ached for her. She was worrying about hurting Melia's feelings, when Melia was . . . Well, Melia was only acting her side of the friendship, even if she did it so naturally she couldn't tell herself where the lines blurred.

"Who was Dugald Stewart?" I asked, as we passed his monument, a coterie of tourists taking photos on their phones. I'd left mine in the flat, the better to tune out the voicemails arriving from Melia.

"You've asked me that before," Clare said. "He was a famous moral philosopher."

"Oh yes, the common sense guy."

"Exactly. We could do with a few more of those about the place."

"True." And for a brief moment on that hill it felt as if common sense really were all that was needed to save us.

On the train home—a slow skeleton service of the sort that made you lose the will to live—Clare groaned as she saw the work messages that had accumulated. "Who emails on Boxing Day, for fuck's sake? The world's gone mad."

"Did your couple make their offer on the house in Blackheath?"

"Not yet. Tomorrow, hopefully. Oh, I've had a couple of missed calls from Melia."

We exchanged a significant look, mindful of our conversation on Calton Hill.

"Any voicemail?"

"No. Should I call her back?"

"Leave it till you see her at work tomorrow," I suggested, yawning.

The train was due into King's Cross at 10 p.m. Normally, when heading home to London I felt a rock-solid conviction that I was traveling in the right direction, back where I belonged. Dick Whittington returned, ready to rule his city. But this Thursday evening after Christmas, by the time the houselights lining the tracks began to thicken, before we entered the deep cut into King's Cross, I felt a sensation remarkably like dread.

27

December 27, 2019

"Dread? Why would you feel dread?" Parry asks, and I realize I've lost track of what I've said aloud.

Not long ago, Melia gave me some advice: *The best way to stop yourself saying stuff is to not* think *it.* But how do you stop yourself *thinking*?

"Because of all this." I motion to the space around us, the increasing tempo of late morning, the dizzying number of variables that might make the difference between a good day and a bad one, a good deed or a bad one. "Work, life, London. The craziness of it all. It's overwhelming. Don't you ever feel that after a few days away?"

It is almost ten thirty. I struggle to cast my mind back to the commute this morning. I remember the empty seat where Kit should have been; the strangely cryptic conversation with Gretchen; the welcoming committee at the pier. That self-indulgent sense of isolation at exactly the moment I was singled out: *Is it just me?*

And then this interview. Talking till my throat parches and my heart shrinks. *Everything you know.*

Merchison is suppressing a desire to stretch, I can tell from the tension in his shoulders, the squirming in his seat. If someone yawned, he'd yawn right back. Parry, younger, gym-fit, is holding up better, but his phone has rung two or three times during the latest portion of my account and even he is losing concentration. "Okay, we'll leave it there," he says. "Our apologies to your manager for keeping you a little longer than billed."

My eyes pop. "You don't want me to make an official statement or anything?"

"Not for now. Don't go harassing anyone else involved in this investigation, mind you. If you do, we'll be all over you for perverting the course of justice, understood?"

It's not hard to guess their primary fear: that I'll try to hunt down this other witness and force from her the details they've held so tantalizingly at bay.

"That includes Mrs. Roper," Merchison says. "In fact, keep everything we've discussed to yourself for now, all right?"

I frown. "What, even Kit going missing? Are you not putting out some sort of appeal?"

I had imagined grainy footage of an inebriated Kit staggering off the boat and up the jetty—ideally with the preceding fight scene left on the cutting room floor—played on all the news sites and the local TV news. *Did you see this man on Monday night?*

"Not yet, no." They exchange a wary look, before Merchison explains: "In light of this conversation, we'll need to consult with senior colleagues. It may not be appropriate to involve the public at this time."

I stare, unsure how to decode this. I wonder if budget is a factor. Maybe those big media appeals are only for children and attractive young women, not feckless men with drug issues and debts, gone AWOL in office party season. Not so much tragedy as natural wastage. "You mean, what, you don't want to jeopardize other cases, that kind of thing?"

"That kind of thing," he agrees.

"Can I talk about it with Clare, at least?"

They nod their assent and dictate a number for me to reach them on. "Call us straightaway if he gets in touch."

"Of course." I pocket my phone and get to my feet.

I can't resist the opportunity to double back and take the stairs down, allowing me to track them in my peripheral vision. They remain at the table, phones in hand. Will they stay a while to hammer out a new hypothesis? Or hotfoot it to St Mary's, hoping those houses closest to the Thames path will yield witnesses, accounts by children of having been woken on Monday night by scary drunk men shouting and scuffling?

Or maybe they'll just go back to the station to wait for word that a body has washed ashore.

28

December 27, 2019

I leave by the western exit and hover for a moment in the flat winter light, assessing. When I'm certain I'm not being followed, I allow my shoulders to relax and slowly exhale. *I'm free.*

For now.

I feel as shattered as if it were the end of a long shift. My lower back aches badly. Sciatica? A slipped disc? Middle-aged people's afflictions I've chosen to disregard of late, believing that youth is transferable through bodily fluids. I have a sudden, unbidden thought: *I am almost twenty years older than Melia. When she's forty, I'll be sixty! What are we doing?*

Though the Comfort Zone is a five-minute stroll away, I turn in the opposite direction, towards the river, already dialing Regan to make my excuses: "I'm really sorry, but I've had to go home. It's an emergency, a friend's gone missing."

Her reaction to the news is far more excitable than mine was. "That's *terrible*! I can't believe it! What do they think's happened to him? Who is it?"

"You know the guy I get the boat with? Kit? It's him." Within five minutes, I've ignored the detectives' instructions to keep the inquiry to myself. Already, I'm willing to exploit the currency of this crisis for my own gain. "I'm sure he'll turn up, but the whole thing is . . ." Hearing the sound of the milk steamer hissing and squawking, I stop. The whole thing is what? Impossible to process? Not really happening? "Confidential, so don't say anything, got it?"

"Of course."

"Can you get someone else to help out today?"

"Simona just came in, but it's been dead so far." I hear her catch herself, as if the word "dead" will distress me.

"Thank you, you're a star. I'll definitely be in on Monday, no matter what."

I retrace my steps to the pier. The concourse by the Eye is thickening with tourists, the winter wonderland open for business. I stand for a minute watching the innocents in their knitted hats and leather gloves, talking one another into a cheeky mulled wine or a hot chocolate with whipped cream. As I wait there, alone and unnoticed, it's as if I am the one who might have been abducted, not Kit.

There's no service to St Mary's outside of rush hour, so I board the next boat to North Greenwich. The tide feels stronger, the water more agitated than earlier. Above, the pearl sky is starting to streak with darker cloud. I've never seen the boat this empty. Just me and half a dozen tourists in hooded parkas, their bags strapped across their chests. There's a family of four—Italian, I think. Two sons, less enthused by the riverscape than their parents are, showing each other stuff on their phones. The parents object at first, then give up trying.

The first thing I do is buy coffee and water and listen to Melia's voicemails from the past few days, pleas for me to let her know if I've seen Kit:

"I'm sure it's nothing, but . . ."

"He's still not back, can you *please* call me!"

I text her an apology:

So sorry I missed your calls, my phone was off over Christmas. This is awful about Kit. I swear I haven't heard from him since late Monday night. Please let me know what I can do to help.

I imagine Parry and Merchison reading it, debating whether it's a genuine approach by a bewildered lover or the sort of message composed by someone covering his criminal tracks. Of course, I know they won't be doing anything so sci-fi as reading my texts live. On TV, getting phone records takes a matter of hours, but I've read that in reality it's probably more like days or even weeks; the phone companies drag their heels in their dealings with the police. It will be the other side of New Year, surely. And what about internet search histories? Do the police need the actual devices for that? Will they come to the house and seize all our electronics? I think about the calls and texts and internet searches every one of us makes each day, the inferences to be made, cases to be built.

What the police *will* do soon enough—today, I'm supposing—is phone Clare. At the very least, they'll want her to confirm the time of my arrival home on Monday and my whereabouts since. I pray they don't tell her about Melia and me. If they could just hold fire for a few days, ideally a week.

Even before the boat reaches Tower Bridge, both Steve and Gretchen have phoned, one after the other. I let them go to voicemail and then listen to the messages straightaway.

Steve: "Jamie, did you hear Kit's gone walkabout? Let me know if you hear anything, will you?"

And Gretchen, more distressed: "Jamie, is this true about Kit? No one's seen him since our night out? His phone's turned off, I just tried. Sorry if I was weird earlier, I had stuff to think about. I'm off to Marrakech for New Year—I hope that doesn't look bad, but I booked it just before I heard the news and I won't get a refund if I cancel. Anyway, I'm rambling. Please phone me if there's any news." There's an odd pause before she rings off, as if she was considering adding something but changed her mind.

Or maybe that's just me, imagining secrets where there are none. I text her:

Yes, it's true. I've already met with the police. Really hope it's all some misunderstanding.

I send a similar message to Steve and then sit back, my shoulders sinking low in the seat. I've never been so aware of the rise and fall of the vessel; at Canary Wharf it seems to have trouble docking, the deckhands stern-faced as they feed the rope through expert fingers. On the move again, the eastern sky darkens to smoke-gray, as if we're sailing into a bonfire.

A new text pops up from Clare:

How did it go with the police?

A bit worrying, TBH. Skipping work & heading home.

I'll try to finish early.

At North Greenwich, the service terminates and I'm thrown off balance by the movement of the pontoon beneath my feet, the swelling tide below. I walk down the eastern side of the peninsula; the riggings of the boats rattle in the wind and jar my nerves. As I pass some of the apartment buildings where I've had assignations with Melia, I look up at the blank windows and picture the vacant glazed spaces within, the cold finishes and smart technology that await their occupants. They're strikingly devoid of decorations, as if the festive season has been canceled in this place, life lived in the near future. There's just one figure visible on the matrix of balconies, a woman dressed in running gear with a water bottle in her hand, the railings of her balcony making it look as though she's behind bars.

I follow the home curve of the river, the Thames Barrier glinting ahead, before I turn inland for the train station at Charlton. On the deserted train, I have four seats to myself and sit calmly, watching southeast London slide by. You'd never guess I was a man who'd once brought a network to its knees, or whatever Twitter claimed happened.

I remember the therapist saying, "Could you go on the Tube again if it was just you? An empty carriage, no one else."

"Yes," I said. "I think so."

"So your fear is associated with the other passengers as much as with being underground."

Not a question, nor a judgment. A conclusion.

The memory dislodges a more recent one: that odd segue in the police interview between their warning me about "other versions" of what happened on Monday night and probing the episode on the Tube. Why had they made the association? The discussion might reasonably have proceeded with no reference to the Tube incident at all, so it must have been relevant to some unspecified hypothesis of theirs, something more than a demonstration of my—what was it?—"impulsive streak," that was it.

My imagination twists. What if . . . what if this other passenger had something to do with the earlier event? That one hater who'd emailed me those horrible messages: had something happened to her baby and caused her to develop some psychosis, to become fixated on me? Had she been *stalking* me?

I leave the train, walk alone down the platform. No, it's a crazy leap, not to mention egocentric. People like me don't have stalkers.

Do we?

———

Senseless, I know, because Clare won't be home for hours yet, but it's with a terrible foreboding that I enter Prospect Square and approach number 15. By the time I've put my key in the lock, I'm fully expecting it not to fit, for the locks to have been changed, or at the very least for me to find bin liners of my clothes heaped in the hallway. Smashed photograph frames, my passport savaged, toothbrush snapped in two.

But all is as it should be. My clothes are alongside Clare's in the wardrobe in the master bedroom and the kitschy photo of us at a tea ceremony in Kyoto remains on the mantelpiece. My passport and toothbrush are intact.

I make a coffee and sit on the sofa with the iPad to search online for news of Kit's disappearance—information might have circulated in spite of the police's preference to keep investigations below the radar—but there is nothing. I check the name "Sarah Miller" and find three hundred million listings. There are thousands on LinkedIn, almost two hundred of those in the UK. Am I really going to track down everyone and demand to know if she took the river bus to St Mary's on Monday night? And if I do by some miracle identify the right individual, will she cooperate? Like me, she'll have been asked not to talk about the investigation and she might report my approach to Parry and Merchison, make me look more suspicious, not less.

I check on Kit again. Still nothing.

I know I ought to be careful of my online activity from now on. If the police do suspect me of foul play and are monitoring it, it might look like unusual levels of interest.

On the other hand, wouldn't any friend be searching constantly for updates? Wouldn't any friend be on the streets scouring in person, out of their mind with worry? Making notes of remembered details that might prove useful, scraps of conversation that contain clues.

If the police even believe I was a friend in the first place. I text Kit's phone for the first time since Monday night:

Where the hell are you? Everyone's worried sick!

But the message fails to send.

29

December 27, 2019

Clare comes home at five thirty—early for her, she must have canceled her evening viewings—and hurries straight over to hug me. There is licorice on her breath from the little Italian sweets she eats when she craves a cigarette, the only sign that she is anywhere near as agitated as I am.

"I know we just talked about cooling things with Kit, but I didn't mean for him to literally vanish!"

"I know." I remember my suggestion about adjusting my hours in the New Year and changing to a different boat from him, but right now, the idea that my working life will proceed along controlled lines feels like a fantasy. "Have you seen Melia?"

"No, she wasn't in. She rang Richard this morning. Played it down from what I can gather, said it's not the first time he's gone AWOL, but obviously I knew from you it's more serious than she's letting on. I mean, to report him missing! She must know this isn't just his usual drinking session—I mean, who with? Ev-

216

eryone will've been with their families over Christmas, won't they? Like us."

Like us. The words cause a lurch of remorse.

Clare shrugs off her coat, drapes it over the back of the sofa. "Poor thing, I hope she hasn't been dealing with this on her own. Richard's told her to take a few days' compassionate leave. She won't be able to think straight until she finds Kit. Where the hell is he, d'you think?"

I exhale noisily through my mouth. "I have no idea. Did the police call you?"

"Yes, just now."

Well, they can't have told her of the affair or she wouldn't be talking to me like this. The thought is less relaxing than I'd hoped. There's something dangerous simmering within me. "They'll be ringing everyone he knows, Melia must've given them a list. What did they ask you?"

"Just when I saw him last, which was weeks ago, so no use to them. Also, what time you got home on Monday night."

Which presumably *was* of use to them.

"What did you say?"

"Eleven forty. I looked at my phone when you woke me up, so it was easy to remember. They said you were the last to see him. Is that true?"

I shrug. "As far as they seem to know, yes, but I don't see how I can have been. If he didn't go home, he must have gone to meet someone, or to a bar."

Clare pulls a face. "Maybe he carried on drinking somewhere and went to sleep under a bush or something, in which case he could have caught hypothermia. I assume they've tried all the hospitals?"

"I guess so, they didn't say." It strikes me that in my extended chat with the two detectives I gathered very little information for myself.

"Well, he didn't reach home, that's established," Clare says. "Melia went to bed early, apparently, and when she got up and realized he hadn't come home, she assumed he must have stayed out with you. Then she discovered his phone was dead and started getting worried. She couldn't get hold of you, *or* me—it must have been a complete nightmare for her."

She sets about turning on the lamps I have left unlit, restoring us to normality. The Christmas tree lights, in the window at the front, are on a timer and so have been twinkling for some time and I feel an ache of regret for all the future Christmases that I won't be enjoying here. Because everything's changed now. She leaves the room and a minute later, I hear the fridge door open and close, the musical clink of glassware on worktop.

Then she's back, with two oversized glasses of white wine that must contain half a bottle each. I told myself on the way home that I wouldn't drink this evening—with the police interested enough to intercept me on my way to work, I need to keep my wits about me, remember every word I say and to whom. But the pull is too powerful and I take the glass, swallow gratefully.

"God knows what Melia's feeling right now." Clare arranges herself next to me on the sofa, her face close enough for me to feel the heat of her breath. I have a sudden and terrifying premonition of discovery, of conflict, seeing with hallucinatory clarity her wine flying the short distance from glass to my face. I can feel the cold sting of it in my eyes.

She sinks back, takes a sip. "Should we go round there, do you think?"

I look just past her candid, caring gaze. "I don't know. She might be with the police, one of those family liaison types."

"I doubt it. I mean, would they have the manpower for that? Half our industry was off work today, so it must be the same for the police, all the public services—they can't possibly be laying on the full works. Let's go round after we've finished these. We can't just leave her to suffer, can we? It's been, what, four days? She must be assuming the worst by now. I know I would be with a boyfriend like that."

I take a deep draft of wine and then speak very carefully: "I think you should go on your own, Clare."

She frowns. "Why?"

"Because the police asked me not to go near her." There's a cold prickle at the back of my neck as I realize I haven't phrased this skillfully enough. The sense of premonition deepens and I recognize it for what it is: the slippery, bucking, lunatic impulse to confess.

"Why?" she asks a second time.

"I suppose because I argued with Kit on Monday, so they think I might be involved in his disappearance in some way. And I ignored her calls—maybe that looks bad."

"I didn't know you ignored her calls. Why didn't you pick up?"

"Because it was Christmas and I didn't think they were any-thing important." I can hardly use the excuse I gave the detec-tives: the awkwardness of taking calls from your lover while a guest in your partner's parents' home. "What could we have done from Edinburgh, anyway? Melia's got other friends, hasn't she? They would have helped her."

Clare stares at me, her head tilting fractionally. "Did some-thing happen on Monday you haven't told me about? After you got to St Mary's?"

I shrink slightly from her scrutiny. "No. I didn't see him again, I swear. They've already looked at the security film on the boat, they know I got off first. And even if he *was* walking behind me the whole way, once they check the other cameras they'll see I came straight here."

"So they literally met you off the boat this morning? That must have been a shock."

"Yes." I keep my voice steady. "It was pretty early."

She shakes her head. "I don't understand why they're so inter-ested in you. What motive could you possibly have to harm him?"

I shrug.

"What did you argue about? You still haven't said."

My continued silence serves only to steer her towards her next, most damning query: "Why aren't you *really* allowed to see Melia?" And I watch helplessly as her mind files through the possibilities, her head quite still.

She'll throw me out, I think. *Where am I going to go?* My heart rate accelerates even before she says it, an animal reacting to its predator's pheromones:

"Oh my God, I know what you argued about. I know why the police wanted to talk to you."

"Clare—" I leave her name hanging. There's no script for this; it's a testament of my cowardice that in all the months of my affair I have never rehearsed this showdown. Now that it's happening, I know instinctively I should deny, deny, deny, but sheer stupefaction gets the better of me and I say nothing at all. I'm no longer *thinking*.

A flush spreads over her face and she blinks as if to refresh her vision. "Something's been going on between you and Melia. *You and Melia.*" She repeats her name in an altered tone, disgust thickening her voice like mucus. As I finally begin my denials, she breaks in, right in my face, her breath coming rapidly: "How long? And don't insult me by lying. No more lies."

"Since the spring," I say, at last.

"What does that mean? May?"

"March," I admit.

That's a second shock, I can tell. She's wondering how she could have been unaware of what must have been an attraction from the get-go. She's probably thinking, Well, of course *he* would fancy her, but what would *she* see in him? Or maybe I'm doing her a disservice. Another one. Oh, shit, why the hell aren't I denying it? Denying it and counterpunching with injured pride?

"Where did you meet? Not here?" Not in *my* house. Even in this moment of profound crisis, the inference goads me.

"No, at a friend of hers' place."

"How often? Once a month?" Her words come in gulps. "Once a week?"

"About that, I suppose."

"So you've had sex, let's see . . ." She tots up the weeks, nine months' worth. "Thirty-five, forty times. More, probably. Or is it waning a bit now? Hang on a minute, they got married in August . . ." As the next dirt-encrusted penny drops, she begins to tremble. "You continued after that? That's the lowest of the low, Jamie. Even if you couldn't give a shit about me, what about Kit? You were one of their *witnesses*."

I stay silent. Anything I say will be ammunition smashed back at me.

"Did he find out? Is that what you were rowing about? You need to tell me, Jamie, this is bloody serious, it could be seen as a motive for murder!"

"I know that!" I find my voice. "He didn't find out, no, but he was slagging her off and threatening me and I got angry. I was worried he would go back and, I don't know, hurt her or something. You know what they're like."

There's an uncomfortable sense to this last statement, an implication that I acted to intercept him, but fortunately Clare doesn't pick up on it. "Evidently I haven't got a clue what any of you are like."

I breathe deeply, slowly, knowing I must get this right, that this is now crisis control of the highest order: "Clare, I'm sorry you had to find out this way, I really am. I know there's no way back from it, but I honestly don't think Kit's going missing has got anything to do with me. *Or* her. I told the police I think this might be drugs-related."

But I'm a fool to think I can wrench control of this dialogue:

Kit's whereabouts are disregarded while she processes my betrayal. She's on her feet now, hands shaking so the wine threatens to spill. Her face twists with fury. "All this time she's been acting like I'm her mentor. Women helping women. Women screwing women, more like!"

"Don't fire her, Clare."

She looks for somewhere to put down her glass, stumbling slightly, fighting tears. "I couldn't even if I wanted to. It's not illegal to seduce a colleague's partner of ten years, just fucking rude." Her neck is streaked with high color, hair disheveled from her pulling at it; she looks both wild and destroyed. "I can't believe this is happening. I want you to leave. Get out."

I experience a whoosh of horror. And not only horror but also, farcically, given how much I've risked and how long I've been risking it, *surprise*. Surprise that she's exercising the power that's been hiding in plain sight all these years, even when a well-paid career of mine afforded me the illusion of equality: this is her castle and I've been allowed to be king of it only on a grace-and-favor basis. If it were the other way around and she had been unfaithful to me, I would still be the one who had to beg for the stay of execution.

I keep my voice level. "Come on, that's not fair. This is my home, my home of ten years, I must have some rights. Let me stay until I sort something out. I'll move to the spare room, I'll keep out of your way."

"I know you will, you won't *be* here. I can't speak to you anymore, I can't look at you." She retreats and I hear her in the loo under the stairs, fan turning, water splashing.

This is bad, I think. Trembling, I finish my wine, rehearse my next pleas: *Please, can you just let me stay another week, till the New Year . . .*

The doorbell rings—our online grocery order—and bag after bag is passed across the threshold. The delivery guy tells me he's worked nonstop over the holidays and I fish in my pockets for a tip.

"Much obliged." If he hears the sound of a woman weeping a few feet away, he makes no remark. Maybe it's not the only evidence of domestic dysfunction he's witnessed this shift (isn't it the case that more divorces are initiated after Christmas than at any time of year?).

When he's gone, I knock on the loo door and call out, "Please, Clare, can we talk about this?"

"Go away," she responds, the words muffled by the door between us and by her tears. "Go away."

And I think, with disgraceful relief, that "Go away" is at least a notch of an improvement on "Get out."

30

December 27, 2019

I'm startled awake by the sound of a door thumping shut, a vibration in my body, and I think for a moment I'm on the riverboat, absorbing the sickly bounce of the tide as heating pumps through the cabin, smothering me. (I dream of the river often now.) But then I feel the brief dip in temperature as the outside air reaches my skin and the living-room furniture takes shape.

Having unpacked the shopping while Clare was still holed up in the loo, I'd succumbed to the nervous exhaustion of the day and drifted off on the sofa. For how long? An hour, at least.

I stagger up, grab my jacket, and tear out into the cold. From the doorstep, I catch a fragment of scarlet puffa jacket near the railings on the western side of the square; the faint crack of Clare's boot heels on pavement. She's heading towards the high street.

"Clare? Clare!" I sprint to catch her up. "Where are you going? Not to Melia's?"

She doesn't slacken her pace as she addresses me sideways. "Right first time."

"But why?"

"*Why?*" She gives an openmouthed cackle of laughter, her breath a succession of puffs in front of her face. "Because I've got a couple of questions for the slut, that's why."

The same insult Kit used. They're all calling her that and she doesn't deserve it. But I have to pick my battles. Defending her to Kit was one thing, but defending her to Clare is more than my life's worth.

"I'll come with you." I'm breathing heavily after the dash, recoiling from the bite of the chill on my face. The threatened storm hasn't yet broken, but the wind is low and strong, picking up leaves and runaway litter. A putrid odor reaches my nose.

"I thought you said you weren't allowed?" Clare snaps. "Can't keep away, can you?"

"Listen, I know you don't want to hear it, but I'm convinced all of this is to do with drugs. I think maybe Kit owed his dealers money and they took him down."

"'Took him down'? Are you for real?" Her tone is full of the contempt she normally reserves for politicians on TV and clients who turn out to be time wasters.

"I *am* for real, yes! There's all this knife crime now, it's in the papers every day. People are killing each other over trivial things, like just looking at someone the wrong way. We like to think that this stuff is only ever gang-related, but it could happen to anyone."

"Far more likely he's topped himself because he can't bear being with *her* a moment longer."

"You don't mean that, Clare."

Her snarl begins in profile and ends face-on, just as we reach the high street and draw up at the curb. "Don't tell me what I *mean*." And she marches into the road with only the briefest regard for an oncoming single-decker bus, which blares its horn and brakes. Delayed by this and a pair of cyclists, I scurry after her towards the Lamb, the only pub on this stretch. On the pavement outside, smokers notice our fierce, unhappy faces, out of kilter with the prevailing Friday-night spirit. Will someone report us, I wonder: a wild-looking man stalking a well-dressed woman? A second account of his suspicious behavior in four days? At the thought, I hang back; only when we reach Tiding Street do I draw level again. The street is a far more alluring prospect than on previous occasions, the residents of Victorian cottages clearly recognizing that this is their time of year: there are beautifully decked trees in almost every window and wreaths adorning most of the doors.

Not on the Ropers', however. No tree glitters at their window, no twists of holly and ivy bedeck the door. As Clare rings the bell, holding it down for a full five seconds, a man strides past with a huge bouquet of flowers and I'm assaulted by olfactory memory: the scent of the flowers we brought the night we came for dinner, the night all of this was set in motion. The next thought comes in a furious surge: *What if he's in there, standing right next to her? This will all be over!*

Before I can assess how this thought makes me feel, the door opens. Though I've half-prepared myself for the state

227

Melia might be in, I can tell Clare is rocked by the sight of her. She's swollen-faced, her hair limp and lips rough and chewed. Dressed in leggings and a fleece, she has nothing on her feet, making her a full head shorter than us. Luckily for her, all of this has the effect of stifling the barrage of insults Clare surely had ready and instead we are divided by a strange, downcast expectation.

"Melia," I say into the void, "we're so sorry—"

"I don't want to see you," she interrupts in a desperate, raw-throated voice. Though she raises a hand, she doesn't quite close the door.

"We understand you don't want visitors right now . . ." Clare has found her voice and it's very different from the one I was anticipating: cool, underlaid with compassion, as if she recognizes an injured animal when she sees one. "But can we come in for a couple of minutes? We might be able to help you figure out what's going on."

Perhaps it's a conditioned response to the voice of her professional superior, but Melia surrenders almost at once and without anyone uttering another word we are moving through the small unlit hallway, up the narrow staircase and directly into the living room, where we sit side by side on the yellow sofa.

There *is* a tree, a small potted one on the floor by the fireplace, a handful of baubles, a sparkly "M" at the top. Who chose that "M" for a star, Melia or Kit? There are only three or four cards on the mantelpiece, one I recognize as being from us. Clare always sends them through the post, even to those who live walking distance away. She likes imagining cards on the doormat, swept up and enjoyed over the first drink of the evening.

There is no offer of a drink on this occasion, though Melia looks as if she could do with something hot, her normally glowing skin tinged pale blue. It's very cold and I remember her complaining of huge gas bills. They can't have been cut off, can they?

Still unsure if Clare intends making accusations about the affair, I take the initiative, hardly knowing what I'm saying: "Melia, you probably know Kit and I had a row on the boat on Monday night, but that's the last I saw of him, I swear. I'm sorry I didn't pick up your calls, but I had no idea all of this was going on, and we were in Edinburgh until late last night, weren't we, Clare?"

Melia just blinks at me, otherwise unresponsive to this gush of information.

"Richard filled me in," Clare says, as if I have not spoken. "Are you being kept up to date? Should you even be on your own like this? It's a hugely stressful thing to have to go through."

"I'm okay. I'll be the first to hear if anything happens." Melia looks at her, her distress clearly unadulterated by any additional fear of her friend and colleague. Can't she guess from Clare's manner towards me that we've been discovered? Should I have texted to warn her we were coming? But even if I hadn't had to scramble after Clare the way I did, I'd have needed to be aware of the police accessing my messages, reading meaning where there is none.

She turns her hollow gaze back to me. "I just want to know where he is. Or where his body is."

"His body?" I give a mirthless laugh. "I think that's a bit melodramatic, don't you?"

"Melodramatic? You just admitted you got into a fight with him! Just tell me what happened? After you got off the boat."

"There's nothing to tell."

"Right." She fixes me with emotionless eyes that make what she says next sound all the more chilling: "I hate you, Jamie."

Sensing a frisson of pleasure from Clare, I protest: "What? That's ridiculous, I haven't done anything!"

"Look," Clare says, "we all know Jamie wouldn't harm Kit. He's not capable of it. That will be obvious to the police." I don't care for her disdain, but she continues to adjourn any confrontation about the affair and, for that, I'm supremely grateful.

Melia's attention moves from Clare to me and back again. "Please just go," she whispers. "Both of you."

"We're going. But just answer me one thing first, Melia." Clare shifts closer to her, her eye contact insistent. "Answer me honestly . . ."

"What?" Melia asks, and she gazes at Clare as if with a morbid fascination she cannot hope to break.

"Do you *really* not know where Kit is?"

There's a moment of acute shock. From the street, a car engine starts, a kick of dissent. What Clare just said may not have been intended as an insult, but it's certainly received as one and enraged eyes meet mine before Melia turns on her: "I *beg* your pardon. Why would I be in a state like this if I wasn't terrified something horrific has happened to him? Where is it you *think* I think he is? On a stag weekend in Vegas?" Her tone is hostile, haughty, but she can't sustain it for longer than a few seconds and suddenly her face collapses and she's weeping into her hands.

Unable to watch her, I focus on Clare, terrified she'll escalate the argument, but again she wrong-foots me with her response. She places a gentle hand on Melia's shaking shoulder and her tone dips in apology: "Oh, Melia, there could be all sorts of reasons for his going to ground. I'm sure there'll be news soon. Good news. I'll leave you, I didn't come here to upset you, but let me know as soon as you hear anything. Or if you can think of any way I can help."

"Me too," I say, sidelined by that insistent first-person singular, and we leave her with her face in her hands. I am bewildered by Clare's behavior. Is it purely reactive, the effect of Melia's torment dwarfing her own? Or is it more strategic: she's waiting for a bigger stage on which to expose us for who we are? To assemble witnesses to support her?

I think, for the first time, *Will she take revenge?*

"Why didn't you mention—" I begin, but she interrupts.

"That's my business. I don't answer to you anymore."

"You never did," I say, before I can stop myself.

She comes to an abrupt stop, one foot in front of me to force me to do the same. *Ah, there's to be an announcement.* "I never did, you say? Right. Life won't be so different, then, will it? In case it's not clear, don't think for a second I'm forgiving you. We are over."

We start walking again. I imagine the bristling hostility as a force field around us: if a third party reached towards us, they'd burn their fingers. Heavy with guilt, I remind myself that the fact that I have to grovel is at least part of the reason why I strayed in the first place.

"Clare, about my staying in the house a few days, I—"

She interrupts with a snort of contempt. "Stop begging, it's pathetic. Yes, you can stay in the house. I'll support you till you sort out this crap with the police. It's obvious you're not a murderer and the last thing I want is people thinking I've been living with one all these years."

"Thank you. I'm grateful." And I really am, in spite of all my resentment. In spite of everything.

"But as soon as you're in the clear, you need to go. And when you do, I don't ever want to hear from you again."

I suck my lower lip. "I understand." As we reach Prospect Square, I'm conscious of ravenous hunger. I haven't eaten since early morning. Since then, only coffee and wine. "Will we . . . will we still eat together?"

She rears up with fresh anger. "Yes, Jamie, what shall I rustle up? Boeuf bourguignon all right? Or would you prefer the fish of the day?"

I keep my voice neutral. "I meant I'm going to cook—we've just had all that food delivered. Would you like me to make something for you too?"

"No thanks. I'd rather starve."

We've halted on our doorstep. As she fiddles with her key, she gives an unpleasant scrape of a laugh and I can tell she wants me to ask.

"What?" I oblige.

"I'm just thinking that there's one thing I agree with Melia on."

"What's that?"

"I hate you as well."

And it hurts. Even in the maelstrom of the rest—the pounding of my head, the ghastly arrhythmic drum of my terrified heart—it hurts.

31

December 28, 2019

I wake up on Saturday wretched and unrefreshed in one of the spare bedrooms (*one of the spares*: I know how that sounds). Though I can use the second bathroom (*second bathroom*: ditto), I have to enter the marital bedroom for fresh clothes and when I do Clare assaults me on sight. And I mean assault: first, she's slapping my face with open palms, then she's beating my chest and shoulders with closed fists, the whole time repeating her sentiment of last night: "I hate you!"

"Stop!" I try to seize her arms but she goes on lashing out, striking a particularly unwelcome blow to the tender area of bruising left by Kit's skull. Eventually, she crumples away, sinks onto the bench seat at the end of the bed, breathing hard.

"How can you have fallen for such a bloodsucker, Jamie? *How?*" She groans. "Stupid question. It's not your blood she's sucking. Sex. Always sex."

Rubbing my wounds, I don't point out that she was the one who introduced us. She would only—quite reasonably—tell me to shut the fuck up. "Come on, Clare, something bigger is going on than some meaningless affair—otherwise you wouldn't have felt sorry for her last night. You didn't behave like this with *her*." I run fingers over my stinging left cheekbone, feel the raised lines where her fingernails have broken the skin. There are going to be scratch marks.

"Of course I felt sorry for her," Clare cries. "She thinks her husband's dead and I'm a decent human being! And why does it have to be a showdown between women? You're the one I'm confronting here."

"I know, but if you could not do it physically." As I gather the clothes I need, I notice there's a packed overnight bag by the wardrobe. Downstairs, as I drink my morning coffee, I hear snatches of phone conversation—"Just one night, maybe two"—and try to make sense of the thuds and slams that succeed it. When she comes down, the bag bumping at her side, I ask where she's going.

"If you're going back up to Edinburgh, won't all the trains be booked up for New Year's? You won't get a seat, it'll be awful standing the whole way. Stay here, please. It's your house."

"I know *that*," she snaps. "Are you offering to leave instead?"

I make no reply.

"That's right, you have *rights*. I'm flying, for your information, so there's no need to concern yourself with my comfort."

God knows how much the flight must have cost her the Saturday before Hogmanay. What a wonderful cushion money is.

Without saying goodbye, she closes the door in my face.

Upstairs, there's further ignominy to contend with. My remaining clothes and toiletries from the master suite have been moved into the spare and dumped in a huge heap on the bed. A roll of bin liners has appeared on the dressing table, the message that I should get packing loud and clear. Decide what I'm going to donate and what I'm going to keep for my next life.

I tip the clothes onto the floor and go back to bed.

———

For once, I wish I worked weekends. Delaying rewaking—and therefore decision-making—until the afternoon, I leave the house and walk down to the pier, the commuter who won't take a day off. Okay, it's more than force of habit, I admit I'm hoping Melia might be walking on the river path, fleeing the cabin fever of her waiting game to get some air. But the riverside is deserted, the water a sullen gray, and she is nowhere in sight.

With the powerful need to do something constructive, I retrace my steps from Monday night, from jetty to Prospect Square, checking for the security cameras in which I've so emphatically put my faith. As well as the one mounted on the front wall of Mariners, there is at least one traffic camera, as well as a private surveillance camera above the door of a large house on the western corner of Prospect Square.

Reaching number 15, I pass the gate and return to the river by the second, lesser-known route accessed from the eastern side of the square, which leads down Pepys Road, a dead-end used mostly by construction vehicles heading for the new apartment complex going up, St Mary's Wharf ("Riverside Forever Homes," for fuck's sake). The road ends about twenty meters from the water, at which point the river path is reachable only on foot and via an insalubrious alleyway yet to be improved by the developers. I don't see a single camera between my own door and the stretch of river path leading to the Hope & Anchor, including the black spot I mentioned to the detectives. No drug dealers today, only a couple of homeless guys who've managed to furnish themselves with fags and booze and who call out festive greetings to me from the bushes.

It's as I pass the door of the pub that I think I hear it: Kit's laughter, the distinctive discharge of it, somewhere within. I pivot with a dancer's precision and go inside. Other than the main room overlooking the water, where I've drunk frequently with Kit, the rooms are of the poky, low-ceilinged style I dislike, the stairwells unpleasantly confined, but I sweep systematically from corner to corner. There is no sign of him. The two lavatories are vacant.

I must look forlorn because the barman tries to help out. "Who're you looking for?"

I don't recognize him as regular staff and so I find a picture of Kit on my phone and show it to him. "A friend of mine, a short bloke, about thirty?"

"Oh, I know Kit," he says.

Of course he does.

"Haven't seen him for a few days, mind you—" As if only now registering the inquiry—or my face—properly, he presses his lips tightly together, which I take to be a subconscious sign that the police have been in and asked him not to mention it to anyone.

"Thanks anyway." Since I'm here, I down a double G&T that I really shouldn't be spending money on when I have free booze at home. I take a seat in the main window and send Kit another message: *Where are you*? But the text, like the one sent yesterday, brings only a "message failed" notification. I look out at the Thames, consider its unknowable depths. Is that where Kit's phone is? Down there, on the riverbed? I saw an exhibition once of phones found in the Thames, from the earliest brick models to the latest iPhones. Each one had an owner with a story about its loss. Maybe in the case of one or two sad souls, the story died with the owner.

Feeling a flare of fury, I push my empty glass from me and stride out. This won't work, being haunted by the bastard everywhere I go.

Other than a voicemail left for my father in which I neglect to mention that I'm now a single man soon to be of no fixed abode, my communications over the rest of the day are spartan, characterized mostly by unanswered texts. There's one to Clare to ask how long she'll be away. I imagine her with her family, telling an appalled audience of my betrayal, an excellent whisky at their disposal. Will they express shock and dismay or will they say, Well, we've always thought there was something *shiftless* about him?

When she fails to reply, I make a more specific appeal to Dad: *What are you doing on NYE? Would you like to come to London?*

He won't answer either, at least not promptly. He treats his mobile like a live grenade. I'll need to call his landline to repeat the invitation. Even so, I check my texts constantly. What power these things have, as if words lit on a screen are more significant than those produced by the human voice. I remember presenting the detectives with that text to Kit, like I was a magician, a mesmerist.

I had to show him I wasn't intimidated.

I had to get the last word.

With hours to fill and a taste for G&Ts freely indulged, I replay my police interview, teasing the details from a short-term memory that retains a fraction of the information it would have done twenty years ago. I know why I was singled out, of course—if I were drawing up the list I would have put my name top, too—but why in person and not over the phone? Why two detectives, not one? Someone had convinced them that I warranted intercepting in that fashion and to my knowledge there were only two people they interviewed before me: Melia and this other passenger, possibly named Sarah Miller.

I can't shake the thought of the hater from the Tube. I know I shut down the email account she used to harass me, and I'm certain she never signed her name, anyway, but there was an email address for her that I retrieved from my bank of bad memories when talking to the detectives. Weren't there three letters, initials, perhaps? STM or SBM? Could they stand for Sarah Miller?

What goes around comes around . . . That's what she'd said.

Or maybe Sarah Miller really *is* part of another investigation. *Think.* Maybe there's a more obvious candidate, someone who's been party to the tensions between Kit and me and who may even have rivalrous feelings towards me. And I know he was on the boat that night because I bought him a drink! Adrenaline courses through me as I find Steve's number on the water rats' WhatsApp group and tap out an individual message:

This is Jamie. Have you been telling the police lies about me?

His reply comes within ten minutes:

What lies?

I just want to know. Be honest with me PLEASE!

You been on the sherry, mate? I've told the police nothing. Take it no news on Kit?

In the time it takes for the adrenaline to drain, I have understood that my theory is preposterous. My phone rings—Steve—but I decline the call.

I feel suddenly completely alone.

I search for something to watch on TV that will hold my attention, dismissing episode after episode of dramas that any other week of my life I'd have found perfectly gripping. Finally, I settle on the old movie *Plein Soleil*, the French version of *The Talented Mr. Ripley*, with Alain Delon and Maurice Ronet. Clare and I saw it years ago at the NFT and had disagreed about the ending: the body is thrown overboard and gets tangled up in the boat's propeller, only to be discovered when the yacht is inspected by a new buyer. While Clare was outraged that they'd changed the book's denouement, I hadn't read the book and pronounced the twist perfect.

But as I watch it a second time, in less settled waters of my own, it strikes me as the most heartbreaking thing I've ever seen.

32

December 29, 2019

Sunday. Kit has been missing now for six days and I honestly don't know how much longer I can live with this strain. Suspense is fine in a novel or a movie—just a few hours and then you can decompress—but in real life it's corrosive, cumulative; I swear it shaves time off your life expectancy.

I try to get to grips with my financial position, but am immediately fearful of the string of notifications I've received from the bank confirming the canceling of direct debits from our joint account. Clare must have switched them to her individual account and I can safely assume no longer intends paying a penny of her salary into the joint account.

I log into my individual account and see it for what it's been this last year: pin money. There are not enough funds even to cover the river bus season ticket due to be renewed in a few weeks' time. If and when I set up domestic life alone, I will be in the same predicament as Regan and millions of other residents of this brutal city: sleeping under faulty boilers, sharing a bed with shift workers, eating customers' leftovers. Reading avidly of victims of violent crime, perhaps because it feels as if they're the only ones left who have even less than you do.

————

It is exactly three o'clock when I stroll up to the high street and catch sight of a visibly tearful Melia in the window of Rosie's Café. She's with a friend, a half-familiar face, and by the time I'm through the door I've remembered her square jaw and overgroomed eyebrows from the wedding party—she's the girl who was dancing with Melia on the river path. Her head is bent towards Melia's in earnest attention. No need to ask why Melia is upset, but is she close enough to this friend to have confided the complication of her affair with me? Have I been naive to trust that no one else knows? No one besides Clare, of course—and the police.

It's loud inside, the acoustics crashing, but I weave through the tightly packed tables to reach her. "Melia, do you have a second?"

"Jamie!" She cringes, as if I'm going to whip out a baseball bat and start beating her. Recovering quickly, she motions to the other woman. "You remember Elodie from the wedding?"

"Nice to see you again," Elodie says, but her automatic smile has already frozen: she senses Melia's fear and my instability. She notices the scratches on my face from Clare's attack and no doubt forms her own opinions as to how I came by them.

"I want to talk to you about Kit," I say grimly. "On your own."

Elodie shoots Melia an uncertain look and the edges of her eyebrows draw closer together, a bulge of pale skin forming between them. "Should I leave you two . . ."

"No," Melia tells her. "Please stay. I don't want to talk to him about Kit. Have you been following me, Jamie?"

"Of course not!" My protest is animated to the point of parody: "I saw you in the window and I just wanted to find out what the situation is. Have you heard from him? Is he still AWOL?"

"I said I don't want to talk about him. Please leave!"

"I think you should do what she says," Elodie tells me, fierce with disapproval.

"But if there's any news, I have a right to hear it. I'm being hassled by—"

But Melia interrupts me with a sudden escalation of emotion: "Why won't you just leave me alone?" She begins weeping noisily and Elodie is on her feet, trying to edge past me. Anyone would think we were shooting a movie, the actorly way people pretend not to be listening, but I know they are. I certainly would be.

"Melia? Are you okay?" Elodie asks, an arm around her friend's shoulders. She regards me with indignation. "Don't you think she needs some privacy at a time like this? If you don't go right now, I'm dialing nine-nine-nine."

At this, the other customers fall silent and several faces turn in our direction, with varying expressions of inquisitiveness and alarm.

"It's all right, El, really." Melia wipes away her tears with the backs of her hands, before noticing the paper napkins and taking a handful. "He's going, aren't you, Jamie?"

"Fine. If I'm not allowed to be concerned for a friend." I leave with a bodily impression of the fear I've left in my wake, fear I don't fully understand until I see my face in the mirrored glass of the doorway.

There are the scratches, yes, but that's not nearly the most disturbing thing. It's the look in my eyes: wild, guilty, almost depraved. I may not have killed a man, but I look exactly like someone who has.

―――――

It fills me with both terror and relief when Clare returns late the same evening. She will, of course, have appointments tomorrow, a business to run. As her overnight bag drops heavily onto the tiles and her keys clunk into the dish on the hall table, I emerge from the depths like a house cat overdue its feeding time.

"Oh. You're here," she says, scarcely glancing. She's kicking off her boots, straightening them on the shoe rack. I'm lucky she hasn't yet purged it of my footwear. "I thought you might have gone to shack up with *her* by now."

This was not a suggestion made before she left and so must have struck her while she was away. I fear she's in a mood to withdraw her offer of accommodation, the last thing I need, and I must do as little to provoke her as possible.

"Of course I haven't. We're not together. You saw yourself how she feels about me now. You heard her say she hates me."

An inadvertent reminder that *she* repeated the sentiment.

"On Friday, yes." Still she won't look at me. "Who knows what might have happened since then? I think we've established that whatever it is I'll be the last to know."

It's true that Friday feels prehistoric. If this is how time is going to be now, every beat slower and stickier than it should be, I don't know if I can bear it. I think of that anguished little foray to the river yesterday, how I looked for Melia and thought I'd found Kit. Then, earlier today but already feeling surreal and distant, that ugly altercation in the café. "How are your parents?"

"How do you think?" She shoots me a ferocious arrow of a look, and I answer for myself: deeply upset to be having to console their only daughter, her faithless cunt of a partner having destroyed the holidays for everyone. They must be regretting every last drop of fine wine they served me when I was their guest for Christmas.

"I take it Kit hasn't turned up?" She stands in front of me, hands on hips. Her sweater—ivy green, with a gold thread running through it—is new, one of the presents we opened together under Rod and Audrey's tree, *Nutcracker* decorations rocking above our heads. A week ago, I would have said how beautiful it is, how well it suits her, especially with the ruby-red lipstick, which has bled into the lines around her mouth.

I half-shake my head. "Not that I know of, no."

"It's genuinely bizarre, isn't it?"

I think "bizarre" is maybe a bizarre word to describe a man's disappearing without trace, but I know better than to voice this. Those slaps and punches she inflicted on me, I deserved them, yes, but that doesn't mean I'm looking to repeat the punishment.

"Anyway," she says, "I want to talk to you for a minute."

"Of course." It isn't so much a request as an order and I follow her to the kitchen table for our meeting. She pours herself a glass of wine and takes her customary chair with the sheepskin. Resisting the urge to fetch alcohol for myself, I crumple into the seat opposite. "Is it about the bank account? I saw you've switched the direct debits."

"Yes, the paperwork will arrive in the next few days to close that account. I have no intention of being liable for any overdraft you decide to run up funding *her*."

I swallow my exasperation. "I've just told you we're not together."

"It's none of my business," Clare says, curtly. "This isn't about that."

"Okay." It must be about who gets what, then. Furniture, books, coffee cups: which provenance can be proved, whose claim is greater. Exhausted doesn't begin to describe how I feel at the prospect of negotiating this. *Just keep everything*, I think. When it comes down to it, it's mostly all hers anyway.

"When I was home, I talked to Piers about all this and he had some interesting thoughts," she says, her tone warming a degree or two.

Well, I wasn't expecting *that*. Piers is her cousin, a twice-divorced accountant who is not noted for his interesting thoughts about anything, least of all male-female relationships. "You mean about us?" I say, doubtfully.

"No, not about us. There *is* no us." She lifts her glass and the veins on the back of her hand glow blue on pale skin, river lines painted on old wood. I think of Melia's skin, so fresh and youthful, and feel a surge of conviction that the choice I've made is predestined. However magical I imagine my affinity with Melia to be, I'm hardwired to prefer youth, it's as simple as that. An old goat like me might still procreate with her, but not with Clare. (For the record, I don't have plans to procreate, full stop.)

For just a moment, I think I hate myself as much as the woman watching me does.

"I mean about Kit," she says. "I know you think drugs might be a factor in this vanishing act of his, but we think maybe there's something else going on."

"Like what?" My eyes narrow. Vanishing *act*? Instantly, I'm alert.

"I don't know yet, but Piers thinks it might be financial and knows someone who can help. One of those forensic accountants who can reach out to people better placed to find out stuff that's supposed to be, you know, protected."

"You mean a hacker?" I feel my breathing alter. "You want to 'reach out' to a hacker to dig some dirt on Kit? Are you serious?"

She taps her nails on the wineglass. "I don't mean invade his privacy for the sake of it, just get a picture of what's been going on. Piers says money is the number one reason why people go missing, behind crime generally."

Nerves make me scoff at this. "Well, he's an accountant, so that's the only perspective he has on human nature. What about crimes of passion?"

"Isn't that what we're trying to *dis*prove, for your benefit?" she says, and I recoil from the sudden arctic chill in her tone. "Maybe this will unearth something that supports your drugs theory. Big cash withdrawals, say, activity that shows he was trying to get money, but couldn't, leaving him exposed to criminals. I don't know what this person will uncover, but it would be good to set the police off in a new direction—away from you."

I'm nodding now, vigorously, demonstrating my gratitude. "That's true, but shouldn't we let them do that through their own legal means?"

"We should, but we can't be sure it will actually happen. They're gathering evidence to prove the hypothesis *they're* pursuing, not the one we are."

The one in which I'm the suspect. I get it. "How long will it take?"

"Piers said his guy should have something for us within forty-eight hours."

"Forty-eight hours?" They've already set this in motion, I realize, shocked. And, unless this shady character owes Piers a favor, they must be paying through the nose for him to work so quickly at this time of year. It strikes me that she might in fact be scheming with Piers and his associates to incriminate *me*, not Kit. But then she'd hardly be briefing me on it now, would she?

Unless this is a more elaborate sting of some sort? All that stuff about clearing my name in order to save her reputation: for all I know, she could be working with the police and feeding me lines scripted by them. At the edge of my paranoia lurks that name again, Sarah Miller, and I extinguish it. *Focus.* "How much is all this costing?"

"Don't worry about it," she says. "We'll call it a goodbye gift."

Sensing sincerity, I reach for an expression of grateful

humility. "Thank you. If it turns something up that might help me . . ." I falter. Everything I say now has the uncomfortable ring of testimony—to be quoted back to me at a later date. "I mean, if it helps us find Kit, then wow, okay. Thank you, Clare."

She says nothing, just peers at me with cold curiosity, as if she doesn't recognize me anymore. "He's not on any missing persons sites yet, I checked them all earlier. Any idea why?"

"The police said they weren't issuing any details yet." It seems to me she's doing more detecting than the detectives are. And there I was imagining her this weekend in a Scottish slough of despond, weeping and inhaling whisky.

"Why on earth not? Shouldn't they be appealing for witnesses?"

"You would have thought so, but they specifically asked me not to talk about it with anyone while they updated their bosses. I think it's because of the possible drugs connection. And that's a point, Clare: if this involves their organized crime unit, say, then we should be very, very discreet about these inquiries we're making."

Two words stand out there: *organized crime*. She hears them, all right, but she doesn't back off. "I'll pass that on."

As she leaves the kitchen, wineglass replenished, I say, very casually, "Can I just ask, do you have plans for Tuesday evening? New Year's Eve?"

She rotates, glowering. "Are you serious? What d'you have in mind? Dinner and a romantic stroll along the river to watch the fireworks? Or do you mean you want me out of the way so you can party with your new love?"

I aim for an expression of polite neutrality. "I just told Dad I might be free."

In her face there is dismay, then righteous satisfaction. "You'll have to go to him, then, because I'm staying in and I can't face socializing. I'm sure you'll find it in your heart to forgive me."

"Of course. Sorry." But my apology, like all the others, is profitless. Too little too late.

33

December 30, 2019

Monday morning arrives as a blessed fucking relief, frankly, with Clare and me both due at work and indecently keen to get there. She leaves just before seven and her mug is still warm from her coffee when the doorbell rings.

To my great consternation, DC Merchison stands on the step, legs planted apart, ID brandished, as if I don't already know who he is. He's clean-shaven, smart in a blazer and what looks like a cashmere sweater. A Christmas present, no doubt.

"Another early start," I observe, concealing my unease. "I hope you're getting overtime for all this."

"Do you have a minute, Mr. Buckby?"

The formality is a bad sign, but the fact that he's alone is a good one. This time, I'm not considered a physical risk to anyone. Grateful it's him and not Parry, I draw back the door in welcome. "Yes, a quick one. I'm about to leave for work."

"What happened to your face?" he asks.

"Nothing. An accident."

No doubt he's questioning whether the marks might be linked to my scuffle with Kit on the boat and I let him remind himself that they'd have been evident on Friday if they were. Clearly, I'm just a very unpopular guy.

In the kitchen, I offer him tea and dig out some posh biscuits (lemon, dipped in white chocolate: Clare's favorite). I recognize a pride in myself, one of the last times I'll be able to play host in this house. Pretend all this is mine to share.

On the other hand, when the police visit a beautiful house, do they feel more or less inclined to nail the owner-occupier? More, I'm guessing. He'll probably see the luxury snacks as bribery.

That doesn't stop him from tucking in.

"You must see a big improvement in refreshments at this time of year," I remark inanely. "All those mince pies and leftover chocolates."

I glance at the time on my phone; I'm not going to let myself be detained a second time in lengthy conference. I need my job, minimum wage or no. "I take it you haven't found him yet?"

"How would you know that?" he asks.

"Well, if this was one of *those* calls, you wouldn't be eating biscuits before you break the news, I'm guessing."

"No, I'm afraid we haven't," he concedes, and takes his time crunching. "Did you forget what I said about leaving Mrs. Roper alone? We asked you very clearly to keep away from her and yet you've approached her twice over the weekend."

Jesus, she really has got his ear. He's like her personal security detail. I feel myself twitch, imagining her waking up alone in that icy flat, warming her hands on a mug of tea, the police, not me, her first point of contact. *She's* why he's pestering me at this ungodly hour, not because he has any new evidence to act on. "You're here because I happened to bump into her in a café yesterday? What, am I being charged with harassment?"

He snaps a second biscuit with his front teeth. "You're not being charged with anything yet."

Yet. There's always a yet with this man. On my lap, my hand aches. The bandage is off, scar tissue hardening on the wound; I put it to my mouth and worry it with my tongue.

"You came all the way to my home to tell me that? Is that an efficient use of taxpayer's money?" I remember Clare's comment about the police pursuing their agenda, not ours, and it couldn't be clearer that she's right.

"If it preempts further misguided actions on your part, yes, I'd say it is."

"Misguided actions? What are you expecting me to do, get rid of her, as well?"

There's a moment of horror as I hear what I said: *as well.* I feel myself color. "To be clear, that was a joke. I haven't got rid of anyone and don't intend to. Look, yesterday, that was my fault, I shouldn't have approached Melia and I'm very sorry. But the first time, on Friday, I was only accompanying my partner. I was worried . . ." Worried she might attack Melia physically as she later did me? No, it's too incendiary to tell him of Clare's discovery and the arguments we've had. The fragility of our current standoff. "I won't go near her again, you have my word."

"Good." He nods. He's not taking notes, so this must be off the record. He'll tell Parry, though. He'll log it. Do they have other cases, this early rising team? I hope so. I hope this is the first and last call he'll make today regarding the Ropers and me.

I offer him a third biscuit. "Since you're here, can I ask *you* a question?"

"Shoot."

"We're wondering why you're still not publicizing Kit's disappearance in the local press? Or on missing persons?"

Merchison's tone sharpens: "'We'?"

I couldn't do a better job of advertising myself as a loose cannon if I had the words stamped on my forehead. "Just me and Clare. I told her I thought there might be some bigger drugs ring operation you don't want to jeopardize. Undercover officers, that kind of thing."

The look he gives me is half amused—by my cliché TV terminology, perhaps, or because I think for a moment he's going to share this sort of intelligence with me. "I can only repeat that involving the press and public can, in some cases, compromise overlapping inquiries. We've told Mrs. Roper the same. Understandably, she shares your frustration."

"But how can you control it? There must be others who're worried? What about his colleagues? If he doesn't turn up for work, won't they put out alerts that could get picked up by the press?"

"Please leave us to worry about that."

Easy, I suppose, for them to ask Melia to phone Kit's employer with some excuse, or for them to explain directly the need for anonymity: "overlapping inquiries" seems to be the line.

"And, Jamie? Anyone who takes it upon themselves to circulate an alert will have us to answer to."

"Right." I make no mention of the secret cyber probing initiated by Clare. Safer to play dumb. "I saw a TV drama where the police opened the helpline in an appeal and the public started phoning in. They called them something, the time wasters. Fools and ghouls or something."

Merchison chuckles. "That's a good one. I'll tell my wife that."

"You're married?"

"Five years tomorrow."

"Congratulations." I have no right to compare his obvious pride and contentment in his relationship with my own status—one partnership irrevocably broken thanks to my treachery, the other in sticky suspension. No right to name the jagged pain in my rib cage anything other than a self-inflicted wound.

Only when he's finished Clare's biscuits does he leave and I marvel at a constitution that can process so much sugar this early in the day.

———

I head to the pier for the boat to work, too late for the 7:20, thanks to Merchison, and only making the 7:55 by the skin of my teeth. The boat is still quiet, the no-man's-land between Christmas and New Year's rolling on, the wealthy off skiing or frolicking on some far-flung beach. I'm literally one of only a dozen or so to board at St Mary's and it's impossible not to scan the faces of the last remaining commuters and wonder about the mystery witness. She of the black hair with pink ends is a couple of rows in front of me, and couldn't pay me less attention if she tried, her earbuds like creatures burrowing into the skull. But if she's the one who reported me to the police, wouldn't I remember seeing her that night, one of the more distinctive-looking commuters? And wouldn't she be wary of seeing *me*?

Putting my phone to my ear, I say, loudly, "Sarah?"

Nothing. Feeling foolish, I tuck my phone in my pocket and check out the crew. I don't recognize any of them from that night service a week ago and, even if I did, it would hardly be advisable to start quizzing them about what the police had asked, whether the security footage was formally seized with the intention of being used as evidence in a prosecution. The thought causes me to groan loudly and Pink Ends glances over her shoulder. Her eye lingers, not with sympathy or even curiosity, but with caution, as if she thinks I might be unstable. I smile, but it probably makes things worse, and when we slow to approach the next stop, she moves to a different seat.

I straighten my mind, scan for loose ends. I leave a message for my father: "I'm so sorry, Dad, but I'm going to have to bail on tomorrow night. The thing is, Clare and I are going through a rough patch at the moment and she doesn't really want house guests, not even family." I feel like a heel, both for letting him down and for blaming Clare for it. Crap behavior begets crap behavior, it would seem.

"Jamie, you all right?"

It's Steve—God, have we reached North Greenwich already?—and I remember my text to him, the idiocy of which has been eclipsed by more pressing concerns. With the rest of my row free, I have no hope of avoiding a confab with him.

"You're in late, as well?"

"I overslept." He licks a spot of toothpaste from the corner of his mouth. "What the fuck was that text all about on Saturday?"

"Sorry, I'd been drinking, lost my mind a bit about this Kit situation. Someone's been talking bollocks to the police, saying I'm involved."

He removes his glasses and wipes them clean, turning large blind eyes towards me. "Yeah, well, you must know I would never rat on a mate, even if I did think he'd done something dodgy." He puts his glasses back on and seems to notice the marks on my face for the first time. I watch him decide not to ask. "What's the latest, then? You don't think he's just gone off somewhere without telling Melia?"

"I hope that's what it is," I agree. Already, I'm sensing there's comfort to be gained from this discussion. Steve's instincts are in sync with those I first presented to Parry and Merchison: Kit's gone AWOL because it's the kind of thing he does.

Steve frowns. "He might not even know there's been all this drama. Why's there nothing about it online? If he saw a news report, he'd realize people are worried and he'd get in touch with her. Or *someone*."

"*If* he's online," I point out. "His phone is out of service—all my texts are coming back undelivered."

"Yeah, mine as well."

I lower my voice. "Between you and me, I think the police

think it might be to do with some drugs dispute. Did Kit say anything to you about being in that kind of trouble?"

"Drugs?" Uncertain emotions pass across his face. He's remembering, perhaps, my halfhearted proposal of an intervention a few weeks ago, his own cavalier dismissal of the notion that Kit had a problem. *Live and let live* sounds like bad advice now. "Well, I knew he was strapped for cash, but I didn't get the impression he was looking over his shoulder. I wonder if Gretchen's heard from him."

"She's off now till the New Year. Morocco."

"Really?" We look at each other and I guess his thoughts: might Kit and Gretchen have absconded together for some extended dirty weekend in the sun? No fling has ever been admitted to, but when has that ever stopped the millions of faithless over the centuries? (Let's face it, I should know.)

"You don't think . . .? Would she have had the guts to lie to the police when they called looking for him?" I ask.

"It's possible," Steve says.

"What about the airports? You'd have thought they'd check them as part of their search."

"Maybe it's not something you can do that easily or quickly. Shall we phone her? See if she picks up?"

As I hear him connect to Gretchen, I focus on the glazed dome of the foot tunnel entrance by Greenwich Pier, allowing my mind to dislocate from the present and picture the building going up at the turn of the twentieth century. What crises did men grapple with then? Did their disasters befall them unannounced or did they create them for themselves? Were there Kits and Jamies and Steves among them? Were there Melias?

I know myself well enough to understand that this sudden hunger for perspective, the desire to reduce myself to a speck in human history, is really a ruse to diminish my guilt, my fear.

"Any luck?" I ask, when he hangs up.

"Nope. She's in Marrakech, you got that right, but she thought I was calling *her* with news. I woke her up, so either she's a brilliant actress or she knows even less than we do."

"Well, it was worth a try."

We sit in fretful silence until Tower Bridge, where he disembarks.

"Something bad has happened, hasn't it?" he says, by way of a farewell.

Yes sounds too stark, too brutal, so I tell him, "All we can do is hope," and he heads for the door, limping a little, head down.

I would never rat on a mate. Not an enemy then, as I'd supposed, but nonetheless too late to be an ally. I wonder if he'll mention his theory about Gretchen to the police, should they contact him again.

The tide is the highest I've ever seen it. As we duck through the gold-studded red arches of Blackfriars Bridge, I picture the river bursting its banks and beaching us onto the South Bank, the humans fleeing from the slimy double-hulled monster, everyone screaming.

34

December 30, 2019

The Comfort Zone remains disquietingly celebratory of all things Yule. Plum pudding and ginger latte has been our special for the last two weeks, and even though the thought of drinking one makes me want to gag, it continues to outsell all other offerings. Regan, still in an elf's hat and glittery Christmas makeup five days after Santa's visit, has at least replaced the sprigs of ivy on each table with mistletoe.

She peers at my face and, unlike Steve, demands an explanation. "What happened to you? You look like you were attacked by a cat."

"I kind of was," I say.

"You weren't bitten, were you? If you're bitten you're supposed to get a tetanus jab. Cat's teeth are so small, the skin heals over the wound and seals in the infection."

"I think I'm up to date with tetanus."

"Any news on your missing friend?"

"Not yet."

I can read the mixed emotions in her face: she's charged by the sudden drama in her workmate's life, but repelled by the unseemliness of physical violence. And then there's the perplexing way her brain wants to link the two.

A group of women with babies commandeers our largest table for most of the morning, creating an obstacle course of prams and buggies that could be the difference between life and death, preventing, as they do, access to the fire exit by the loos. Some of the babies are plump and cute, like babies should be, but some are like tiny men, their faces sharp, bursting to escape their mothers' arms and start contradicting authority. I experience a sudden lurch, a memory of the first time I met Kit, his complaints about the mothers in St Mary's—*They'd rather you got hit by a bus!*—in that wicked, laughing way he had when he was in a great mood, meeting new people and pouring all his energy into his own charisma.

At least the mums order hot drinks and I'm grateful for the noise of the steamer, which I normally hate, that mechanical screaming that obliterates all human speech within range.

But in the first interlude, Regan continues her inquisition. "How long has it been? Your friend, I mean." She begins sorting the recycling as we chat and I help in a desultory fashion, flattening cartons and picking out the nonrecyclable crisp packets.

"Almost a week."

"So how long before someone's, you know, presumed dead?"

"I don't know. Years, I think."

"*Years?*" She stops what she's doing and raises her voice. "How are his family and friends supposed to live in limbo like that? Not knowing if he's been viciously murdered?" At this, a couple of the mums look up, frowning—as if their uncompre-hending babies are going to be contaminated by our unsavory conversation. "Do they have to keep his job open for him?"

"I imagine so, legally, but between you and me I doubt he's any great loss to the insurance sector. He thought he was doing them a favor just gracing them with his presence."

It feels good to be able to say something critical about Kit. Just because someone's missing doesn't mean they aren't still a twat.

I don't say *that* to Regan, obviously.

My phone buzzes. Dad has left a voicemail assuring me that he's happy to accept a neighbor's invitation on New Year's Eve, before making a surprising admission: "I wondered, in France, about you and Clare. I hope you can work it out, she's a great girl."

I imagine Clare hearing that and teasing him for calling her a girl. Making no secret of the fact that she's pleased. I wonder if they'll keep in touch after news of our separation circulates. How could he *not* side with her?

Regan misreads my melancholy expression as being related to the mother-baby tableau in front of us. "I bet it puts things in per-spective, doesn't it, this business with your friend? Makes you re-assess. Did you ever want kids, years ago? You and your partner?"

She makes it sound like a geriatric's long-distant dilemma. I haven't told her I've split up with Clare and I agonize for a few moments over whether it could cast doubt on my character if I'm later found to have deliberately misled her. I tell myself not to overthink this stuff. "No. Way too scary."

"I know what you mean," she agrees. "It's totally the most ter-rifying thing I can imagine."

I manage a blissful thirty seconds deluding myself that cuddling an infant while chatting over the top of its head with another adult is indeed the most terrifying thing I can imagine, but then I remember DC Merchison on my doorstep that morning, all too determined to step over the threshold and find a way to prove his gut instinct that I'm not to be trusted. That I'm telling him everything except what might actually be useful.

———

Even though Regan sends me home early, there being so little business after the mums' group, by the time I board the boat home it's already dark as midnight. The bar staff are offering complimentary slices of chocolate log and cleaning up in tips. Festive songs play: *Good tidings we bring* ... which makes me think of Melia of course. I imagine myself arriving at St Mary's and walking up Royal Way, past my turning into Prospect Square and on to the high street towards Tiding Street, until I'm standing under her window like a stalker.

But I know better than to succumb to that temptation. I bite into my cake, icing catching on my upper lip, and start chewing. It tastes stale. The boat is taking its time pulling away from the pier; the river's busy with evening tour boats. The song changes to "Let It Snow."

On the other side of the river, on Embankment, the traffic lights blaze red as far as the eye can see.

———

When I get home, Clare is already there and still in her work trouser suit, not the yoga gear she routinely changes into as soon as she's through the door. In the living room, nibbles have been set on the coffee table, enticingly arranged on a lacquered platter, alongside a carafe of iced water and three glasses. I anticipate a request to make myself scarce.

"Expecting guests?"

"Piers's contact is coming round to talk to us. Kelvin, he's called." She speaks to me as I've heard her speak to the cleaner and other helpers. Scrupulously democratic, emotionally remote, but preferable to the angry contempt that is, in my case, the alternative.

"You mean the investigator? That was quick."

"It was an express service. Anyway, how long can it take? They just sit at a laptop, don't they?"

Cracking pass codes. Breaking the law. Stealing data like a prowler steals jewelry and cash. As I collect a nonalcoholic lager from the fridge and take my seat at this most peculiar of conferences, I feel the wings of foreboding flap in my gut, as if the next couple of hours could alter my destiny.

"By the way," she says, "I rang Kit's office today."

"Really?" I remember my own query to Merchison about Kit's colleagues, his swift shutting-down. "Should we be doing that?"

"I don't see why not. I said I was a family friend."

"What did they say?"

"They said he's on leave. Very diplomatic. I guess it's easy enough to cover it up at this time of year, when they've only got a skeleton staff anyway." At the sound of the doorbell, she jumps to her feet. "That'll be Kelvin."

I'd pictured a whiz kid barely out of school, but he is fortyish, stout of body and thin on top. He presents his findings with a cheerful bedside manner, as if he's a financial adviser reviewing our pension provision. But Clare and I are quickly transfixed by the unequivocally dire, chaotically entwined arrangements of Kit and Melia: student loans, and many other types of loan taken out since, all with iniquitous interest rates; defaults on credit card payments; rent arrears on Tiding Street, plus three months unpaid on the flat before that is still being sought by the landlord; unauthorized overdrafts with excessive charges. Extensions on some of the loans and reductions in payments have been only temporary reprieves and their salaries barely touch the sides of the money pit. Since I've lost regular contact with Melia, they've been given notice to vacate Tiding Street and warned that bailiffs will visit if the arrears are not met.

"It's obvious she can't pay up and is going to be evicted," Clare says. "I hope she's got somewhere to go."

"Legally, she has till the end of January," Kelvin says, "even if bailiffs take the furniture before then."

"She has friends," I say, thinking of Elodie and her 999 threat. It's striking that we all speak on the assumption that Melia is, for the foreseeable future, a single woman.

"Really, they should have been getting advice about this," Kelvin says. "If nothing else, they could have rung the National Debtline, got some pointers on restructuring."

"They're too proud for that," Clare says, astutely. "I think they've had their heads in the sand."

In white powder, more like, I think, chewing a stuffed olive. Though Clare and I have not shared so much as a bowl of peanuts since her discovery of my affair, I've helped myself to a plateful of snacks, confident I won't be chastised. Appearances are important to her; she won't humiliate me in front of a stranger.

Kelvin is reaching the end of his roll call of shame. "On December the second, they took out a new credit card and were able to withdraw almost ten thousand pounds on it."

"Ten grand?" Clare echoes. "Well, they didn't use it for the rent, obviously."

"They paid off one of the other loans?" I suggest.

"There's no evidence of them doing that. Since it was withdrawn in cash, I'd suggest it was for personal spending, something they didn't want to be traced." He pauses, looks at Clare, as if for her approval. Evidently, it is given, because he expands his chest as if poised to say something significant. "If you want my opinion, you and Piers could be right."

"Right about what?" I ask, but he doesn't respond. I turn to Clare. "Please, tell me."

The look she gives me then makes my stomach drop. It's a deep, complicated look, expressive of extreme and conflicting emotions. It's a look that says, *Much as I hate to help a bastard like you, I'm about to because what's going on here is too fucking serious for party politics.*

Cowed, ashamed, and seriously spooked, I ask again what they're talking about.

Finally, she tells me: "We think Kit and Melia are setting you up."

35

December 30, 2019

There is a moment of hideous breakneck freefall when all I can do is gawp. Finally, I recover my vocal cords: "Setting me up in what way?"

Clare's expression deepens. "They're pretending something terrible has happened to him, something *you* caused, so Melia can claim on Kit's life insurance."

Something you caused. My heart rate accelerates and I think I'm going to be sick.

"It's a really great policy, as you can imagine, given who he works for. The basic payout would be well over a million."

I put down my plate. "You think this because they withdrew a bunch of cash?"

"Yes, you need cash when you go into hiding, you can't go using ATMs, you can't do anything that can be traced to your old identity." Clare looks to Kelvin for confirmation and he gives a quick nod.

"Old identity?" The muscles in my cheeks are numb with shock. "I don't understand."

"I know it sounds crazy, but Piers and I discussed it in depth and if you think it through, it adds up. They may have been planning it for some time, months probably. Your little fling with her might have been strategic—I assume she was the one who initiated it?" Again, Clare glances at Kelvin, who this time looks down at his sparkling water. He has turned pink, but for a white zone at his hairline.

My mouth is so dry my tongue is sticking to the roof of my mouth. I peel it away to repeat, "Strategic?"

"Yes, to create a motive for you to kill Kit. You said the police as good as accused you when they interviewed you. *And* you said you thought Kit suspected something about you and her. Well, I bet he's known all along. It may have been his idea in the first place."

"Jesus, Clare." My senses are under attack: as well as the dry mouth and stiff face, there's a burning sensation behind my eyes, a jangling in my ears.

She continues: "Think about it. It's not a coincidence that you were the last person to see him—they planned it that way. Last Monday was the perfect night to do it, Christmas drinks, everyone wasted. It would have been easy for him to start an argument, make sure there was a camera nearby. The fact that you went off to Edinburgh the next morning was a bonus—it makes it look like you couldn't get out of town fast enough. Meanwhile, Melia gets him into hiding and reports him missing to the police. Confesses to her affair, says she was scared you were jealous or possessive. She doesn't even need to accuse you directly, it's their job to put two and two together and you can bet your life they will. Have they been in touch since Friday?"

"Yes." I gulp, straining to process her narrative, rattled off with a terrible ring of plausibility. "One of the detectives came round this morning."

"The police were here this morning? In the house?" Her voice rises an octave. "That's not a good sign, Jamie. This drugs thing is a total red herring, probably meant to lull you into a false sense of security. They're playing you—Kit and Melia are playing you!"

I know when Clare's convinced, and she's convinced. Her intensity is infectious, making my pulse pound. I turn to Kelvin for a more balanced appraisal. "Tell me about this insurance policy. They don't pay out on missing persons cases, do they?"

"Not unless the insured person has been declared dead," he says, simply.

"Don't you get it?" Clare cries. "People tend to get declared dead when someone's been found guilty of their murder! And you don't always need a body to prove it. We've seen it on those true crime shows, it can really happen!" She is becoming upset, pulling furiously at the roots of her fringe until a strand of blonde hair stands on end.

I try to steady my breathing, wrench the momentum from her. "Let's talk this through. You're saying Kit's faked his own murder and disappeared intentionally. Where do you suggest he's hiding? Rio? The Costa del Sol?"

I've intended a level of sarcasm, but she answers me straight: "That's a point, it would be good to know if his passport's missing. The police would have checked that, right? Or he may be closer than we think, people often are when they go into hiding. You remember that guy who faked his own death in a canoeing accident? He turned out to have been living a couple of doors down from his 'widow' all along."

As I flush deeper, the wounds on my face smart. "You're saying he's still in St Mary's?"

Kelvin, who has been chewing a fingertip, lets his hand drop and chips in: "I don't know. There aren't many properties you can rent for cash. And ten thousand pounds won't last long in London."

Clare's eyes gleam as a new idea takes root. "What if they're not paying? He could be squatting somewhere. We could start by checking the flats Melia has shown over the last few weeks; sometimes they're empty for days at a time, even weeks. She could move him from place to place, tip him off if there was a viewing or cleaners coming in or whatever. For all we know, she took this job with this in mind. Set it all up and then looked around for a fall guy. She's incredibly attractive, Kelvin. She could have targeted anyone and he'd have fallen for it. I'll show you a photo on my phone . . ."

She could have targeted anyone: as Kelvin concedes Melia's exceptional visual appeal (a wedding shot, I gather), the phrase rings in my ears, disturbs my equilibrium. I repeat my mantra: *Trust me, Jamie.*

"The police need to check her phone," Clare adds. "See if she's been communicating with an unknown number. Ask them, Jamie, when you next speak to them."

"Surely if she'd gone to these lengths she'd be using an un-traceable pay-as-you-go?" Kelvin says.

"Maybe, but she's not a professional criminal, she'll make mistakes. Like the paper trail for this loan you've found, which is good for us. Good for Jamie." There's a catch of tenderness in her voice, but she corrects herself quickly, remembering that we're separated now, there is no "us," and it causes a reciprocal pang in me. I was wrong to think she had any nefarious agenda in commissioning this investigation; only a very special person would have the grace to defend her cheating ex like this.

I sink my teeth into my lower lip till I'm close to breaking the skin. "I'm not sure, Clare. It's a bit extreme. I mean, he must have had other options, mustn't he? He could have applied for bankruptcy, for instance?"

"Not if he wanted the insurance payout, he couldn't."

"I really don't think I was targeted," I say, absorbing an abrupt roll of emotion.

There's brief silence. The air between Clare and me is charged, combustible.

"There is another possibility," Kelvin says, with delicacy. "What if this isn't an attempt to frame anyone, but just a long-term fraud that Jamie has somehow found himself tangled up in?"

"Go on," Clare says.

"Well, it's true you'd get the payout more quickly if there was a murder conviction, but you'd probably still get it anyway, just later. It takes about seven years to get a legal declaration of death, according to my research."

"Seven years? Even with Kit working for an insurance company?"

"Yes, I've looked at De Warr's standard policy for employees and there's nothing to suggest it would be paid ahead of normal schedules. It's not like being in a plane crash, anything could have happened to him. The question is, is it worth seven years of living off grid?"

"Exactly how much are we talking about?" I ask. "Clare said over a million?"

"It's actually two, or near as dammit. The death in service cover adds a chunk. He'd really have to trust his wife, though. The check, when it comes, will be in the name of Melia Roper."

Kit updated the details promptly then, I think. It seems a very long time ago, champagne in Greenwich, but it was little more than four months.

Clare inhales, her widening eyes signaling yet another brain wave. "I bet that's why they got married. It validated the policy in some way."

"It certainly increases the payout," says Kelvin.

"We have to tell the police about this." Clare's all set to dash to the police station right away and my heart gives a violent kick.

"It's definitely a theory worth pursuing," I say. "Wow. This is a lot to take in."

"You're not on your own," Kelvin tells me, by way of a conclusion, and I see that in spite of the talk of my "fling," he assumes we're still together. He admires Clare for defending her man with such energy and intelligence.

He gets up to depart. I hear them at the door, her reassurances that his name will not be invoked outside these walls, certainly not in any conversations with the police. I hunt in the fridge for another alcohol-free lager and when I return to the living room Clare's on the sofa with her laptop. "What are you doing?"

"I'm looking up a number for your guy on the St Mary's Police website, but they don't seem to list detectives, only PCs."

"I think they're based at Woolwich, it'll be a much bigger team." I move close to her, careful not to make physical contact. "Wait, Clare, before you put your name to anything, have you thought how you'll explain how you got this information? I don't want you getting in trouble on my account. I've already put you through so much, I don't want your job to be at risk as well."

She pauses. In a heavily regulated business like estate agency, the slightest hint of financial impropriety can lead to suspension, and colluding with a hacker is more than a hint. "You're right," she agrees. "Maybe it's better to send it anonymously. You know, like a tip-off. Let's see if they have a special email address for that on the Woolwich site. Oh, good, they do."

I peer over her shoulder, struggling to focus. "If it's just some admin address, they might not see that for days. I'll ring first thing in the morning and get DC Merchison's email address. If you forward me Kelvin's file, I'll make sure neither of your names are on it before I send it on."

"Good plan." Her fingers move across the keyboard and my phone pings as the file hits my inbox.

"Thank you," I say. "Thank you for everything."

Whenever I say thank you now, she never says you're welcome. Usually, she leaves the room, but on this occasion she is not finished. "When you speak to him, there was one other thing I remembered. About Kit."

"What?"

"That photo they showed us when we went there for dinner. The one on the mantelpiece that Kit used for the coke."

I take a swallow of my crap placebo lager. "Melia in *Cat on a Hot Tin Roof*? I remember. What about it?"

"When we went round on Friday, it wasn't there."

"I didn't notice. Why's that relevant?"

"Just that, if he deliberately disappeared last Monday, if he knew he was never going to be able to come back, he'd have chosen a few sentimental things to take with him."

"He must have loads of photos of Melia on his phone," I point out, but she dismisses this with an impatient gesture.

"You heard Kelvin, they'll both have switched to something untraceable. He can't go turning his old phone on, he'd be tracked. So he grabs the photo at the last minute, something familiar, something he can hold in his hand. It's hard to isolate yourself, emotionally, I mean. You need things to connect you, especially in a long game like his."

I try not to shrug. The missing photo seems an inconsequential detail to me. It could have been moved to the bedroom or one of them could have hurled it at the wall during one of their rows. But I don't like the way Clare's building a case. If she's remembered this detail, she'll remember others too. She's a natural investigator.

"Okay, I'll mention it," I say.

Satisfied, she sets aside her laptop and stacks the glasses and plates, removing them to the kitchen. Freed from her scrutiny, I allow my expression to change from gratitude to horror.

I take out my phone and, instead of downloading the file to send to Merchison in the morning, I compose a text:

How are you bearing up? No need to reply if you don't want to.

Then I select Melia's name and hit "Send."

Almost instantly, she replies:

I asked you not to contact me.

I close the thread, lock the screen, and toss the phone onto the nearest armchair, calling to Clare that I'm nipping out to get some cigarettes.

She reappears in the doorway. "Don't think you're smoking in here!" she snaps.

"Of course not," I reply, meekly.

Fifteen minutes later, having duly picked up a pack from Sainsbury's Local, I arrive on the corner of Tiding Street. I wait for a couple at the far end to go into their house and turn on the lights, before I approach the Ropers' door, head down, and ring the bell.

Melia opens up without revealing more of herself than a swoop of dark hair, fingers curling around the edge of the door. "I got your message. Obviously."

"I wasn't sure you'd remember." But it's a stupid thing to say because Melia remembers everything and our emergency code is hardly a minor detail. Messages in plain sight, that's what we agreed. No extra phones to be discovered, no secret threads.

I asked you not to contact me means "I'm here, come now."

How are you bearing up? means "We have a problem."

(*I hate you* means "I love you.")

"So what's up?" she says, bringing her face into view. Her eyes shine, her skin glows. She has not been crying today. "What is it, Jamie?"

"It's Clare," I tell her, and the choke in my voice is like stage fright. "She's on to us."

36

December 30, 2019

Neither of us speaks again until I've followed her up the stairs and the door is closed behind us. Without warning, she barges me to the wall, her face upturned, and begins kissing me very fiercely. I'm shocked by how powerful my response is: a leap in body temperature, a flaring of every nerve on the surface of me.

"Your heart's going nuts," she says, more in wonder than alarm. "Tell me what's happened—she knows we're together?"

For a moment I've forgotten Melia isn't aware of the scene on Friday before we came tearing round here, or about Clare's weekend flight to her family. "She does, yes, but that's not the issue. What I mean is she knows about *this*."

Melia takes a step back and we face each other across the narrow hallway. Her deep intake of breath is audible. "*What?*"

"She's dug up a whole load of stuff about your and Kit's finances and she's basically guessed. She wants to tell the police you're trying to frame me for murder to get the early insurance payment. She's worked it all out, Me, it's incredible."

278

Melia's eyes are clocks, their hands spinning madly, too fast to track. "When did this happen?"

"About an hour ago. She had this guy around to brief us. He's a financial investigator she hired, and he used some dodgy hacker to get confidential data."

"What data? For fuck's sake, why would she do that?"

To help me, I think. Because no matter what she claims, Clare doesn't hate me. She loves me. "Because she's a problem solver," I say. Also true. "She's a lot more impressive than the detectives, I have to say."

There is a pause. "But she hasn't told *them* her theory?"

"No, she's literally just told me. I've said it's better that it comes from me and I'll email the file to DC Merchison. I won't, obviously, but I'll have to come up with something credible to fob her off. She's invested money now, so she'll want results. I'll have to fake some sort of email from the police."

As she listens, Melia's shoulders relax a notch. "You don't need to do that. The main thing is to delay it till after tomorrow. Tell her Merchison's taken a couple of days off for the New Year and you'll contact him as soon as he's back. By the time that comes around, it won't matter and she can tell him her theory herself if she still thinks anyone's interested." She smooths her hair behind her ears. "To be honest, they've probably already considered it if they've done their own financial digging. How can they not? I told them we're in terrible debt and De Warr will tell them what a great life insurance policy he's got. If Clare can figure it out, they can."

It's remarkable how quickly she's regained her composure.

"There's a recent loan for ten thousand that she and this guy thought looked suspicious," I tell her. "What was that for?"

"For everything." Melia motions with both hands, fingers tightly arched, as if all the strain she carries is in them. "To keep everything going until payday."

It's warmer in the flat, I notice. The heating's on. Now is not the time to discuss her rent arrears. "The point is it doesn't matter what theories anyone comes up with about Kit, so long as they don't act on them till the New Year. After that, they'll be starting from scratch, won't they?"

We look hard at each other. *If everything goes to plan.* I feel my pulse steadying. "You're right. Yes. Okay. I just wish they'd issued some sort of appeal or involved their missing persons unit. Make it officially known that he disappeared last Monday."

She nods. "That's what I thought, as well, and I've asked them so many times to do a press release. I even threatened to do it myself. But they got their boss to call me, some kind of inspector. She said it was crucial we let them handle it their way, doesn't want it encroaching on some other investigation they've got going on. She said my personal safety could be at risk."

"Seriously?" This is far more than has been shared with me.

"I actually think it's a good thing, Jamie. It sounds like they're considering something a bit more underworld. I told them I was worried about his coke habit and you mentioned the drugs, as well, right?"

"Of course, exactly as we rehearsed." That was my MO for when the cops came calling: no matter where their questions led me, I was to find a way to get the drugs angle on the table, ideally with a mention of the stretch of the river where druggies and the homeless fraternized. Even if they didn't leap on it—which they didn't—it would be seeded.

"Good. So the only thing that matters is they know he was last seen on the twenty-third. It's all on record and his disappearance is being investigated in a low-profile way. They've checked CCTV material, interviewed witnesses—that's more than enough. A media appeal might have made things worse. We don't want journalists and the public poking around, noticing things tomorrow night."

"You're right." That reminds me of the other fly in our ointment. "There's something else. Not big enough for me to have busted out the code red, but I have to admit it's been on my mind."

"What?" She's by my side, her hand on the back of my neck, thumb tracing the bumps of my spine. "Tell me."

"There's some other passenger from the boat home that night who's giving the police information. I haven't got a clue what they've said, but the police implied it's something incriminating, something beyond what they saw themselves on the security video."

"What other passenger?" she says, sharply.

"I don't know, but I'm worried someone might have been following me that night."

"Following you? Who?"

"I think it's a woman. Maybe someone I've pissed off in the past."

"If you don't know who they are then you can't have pissed them off *that* badly." Her gaze shrinks to a narrow strip of amber.

"It sounds like paranoia. And even if you were followed, how can what they say possibly be incriminating? The police must know you went straight home from the street cameras."

"They haven't actually confirmed that with me," I point out.

"They will, Jamie. You didn't do anything, they can hardly fake evidence. Come on, babe, we knew there might be a few difficult questions, we can't control what the police ask, what everyone thinks they've seen. All things considered, it's going really well." She pauses. "When *did* you last hear from the police?"

"This morning, first thing. Merchison came round. Warned me to leave you alone."

A small smile slides across her lips. "Bless them. They're very protective."

"Little do they know they're protecting the wrong person."

"They certainly are." Sensing my exhaustion—or is it fragility?—she says, "It's not long now, we're almost there. I doubt you'll hear from them again. It's down to me now."

I feel inadequate then, a fraud, leeching strength from her when I'm the one who should be supplying it.

"Stick to the plan, Jamie. We've been through it a hundred times, we're word perfect."

She steps towards me and we kiss again. My last doubts roll away and my mind dares consider the next thirty-six hours.

"Who've you got staying here tomorrow night?"

"Elodie."

"The girl you were with yesterday?"

"Yes. She's very concerned about me. She knows I just want a quiet night in, so there'll be no persuading me to go out and party. She'll be out for the count by twelve thirty with the sleeping pill, won't wake up till late. How about you?"

"Clare's going to be home."

"You definitely don't need a pill for her?"

"No. Once we've gone to bed in our separate quarters she won't come looking for me—unless it's to hold a pillow over my head." I'm recovering my confidence now, my humor. My arrogance.

"Separate quarters," Melia echoes. "So she really knows we've been seeing each other, wow. Should I be fitting extra locks to my doors?"

I grimace. "She found out on Friday, so if she was going to kill you, she'd have done it by now."

"Friday? Are you serious?" Melia nuzzles me. "Tell me everything she said. Can you stay a while?"

She leads me into the bedroom, a tiny room heaped with shoes and bags and books and chargers and myriad other possessions. The small wardrobe overflows, the mantelpiece holds an ugly tangle of fairy lights either dead or forgotten. I wonder if the bedding has been changed since Kit last slept here. Between stretches of kissing, I describe Clare's discovery of our affair, unsure what to make of the obvious arousal it causes in her, and soon too absorbed in my own pleasure to care.

———————

Thirty minutes later, I surface from Melia's sheets as if from under a mask of fresh oxygen, renewed, recalibrated. Disgracefully, since I've just been wrapped around his wife in his bed, it's only as I leave that I remember to ask, "How is he, by the way?"

"He's okay," Melia says. "Not great at killing time, but that's Kit."

I picture him, sullen in his solitude, restless for playmates, stewing in his own resentment.

Just you wait, Jamie.

Just YOU wait.

We're not so dissimilar in the end, Kit and I. We're both happy to sell the other down the river.

The only difference is, one of us knows the other is doing it.

37

December 31, 2019

New Year's Eve in London, city of nine million. A day and night of mindless drunkenness, of emergency departments split at the seams with the survivors of pub bust-ups and party mishaps. Of carnival and carnage.

A perfect night to bury a crime.

Every minute of today must be accounted for. The Comfort Zone closes inconveniently early, at 4:30 p.m., and knowing Clare will likely stay at work till at least 6:30, I head from St Mary's Pier to Starbucks on the high street, laptop bag heavy on my shoulder. I've chosen the venue both for its security camera and its array of perky staff, at least one of whom will remember our banter about my unusual order: Earl Grey with steamed almond milk on the side. No one ever orders that. I tell the server I work in a café myself and have never been asked for it.

Something DC Parry said bubbles to the surface and gives me momentary trepidation: *You seem very confident of the cameras. Almost as if you've gone out of your way to be seen.*

In other words, an innocence too ostentatious might easily be construed as guilt.

The Wi-Fi was playing up at home this morning, I rehearse. Following a change in circumstances, I wanted to start applying for new jobs, had a quick look in my break. My search history backs this up, including a browse of the website of a big chain of coffee shops, and in my sent folder is an email to the manager of a café in Greenwich, inquiring about a weekend manager's vacancy. Even so, there's a chewing sensation in my gut, like parasites devouring me from the inside.

Arriving back home at the same time as Clare, I'm on tenterhooks in case she's had some mercurial change of mind and decided to escape me for the night. I am trading on the power of association by having a bath midevening and putting on pajamas, nice brushed cotton checked ones that her parents bought for me a few Christmases ago. I wonder what Melia imagines I wear in bed; would she think pajamas only for old men? We've never spent the night together. If you add together the hours we've been together, does it qualify as long enough to love? Long enough to trust?

I ignore these questions and concentrate on Clare. The pajama ploy works and by nine o'clock she's dressed for bed too; we're sitting together in front of the TV watching ancient episodes of *The Big Bang Theory*. Anyone looking through the window would think us a normal couple opting out of the party scene in favor of an intimate night alone, not a pair trapped by their estrangement, by the undisclosed machinations of one of them and the misplaced beneficence of the other. Clare's drinking chilled Chablis, but I'm alcohol-free. Even sobriety may not be enough for me to navigate tonight.

During a scene on TV in which two characters break up, she suddenly clenches. I wonder if she's thinking how much she hates me. The sheer audacity of my still sitting here in her house, abusing her generosity, disrespecting her.

She sighs and I dare ask: "What?"

"I'm just wondering when that detective of yours is going to pull his finger out."

So it's not her hatred of me that consumes her. I should have known. She is a woman of great focus, Clare, and her focus has turned away from her own humiliation and towards crime fighting. But I have no doubt that it will return and when it does I will need to be ready to go.

"The moment he's back at his desk, I'll be on to him," I assure her. "The day after tomorrow, his office said. Then I'll send Kelvin's report. I've already drafted the email with our theories. All in my name, as we agreed. You're not mentioned."

She nods, satisfied. "I went to check on a few flats on our rentals roster today. The ones that haven't had any viewings over the break and I reckon Melia might think are safe to squat in."

"You did?" Jesus, even at the eleventh hour, she's blindsiding me with her resourcefulness. "Any signs of habitation?"

"No." She groans. "Not that I would have known what to do if I *had* found him. It was silly to think I could take him on on my own. He'd have killed me, probably."

"Of course he wouldn't!" I protest.

"Why not? If he doesn't mind destroying *your* life for monetary gain, he'd probably be happy to destroy mine while he's at it. Happier, probably, since I represent the land-owning elite he hates so much."

I smile but she doesn't reciprocate. "I really hope you're not right about all of this, Clare."

"So do I. But in a way, if I'm not, then it's more than likely he's already dead, which is hardly a great alternative, is it? Better that we prevent his crime and save your skin. None of this is worth losing a life over."

As her attention returns to the screen, a chill passes through me, exactly like you read about in stories of the paranormal. Something deeper than bodily; a recognition in my soul of the wickedness I've allowed to take residence.

Astonishing, really, that it's taken this long for it to happen.

————

2020 has a sci-fi ring to it, I feel, like it might be the year of alien landings or the one when the gamma rays get us. We don't bother waiting for the countdown to midnight: we've each experienced almost fifty of these before, after all. Instead, just after eleven thirty, I tell Clare I'm heading to bed. To my surprise, she follows closely after, intercepting me on the first-floor landing, outside the door of the spare bedroom.

I wait politely for her to say whatever she wants to say. Something to emphasize the mistakes I've made: *I hope you know what you've thrown away.* Yep, if I had to put money on it, that's what she'll say.

"Do you think it's completely impossible . . .?" she begins.

I feel my brow pucker. "Impossible to what?"

"To rewind."

"Rewind what?"

"Life. Just a few months. Pretend none of this happened."

Both the sentiment and her expression are oddly childlike for her, reflecting a rare rawness of emotion, a leap of faith she seldom allows herself to make. Reflecting also, perhaps, the whole bottle of Chablis she's drunk. I choose my words with care: "If I had a superpower that's the one I'd choose."

She takes her time absorbing this piece of diplomacy. "Do I even want to myself, that's the question."

And yet she doesn't make a question of it, and that's what saves me, that missing question mark. I hover in my doorway and watch as she goes up the stairs to the master bedroom on the second floor, the room where we slept together for ten years. She closes the door behind her, spends a few minutes in the en suite, and then her lights are off. I can hear the faint drone of her radio: she likes to fall asleep to audiobooks, used to listen through earphones so as not to disturb me, but now she can play her stories out loud.

In my bedroom, as fireworks crack and whistle in the distance, I check a few news sites online, text family and friends: *Happy New Year from us!* Establish that I am here, at home, with Clare. Then I select a radio drama from the iPlayer, one with a running time of almost two hours, and hit "Play." I turn the volume down and slip the phone under my pillow so I can't make the mistake of taking it with me.

At 1:20 a.m., I pull on trainers and a hoodie, both items too big for me and purchased with cash. I creep downstairs in the dark and leave the house.

There's not a soul on the street, though I can see party lights in several houses where gatherings continue into the night, well-dressed silhouettes at the windows, wineglasses raised. Drunk people make poor witnesses, I remind myself—I was one of them myself on December 23rd. I'm as confident as I can be that no one is watching as I move, soft-footed, towards the eastern exit of the square. Melia is right: my little visit from Merchison yesterday was the end of it. I've considered Kit gone since I was notified by the same officer on the 27th and, come tomorrow, I'll be exonerated on those very grounds. Meanwhile, word will reach police ears of my clashes with Melia, designed to emphasize that we are foes, as far from coconspirators as you could imagine. It will all be on record, incontrovertible, both our alibis for the night of the killing as airtight as each other's.

As for any thoughts I've had of this other passenger having some historic grievance against me, following me, waiting for me to trip up, Melia was right about that, as well. Paranoia, nothing more.

I take a left onto Pepys Road and head down to the river. As expected, I pass no one, only a skinny fox scavenging for food. A year from now, when the St Mary's Wharf flats are completed and their buyers installed, it would be a different story. There's a smell of sulfur in the air, of spent fireworks, stirring memories of childhood bonfire nights, Debs by my side, both of us in scarves knitted by our mother. Never, not for a nightmarish second, would my mother have imagined her son capable of doing tonight what he's about to do.

I reach the river path. There's no lighting on this stretch and no passing vessels, so I hear the water before my eyes adjust sufficiently to see it, the slap and squelch of high tide. When I draw to a halt, I realize I'm shaking badly. Maybe because I know that where I'm standing is a black spot and I'm entirely alone and unguarded, hunter become hunted. The bar manager at the Hope & Anchor first drew it to my attention after my bike was nicked from where I'd locked it to the nearest bench. Their camera range didn't extend that far, he explained. It's I who told Kit and Melia about the spot, unaware, then, of their future uses for it.

My night vision is sharpening; I'm about twenty feet from the bench. Whatever celebrations were hosted by the Hope & Anchor are over, all its windows dark. There's a sudden gust of high spirits from a party boat on the far bank and I'm reminded of when I told Kit about the *Marchioness* disaster. I feel a lurch of grief for the victims that terrible night, for all the dead who fall from memory with the passing of their own generation.

The innocent deserve better.

Without my phone, I can't check the time, but it must be close to our agreed rendezvous of 1:30 a.m. Minutes tick by and I start to think they're not coming. I'm shocked by the depth of my disappointment, by the phrase that rears in my mind: *I'm ready*. I'm ready to leave my home, my life. I'm ready to bundle every last possession into a sack and sink it in the Thames. To start my life again with the woman I love.

And then, quite suddenly, there they are, approaching from the same direction I came from myself.

Kit and Melia. Husband and wife.

Victim and killer.

On Melia's back, a small, stuffed backpack. In Kit's hands, nothing but a cigarette, which, as I watch, he tosses suddenly to the ground, too cool to extinguish it, like he thinks he's James Dean.

It's three, perhaps four, weeks since I last saw them together and, watching their advancing forms, I'm reminded of our first meeting, of their reflective, twinlike qualities. If Melia and I fit, they match, each an impression of the other. And it feels, for an instant, unimaginable that they should be parted, as they have been these last days, Kit holed up in the kind of cheap and nasty hostel that he of all people would consider far beneath him. Accommodation arranged with every effort to avoid detection. False name, false address. False dawn.

Because Clare's deductions are spot on, in case that's not yet clear. What she thinks Kit and Melia are doing is exactly what *he* thinks: a disappearance to lead to an insurance claim, a fall guy to expedite its payment from seven years to one. The perfect fraud.

Think again, Kit.

38

I take a pace forward and place myself in their path. I haven't rehearsed my first words and when they come they are dismayingly prosaic and utterly right: "Well, well, who do we have here?"

They both stop dead, just a few feet in front of me. Kit is a step closer, close enough for me to witness the shock flooding his pale features. He's let himself go in his eight days of lying low, excursions limited to late-night walks in the dark with Melia along the deserted river path. He's needed the human contact, needed his Melia maintenance. I haven't asked her if she's slept with him, but it seems unlikely that she would have undressed in some squalid hostel. A kiss, perhaps, with this bearded, semi-vagrant Kit.

It's good he looks so rough. That will help.

He has recognized me, of course, and is instantly combative, an animal sensing a trap. "What the fuck are *you* doing down here, you prick?" His voice has the hoarseness of disuse. He turns to Melia, anger and panic exploding from him: "Can you believe this? This is a fucking disaster, Me!"

"Kit, wait—" she begins, but he speaks over her, spinning back to me, his mouth twisted with contempt.

"Why are you lying in wait like some fucking psycho? What do you want?"

"I'm not lying in wait, don't flatter yourself." My tone is lethally cold. "I've just been to the New Year's party at the Hope and Anchor. Getting some air before I head home. Back to my lovely Georgian town house."

Though the line about the party is rehearsed, the taunting detail about the house is unexpectedly real, a last opportunity to lord it over him. I watch him grapple with the claim that this meeting is coincidental. He wants to believe it. He has little choice *but* to believe it.

"Kit." Melia tries again, but he ignores her and edges closer to me, so close I can smell the confinement on him, humid and sour.

"Don't you tell a soul you've seen me, all right? I need your word on that, Jamie."

"Or else?"

"Or else I'll kill you." His eyes flick to the river. He would do it, as well. He would tip me over the wall and watch me drown. I picture my own face on the surface, stealing a final breath before the water turns it black, and suddenly, before anything, above all else, I crave a confession.

"I know what you're doing," I say, straying from the script. "You're in hiding, you can only come out at night like the vampire you are. You're setting me up." My voice breaks with sudden, rogue emotion: the lowest, bleakest sense of lost friendship, of betrayal. I'm breathing heavily, starting to forget Melia is there. "You really would see me rot in jail, wouldn't you? Just for a payout."

"What the fuck?" He denies it, of course. "You're losing your mind, Jamie. Must be dementia at your age, eh? Just go home, yeah. Forget this happened. No one would believe you, anyway—I hear the police are all over you already."

I brace, feel the strength gathering in my shoulders. "I'm not going anywhere. Not until I hear it from your lips, that you've set me up."

He continues to protest, at the same time shoving me, so I slam against the river wall, adrenaline stifling the worst of the pain. Our body heat is magnetic, we're clinging as if we're down a well together, nothing to clutch but each other. This is not brawling, as it was on the boat, but mutual primitive terror. "Say it," I growl. "Say it."

A figure moves in my peripheral vision with a dancer's grace, a steel blade raised that will slice through clothing like butter. The angle of entry has been studied on websites that supply such information, googled on borrowed devices.

There is an instant of acute horror when Melia looks beyond him to me and I think, *She's going for me, not him*, but it's delirium, of course, the final, most fantastical projection of my paranoia.

She loves *me*.

She chose *me*.

Now Kit utters a succession of noises unconnected to rational language. I couldn't have asked for a more perfect expression on his face as he collapses against me: surprise dawning, but not allowed fully to rise. A beautiful sunrise blotted by a flock of swallows—or maybe a toxic ash cloud.

I step back and let go of him, and he's falling to the ground with a heavy thwack. He's remembering language and saying my name, begging for help, crying for his mum. But all too soon his airways are filling with blood and he can no longer voice his terror. There's a scraping noise from one of his hands, before defter fingers than his remove something from his grip—a phone. Then, with a clean arc, it flies over the wall into the water.

An arrow of steel follows.

We wait, and, as his final breaths are drawn at our feet, we stare down at him. *Bless him*, I think, unexpectedly. There was no guarantee I'd be found guilty—or even charged—and without a body there'd have been those seven years to endure before he could be declared dead and the insurance payment made. That's trust for you. That's love. Of course, his clear preference was for plan A, the swifter, more ruthless solution. All he'd have needed then was his new passport and he'd have been off somewhere hot and cheap while he waited for Melia to join him.

Sorry, Kit, there's no passport. A murder conviction without any evidence of human remains? Come on, that happens once in a blue moon. Of course insurance companies want a body.

And that's what they're going to get.

"Let's get this finished," Melia says, and together we drag him behind the shrubbery on the far side of the path. There is blood by the wall, but that can't be removed and in any case may prove a useful guide for the early morning runners and dogwalkers who will stride past in a matter of hours, hungover and resolved to cleaning up their act. New Year, New Me. One of them will find him, led by a dog's inquisitive nose, if not their own eyes.

When the police tell Melia where Kit's body has been found, she will confess she knows the spot. She knows it because he has told her he meets his dealer here. She doesn't know the dealer's name, no, but she'll remind them of his debts—debts that any financial investigator can confirm. She's feared that since his disappearance he's fallen into semi-vagrancy, like some of the other addicts she's seen; she's searched and searched—even going out in the dead of night—but never been able to find him. She's been so worried, what with knife crime being on the rise, practically an epidemic.

"Are you all right?" I ask her.

"Yes, I think so. You?"

"Can't stop shaking."

I feel her grip on my arm, firm and steadying. "Keep going."

In the breath of the sleeping river, we change out of our clothes and shoes and into fresh ones carried by Melia in her pack. The old go in the pack and are tossed into the water. At home, I'll undress and put everything in the washing machine, just in case some fiber from him, some spot of blood, has attached itself. Melia will do the same.

We've been through the scenario, the psychology, scores of times, we both know the script by heart, but I still confirm my next line before we part. "As soon as I hear he's been found, I'll send you a text message of condolence. Clare and I will send you a card."

"Thank you." There's grace in those two words, a sense of something still spared for her former lover. "I'll invite you to the funeral. You and Clare."

"We'll come."

"I love you," she says, as gentle engine sounds rise from the water; scraps of human voices. I repeat the words back to her in a whisper.

"It's just us now."

I repeat this too, though it is not quite true. There's still a way to go in this plot of ours, still other players to handle—not least Clare, who, as she keeps proving in new and dangerous ways, is no fool. But the hardest part is done. Melia will have her dead body, get her payout, and all that will remain will be to decide where to meet, where to locate our future together, where to spend her money.

I take one last look at Kit, a form now, not a man. The departed. I have a grotesquely clear memory of him sitting next to me on the boat that first morning, grinning and preening, saying, *I plan to stay alive.*

Well, death is what happens when you're making plans, if you'll allow the misquote.

39

January 1, 2020

A word of advice to would-be killers: when you're waiting for a body to be discovered, don't look too expectant. Don't pick up your phone before it rings. Don't watch the window or spring to the door at the faintest scuff of a footstep on the pavement outside.

"Waiting for a delivery?" Clare asks.

"No."

"You're so jumpy this morning. You look terrible, actually." When she makes these remarks now, it's without any implicit offer of comfort; in fact, she's borderline pleased. I wonder what she'd say if she knew how close I was to vomiting—*because I've helped kill a man*. My upper body is aching from last night's scrap, that shove against the wall. I can feel a huge bruise blooming on my lower back.

"I didn't sleep that well," I say, testing.

"Really. I was out like a light." She can't know that her callousness is the very answer I'm praying for.

With or without Clare commenting on my jitters, this is torture. The day is a bank holiday, of course, with no work, no public services. I can't go out for fear of being unaccounted for within the window of Kit's time of death and when, in the afternoon, Clare straps on her Fitbit and announces she's going for a walk, I use the Wi-Fi to establish my presence at home. I permit myself a check of the local news, but there is no report of a stabbing by the river. Maybe there aren't so many dogs on riverside walks, after all. Maybe they're being kept on a short lead to stop them from nosing the vomit and broken glass left by last night's revelers.

Sitting there, in the ground-floor window so as to be easily observed from the street, I become obsessed with the certainty that Clare will be the one to find him—of all people, her! I imagine her crouching next to the body, crying softly as her fingers fumble for her phone, her heart swelling with sympathy for Melia, the one person she should be condemning to hell. Is he even still intact? Might foxes have mutilated him—or time itself, every hour of death removing more of what was recognizable in life? Will the odors of his decomposition be evident yet or will they be suppressed by the low temperature?

Obviously, I can't google "rigor mortis" or anything else to do with dead bodies.

But, mercifully, Clare isn't the one to find him. She returns with a spring in her step and pours herself a posh pressé. She's doing Dry January, of course. I'm doing it too, but only because I'll keep my story straighter if I'm sober. We speak very little.

She is regretting, perhaps, her drunken half-suggestion of rec-onciliation last night, affronted that I didn't jump on it as I should have.

There are dead bodies and then there are rejected live bodies.

Remarkably, by the time we go to bed, Kit remains undiscov-ered. "If I don't see you in the morning, phone me after you've spoken to the police," she says, and there is a horrified second or two before I realize she's talking about Merchison and my promise to pass on her theory about the Ropers' fraud, the notes from Kelvin to support it.

"No problem," I say.

January 2, 2020

Having assumed I'd be absent from work the next day, dealing with traumatic developments in St Mary's, I'm disorientated to find myself back behind the counter of the Comfort Zone following a routine passage on *Aragon*, which has replaced *Boleyn* as the carrier of the 7:20 a.m. tranche of westbound commuters. It was full of new faces, drudges who'd made the change, eyes tracking the riverscape just as mine did on my maiden voyage.

"Your scratch has almost healed," Regan tells me.

"It wasn't anything serious."

She has details to share from a New Year's Eve house party where a man had had to be prevented from defenestration.

"He's only thirty," she says, unaware of the ghastly parallel.

"That's no age to die," I agree.

"He's really depressed, apparently. Had his hours cut at work, couldn't pay his bills. I really worry about that, as well."

"If there's any danger of that happening to you, I'll give you my hours," I tell her, earnestly.

"You're so lovely, Jamie," she says, and makes us both an oat flat white. A *pain aux raisins* gets knocked to the floor and she gives it a wipe and begins eating it, unwinding the pastry until she's left with the stodgy, raisin-studded heart.

All the conversations I eavesdrop on this morning are about finances, personal (too much spent over the holidays and not enough earned) or work-minded (deals, subsidies, compensation, revenue). For once people have cash for tips. "We need to position the pot more prominently," I tell Regan, and I remember my promise to Melia that day she helped out that I'd share my tips with her.

We are different people now. Killers.

A whimper escapes me, but Regan doesn't appear to hear. All morning, she plays music that sounds as if it was recorded underwater and it starts to torment me, makes me want to tear off my skin in strips. And still no news! I agonize over whether to phone Merchison. If I don't, Clare will want to know why, but if I do and he's speaking from the crime scene, will he wonder at the coincidence of the call?

My only phone call is from Gretchen.

"How was Marrakech?" I ask.

"Good. I've just got home from Gatwick this minute." But she doesn't sound good, she sounds as overwrought as I feel. "Can I come and meet you in your break? I need you to update me on Kit."

"Okay," I say.

Well, the latest update is we stabbed him to death . . .

Stop this. No matter how confident I am that I would never give this inner commentary voice, merely to think it puts it in danger of being extracted from me in extremis or perhaps volunteered in sleep. No, instead, such knowledge must be completely suppressed.

We are not different. We are not killers.

I meet her at the pier after the lunchtime rush. She suggests the café at the Royal Festival Hall, but, fearing some posttraumatic attack if returned to the scene of my interrogation, I lie about building works and steer her instead to the bar at the NFT.

We collect our drinks and sit on uncomfortable wooden benches alongside young people wearing huge earphones and thumbing apps on their phones. Young brains multitasking. Gretchen has no tan from her Moroccan sojourn, only smears of pink on her cheekbones and nose. There's a chain around her neck with a pendant made of what looks like a tarnished Berber coin.

"Did you have a good time?" I ask.

"Not really. I shouldn't have gone. I couldn't stop thinking about Kit."

"I know." I breathe deeply, feel the painful expansion of my chest. "It's been awful not knowing what's going on."

"So there's really no word from him? Complete silence since our night out?"

"As far as I know, yes."

"It feels like *ages* ago! It must be ten days now." She fixes me with the intense gaze of a mesmerist. "You know, don't you?"

"Know what?" Feeling a tremor in my left cheek, I massage the spot with my knuckles. They're a little grazed, I notice, from recent exertions.

"That we were kind of seeing each other. Behind his girlfriend's back."

"Ah." It's hard by now to know if complications help or hinder. If subplots mask the main narrative or serve to shine a light on it. "I didn't know, no. I mean, I wondered, but I didn't think it was any of my business."

"That's decent of you," Gretchen says, and it's the second time today I've been told what a good guy I am. As she regards her untouched Diet Coke, her mouth stretches into a glum line. "Don't get me wrong, I knew it meant nothing to him. We stopped when he got married, obviously. Not that *that* did him any good. He was so adrift, wasn't he? He wanted us to think he was so strong, but we kept forgetting he was an actor."

Her past tense is emphatic. I've read that its use is a red flag to the police; the innocent are less likely to do it. "I'm not sure I know what you mean, Gretch."

"Really? You don't think . . .?" She continues to gaze at me, tears pooling. "You don't think he's taken his own life?"

I don't tell her that Clare made the same suggestion before launching her insurance fraud investigation. She reminded me of Kit's rant about suicides at the train station the first time he and Melia came to dinner: *I'd fuck off and do it privately*, he'd said. Was this what he had done? Clare asked me.

I was quite forceful in my disagreement then and I repeat it now. "No, Kit would never kill himself."

If he did, his insurance policy would be void.

Gretchen flushes. "But when he saw the cleaner on the building that time, he assumed it was a suicide, didn't he? Steve told me that's what he said, you know, the morning he was in that weird mood? Maybe that was a cry for help that we totally ignored?"

"No," I say again. I keep my voice low and steady, banish my knowledge that she needs only hold on a few hours and she'll know he's dead, thought to have been knifed by some druggie. "I'm one hundred percent sure he wouldn't do that. I've told the police the same. He wasn't suicidal. He was a total hedonist. Still is, hopefully!"

Tears of relief drop onto the table and I put my arm around her shoulder as our young neighbors regard us blank-eyed. I hope this brings an end to our discussion, but evidently Gretchen has more to say, more to confess.

"The thing is, Jamie, there're texts I sent him that make me look like some kind of stalker. I'm terrified the police will see them and think they pushed him over the edge, you know? Have they got his mobile phone? Can they see texts even if they don't have the phone?"

"If they get the records from the phone company, they might. I showed them mine from that Monday night voluntarily." I sip my water. "But if yours are from before he got married, they won't be of any interest to the police. That was back in August, months before he went missing. They won't look back that far."

She shakes her head, flattens her hair with her palms. "Some are more recent than that."

"How recent?"

She groans. "That night. After I got off the boat. He'd upset me about the Christmas present, about all kinds of things. Like, he was all over me in the bar, and then on the boat he was horrible, kept saying he'd made his choice and I should get off his back. Then when I heard he'd gone missing . . . The whole time I was on holiday I was convinced the police would fly out and arrest me." She's weeping freely now. "Even at Gatwick this morning, I thought I was going to come through Arrivals and be arrested."

Well, that answers one question: the police haven't yet accessed Kit's communications; or if they have, they have not yet seen fit to contact Gretchen about it. It all points to their having moved away from theories involving his drinking buddies and towards those involving his drugs ones.

I take her hands in mine. "There'd be nothing to arrest you for. What exactly did you say in these texts?"

She flushes. "I said I hoped something terrible would happen to him. It could definitely be seen as some kind of a threat."

My eyes widen.

"What do you think? Should I go to the police? Show them the messages, like you did?"

"No. I wouldn't do that." I squeeze her fingers, feel the fine bones of her knuckles. "Don't torture yourself when he might still be alive." I'm so deep in character now, I'm convincing myself. "You know, Clare thinks he's in hiding, trying to pull off some sort of life insurance scam—I'm about to phone the police and raise it with them."

Gretchen's mouth falls open. "No? That's completely insane!"

"Maybe, but it shows there are lots of theories in the mix." I watch as she uses a paper napkin to mop her face. I only have a few minutes before I need to be back at work. "Gretchen, you remember on the Monday night, did you notice anyone else on the boat home?"

"There were quite a few people, weren't there? That group of students . . ."

I vaguely remember a gaggle of young people sitting at the front, filling a whole row. Had I caught the eye of one of them? Tossed out some drunken remark? "Yeah, they got off when Steve did, I think, at North Greenwich. I mean anyone who seemed particularly interested in us. Someone you've seen before, a woman maybe?"

"Sorry, I don't remember. I was pretty drunk—and I was concentrating on Kit. Why?"

"The police mentioned someone, some other witness who's come forward."

"Maybe someone he knew? Someone else he'd slept with? A member of the crew, even? He was always bantering with them."

This is not something I've considered, and the idea of an unknown person from Kit's side, with an agenda entirely separate from his or mine, is too horrifying to contemplate.

Gretchen begins to rock a little, eyes half closed as she speaks: "Please be okay, Kit. Please. If anything's happened, I'll never forgive myself."

Her anguish is so genuine I'm moved. I urge her to go home and get some sleep, to stay as positive as she can.

"See you on the boat tomorrow morning?" she says, as we hug goodbye.

I swallow. Over her shoulder, behind the strolling tourists and the buskers, the river stops moving: a trick of the light, corrected with a blink. "Absolutely. See you then."

40

January 2, 2020

Almost as soon as I return to work, things start to happen. Clare calls first: "One of my team just did a viewing in St Mary's Wharf and says there're police down near the Hope and Anchor. Apparently, they've found a dead body. They've got one of those blue tents up, forensics people in big suits. I'm looking online and they haven't named anyone, but you don't think . . .?"

"Kit?"

"Yes, I have a really strong feeling it's him." She sighs. "Maybe I got it wrong about the insurance fraud, maybe you were right about the drugs debt. Did you speak to your detective?"

"I've left him a message," I lie. "If it is Kit, then he'll be busy at the scene."

As Clare is distracted by a voice in the background, I try to regulate my breathing. With each inhalation, I feel a spike of pain in my chest. "Jamie? Someone's just told me it's a male body. Another knife attack, apparently, so the media'll be all over it."

"Poor Kit—if it's him."

"The police will drop you like a ton of bricks now, so there's that, at least."

"Yes." And I feel a terrible jubilant skip of my heart.

"Well, I just thought you'd want to know," she says, and her voice has turned cool as she remembers, perhaps, that she pledged her support only while I was under suspicion.

"Thank you, Clare."

We end the call with an equal measure of formality, almost as if we expect never to speak again.

"Was that about your friend?" Regan asks.

"We're not sure, but they've found a body by the river in St Mary's." My senses are weirdly heightened: customers' mumbles as intolerable to my ears as a bass drum, the buttery aroma of a new batch of cinnamon buns sickening.

"Don't jump to conclusions," she says kindly, and lays a hand on my arm. "It could be anyone. You said knife crime?"

"Yes, that's what Clare's heard."

"Wow. The epidemic continues. I wonder who he had beef with."

My eyes shine. Everything I see sharpens and then blurs. "I really can't imagine."

An hour passes and no further information reaches me. Little more has been reported online than what Clare's already told us, the identity of the victim not yet released. It starts to rain pretty heavily and I picture the scene on the river path, the extra precautions the forensic team will have to take to stop the weather obliterating physical evidence. I wonder if it's acceptable—or natural—to ring Merchison and ask outright if it's Kit. Isn't it stranger *not* to? I decide I'll finish the rash of late-lunch food orders I'm preparing and then I'll call.

I have my back to the counter as I plate up sandwiches for a table of Chinese students, when I sense a gathering on the shop floor, a change of mood. "Mr. James Buckby?"

I turn. On the other side of the counter stand two uniformed officers. With a sideways look to the street, I spot a squad car a little way up, parked with its wheels turned as if in haste. This, I was *not* expecting. Melia and I have not predicted it or prepared for it, but now they're here it seems reasonable enough that I should be notified in person—almost touching, actually. Parry and Merchison must have requested it as a courtesy, given the suspicion I was under, the time they spent grilling me.

Unless there are additional details they hope I can supply. I motion to Regan that she should complete the food orders so I can give the officers my full cooperation. They are both younger than me, a man and a woman, each fair-skinned and flushed, presumably from overheating themselves in their car. Raindrops spot their dark shoulders like fresh dew. I try to remember the face of the colleague at the Royal Festival Hall, the one I saw Parry talking to; I think it might be her.

"This is about Kit, isn't it? Christopher Roper?" If I've learned anything in my dealings with the police, it's to be as truthful as possible. Withhold, yes, but when you do speak, avoid lying. "My girlfriend phoned me earlier and said a body's been found by the river. We were worried it might be him. It's not, is it?"

I expect them to be discreet, to move me out of earshot, but they confirm the matter openly and at once. "His wife has just made the formal identification."

Oh Melia, that can't have been a pleasant job. What did he look like, his flesh drained of blood? Were his dreams—ill-spirited though they were—still visible in his eyes?

"That's awful. Poor Melia." Feeling my legs tremble, I plant my feet heavily and place a hand on the counter. Behind me Regan is cutting the sandwiches; I hear the light sawing, the chime of metal meeting plate. "How did it happen? My girl-friend said it was another stabbing, is that right? We were just saying, weren't we, Regan? How worried we are about this knife-crime epidemic."

Regan turns and nods energetically, honored to be included in the drama.

"We're not in a position to share that information," the male officer says, as if I'm delaying them with idle gossip. Darting around me, Regan delivers the order to the table in the window and returns to stand at my shoulder.

"Well, thank you for letting me know," I say. "I know we're not family, but Clare and I were close to him. We'll phone Melia and see if we can support her in any way. She and Clare are good friends." I'm pleased with my handling of the scene so far. I'm appropriately saddened but with a touch of relief in my posture: *At least we know now*. I have to say, now it's unfolding it feels like genius. *She's* a genius. Melia. My Melia.

"Where were *you* on New Year's Eve, Mr. Buckby?"

Though the question has a level, just-out-of-interest tone

to it, I'm taken aback to be asked it. "New Year's Eve? I was at home all night with Clare. You've got her details, if you need to check with her." That's the fourth time I've mentioned her in the space of a minute; didn't I do the same with the detectives? Like she's my talisman, my proof of integrity. I gulp at the thought of the misery I've caused her, while *still* I exploit her virtues for all they're worth. "We watched TV and then we went to bed just before midnight."

"Just *before* midnight?"

"Yes, we didn't bother staying up. We've seen it all before. I leave the partying to Regan here."

Regan is alone in chuckling at this.

"And yesterday morning?"

"Nothing much. Pottered about. Clare went for a walk in the afternoon, but otherwise neither of us left the house again until coming to work today. I was going to ring DC Merchison this afternoon, actually, because Clare and I have some information about a loan Kit recently took out. It might still be useful, even though . . ." I trail off. *Even though he's dead.* "I'll email him, shall I? When I get home."

"What was the name again?" The male officer's eye contact is impersonal, almost robotic.

"DC Merchison. The one who interviewed me when Kit went missing. He's been my main point of contact since then. Based at the Woolwich station, I think he said."

"When was this interview? Yesterday?"

I frown. By my side, Regan shuffles. I hear her speak in hushed tones to new customers, asking them to wait. I think of theater ushers shushing late arrivals. "No, last Friday. The twenty-seventh, wasn't it?"

Like the date isn't stamped onto the inside of my eyelids.

"The twenty-seventh of December?"

I try to keep my patience, not wanting to irritate them, but really, this is sloppy. "Yes, just after he was reported missing. I was the last person to see him, they said, on Monday the twenty-third, on the late-night riverboat to St Mary's. We had drinks with our commuter friends—you'll have it all in your report."

"That's right," Regan confirms, keen to contribute. "Jamie didn't come into work on the twenty-seventh. I can show you his text?"

The officers glance politely at her before returning their attention to me. "Our understanding is that Mr. Roper was reported missing yesterday morning," the male officer says.

I shake my head in disbelief. This lot are hopeless. "I thought . . . Clare and I understood he hasn't been seen since before Christmas? Since that night of the drinks? That's what your colleagues told us. We saw Melia last Friday night and she was distraught about it. She'd raised the alarm over Christmas, when we were up in Edinburgh."

The female officer interjects now; she has the air of being better briefed than her coworker. "There was some confusion as to his whereabouts over Christmas, that's right. He was out of town and neglected to keep in touch, I believe."

I stare at her. *Out of town?* We've ventured deep into cross purposes now and it's crucial I don't panic and display how urgently I'd like this discrepancy to be resolved. "I think you might be mixing this up with something else. Phone DC Merchison, he'll help you join up the dots."

The two of them confer and finally she gets on the phone to connect with Woolwich CID. I remind myself I'm still devastated by the news of Kit's death and adjust my expression from impatience to appalled sorrow. "Poor Kit," I say to Regan, in an undertone. "This is so awful."

"It's terrible," she echoes, and links her arm through mine. "There's no way I'm telling my mum about this."

A pair of neglected customers give up and leave, but by the time the officer disconnects the call, all remaining clientele have turned to watch us.

"There's no DC Merchison at the Woolwich station," she says.

I blink. "I must have got that wrong, then. Blackheath or Greenwich, maybe?"

"My colleague has just searched the database and the name isn't coming up anywhere in the Met."

"Then maybe he's listed under a different name? Or new and not in the system yet?" He didn't *seem* new, though. He seemed the more experienced of the two, but then he might have recently transferred from a different force. I struggle to stop my face from twisting in irritation. "There were two of them. The other one was called Parry. Ian Parry. Try him."

As she dials a second time, an argument kicks off outside. It's an exchange of hostilities we hear every day, usually between motorists and cyclists and born of the fear of the near-miss, but this time it feels linked to me, a projection of *my* terror. When

I remove my focus from it, my eye falls on a pile of flyers Regan placed earlier on the shelf under the noticeboard: *London Philharmonic Orchestra at the Southbank Centre, introducing soprano Sarah Miller!*

The officer is off the phone again, her face that of someone whose tolerance for time wasting has been used up. By the time she confirms it in words, I'm already experiencing the collapsing sensation that comes with a realization so diabolical the brain has no immediate means to process it:

There's no DC Parry, either.

41

January 2, 2020

My diaphragm contracts and an ungodly groaning noise escapes me. Vomit rises and I'm holding it in my mouth, my swallow reflex in paralysis. Sweat pours through my skin ducts, drenching me in seconds. I close my eyes.

Let me understand this: Andy Merchison and Ian Parry interviewed me about Kit for almost two hours—that much I know to be true—but whoever they are, they are not detectives employed by the Metropolitan Police.

And only one person has had the means to convince me that they are.

Oh, Melia.

You are not who you said you were.

I thought you were deceiving him. He thought you were deceiving me.

You were deceiving both of us.

As if from deep underground, I hear one of the officers say:

"Can we ask you to come with us to the station, Mr. Buckby."
Beside me, Regan gasps in shock.

I open my eyes, finally succeeding in swallowing the vomit.
"If you think I can help sort out this misunderstanding, then
sure, but I have to say I'm very confused. Several people can
vouch for my earlier interview, I can give you their names."

This is pure bravado. Clare, Steve, Gretchen, Regan: all the
people *I* told about it. And Melia herself, of course. I'm a long
way from fathoming how she did this, but my instinct is that its
execution will have been flawless. My fingers itch for my phone,
but it's in my coat pocket in the staff room. "Would it be okay if
I get my things from the staff area?"

The officers agree to this. There is a sense that we are all
reasonable people with no appetite for dramatics. As I leave the
counter and advance between tables to the back of the shop,
Regan engages them with supplementary questions of her own;
I can't hear her words, but can tell by her tone that she's defending me, indignant that my account should be doubted. Next,
she's giving her name, address, and phone number.

As I gather my possessions and force my arms into my coat
sleeves, I feel spasms traveling up and down my body, like mice
running under my clothes. Free of the officers' scrutiny, I've lost
control of my nervous system, wouldn't be surprised to find I've
pissed myself or begun bleeding from my ears. In the doorway,
I pause. To my right, between the customer loos opposite and
where I'm standing, is the fire exit, which leads to the alley behind
our block where other staff sometimes go for a smoke among the
bins, slotting discarded butts into the cracks in the mortar.

It is then that the impulse makes itself known. Even as I register it, I'm warning myself against acting on it, because it never works on TV, not even for the innocent.

It only ever makes things worse.

But I do it anyway. I turn off my phone and then I slip through the fire door and run.

————

Somehow, I've forgotten it's raining, raining hard. The drops on my face are cold and sharp like a punishment, but I register a flare of satisfaction that I'm wearing trainers with a good grip; my foothold is solid as I thunder over wet cobble and paving stones.

Muscle memory leads me to the river: along the alley and into the open—close enough to read the registration of the squad car the officers arrived in—then between the National Theatre and the Royal Festival Hall and down to the London Eye, where I can lose myself in the canopy of umbrellas. The tightness in my lungs is agonizing and I pull air, hands on hips as if to remind myself how to stand as I check the river bus departures screen: the next boat, an express to Greenwich, is docking.

I slap my wallet against the electronic reader, sprint down the jetty, and board just in time, ducking low in my seat in the middle bank as far from the windows as I can get. Still breathing heavily, I try to evaluate the logistics of my flight. The police can't possibly be tracking me: yes, I used the card reader and of course there must be forests of cameras at the Eye, one of the city's biggest tourist attractions, but neither could conceivably have been accessed so quickly. Plus there's my cleverness in turning off my phone while still at work.

But, as we pass London Bridge, these points of advantage are exposed for what they are: temporary, fraudulent, and, in the end, easily construed as evidence of guilt. The grotesque truth is that my carefully plotted timeline, my meticulously secured alibis, Melia's and my rehearsed scripts: they're all meaningless because Kit was never reported missing when I thought he'd been.

When *he* thought he'd been, too, I've no doubt.

The two imposters who interviewed me must have been paid and prepped by Melia. The £10,000 loan that Kelvin unearthed, that feels like the right sort of fee for an acting job like this: one big interview, a house call or two, phone conversations as and when *he* gets in touch—their target and their dupe. Expenses would have been minimal, the costumes the actors' own and their only props a pair of fake IDs. A cheap disposable phone to field my calls must by now have been hurled into the river or crushed to pieces in the back of a garbage truck.

This is as much as I can calculate of the "how." The "why" is clearer: she's framed me for Kit's murder. What did the officers say just now? *His wife has just made the formal identification.* There was no hint—and nor do I have any hope—that she is under suspicion, much less arrest.

Clare's words haunt me: *Your little fling with her might have been strategic . . .*

How could you do this to me, Melia?

The boat leaves the central zone and picks up speed. Still, the riverside paths and roads are free of flashing blue lights. Still, there's no message over the PA for a member of the crew to make contact with his captain. But even if the police don't know where I am, the fact remains that I have nowhere to go. I can't go home. I have nowhere to hide, no one to protect me. My past with the woman I used to love can never be resurrected, my future with the woman I love now only ever existed as fantasy, as bait.

Greenwich comes into view and my fellow passengers press towards the exit, eager to get sightseeing, even in the rain. Thanks to the screen their queue creates, we've docked before I see it: a police launch, skimming the water behind us, dispatched, presumably, from the river police station at Wapping.

They know where I am!

The sight reignites the flight instinct and I shoulder my way to the exit, ignoring the grumbles, mouthing apologies with the taste of bile in my mouth. The moment the rope is raised, I tear past the crew and hare up the jetty to the open concourse, where I scan the options in front of me, my left ankle deep in a rain puddle: the *Cutty Sark*, with no queue in evidence; the terracotta entrance to the foot tunnel; the Greenwich streets, with the park—and southeast London—beyond; the Thames path east- and westward, both directions obstructed in places, if I remember rightly. Behind me, heavy footsteps, urgent voices; ahead, a uniformed security guard attached to the *Cutty Sark*, not looking my way but with his radio to his ear.

For fuck's sake, Jamie, choose!

Instinct leads me to the right and I slip into the doorway of the tunnel entrance, fed automatically to the left down a wide spiral stairwell. Round and round in a sickening corkscrew, my wet foot squelching loudly, my brain struggling to fathom what my body is doing. If I get to the other side of the river, I can run from there. Find somewhere to hide, think of a way to contact Clare.

No, not Clare, they'll be expecting that. Not my father or sister, either. Who, then? Who do I have left in the world? In my fixation with Melia, I've isolated myself. I've put all my faith in a false god.

At the foot of the stairs, the narrow tiled pipe beckons, the squares of fluorescent light along the curved ceiling receding down the shallow slope. There's a swarming sensation in my head before I'm even twenty feet in and I hear myself shriek as something whips past me, a man on a bike, riding one foot on the pedal, swooping into the dipped center, before disappearing from view. Now there are voices behind me, disembodied, their echoes sinister, and before I dare look a knot of tourists overtakes me.

I try to accelerate, but all I feel is an unbearably heavy wading motion, as if my coat is made of plates of iron. The world is suddenly odorless but for my own sweat, my rank breath. I reach to touch the tiles, to check the world is physical and not locked inside my mind.

I call out to the group bunched in my path. "Please, can I get by? *Please.*"

Startled faces turn, there's even a faint recoiling, confirming the otherness of me. Then someone makes way and I finally pick up speed, rushing and rushing, opening a gap between us. I'm almost at the midpoint of the tunnel, deep under the water right now. The concave walls enclose me, the dot at the end out of reach. I register the aching rumble of a train somewhere in the earth nearby. I think, *Why the hell am I here?* I'd have been better hiding in a building, the toilets of a bar. Now my destination is narrowed to the exit on the other side. Narrowing and narrowing into a cone . . .

"Grab him, he's falling!"

The last words before my hearing fails, my vision blurs. I feel the brakes in my body, the loss of power, and everything turns to black.

―――――

When I come to, the first thing I see is a man's face bright with concern. He is taking my vital signs and his fingers are gentle. He is in a hi-vis jacket, but I do not think he is police.

"Why did the train stop?" I say, which surprises me as much as it does him.

"You're not on a train. You're in the Greenwich Foot Tunnel. You fainted and someone pressed the emergency button."

"The emergency lever. I pulled it. I needed the train to stop. I have to get out."

"Stay nice and still while we wait for the medics. They'll have a stretcher with them, so you don't need to move. It will only be a few minutes."

I focus on details. The glaze on the tiles, cracked, each rectangle its own parched riverbed. A stalactite on the ceiling—calcium has formed in the gaps. I know these things. How far above is the water? I know this fact, too, I do.

"Stay right where you are," the voice commands, and I see the stalactite drawing closer as I rise to my feet.

"No, no. I can walk."

"You really need to stay still in case—"

I battle through the onlookers, staggering on. They don't know if I am a threat or a form of entertainment. There are silhouettes in the circle ahead. I can hear the man in the neon vest coming up behind me and calling, "Sir, please come back!"

Uniformed police are coming towards me now. They are bowling pins, toy soldiers. A fearful, accented voice asks: "What has this man done?"

Another, local, bolder: "Keep out of his way, he might have a knife."

Undeterred, someone walks right by my side, phone held brazenly in my face.

Three police officers surround me. One speaks into his radio, another addresses me directly:

"Was that *really* necessary, Mr. Buckby?"

I know the voice and my heart leaps: Merchison!

But no, not him, of course not. He is neither officer nor friend, but Melia's puppet. Like Parry, he speaks only her words.

There are hands restraining me now, because I can no longer be trusted not to bolt, and as I emerge above ground, daylight snapping and crackling around my face, the police arrest me on suspicion of murder.

42

January 2, 2020

This time we go to a police station. Of course we do. Why would detectives from the Metropolitan Police interview someone in the middle of winter at a terrace table outside the Royal Festival Hall? We drive west down roads rinsed clean by the rain, passing Londoners reborn with optimism as they raise their faces to the emerging sun—*that used to be me!*—until we reach a featureless mid-rise building in Woolwich that I've never had occasion to notice before.

Before I met Melia.

There's a booking-in process that takes an age and gives me time to recover from my absconsion, my confusion in the tunnel. To clarify my situation to myself, understand my rights. "Have you arrested anyone else, as well?" I ask the custody officer, but am told to worry about myself and leave police work to the professionals.

Eventually, I'm introduced to the duty solicitor and taken to a room far removed from the large interrogation chambers you

325

see on TV, where officers get buzzed in and out and chief inspectors watch through a one-way mirror as suspects pace like caged tigers. This is small and oppressive and could be a unit at a job center or a parking office: we sit on rough-textured plastic seats at a smeared table, on which there is digital equipment of some sort. A wall-mounted camera in the corner with an all-seeing eye. There's no offer of coffee, but I am permitted a plastic beaker of water.

The solicitor sits by my side. Evan, a good Welsh name, even if his accent is pure home counties. I try to bring to mind our pre-interview conference—he was briefing himself as we spoke and there was some grumble about disclosure. He is about my age and wears his world-weariness in extra kilos around his waist. Once or twice he yawns and I smell cigarettes on his breath, which makes me think of Kit and me on the stoop, looking out over Prospect Square.

How the hell do you get to live in a place like this?

He thought I had it all and didn't deserve it, when in fact I was busy preparing for exactly what I deserved: nothing.

A detective comes in. A real one. I don't absorb his name, but he is so totally unlike Merchison and Parry I could weep at my stupidity. It's not just his appearance—unremarkable, mid-priced suit, complexion that speaks of long-term dietary compromise—but also his sour odor of institution, of overwork. He is in his early forties and has rounded, boyish features, with a bright, obliging manner that feels hackneyed, as if he's signaling to me that he is not to be surprised, I am no one he hasn't sat face-to-face with a thousand times before.

He says he is recording our interview and activates the equipment, checking that I can clearly see what he is doing. The time and place are stated, as well as the names of all present. When asked to give my address, I have a profound sense that I will never set foot in Prospect Square again. I am the outcast now, the dispossessed.

"Okay, Mr. Buckby." He insists on eye contact before beginning. "Perhaps you'd like to start by telling me why you took it upon yourself to take off the way you did this afternoon when our officers spoke to you at your place of work?"

"Because I thought . . ." My voice is a mumble and I clear my throat, raise the volume to a more confident level. "I thought I must have been framed for Kit's murder and I got scared. I'm sorry. It was a crazy thing to do, I didn't mean to waste your time and budget."

He gives me a sarcastic *Well, that's all right then* kind of look and I understand that what little benefit of the doubt I might have been entitled to, I've squandered. He is entirely disinclined to believe a word I say.

"What made you think he'd been murdered? You hadn't been told that by our officers, had you?"

"No, but my partner had phoned earlier and said she thought it was a stabbing."

"Did she now? Her job is what?"

"She's in property. What I mean is, she was in the area and she overheard someone say it was a stabbing. She didn't see the body with her own eyes."

The body. I can't connect with what I've done, what Melia has done. It's evening by now and the river bus commuters will

327

be arriving home. Are the police still there, rainwater dripping from the tent, cordons in place?

"Right. Well, what *I'm* interested in, if we're going to get anywhere tonight, is what you've seen with *your* own eyes. Okay?"

"Yes."

"Where were you on Tuesday night of this week?"

"At home." I repeat the answers I gave the uniformed officers in the café. Again, Clare is invoked. If I've established anything in the time between arrest and now, it's that this is Melia's word against mine, whether she is questioned as a suspect or as the victim's family or both. I have Clare to alibi me and she has Elodie. Surely someone as successful and respectable as Clare will be more convincing than Elodie? I try to remember her profession, if I was ever told it. Most of the Ropers' friends are "creative," so if there's any justice in the world, Elodie will be flitting between casual jobs, constantly demonstrating her unreliability. An uneasy voice corrects mine: Melia will not have picked her at random. I shudder.

Bright eyes grip mine once more, demand my focus. "Let's look at the period between midnight and six in the morning on Wednesday, Mr. Buckby."

That must be the time of death. "I was in bed. I sent some New Year's messages to my family, then I listened to a radio drama. I slept from about one to eight thirty in the morning."

"What radio drama was it?"

"Just an old Jeeves and Wooster thing."

"In a lighthearted mood, were you?"

"Not really, it was just good to fall asleep to."

"Because you were keyed up about something?"

"No, not at all. But I could hear fireworks going off, a bit of party noise from the square outside. I just wanted to relax. I'm sure you could check my phone, or search history or whatever."

"I'm sure we could. What was the Jeeves and Wooster story? Fill me in."

His style is relentless: this is no game of cat and mouse, but the lightening of an unmanageable workload with optimum efficiency. I'm of no fascination to him, only an arrogant chancer who believes his life is worth more than other people's and who has been wicked enough to act on that belief.

I wouldn't have a hope even if I did disagree with him.

"I can't remember," I say, truthfully.

"Try. Give me some idea of the story."

I strain for a likely detail. "I think it was the one where he helps his friend break off his engagement."

"Sounds like an episode of *Friends*." There's a pause, a moment of amusement shared with Evan rather than me, a split second of security I'd be a fool to put my faith in. "Thank you, Jamie, that sounds very complete. A nice, civilized early night. The problem is, we've got this."

It is a photograph, in black and white. As I peer at it, tilting my head to rid the surface of the glare, discussion ensues between the two of them about disclosure. Evidently, the item should have been submitted to us before the interview. Evan suggests a break, a private conference, but I wave away the idea. "It doesn't matter whether I saw it before or not, because I can't tell what it is."

This is true. There is little discernible variation in the dark tones of the image. But then I see the time stamp in the corner—01/01/20 01:43—and I brace in my seat. The atmosphere in the room heightens and quickens and contracts. Everything slams into everything else.

My interrogator resumes: "This is an image sent anonymously through our witness appeal channels. It's been taken without a flash, so you're right, you can't see anything much, but if you look at this enhanced version our techies have sorted out for us . . ."

A second picture is placed alongside the first. Now I can make out two figures against a low wall, their torsos crushed together. They might be lovers if you cared to interpret it that way, but I know they are fighting. Fighting over a woman, fighting for their lives, though neither knows it yet.

Only one face is visible to the camera.

"Can you identify either of these figures, Mr. Buckby?"

Again, Evan attempts to interrupt the questioning and, again, I dismiss him. I touch my own face in the photo with a tentative finger. "This looks like me, but if it is then the time must be faked. Like I say, I was at home then. Clare will confirm that."

The detective ignores this, making a comment for the purposes of the recording that I have identified myself in the evidence. "And the other person?"

"I have no idea."

"You don't remember who you were with?"

"The date's faked, so if I don't know when it was taken, then I don't know who I was with." I cling to my line: everything is faked now, it's an established problem for seekers of the truth.

But the police are seekers of convictions, which is not necessarily the same thing.

"Do you recognize the location, Mr. Buckby?"

"No idea," I repeat. The black spot is out of range of all cameras and we were alone, which means Melia must have taken this photo, careful not to use flash, as the detective points out. I would have noticed that and so would Kit.

Witch. Double-crosser. Right in front of our eyes—except our eyes were on each other.

I pick up my water beaker, but it's empty. I chew at the rim, as if that will yield liquid. "Could I have some more water, please?"

Evan slides his cup towards me and I pour the remaining liquid down my throat. I say thank you but do not meet his eye.

"We believe the second figure is your friend, Mr. Roper," the detective says.

"It could be," I agree, "just not any time recently. As I keep explaining, I haven't seen him since Monday the twenty-third of December. I thought he'd been reported missing and I wasn't the only one to think that. For God's sake, Merchison and Parry detained me for half the morning on that basis!"

"Ah, yes, the famous Merchison and Parry." An audible lungful of breath, followed by a theatrical sigh, tells me what he thinks of the allusion. "You were interviewed under caution, were you?"

"No. It was only an informal chat."

He chuckles. "An informal chat that took up half the morning. Right."

"Yes, *right*. Someone needs to investigate *them*. If they're not in the Met, then they should be charged with impersonating a police officer. That's an offense, isn't it?" I've said this several times to police staff since being arrested, but it's clear that all, including this one, the one who counts, think I'm making my inquisitors up, that they're phantoms, delusions. Names plucked from some magazine ad or a label on a box that caught my eye in the café as I spoke to the uniformed officers: Merchison & Parry, purveyors of traditional gingerbread. My face floods as I remember Sarah Miller, soprano. Merchison must have seen her name on a poster or a flyer in the RFH, then doodled it in his pad, making himself look like a real detective, noticing things. What else was in that pad? A shopping list? Ideas for anniversary gifts for his wife? Does he even *have* a wife? A spike of fury pierces the deadweight of self-pity in me and I feel my face flame.

"Let's leave that issue for now and return to the photograph, if we may. Is it possible that this could have been taken on the stretch of the river where Mr. Roper's body was found earlier today?"

"I wouldn't know which stretch that was," I say, teeth gritted.

"I thought you said your partner told you? It might interest you to know that we're checking all CCTV footage from cameras in St Mary's on New Year's Eve, including the roads between your house and the river."

I feign a shrug. There'll be nothing on the main route, I'm confident of that much, but any amateur could find the alternative access path with a cursory google and my precautions strike me now as utterly woeful. Melia assured me it was clear of security cameras and because I had no reason to doubt her my own reconnaissance was far from exhaustive. Might there have been a distant camera I wasn't aware of, somewhere beyond the gates of the St Mary's Wharf construction site? A camera she alone knew to evade?

A bulb flickers overhead—or maybe I'm imagining it. "This time stamp has been faked," I repeat, blinking.

The detective's gaze does not waver. "We've tested its authenticity and we're satisfied it meets evidential requirements."

Otherwise, they might not have had enough to arrest me. And I don't need my new friend Evan to take me aside and explain it is likely going to be enough to bring a charge all on its own.

I have a memory of myself in Rosie's Café, haranguing Melia. *Have you heard from him? Is he still AWOL?* Lines rehearsed to show concern for a missing person, but might they just as easily have been those of a man hunting another man with the intent of doing him harm? My face that afternoon was crazy-eyed. I'd looked *deranged*.

Just as I know I do now.

"It was Melia," I say, abruptly. "She took this photo. She's set me up."

As my solicitor tries more strenuously than ever to intervene, to somehow negate this last catastrophic offering, I raise a hand, insist I know what I'm saying. The detective lowers his shoulders, adjusts his gaze. He was not expecting a confession so quickly, but then this is not my first interview, no matter what he prefers to think.

"You mean, you *were* with Mr. Roper at one forty-three on the morning of January the first?"

"Yes. We were by the river in St Mary's. Just along from the Hope and Anchor."

He taps the photo. "And this is him in the photograph with the person you've already identified as yourself?"

"Yes." I take a breath and expel the truth: "But I didn't stab him. I admit I'm guilty of not reporting a crime or whatever that's called, but not murder. She did it." When he makes no immediate reply, I raise my voice: "Look at me, surely you're trained to tell if someone's telling the truth!"

His mouth tightens, as if to warn me that more challenging individuals than me have sat in this spot and spat out their lies, their avowals and confessions. "To be clear, when you say 'She did it,' you're talking about . . .?"

"Melia, of course! I just said!"

"Melia Roper, Christopher Roper's wife?"

That's the moment when I see my future—*hear* it. The way he says her name, the incontrovertible rejection in his tone. That's when I know beyond a shadow of a doubt she is not sitting somewhere else in this building being subjected to a parallel interrogation, but is at home being comforted and cared for. Elodie is going to turn out to be a special-needs teacher or a social worker and she will swear on the lives of our city's vulnerable or her own babies that Melia was in the flat with her all night, a unit so compact she couldn't have failed to notice her friend's absence (unless she was drugged, of course). Clare, meanwhile, will freely explain we weren't sharing a room; we weren't even on the same story of our big rich-person's house. I could have been doing anything while she slept, a bottle of wine in her system.

"Mr. Buckby? Mr. Buckby?"

My head is in my hands, fingers pressing eyes into the sockets, and all of a sudden they're saying my name as if releasing me from a spell.

"I strongly urge you to take a break," my solicitor says, and reminds the detective of my fainting fit in the tunnel, my disorientation on regaining consciousness. *He doesn't know what he's saying.*

But I do, and for the last time, I silence him. "No! I want to talk. Let's get this over and done with."

The detective is pleased. His body language opens, his tone relaxes. "That would be my preference, as well. I'd like to bring in a colleague, if I may."

The photos are withdrawn, papers put back in order, recording equipment checked. The solicitor is messaging on his phone, canceling plans. The deflation in his manner tells me he thinks he's done all he can and is now a bystander, not a player. Well, I don't want his law. I no longer care about my rights.

Soon there are two men facing me across the table. By coincidence—or illusion—they are of similar height and build to Merchison and Parry.

"Let's start at the beginning, shall we?" the new arrival proposes. "Tell us everything you know about Mr. Roper. How long have you known each other?"

I gape. These are the same questions I was asked on December 27th, the exact wording. I feel like I'm losing my mind, though in truth it's been dislocated for me, by an angel who turned out to be a she-devil.

I clear my throat and a phrase grips me, more than a phrase, a sensation: *fear of falling.* Oh, Melia, maybe it would have been better if we'd fallen from the cable car that night. We'd have died on impact, rolled along the riverbed in our capsule, figures in a snow globe waiting to be shaken back to life.

"Almost a year," I say. "We met last January."

43

January 2, 2020

You know what's funny about all this? (And when I say "funny," I mean sick, fucked-up; wildly, suicidally *bad*.) My second version is really not so different from the first. I was never actively lying to Parry and Merchison. I didn't need to. It was really just a matter of deleted scenes.

Like that evening in late March, the bedroom with all the mirrors. That confessional exchange of frailties—and, yes, I know they are in fact vanities, but perhaps vanity is the most profound frailty of all? Mine, the shame of being virtually as impoverished as she was, hers the fear that she could never attract, or be attracted to, a partner with the means to free her from debt and help her reinvent herself and rise.

"You know what I've just thought?" she said. We were still in the bedroom, but dressed and about to leave. I was putting on my shoes, she was fixing her hair in one of the mirrors behind me.

"What?" I glanced up at her and saw that something maverick had been stirred in her. Her eyes glittered gold.

337

"Kit's got this life insurance policy. It's part of his work benefits, all permanent employees his level get it. So apparently, if he dies, I'll get a crazy amount of money."

"You're the named beneficiary, are you?"

"That's it. *Beneficiary.*" She said it like it was some erotic term.

It was immediately clear to me that I should treat this as jest and nothing but. "How do you plan to do away with him? No, don't tell me. You can't trust me not to squeal when the time comes."

"Really? That's disappointing." A held beat as her gaze drifted from her own reflection to my face, and then she sighed. "You know I'm only having a laugh, don't you?"

"Of course. Besides, those policies only kick in after a certain length of service."

"Two years," she said.

I paused. *Don't ask.* "How long has he worked there?"

"Twenty months this week."

I noted the precision and said nothing.

"What about Clare?" she asked. She had her back to me now and was fiddling with her bag, looking for keys.

"What about her?"

"Does she have a policy?"

"I don't think so. I'm not sure I'd be her beneficiary, anyway. She has a cousin she's close to and he's got three kids. She's always said she'd leave everything to them."

Those mirrors, that night, a great arrangement of them! I remember our gazes connecting suddenly in reflection and I was disorientated by the flicker of malevolence I thought I saw in her face. Only when laughter broke across it did I recognize her again.

"Bummer," she said. "Kit it is, then."

———————

And like another evening, the one on which the plan surfaced. September, the first time she and I had met since the wedding, just after my holiday in France with Clare and Dad. A reunion so sweet, so ripe—and yet, by the time we parted, there was already that fine, dry dust that denotes the beginning of rot.

I remember being bewitched by her. That's honestly the only word to describe it. The sight of her, the feel of her, the scent of her, it all filled me with a new recklessness, a daredevil pleasure indistinguishable from freedom.

I thought, *Nothing in my life is important except this.*

(Which is very different from *Nothing in my life is as important as this.*)

"Tell me why you and Kit got married," I said. "It can't have been on impulse, you have to give notice."

"I know. I did it because I've had an idea." Such a simple statement, and so stark, that use of the singular, as if Kit had no agency at all. If I could go back to that moment and suspend time, start living backwards, all the way back to birth, I would. "I've been thinking about it for a while, going over all the details, seeing if it could work. And I'm a hundred percent certain it could."

"What idea?" I said, because time was not suspended; it proceeded as it always did, a pace or two ahead, tugging me forward by a leash clipped to my collar.

"How we can deal with Kit and claim the insurance money."

I raised an eyebrow and smiled as if at an imaginative child. "When you say 'deal with,' you don't mean . . .?"

She pressed her lips together in private judgment; when released, they puffed open like a flowerhead. "I do."

My face was trapped in that smile. Inside, confusion roared. I felt as if I'd missed a link in the plot development, my understanding obscured by a fit of amnesia.

Her mouth moved a fraction closer to my ear. "That's why I had to marry him. You get more. There's a death in service thing, as well as the life insurance. Almost two million pounds."

"As much as that. Wow." Though I was still chuckling, I was aware of the tension in her body, the weight of expectation on me, and my heart quaked.

"Help me, Jamie." Her gaze was persuasive, the kind born not of envy or revenge but of the pure, primal will to succeed. "You've got nothing, I've got nothing. This is a solution."

"It's not a solution, it's a crime." At last, I brought some condemnation to my tone. "*Two* crimes if you consider the fact that the payout could be treated as fraud or money laundering. If you got caught, you'd go to jail for, what, ten, fifteen years?"

"We wouldn't get caught."

The transition from singular to plural was seamless and deadly.

I fixed her with my gravest frown. "Melia, come on."

"I knew that's what you'd say," she said, with simple acceptance. She rolled from me, releasing me from her body heat. "It's fine, it would be weird if you didn't."

"Well, to be fair, the last time you had an idea, we went on a cable car ride."

A giggle slipped from her then, as if she couldn't resist my humor even when absorbed in the grimmest of thoughts. It was—excruciating to admit now—flattering.

"Just let me tell you how it would work," she said. "Think of it as a fantasy, the plot of a movie."

I know it sounds insane that I even listened. I know I should have walked away. I should have protected Kit.

I should have protected myself.

The fact was I loved her. I was demented with the pleasure of being reunited with her, of the prospect of being a part of her future. Like I say, I was bewitched. Spellbound. And, for what it's worth, she wasn't wrong in her evaluation of my lot. Clare and I weren't married and common law rights were a myth. In the event of a split, even if some lawyer agreed to negotiate for me I couldn't afford to pay them. My job paid a pittance and at any time I could have nowhere to live. I'd be bed hopping like Regan; scavenging like the foxes in the square.

It was not straightaway, no, but at some point after that liaison the erroneous but alluring theory began to form in my mind that owning nothing was the same as having nothing to lose.

And it wasn't as if *I* would be the one to kill him. My alibi would be impregnable—as impregnable as a prison cell.

The real question was, would I be able to consider a future with a killer?

Evidently, I could.

And evidently Kit could consider a future with a new identity in a country far from his own, while an innocent man—me!—was jailed for a crime he didn't commit. That *no one* committed.

According to Melia, he was disgracefully easy to get on board with her fraud scheme—sorry, her fake fraud (how ironic is that?). He was all too willing to abandon his job, his friends, his debts, for the unearned wealth and life of leisure he considered his right.

Even if Melia hadn't warned me, I could have pinpointed the day he'd bought into her plan. He changed towards me, maybe because he knew she'd have to sleep with me for it to work, and yet he couldn't fall out with me, at least not for long. He needed me in his life, his rival and enemy, to be available for an argument on the night he was to disappear. Without me, there'd be no murder theory, only a senseless disappearance, which meant no money for years.

I got used to the rhythm of it. He'd say something abrasive ("You're a fucking *dinosaur*, Jamie") and then he'd regroup to suggest something sociable ("No hard feelings, mate. Time for a quick one at Mariners?"). Of course, he didn't know that I was wrangling an almost identical dilemma: I couldn't stand the sight of him, but I needed him in range. It both fortified and desensitized me to understand that we thought each other equally worthless and therefore equally worth sacrificing.

"I can't believe he's willing to live with a false identity for the rest of his life," I told Melia.

"What's the alternative? Live like paupers forever? And I'd have to, as well, don't forget. The idea is we'd have each other and that's all that counts." She pulled a nauseatingly romantic expression, before letting it fade to dispassion. It was an interesting thing, her alteration, her hardening of resolve. A mutation, fast-moving and deadly, and yet quite undetectable on the surface.

"You wouldn't be able to stay in Europe, if you were really doing it. It would have to be South America or somewhere without an extradition agreement with the UK, virtually off grid."

"*If*," she echoed, adding, hard candy in her voice. "Maybe I'll let him choose the destination. It's the least I can do."

————

Kit being Kit, he struggled at times to stick to his script. It was the failed actor in him as much as the unreliable libertine. With a fortune tantalizingly in reach and nervous tension escalating, he consumed more booze and drugs than ever, risking his job exactly when it was vital he keep it. Melia managed him, talked him up, talked him down. It was a tribute to her that he was able to complete the course, even if the finish line he staggered towards was marked with a blade, not a ribbon.

She's a total slut . . . Just you wait, Jamie! I fucking mean it! It made my blood run cold that he would almost give himself away like that. Not only in his words, but also in his eyes, projecting like a silent movie just for me: months of hating me for having her. Months of longing to tell me it wasn't real, that she was using me.

Well, he was right about that.

Yes, it was a long game, a bluff of moving parts. Every step was debated and dissected, our logistical queries checked on public computer terminals or colleagues' borrowed laptops. "I'm thinking just before Christmas for getting him into hiding," Melia said. "There's a lot of crime over that period, a lot of noise. When I report him missing, the police will be stretched to capacity."

"You mean, you don't want them to investigate *too* well?"

"Exactly. It needs to all be official, but the last thing we want is for them to actually find him." Holed up in his grotty B&B in Thamesmead, with long-stay rooms for cash and a helpful leniency regarding ID. It was a temporary option, as far as Kit understood it, but in reality his final home.

With my train to Edinburgh booked for Tuesday morning, drinks with the water rats would be scheduled for the Monday night. Kit was primed to initiate a row in the stretch between North Greenwich and St Mary's, making sure the cameras caught it nice and clear. Once off the boat, he'd turn onto the river path towards the Hope & Anchor, careful to obscure his face when in range of the pub's exterior camera, and then on to Pepys Road, where he'd be removed to his hideout by an unlicensed minicab arranged by Melia, complete with generous tip to buy the driver's silence.

"Don't get too provoked, Jamie. Don't *actually* lure him off and kill him."

We shared a laugh at that.

"When exactly will you phone the police?"

"I'll give it a day or two. That's what I'd do if I really didn't know where he was."

"Wouldn't you ring me, though? When he hasn't come home on the Tuesday morning? You'd know he'd been out with me the night before."

"I'll ring you," she agreed. "I'll try a few times, but let it go to voicemail. We don't want the police thinking we've been speaking." Colluding. Conspiring.

"You'd try Clare, as well, wouldn't you? That would be the natural thing, if you couldn't get hold of me." She'd be more likely to pick up, but it wouldn't be the end of the world if she did. "She's sure to say he's off partying somewhere, he's done it often enough before."

"By the time you come back, the police will have taken a statement from me and will want to speak to you," Melia said. "My guess is they'll phone you at work on the Friday. And, Jamie?"

"Yes?"

"When you talk to them, they'll be clever. The best way to stop yourself saying stuff is to not *think* it."

"I'll remember that," I said.

As for the crime itself, time and place were quickly agreed: New Year's Eve, the black spot east of the Hope & Anchor. Melia would arrange to meet Kit for one of their long nocturnal walks (they would each have an old-style pay-as-you-go phone for their untraceable messaging), and I'd be waiting, concealed by the night, ready to distract him for a minute or two while she prepared her attack.

Initially, Melia thought we should dispose of the body in the river, wait for it to be washed up, but I'd read extensively on the dangers of the tidal Thames. "The undertow can keep bodies down there for days, even weeks. What if it screws up our alibis? Or the body comes back so decomposed you can't see any wound? We don't want it declared a suicide."

Suicide meant no money, hence my vociferous denials to Clare and Gretchen that Kit had ever had any such intentions.

As for the knife wound, "Leave it to me, I'll research how to do it properly," Melia said, as if talking about growing tomatoes or reupholstering an armchair. "The last thing we need is him living to tell the tale."

"I can't believe you think you're capable of this," I remarked, in another apartment with high windows and floors as smooth as glass. The dusk had come a little earlier then, the light lower.

"It's not like I'll enjoy it," she said. "It's just got to be done."

"I don't believe you," I said. They'd been together for years, been in debt for as long. "What changed? What did he do to make you hate him?"

She shook her head. "He's going to destroy himself anyway, look at the way he lives. This way, we get something out of it. A future, you and me."

"Until you decide to do the same thing to me," I said. It was meant as a wisecrack, but she answered with the utmost sincerity.

"No, we're different, Jamie. We're special."

Clare was an unexpected obstacle.

It goes without saying that ideally she wouldn't have found out about the affair; that was a variable of which I lost control, thanks to having been unsettled by my "interrogation" that morning. Had she not done the decent thing and let me move into the spare room, I would have had to beg for a reconciliation, a last chance.

She rocked the boat a second time by storming off to her parents, when I needed her to be at home for New Year's Eve to alibi me. She came through for me again, but not before I'd had to line up Dad to understudy her, an alternative that would have been far from ideal.

Then, a third time, when she guessed the plan. The fake plan. She had a better nose for a bluff than I did.

When I remember New Year's Eve at home with her, my pulse slows a fraction. I picture her in her pajamas standing in front of me on the landing, making her suggestion: *Do you think it's completely impossible . . . ?*

The suggestion that I now understand was my last chance in every conceivable way.

Dear God, I should have fallen to my knees to take it, weeping with gratitude.

———

And so the police hear out my true confession—hours of it; by the end, I've almost lost my voice—but thanks to my having established myself as a fantasist regarding a certain nonexistent detective double act, they make no bones about considering my account the improvised alternative reality of an unhinged mind.

"So you told these other 'investigators' that Mr. Roper disappeared because he owed money to drug dealers, but now you're saying it was an insurance fraud gone wrong and he was killed by his wife?"

"A *faked* insurance fraud."

"We can't keep up with your imagination, Mr. Buckby."

"It's not imagination," I cry. "It's the truth!" There's a kicking sensation inside my head and my eyelids crunch as I blink. "Melia persuaded him I'd be convicted for his murder without there being a body."

As the three of them regard me with opposing emotions of pity and pitilessness, the bright-eyed detective says, "Well, the fact that there *is* a body would appear to contradict *that*."

Even so, I persist with my truth during the months of remand that follow. I persist with it even in the face of Melia's reported denials, of the ever more convincing case being assembled by the prosecution. My defense team is sympathetic, but pragmatic, repeatedly explaining to me that it is not what I have done or not done that matters, but what they can prove I've done or not done.

For instance: when my phone search history is examined and the words "How to inflict fatal knife wound" found in a private browsing mode that I wasn't even aware existed, I can *claim* the search was made when I gave Melia my pass code so she could download her favorite songs for me, but I can't *prove* it. (Our first meeting after the wedding, too, before I'd even agreed to her plan. She was already setting me up!)

For instance: when it's discovered that a knife is missing from the Comfort Zone—the very one I loaned in the first place—I can *claim* Melia took it during that single, helpful visit of hers, but I can't *prove* it.

And, when my team requests access to the security footage at the Royal Festival Hall and it's discovered that at no time are Merchison's and Parry's faces captured with any clarity, but only mine, I can *claim* they'd studied the angles in advance, but I can't *prove* it.

Oh, and when a hoodie is found in the bushes of Prospect Square with both my hairs and traces of Kit's blood attached to it, I can *claim* Melia kept it back that night and tossed it over the railings, but I can't *prove* it.

I could go on.

I'm urged to consider a manslaughter plea, but I do what they do in movies and I refuse to compromise. I make my "not guilty" plea to all who will listen, including judge and jury.

But in the end, it will come down to who they believe: her or me.

Well, I think we can all guess which way *that's* going to go.

44

Some months later

I won't dwell on the trial. Just as she has been a highly credible witness with the police, so Melia is with the court. Attending in the company of a victim liaison officer, she is dressed in slim black trousers and white blouse, the prim and servile uniform of a waitress. Her hair is demurely styled, soft on her shoulders, her brave eyes shining with grief, and I'm guessing she intends the silver heart pendant at her throat to be taken for a love token from her dear, departed husband.

I study the jurors' faces when she gives her evidence and I see they want to, variously, mother her, befriend her, comfort her, fight for her, or fuck her. She's got "it": something for everyone. They should have invited agents and casting directors to judge her performance alongside the legal professionals and sworn good citizens.

Don't get me wrong, my barrister is excellent and challenges her on her inconsistencies, but she is consistently earnest and agreeable—even apologetic that her messages might have been mixed or misunderstood.

Her fingers reach frequently for that silver love heart.

The way she tells it, the faked disappearance and insurance fraud scheme simply didn't exist. Kit would never have been stupid enough to agree to a plan like that, even if she'd been stupid enough to suggest it. Yes, it *is* true that on December 27th she told her boss and a couple of Kit's friends that Kit had gone AWOL over Christmas and she was sick with worry, but she wouldn't have dreamt of notifying the police, not when she knew how much he liked to party. He'd stayed out all night several times in the months preceding his death, on one occasion with the defendant himself, whose partner had told Melia personally how angry she'd been.

Richard backs her story up: she'd told him Kit had gone missing but made no mention of having reported his disappearance to the police; rather, she expected him to return at any time. The idea that the police were involved had entered office channels via Clare—and Clare's information had come directly from me.

Yes, she'd tried to get hold of the defendant a few times during this anxious period, *and* his partner, who was also her friend and colleague, but neither of us picked up her calls. And yes, it was true that on the occasion of our visit to her flat on Tiding Street, Clare and I had spoken about liaising with the police, but Melia had not fully comprehended such references and had thought the exchange hypothetical.

Then, sure enough, Kit reappeared on the Saturday after Christmas with his tail between his legs, and in the chaos of the holiday season she hadn't thought to let people know. She "kind of feared" others guessed they had a volatile relationship and felt a bit embarrassed about her earlier "overreaction." According to her, Kit then began some sort of amateur rehab program in the flat, supervised by Nurse Melia. Attempts by the defendant to contact her by text message were rebuffed because she wanted to concentrate on her husband's health and in any case regretted her extramarital fling. Of course there wasn't any lovers' code, she wasn't a teenager! *Do not contact me* meant "Do not contact me." A distressing incident in a local café on Sunday the 29th reinforced her belief that her relationship with the defendant had been a disastrous error of judgment—and Kit's friendship with him, too (his alcohol abuse had got far worse since they'd begun commuting to work together).

And so the lie turns the truth into a madman's conspiracy theory, with a string of plausible witnesses to support it, such as the bartender at the Hope & Anchor, who recounts my visit on December 28th in search of Kit: I'd struck him as "unstable" and "paranoid," it transpires. He had wondered about my scratched face and injured hand.

It was a burn! (It really was a burn.)

And such as Elodie, who for good measure had heard Melia phone Kit from the café on the afternoon of the 29th to check on him. She confirms the "harassment" on my part: "He was desperate to find Kit. I would characterize him as not in control of himself. To be honest, he scared me."

Can Elodie tell the court her profession? Yes, she is a carer in a nursing home for elderly ex-servicemen and women.

Of course she is.

No, Melia is terribly sorry, but she can't name anyone else who saw Kit during those fraught few days of withdrawal, but he was obviously alive, wasn't he, since it is an undisputed fact that he died in the early hours of January the 1st. On the night in question, newly sober and inexplicably nocturnal, he had ventured out alone "to get some air." It was the last time she saw him until undertaking the grim task of identifying his body on Thursday the 2nd.

Faithful Elodie had been nowhere near Tiding Street, of course—Melia has no explanation for why the defendant would insist this to be the case or allege that she should want to drug her friend—but it was true that Melia did phone her at 2:30 a.m., when Kit failed to return from his walk. Elodie, coming to the end of her night's partying, advised waiting till morning and they prayed jointly that poor Kit had not bumped into some bad influence from his old life and been tempted into a late-night bar (a glance in my direction as the words "bad influence" are uttered).

As for the photograph of Kit and me, she knows nothing of it, whatever the defendant maliciously claims.

Who, then, captured this crucial evidence? This is put to a member of the investigation team and the court is told that the image was anonymously submitted by email. A subsequent police appeal for the mystery photographer to come forward has led to several claims, including a man in and out of local homeless shelters and known to the police as a rough sleeper.

"Do rough sleepers have mobile phones?" my barrister asks.

"Everyone does," says the officer.

"Mobile phones equipped with data to send material by email?"

"Incredibly, it's not out of the question."

Is there not then a case for charging this man with failure to report a crime?

Without firm identification, no charge can be brought. In any case, at the time the photograph was taken, no crime had been committed. It may even have been snapped accidentally and only recognized as potentially significant following the news of Kit's death. (He's a good citizen, this homeless guy. Someone give him a medal.)

All of which leads nicely into a reiteration of the time of death: any time between immediately after the image was captured and three hours later.

———

Clare witnessed my duping, of course, but now she suggests *I* sought to dupe *her*. She accepts Melia's explanation of Kit's return, understanding on reflection that with Melia off work and the two women estranged over my betrayal, her only information about Kit's disappearance came from me.

No, she did not personally witness the arrival of any police officer at her home on the morning of Monday, December 30th.

Merchison must have waited for her to leave the house before coming straight to the door, ID in hand, to tick me off and secure my continuing faith in his investigation.

One of the worst moments of my life is when, challenged with my claim that she personally took a call from one of the detectives, Clare says it might in fact have been from me, disguising my voice. "I can't say for sure it was him, but I can't say for sure it wasn't."

Ask Gretchen and Steve, I want to scream, *they had calls from the police too*!

But, when it is their turn, they say they were in fact phoned by Melia, not the police. It was a fatal assumption on my part. She concedes she didn't think to text them to inform them that Kit had turned up and they both accept her explanation that she believed Kit had been in touch directly. They were his friends, after all, not hers.

Steve bears witness to my erratic behavior in the days following Kit's "disappearance"—a hostile text accusing him of lying to the police; garbled theories about drugs deals and a trip to Marrakech. (So much for not snitching on a friend—but then standing in a witness box is different from propping up a bar, and he was always closer to Kit than to me.)

Gretchen, for her part, admits to her affair with him, but somehow it only serves to redress the balance in terms of Melia's own infidelity.

Even that airhead Yoyo from the bar on the 23rd is invited to add her two pennies' worth about me: "I found him very menacing."

"Towards Mr. Roper?"

"Yes, he said, 'Fuck you, Kit.' It was like he *hated* him."

Kit must have told Melia about that. Every single detail she's thought through, every single witness has been manipulated.

Except . . . not Regan, surely? The two have never met, so there can be no question of manipulation.

Regan agrees that I spoke repeatedly of a friend who'd gone missing. "We talked about it a lot after he found out about it from the police. He was so upset. Kit was a really good friend of his." Yes, it was definitely Friday, December 27th, when the defendant was questioned. She is one hundred percent sure and her colleague Simona can confirm it.

Finally, an account that echoes mine from a witness who has no reason to perjure herself!

But did she see the detectives with her own eyes? Did she have anyone's word but mine that the disappearance was fact and not fiction? Was she shown any media reports or missing persons appeals regarding Christopher Roper?

"No, but—"

Was it possible her colleague could have made up the drama in order to excuse unauthorized absences or other negligent behavior?

"It's possible," Regan says, with reluctance.

It's all downhill from there. Was she aware of a knife going missing at any time during the final weeks of the year?

"Only the one that belonged to Jamie and I guessed he must have taken it back home at some point."

"This was the twelve-centimeter utility knife by the brand Global, originally bought by Clare Armstrong?"

"Yes, it was really sharp. I assumed he needed it back for Christmas."

For "Christmas," read *killing*, suggests the prosecution.

Was she aware of the defendant making any special arrangements for transporting a professional chef's knife home, given that the law prohibits the carrying of articles with blades exceeding three inches in any public place?

Regan nervously pushes up her sleeves then, exposing her spider tattoo to the jury. "No."

The prosecution barrister allows a generous pause for the jurors to picture the defendant traveling home on public transport with a lethal blade in his bag; the massacre that might have been. How, at any time, I might have stabbed a customer for no other reason than he chose a chocolate croissant over a plain.

Management has since provided a replacement knife, Regan offers, as if that might help me.

"Were you aware of a friend visiting Mr. Buckby on November the twenty-sixth?"

"I don't think so. He didn't really have friends visiting."

"This would be someone who helped him out behind the counter."

"No one helped," Regan corrects them. "You're not allowed in the service area unless you're staff. I'm the manager and I would know."

Of course she would.

I won't go on except to say that the jury need only a couple of hours to agree on their verdict. By then, everyone present knows what I've been warned from day one: that for murder convictions in the UK, there is a mandatory minimum sentence of fifteen years.

45

Some months later

Dear Kit . . .

I never said that when you were alive, did I? I never used that phrase, that endearment. All those "mate's" and "wanker's" and "twat's." Lads together, across the generations.

But now I say it all the time. In the hours upon hours I've been gifted in which to reconstruct the events that led me here, to revise everything I thought I knew about my crime and punishment, it's you I'm addressing. Not Melia or Clare or my legal team; not the guard I like best who used to be a barista at Pret and with whom, in another version of events, I might have worked alongside making flat whites. And certainly not God.

No, in my head, it's always you. Maybe it's because you know how it feels to be screwed by her (in both senses of the word). Maybe it's because there's no one else left for me to appeal to.

Or maybe I just miss you.

It's not terrible here. I'm warm, well-fed, safe enough. The young inmates frying their brains on spice have no interest in a Gen X nonentity like me and in any case it's not like on TV, where the entire prison population is let loose at once to mill around yards and gyms and canteens, the alphas choosing their allies and enemies, the betas hiding deep in the herd. No, it's lockdown most of the day, all of the night.

You'd think it was a claustrophobe's worst nightmare, wouldn't you? But it turns out that being sealed into a confined space, for the most part prone on a metal bunk, doesn't present the same threat to the nervous system as a crush of seven commuters per square meter in a rush-hour train. In this carriage, there's just me and Nabil. And it's not like we're underground, either, we're on the first floor of the house block they've nicknamed the Premier Inn—albeit one with welded steel doors that only unlock from the outside.

And, get this, it's the nearest prison to home—or what used to be home. About a twenty-minute drive from St Mary's. Not too far from the river, in fact, though you can't see the water from here. You can see the sky, though—even when I lie on my bed, I can see a little corner of it—and it's always gray, Kit. It's always gray, even when it's blue.

There's philosophy for you, my friend. There's retribution.

————

Yes, yes, of course I should have paid more attention to the psychological flaws of the thing. Beginning with this: why would a hot twenty-nine-year-old begin an affair with an unprepossessing geezer knocking on the door of fifty? Or, if we accept that she launched it in the belief that he was wealthy, the co-owner of a grand house with its expensive glimpse of the Thames, then why would she continue once he'd come clean and disabused her of this notion?

Two possible reasons. One, she'd fallen in love with him—people say that all the time, don't they, romantic sorts? "By the time I found out, it was too late, I was already head over heels . . ." Because of his winning sense of humor, perhaps (*Oh! Clare* said *you were funny*). Two, she'd begun to intuit a different kind of usefulness to his presence in her bed, his heedless devotion. That little idea she had, maybe it took root earlier than she let on. Clearly this was a woman who could think on her feet—and her back.

And then there are the logistical questions I *did* think to ask, but not loudly enough, not using the correct channels. If once, just once, I'd gone to the police station—*any* police station—in person and asked for Parry or Merchison, or even if I'd phoned one of them through the station switchboard and not on the number they gave me; if I hadn't shut down Clare's attempt to locate them online quite so efficiently.

They don't seem to list the detectives . . .

Making me think they couldn't issue a public appeal because they were investigating some big drugs ring, that was a masterstroke on Melia's part. She's got a real eye for authentic detail, hasn't she? She should write crime drama for the telly.

Oh, there were countless misconstruals on my part. Like when Elodie said, "Don't you think she needs some privacy at a time like this?"—meaning not while Melia despaired of her husband's disappearance, but while he undertook some homespun cold-turkey program a couple of streets away! Just one further question from me might have brought our cross purposes to light.

It's clear now that Melia counted on my compliance, my cowardice, my lack of imagination. I followed her breadcrumb trail like a middle-aged Hansel, into the lair of a wide-eyed, open-legged witch.

And so did you, Kit, so did you. Talk about divide and rule! What if you and I had compared notes, even just a single time? What if I'd heeded your warning, that night on the steps at Prospect Square? *Don't do it, will you?* You *don't need to fall for her drama* . . . You'd be alive and I'd be free.

But you know what they say are the two most heartbreaking words in the English language?

What if.

Or, if they don't, they really should.

————

I have to tell you, I think they overdid it, her detectives. Actor friends of hers, I'm guessing, because to the unsuspecting eye they were really very good. Naturalistic, composed, fluent. You probably know them, perhaps from drama school or from some get-together for struggling actors.

You knew nothing about their gig, of course. Like me, you thought you'd been reported missing to the police, not to two imposters. You thought the last-ditch loan for ten grand was for your new passport, your day-to-day needs in hiding while Melia set about getting me convicted, not pay dirt for a pair of out-of-work actors.

But, as I say, I think they got carried away; they kept adding their own lines. I can't believe Melia briefed them about the claustrophobia—they must have googled my name and found the news reports. I was pretty unnerved at times, even knowing I'd done nothing, that there was no body for them to find—not yet. What if I'd been rattled enough to pull out? That would have been the last thing she wanted.

Or maybe she just knew she'd be able to talk me back around, no matter how I reacted. The washed-up middle-aged man who'd fallen for her so predictably. (A blow job on a cable car, did she tell you about *that*?) Her greatest challenge was probably hiding her contempt.

I'm really attracted to you, Jamie . . . Sometimes, often, I wonder where the three of us—the four of us—would be if she'd never said that. Those words that were not so much fateful as fatal.

————

As for the other passenger, the mystery witness, she didn't exist. How twisted is that? There I was, agonizing over her identity, her potential to subvert our careful planning and sabotage my defense—even resurrecting my guilt about that woman on the Tube, who had probably cast me from her mind the moment she hit "Send" on her last vindictive email—when all along the men pretending to be detectives simply made her up! For a while, I thought Melia must have written her into the script to keep me on my toes, but then I remembered her reaction when I brought it up (*What other passenger?*), that rare moment of disbalance, and I knew they'd been improvising.

No, that little sadistic touch was theirs, not hers.

They had a fine old time of it, Merchison and Parry.

46

Soon after

So, listen, Kit: I might be able to visit your grave myself—and sooner than I thought. I think I might have new grounds to appeal.

I know!

I've sent a message to my brief and hope to get him in for a meeting as soon as his schedule allows.

Let me tell you, visitors are like hens' teeth here—if someone your age even knows what that means—or at least they are in my case. Dad and Debs visited at first, but when Dad passed away following a stroke, three months after my conviction, my sister as good as told me I was responsible for his death and said she couldn't bring herself to see me again—not until "time heals," anyway. I wasn't permitted temporary release for his funeral because I'm Cat A, but Debs at least wrote to tell me it had gone as well as could be hoped and attached a graveside photo deemed by my overlords safe for me to view. Clare was there, of course, looking older, thinner, but that might have been the black clothing, an unforgiving color for the middle-aged.

And so, unbelievably, was Melia. She wanted to pay her respects, apparently, after Clare had paid hers at a "moving" memorial service for you. Women together, burying their men. "If anyone knows how we all feel, it's her," Debs wrote. "She's still grieving too."

Seriously, Kit, is there *no one* who sees through this woman, besides you and me?

Oh, and Clare told Debs they played "She's Not There" by the Zombies at your service, the song we were listening to on the steps of Prospect Square that time. I didn't know it had become a favorite. If they'd had any idea I was the one who introduced you to it, they wouldn't have allowed it. *It's too late to say you're sorry*, remember?

Anyway, in recent months, I've had only one visitor. That's right, out of all the Visitor Orders I've sent out, only one has been used. No, not by Clare, regrettably, but that was always going to be a long shot; not Steve or Gretchen, either, or any of my older friends, the ones I virtually ignored in that last year of liberty—they all think I'm a murderer and presumably couldn't delete me from their contacts, their memories, fast enough.

No, it was my old mucker Regan. Oh, of course, you never met her, did you? I think you'd have found her a bit guileless for your tastes, but she and I always got on fine. Innocent times at the Comfort Zone, eh.

We sat in the visits hall on spongy blue seats, divided by a low table. The mood in the room was upbeat, with many of the men receiving visits from their wives or girlfriends, and supervised mostly by volunteers. She let me hug her and I smelled the outside world on her clothing, on her hair. The plastic coating of the hi-vis bib I was required to wear crackled between us.

"This is so great!" I beamed at her, stirred with sentiments I hadn't felt in months.

"Yes." Through the masterwork that was her makeup job, she looked uncertain and I tried to put her at her ease.

"How's the café?"

"Oh, I left ages ago. I'm assistant manager in a branch of H&M in Victoria Station now."

"Where are you living these days?"

Her lengthy complaint about a studio in Hounslow partitioned to accommodate her and a friend, who was newly and lustfully coupled with a man prone to psychotic episodes, would have elicited more sympathy had I not been flat-sharing myself in a twelve-by-eight-foot cell. I wondered if the aromas compared. Everywhere you go here, including the visits hall, the bodily smells of fifteen hundred overheated, underemployed males are discernible through the disinfectant.

"You got here okay?"

"Fine, though there were these really scary dudes waiting at the gate. They offered me drugs, can you believe it?"

I gestured dismissively. "I'd be more surprised if you said there *weren't* dealers at the gate. There are over fifty different gangs in this place, they all have mates meeting them when they get out and those mates aren't likely to be astronauts."

"Oh, right."

I saw I'd offended her; my social skills were not what they used to be. You forget that outside decent people go on living by the same discretionary codes they always did, the same regard for the feelings of others. "Thank you for coming today, Regan. I didn't think you would. And for standing up for me in court. That meant a lot."

"I didn't . . . I mean, you were so . . ." She faltered, swallowing nervously. Her fingers tugged at the ends of her hair.

"I was so what? You can say anything, Regan. I'm just happy to be making eye contact here." With a woman, a human being who once knew me as good, even honorable.

"You were so *real*," she managed, at last.

"What do you mean, 'real'?"

"At work, when you heard he'd been stabbed. When the police came. You were so believable, when all along . . ."

My smile faded. "Why did you come today?"

"What?"

"If you think I stuck a knife in my own friend, why would you want to see me?"

Her brow creased as she pressed back in her seat, defensive now. "I've always wanted to see inside a prison. I've never had the opportunity before."

Good God, she was serious. I'd forgotten her fascination with street crime. As if to demonstrate her thirst for knowledge, she did a theatrical one-eighty, eyes on stalks as she checked out the other cons in the hall. She wanted to ask what he'd done to get put in here, and that one, too, the one on the far side with the older male visitor drinking orange squash. Who was the scariest, the most dangerous? Were any of them kiddie fiddlers or gangsters or celebrities? She probably thought she'd be allowed to bring her mobile in, Instagram a few pictures of the lags' shower facilities. Maybe she expected there to be a gift shop on the way out where she could buy a mug or Christmas cards designed by the inmates' kids. The latest John Grisham novel.

"Glad to be of service, Regan," I said.

When she left, I knew I'd never see her again. Either that or she'd try to start a romantic relationship with me. Finally, the secret to being visible as a middle-aged man: wear the neon bib that identifies you as the offender in the room. A little crackle of plastic to get the juices flowing.

———

Sorry, I digress. The mind lacks discipline. I was talking about a visit to your grave. New grounds for appeal.

So what's happened is this: a mate of Nabil's rigged up our computer so it picks up cable TV and there we were, watching a BBC police drama called *Hackney Beat*, when I saw a familiar face on-screen.

None other than DC Ian Parry.

He was playing a suspect, actually. Evidently, there's a thin line between hero and villain in casting (as in life). They'd made him look unkempt, a school-of-hard-knocks type, but you could tell he was a professional actor, a man with good teeth and a honed physique who wants to be a star, not a civilian. The credits rolled just slowly enough for me to get his name: Simon Whiting.

"I don't fucking believe it," I said, under my breath. My nervous system didn't know what to do with the development, not at first, lashing adrenaline about and making me think of the ambulances that come sometimes when an inmate has overdosed.

"Bullshit, innit," Nabil said. He thought I was expressing dissatisfaction with the clichéd ending to the story line—criminal in cuffs, cops in the pub, pints raised in celebration—and I played along; I had no intention of sharing this frankly dynamite piece of news. You'd think we'd spend hours talking, wouldn't you? Honing our histories from our bunk beds, dreaming up our futures, keeping each other hopeful, but it's not like that. We have to shit in each other's presence, but we couldn't give a shit about each other.

———

Meetings with briefs take place in a special room, out of earshot of staff for confidentiality reasons. Mine doesn't want to be here, I can tell by the way he opens his laptop to create a screen between us, and by the way he struggles to transform a dead-eyed stare into a friendly, cooperative one the moment he realizes I've noticed. It's an odd thing, seeing yourself held in such low esteem in someone else's eyes. Not because I'm an inmate—he has scrupulous respect for prisoners' rights—but because he thinks I'm a fantasist.

"So you have some new information, Jamie?" he says, typing. I imagine the line: *Latest hare-brained theory . . .*

"Yes," I say. "I know who Ian Parry is."

"Ian Parry?"

I remind him of the account I've given over and over of the false police interview. Even when it was discredited in court and subsequently minimized by my defense team, I've never wavered, never betrayed a shred of doubt. "If you google Simon Whiting and Melia Quinn, I bet you'll find a link straightaway. They know each other. I'm pretty sure they were in *Cat on a Hot Tin Roof* together years ago."

His fingers pause on the keyboard. "*Cat on a Hot Tin Roof.*" Not a question, merely a polite repetition.

"Then once you find him, he'll be able to tell you who Merchison is."

It came to me last night, Kit: Simon Whiting and the actor playing Merchison must have been in the photo on your mantelpiece. In fact, wasn't it *you* who said one of the cast was called Si? That's why Melia removed it from sight. Once I'd met them, she couldn't have me turning up at the flat unannounced and recognizing them in the picture. Clare noticed it was gone, but for once her theory—which I disregarded, anyway—was wrong.

My solicitor checks something in his notes on-screen before saying, in a measured tone, "Mrs. Roper was last employed as a lettings agent, I believe."

"Yes, she was, but I'm talking about before that. She went to drama school and then she was an actor for a couple of years." I lean in a little, try to galvanize him with my positive energy. "This could lead to the kind of new evidence that means we can appeal, right? Come on, if Simon Whiting confesses to this masquerade, we must have a chance?"

He nods, respectfully vexed, before reminding me that the police case is closed and there is next to no chance of securing additional manpower at this stage. "But I can see if someone in my office is available to follow this up. I can't promise anything, but if we do manage to make contact with Mr. Whiting, and if he does disclose anything new and helpful—"

"He will," I interrupt.

"Then I'll be in touch. But you need to know it's unlikely we would get permission to appeal even if his account *did* match yours. I don't have to remind you that the alternative would have been a conspiracy to murder conviction, which in itself carries a heavy sentence."

"I know that," I cry, "but I'd plead guilty to that, wouldn't I, because it's true! Don't you see it's the principle? I'd rather be in here for the crime I *did* commit."

I'd rather know she wasn't out there, living her best life—at the expense of mine.

And yours, of course, Kit. Especially yours.

———

I try not to calculate the exact fraction of attention my case will occupy in the solicitor's mind over the next few weeks. I try not to think about the myriad variables—both professional and private—in his and his unnamed junior colleague's lives that might have a bearing on the act of looking into my lead. Waiting is both my occupation and my goal, after all, my raison d'être.

Oh, but there is *something* of note to tell you during this fallow period: news from Debs in an otherwise dry and guarded letter, the same one she writes to me every other month:

I thought I ought to let you know, in case you hear it in a more upsetting way, that Clare is getting married. Her fiancé is your friend Steve . . .

Well, how about that? Clare and Steve. She used to complain all the time about there not being enough relationships between older women and younger men. It was always the other way around (and look where *that* got us). I'm not at all upset. Just glad to hear someone's had a happy ending.

Bodes well for my own, eh?

————

Finally, my brief is back in touch and a second meeting arranged.

He looks weary this time, even a little seedy. His suit jacket is a bit shiny around the lapel—not nearly as dapper as your work clothes, Kit. There is a sense that he doesn't expect our conference to last long, and my nerves flare: it must be because the news is good—he needs to get on with the official application for permission to appeal!

"Did you speak to Simon Whiting?"

"We did. As you know, when we originally examined footage from the Royal Festival Hall security cameras, we were not able to make a positive ID of your companions. Well, when our investigator approached Mr. Whiting, we didn't exactly spell that out."

"You mean you let him think you'd got the ID somehow?"

"Let's just say he was friendly and helpful. Said he remembered the occasion well because it was just after Christmas and he wasn't working. He and the other friend bumped into you by the London Eye, recognized you from the Ropers' wedding and the three of you had a coffee together."

I shake my head, emphatic, impatient. "No, no, that's a lie. They weren't at the wedding. And why would I go with them unless I thought I had to? I was on my way to work, same as usual. Melia must have told him what to say if someone came asking. She'd have briefed both of them, she's totally thorough." I think for a moment. "Can you get the CCTV video from the pub? The big one on the river at Greenwich. The Stag, it's called. That will prove they weren't at the wedding. It was August 2019, a Saturday. I can let you know the exact date."

He looks singularly unimpressed by this suggestion. "I'd say that's highly unlikely after so long, Jamie. And even if they failed to appear on the footage, that wouldn't be proof that they weren't there."

I glare at him, feeling my temper rise. "So it doesn't help me when they *are* on camera and it doesn't help me when they *aren't*?"

"In this instance, no." He holds my eye. "And it's likely Mrs. Roper would vouch personally for their attendance."

There is a moment of stillness, of pure understanding. My voice sharpens, then breaks: "You don't believe me, do you? You never have."

Sensing the force of my emotion, he adjusts his tone. "We are postconviction here, Jamie. It's not a question of believing your account: *that* has already been judged. The only thing that's of any relevance is whether I believe you have grounds for an appeal."

"And you don't?"

His chest rises and his chin tucks into his neck. "I don't, no. Everyone else involved has credible explanations that are consistent with one another's, including this Simon Whiting's."

Only mine is inconsistent. Only mine is incredible.

He closes his laptop and slides it from the table, holding it to his chest like a clipboard—or perhaps plate armor. "You want my advice?"

Not really. "What?"

"Make a structure for yourself here. This is your life now. There are opportunities here, take them. Apply for a role of some sort. Make the experience count for something, because you *will* be out, one day, if you follow the rules and behave. Make your peace with it, Jamie."

He's on his feet now, looking down at me with eyes that will soon see the cars on the road, the dogs in the park, the schoolkids in the playground. The pint of lager on the pub beer mat. "I wish you luck," he says.

As if luck has any more of a shot against deviousness, against wickedness, than the truth ever did.

47

Finally

You've been drifting from my thoughts, Kit. It's inevitable, I suppose; we can't cling on forever. Even in places like this, there are new friends, new lifelines. Did I tell you I have a job in the health unit now? I'm working towards enhanced status, which means a cell to myself. There is responsibility and there is reward.

You know, I'm not sure I ever really linked the two before. I know *you* didn't.

Today is my fiftieth birthday. In an alternative version, we might have had a few drinks together after work. If we'd gone to the Hope & Anchor, you could have nipped out to meet your dealer while I got the drinks in. And when you came back, I might have accepted a birthday line, just one, mind you, to your five or six or however many you needed by the end to get the engine turning. So it seems as auspicious a date as any to let you go. It's the right thing, the sane thing (I've been reading about mental health a lot, lately).

But, before I do, I thought you might like to accompany me to the visits hall one last time. We have a VIP guest, you see.

That's right, *she's* coming. Your siren and mine. Our shared sorceress.

It's been proposed to me as part of some victim's family support initiative for which she volunteered and I agreed.

Why?

Because I've still got things to say, Kit. I've still got things to say.

Though the meeting with Melia takes place in the main visits hall during standard hours, it is supervised by a dedicated guard in case I take it upon myself to assault her. And my animal instincts *are* engaged, I admit, even before I see her, even before I know she's arrived on site. I'm a black bear who's scented his next meal in a bin far away.

Except I'm *her* meal, aren't I? I always have been.

She doesn't look me in the eye at first when I take my seat opposite her. I can see she has dressed with care so as not to attract the convict's eye. Every inch of her is covered, but for her fine, pale hands and smooth heart-shaped face. Her hair is pulled from her forehead and twisted at the nape over a high-necked black jumper. She has some coins in her hand, has obviously been briefed that she can buy tea or coffee, but she makes no attempt to do that, remaining in her seat with her knees jammed together, her gaze lowered.

We are not allowed to touch, of course.

"Hello, Melia."

Only now does she look up. She looks up as if mesmerized and there's a collapsing sensation inside me—frightening because I don't know what it is that's collapsing. My resolve? My pride? My lunch? The realization that no matter what words and images I've learned to remember her by, she is still breathtaking, she is still luscious, and I may still be in her thrall?

If I hadn't been transfused with blackest loathing, that is.

"Hello, Jamie," she says, and her voice—like her beauty—is just the same. A low murmur, intimate, undivided.

I'd be lying if I said I hadn't thought long and hard what my first question would be. "Has your insurance check come through yet?"

She answers politely. "Yes, thank you."

Two million pounds: in the end, not the value of one man's life, but two. A million apiece for me and you, Kit. I wonder if she's stayed in St Mary's, upgraded her accommodation, somewhere closer to the river, perhaps, because she'd want the wow factor. I wonder if, when she passes the spot where you bled to death, if she pulls up, face raised to the heavens, says a little prayer in your memory. "I hope it's worth it," I say.

"Jamie," she says, with a tut (as if *she* is in any position to upbraid *me*!).

I hold her gaze and search for shame, self-reproach, *anything* real. "Why are we doing this, Melia? And don't give me that crap about victims' families because I don't believe it for a second."

"I know you don't." She checks her volume, casts a glance towards the guard. We are speaking as quietly as possible without being inaudible, we conspirators of old. "I came because I hoped we could . . ."

She can't say it, it seems, but I see it in her eyes: a plea for forgiveness. And a plea with the faintest eroticism to it, like she is seducing a priest. It's still a game to her, a game to be won.

Well, I'm not playing. I pluck the first thing that comes into my head: "You heard about Clare and Steve, did you?"

A flicker of dismay suggests she had hoped to tell *me* that news. "I heard, yes. They met at our wedding, of course." She glances about her then, her eye lingering on the drab furnishings and the locked doors. A faint flinch crosses her face and I sense she is considering the limitations of prison life for the first time. No wine, no sex, no fun. No dancing by the river in the afternoon sun with friends and lovers.

I wonder who she's sleeping with now. It will be a different sort of worship, a different balance of power, now she has money.

"Must be upsetting for you," she suggests.

"Not at all, good for them," I say. "Though I always thought Steve might get together with Gretchen."

She shrugs, displeased with that suggestion.

"What? I'm not allowed to mention her? Obviously it came out in court, but did you know at the time that Kit was shagging her? Was that why you did it? It wasn't just the money, was it? Wasn't it enough that you were doing the same yourself?" It has been obvious to me for some time that this has been a more traditional story than I credited it; I simply failed to spot its classic theme in time. Sexual jealousy. The jury bought it as a motive, they just weren't permitted to see whose jealousy it was.

"Don't be ridiculous, Jamie." Melia speaks with the degree of disappointment that might meet the discovery of a chipped fingernail, but I am as familiar with her body as anyone ever will be and I spot the stretch in the tendons of her neck when she is angry, the thrust of her jaw. Those amber eyes seethe and brighten and I feel a rush of pleasure that I still have an effect on her.

"Anyway, I don't want to talk about them," she says. "I want to talk about us."

I snort. "What is there to talk about?"

"Just that . . ." She bites her lower lip, touches the end of her pretty little nose with her fingertips, as if to check her assets are still intact. "I want you to know that I'll still be here. Later."

"*Later?*" I can't believe I'm hearing her correctly. She's put me in jail, she's destroyed my life, and she wants me to still want her: that's narcissism, that's Melia. "You remember I got a fifteen-year sentence? Fourteen still to go? You want to put a date in the diary for a drink? No, thank you." The "no's" are flowing freely today. If only I'd said no to her more often before. "If you're running out of buddies out there in the free world, what about Parry and Merchison? Oh, hang on, they're not their real names. I know it's Simon Whiting, not Ian Parry, but you're going to have to help me out on the other one."

There's a splash of shock in her eyes and she lifts her chin. I've rejected her and now she'll want to punish me. "I'm sorry, I don't understand who you're talking about? Oh, yes, your imaginary friends. Do you know how desperate you sounded when you tried to talk about them in court? People were embarrassed, even your own lawyers."

379

"Bullshit." I've broken the rules and sworn, but, helpfully, a couple of tables away a prisoner and his visitor have raised their voices in sudden argument and the staff's attention is diverted from us, including that of our designated guard. I take advantage of the interlude to say the only thing I truly want to say in this meeting: "You're a cunt, Melia. And don't think Kit didn't know that too. He probably thought he'd let you do the hard work and then take his half and be on his way. No wonder he was always off his head, staying out all night. He should've left you for Gretchen at the first opportunity—she's worth a thousand of you." All of this is said in a gritted, cheerful tone so as not to alert the guard to the presence of anger. Anger pure as rapture. "Money is never going to buy you a soul, so don't think it will."

Outrage transforms her face, turns it ugly. The tears come slowly, seeming to suspend. A single facial convulsion and they'll fall. It makes me remember other tears, other convulsions. In bed, the way she screamed and groaned, right from the first time, in the apartment with the planes flying in, the view of the cable cars, twinkling like charms on a chain.

"I want to go now," she says, blinking, resetting her beauty. "This was a mistake." She signals to the guard, who summons our volunteer. The volunteer reminds me that the visit has been a gesture of forgiveness on the part of the victim's family, an act of courage.

Shame on you, Jamie.

Melia is on her feet, casting about, trying to remember which door she came in. I'm not sure how many doors there are between here and the outside, it is probably in double figures, but what is certain is that every key will turn in her favor until she gets back to the visitor center to retrieve her phone, find her car, drive away. Or maybe she'll walk to the train station with the other sorry visitors, tense with the strain of their day's errand, the vapors of incarceration rising from their clothes.

Then I hear the volunteer say to her, "We'll just let them know you're leaving earlier than planned and they'll arrange for someone to drive you back to the pier."

The *pier*? Without thinking, I call out: "Melia? Did you get the river bus here?"

She spins, responding instinctually to my urgency. "Yes. I was in town and I saw there was one due and I . . ." As she pauses, the volunteer signals to the guard to wait. A raised finger, one minute. "I realized I'd never taken it and I wanted to see what it was like. I wanted to picture you and Kit. Before . . . before everything."

As we stare at each other, the guard at my side tipping closer, poised to remove me, something honest and sorrowful passes between us, something neither of us could have planned: love. Not for each other, but for you.

For you, Kit.

————

There is an unscheduled spring in my step as I leave the visits hall. Don't get me wrong, it's not that kind of ending, there's no plot twist seeded, no comeuppance for the devil yet to be delivered—at least not by my hand. What there is is acceptance.

I accept that just because Melia should be behind bars and isn't doesn't mean I'm not right where I deserve to be.

I accept that just because friends of hers lied about their collusion with her doesn't mean I should be excused mine.

I accept that when I'm released, years from now, there'll be no one at the gate. I'll be alone in my future, every step, every misstep, my own.

As I walk past the chapel, alongside the little green where visiting kids are encouraged to play, I hear seagulls. And you know what? Until this encounter, until that parting exchange with Melia, until those seagulls, I haven't given our hours on the river a single thought. Not the happy ones. But now I'm picturing it, I'm picturing it so clearly.

Down the jetty and over the gangway we go, through the open cabin doors. You and me in our cream leather seats, with our coffees and our phones, our beers and banter and folded-up copies of the *Standard*. Our entourage, our crew.

Oh, Kit. If someone had told us then that within a year one of us would be dead and the other set to be convicted for his murder, we'd have laughed him out of town. We'd have leaned back in those seats, watched our majestic, heartless city glide by, and we'd have said, "This is the life, right?"

Get us.

EPILOGUE

It's his voice she notices first. Amid the mundane chatter of the other passengers, it is patient and affectionate. He's on the phone, reassuring someone who's rather anxious, by the sounds of it. "No, I'll be all right, I promise. I'll find somewhere more central as soon as the divorce is final. I'm fine, Mum, I don't need any help. What? No, on the boat into town to meet someone from work. It's actually quite relaxing."

Instinctively, her fingers go to the knot at the nape of her neck to release her hair. She can see from the ghost of her in the window that she has a pretty blush to her cheeks.

He's right, traveling by river *is* relaxing. She wasn't really in the mood after that awful experience at the prison, but the staff went beyond the call of duty to return her to the pier and she didn't want to appear churlish. She *was* there, after all, as a victim, and it was important to stay in character right to the end. Call it her professional training. Besides, she already had the all-day ticket and it had been a serious extravagance to buy it.

At least Jamie believed her about the money. Okay, so maybe he'll find out another way, from his solicitor or whatever grapevine he has in that terrible place, but she certainly wasn't going to be the one to tell him that the insurance claim was rejected. A technicality to do with the number of sick days Kit took, a requirement to consult the company doctor that he'd failed to meet. Small print, but basically the work-shy fucker had invalidated the policy.

Invalidated everything.

She has two more weeks in Elodie's spare room before Elodie's cousin comes back from working overseas. It's the cousin's flat, not Elodie's, so there are no negotiations to be had there. Then she is homeless. Which means she has two weeks to find a job, because you can't get a job without an address, even if you can't get an address with the kind of debts she has—Kit's, too, of course. What was his is now hers.

She'd thought seeing Jamie would remind her how lucky she was, how free. That was why she took part in that stupid support initiative, he'd never have agreed to see her otherwise. But what's the point of freedom if you can't afford to experience it in style? Jamie probably eats better in that hellhole than she does out here.

She didn't mean what she said about reconnecting when he's out. Jesus, he'll be in his midsixties by then, a broken man. A *poor* man. It was just a momentary craving to have an impact, to kick up a bit of lust and trouble, to remind him he once worshipped her. She was his Cleopatra, unfurling before his eyes.

Except the bastard rejected her. What was his problem, holding a grudge like that? She giggles at her own audacity—she is not *entirely* without self-awareness—and the man on the phone who's about to get divorced glances over his shoulder to locate the source of merriment. Leaning forward, she has a clearer view of him between the headrests. He's in his mid- to late-forties. Stylishly dressed, an expensive tan, obviously has money. He's nice to his mother.

"No, I'm feeling good. Really, it's the right thing. Great, I'll call you again at the weekend. Bye, Mum."

Off the phone, seeing her clearly now, he colors very faintly.

She rises from her seat, a hand passing across her face in mock horror. "Oh, God, I hope you didn't think I was laughing at *you*?"

He grins. "Of course not."

"It was just a private joke, I was laughing to myself." She groans. "Okay, so now you think I'm a crazy person."

"I don't think that at all," he says, his grin stretching. As she stands in front of him in the aisle, she can tell he is doing his best not to lower his gaze, give her a proper up-and-down appraisal the way older men always want to but know is not acceptable, not anymore. Time's well and truly up, they know that. But they can still dream.

She perches on the edge of the aisle seat just across from him and smiles. A sweet, sinless smile, especially for him.

The next bit comes quite naturally. No need to prepare.

ACKNOWLEDGMENTS

My grateful thanks to the S&S (UK) dream team of Suzanne Baboneau (our first book together and what a joy!), Ian Chapman, Sara-Jade Virtue, Hayley McMullan, Jess Barratt, Polly Osborn, Gill Richardson, Dom Brendon, Maddie Allan, Rich Vlietstra, Joe Roche, Louise Davies, Alice Rodgers, Clare Hey, Pip Watkins, and Susan Opie. And, of course, to the brilliant Jo Dickinson for early helmsmanship—we miss you!

A huge thank you to Loan Le, Libby McGuire, Lindsay Sagnette, Dana Trocker, Min Choi, Nancy Palmquist, Megan Rudloff, Maudee Genao, Jill Putorti, Paige Lytle, and the rest of the fantastic team at Atria/S&S (US). This is our first book together and I look forward to collaborating on many more! Thank you also to Danielle Perez at Berkley/Penguin Random House for invaluable early editorial guidance.

Thank you to my agent Sheila Crowley, aka the best in the business, and to the multitalented and tireless Curtis Brown team: Sabhbh Curran, Emily Harris, Katie McGowan, Callum

Mollison, Luke Speed, Anna Weguelin, and Alice Lutyens. Also to Deborah Schneider in NYC.

Heartfelt thanks to the booksellers, journalists, and bloggers who continue to support and promote my work so generously and to the many fellow authors and publishing folk who have taken the time to read this book ahead of publication. I know how hard it is to rise to the top of that TBR pile!

There are no experts to thank this time—my characters' crimes are strictly amateur—but I must acknowledge the influence of noir movies like *Double Indemnity* and the greatness of Barbara Stanwyck. Also, the book was written to a soundtrack of the Kinks and Lana Del Rey (particularly her 2019 cover of Sublime's "Doin' Time," a song that features in the story).

I raise a glass, as ever, to my friends (including Mats 'n' Jo) and family, especially Nips and Greta.

Finally, thank you to every reader who has chosen *The Other Passenger* for a temporary companion. I so hope you enjoy taking this trip with Jamie and Kit and that you will keep any commuter adventures of your own crime-free.

ABOUT THE AUTHOR

LOUISE CANDLISH is the *Sunday Times* bestselling author of fourteen novels, including *Our House*, which won the Fiction Crime & Thriller Book of the Year at the 2019 British Book Awards and was shortlisted for several other awards. It is soon to be a major ITV drama made by *Death in Paradise* producers Red Planet Pictures. Louise lives in London with her husband and teenage daughter.